CARNEGIE HILL

JONATHAN VATNER

CARNEGIE HILL

THOMAS DUNNE BOOKS
ST. MARTIN'S PRESS ❧ NEW YORK

First published in the United States by Thomas Dunne Books, an imprint of St. Martin's Publishing Group

CARNEGIE HILL. Copyright © 2019 by Jonathan Vatner. All rights reserved. Printed in the United States of America. For information, address St. Martin's Publishing Group, 120 Broadway, New York, NY 10271.

www.thomasdunnebooks.com

An excerpt from *Carnegie Hill* titled "All the Days of Thy Life" was published in *West Branch Wired* in March 2019.

Library of Congress Cataloging-in-Publication Data

Names: Vatner, Jonathan, author.
Title: Carnegie Hill: a novel / Jonathan Vatner.
Description: First edition. | New York: Thomas Dunne Books/ St. Martin's Press, 2019.
Identifiers: LCCN 2018055679 | ISBN 9781250174765 (hardcover) | ISBN 9781250174772 (ebook)
Classification: LCC PS3622.A8825 C37 2019 | DDC 813/.6—dc23
LC record available at https://lccn.loc.gov/2018055679

Our books may be purchased in bulk for promotional, educational, or business use. Please contact your local bookseller or the Macmillan Corporate and Premium Sales Department at 1-800-221-7945, extension 5442, or by email at MacmillanSpecialMarkets@macmillan.com.

First Edition: August 2019

10 9 8 7 6 5 4 3 2 1

For Jules, who never forgot

He discovered the cruel paradox by which we always deceive ourselves twice about the people we love— first to their advantage, then to their disadvantage.

—ALBERT CAMUS, *A Happy Death*

PART ONE

1

THE MEETING

Unsure of the proper attire for a co-op board meeting, Pepper decided to err on the side of stuffiness. She settled on a heather-gray skirt-suit with matching cloche, a raw-silk blouse, nude hose and heels, and a three-carat diamond choker that Rick had given her the past Valentine's Day, two months after they met. He was possibly the most successful asset manager under forty in New York, and he loved to spend money on her. She didn't need it, but she also didn't mind it.

Pepper had been dressing up a lot lately. It was a shortcut to looking mature, even if she didn't feel that way. Despite being on the verge of thirty-three, she still felt like a teenager on the inside. Maybe it was because she'd lived at home until a few months ago. Or because she'd never had a job that felt like a career. Or because she wasn't married yet, unlike most of her friends, including her younger sister, Maisie. Or because she didn't have sturdy opinions about politics and religion and everything else that people argued about. Or because she still used her parents' credit card and resented them for giving her advice. She didn't know how other people grew up; she was in therapy with Dr. Riffler to figure that out, but in almost three years, she'd gotten nowhere. She hoped that her new life with Rick in the Chelmsford Arms would speed things up.

Among the fears her mother had instilled in her—forgetting to wash off her makeup at night, eating more than a bite of dessert, airing too many opinions in mixed company—one of the biggest was the fear of arriving at a gathering empty-handed, so she perused the bottles in Rick's commercial-grade wine refrigerator, his main contribution to their shared life. Even though he earned a good living as a wealth manager, his furniture had been a pastiche of sidewalk and Craigslist finds and the detritus of former roommates, and all his books were ragged and swollen as if they'd been laundered. But he invested in wine, sometimes spending thousands on a bottle at auction, and she liked scanning the labels in search of a tempting vintage. The whites were kept at forty-five degrees on the left-hand side, the reds at fifty-eight degrees on the right. Anything from the top two rows was for everyday drinking or hostess gifts. The middle rows were dedicated to a gradient of special occasions: holidays on top and birthdays toward the bottom. She'd never seen him open a bottle from the very bottom row, ancient Bordeaux with inscrutable, handwritten labels. Their musty secrecy gave her a chill.

Pepper chose a Sauvignon Blanc from the top row and ran it by Rick, who was drinking a chocolate protein shake one determined gulp at a time while replying to Facebook messages, probably from people he'd met once in person and then had become bosom buddies with online. He was kind to everyone: his two thousand Facebook "friends," strangers in elevators and in restaurants, even telemarketers, panhandlers, and street poets. The truth was that his effusive friendliness often annoyed her. He couldn't meet someone without trying to charm them.

"Okay if I take this to the meeting?" she asked, showing Rick the label.

"Ooh, that's a good one," he said. He was so handsome—a dark wave of smooth, gelled hair, powerful nose, dimpled chin—she could barely look at him without getting wobbly. He didn't quite have the face of a model or actor, but diet and exercise, styling and attention to detail amplified his inborn gifts. For better or worse, he knew exactly how good he looked. "It's like eating a pear off the tree, with just a hint of cat piss. They're gonna splooge."

"Maybe I should pick a different one, then—you know, save them the dry-cleaning bill."

"They're going to do it anyway when they see you. You look fucking amazing," he said, and kissed her neck. She kissed his neck, too, and then they were making out in the middle of the kitchen. Part of her wanted to skip the meeting to make love; only when she met Rick did she discover that sex didn't have to be a tepid, churning affair. But he'd still be in the mood when she got back. She could nudge him awake at three in the morning, and he'd be ready to go.

"Is the hat too much?" she asked, angling her face away. "I mean, I'm not leaving the building."

"The hat makes the outfit. It says, 'Bow before me, mortals.'" He palmed her butt.

"Perfect. I was going for Penelopia, Goddess of the Co-op." Pepper's given name was Penelope, but she didn't feel quite mature enough to fill out such a roomy name. Since moving into the Chelmsford Arms, however, she'd been introducing herself with all four syllables. Her nickname was better suited to a little girl, or maybe a bunny.

Rick shook his fist. "Ruler of the Assessment and Creator of Bylaws."

"Wielder of the Signatory Pen and the Construction Shovel." She raised her arms over her head, untucking her blouse. She quickly tucked it back in.

"Your glory shines upon the preferred vendors."

She kissed him one last time, touched up her lipstick, and headed for Patricia Cooper's apartment ten minutes early, propelled by a gust of anticipation.

◄●►

A rickety black woman in a white blouse answered the door and invited Pepper into the dining room.

"Are you Patricia?" Pepper asked.

The woman laughed and touched the back of her head, smoothing her straightened salt-and-pepper hair. "Oh, no. Isn't that something!" She left the room.

The real Patricia, in an embroidered silk robe and burgundy velvet slippers, stood in the dining room, gripping a scroll-back upholstered chair with her clawlike hands. She had small, sharp eyes and a cloud of hair dyed reddish brown, and the way she angled her face downward reminded Pepper of her mother's habitual glare. A chatty Pomeranian with a crazed smile danced a semicircle around Patricia.

"Ms. Bradford! You're the first to arrive," Patricia half exclaimed, speaking through her teeth as though her jaw were wired shut. She pried the wine from Pepper's hands and clutched it to her chest. "Thank you, dear."

"Am I too early?" She felt a lingering embarrassment about having mistaken that other woman, who was probably some kind of helper, for the president of the board.

"Not at all. The others will arrive shortly." She motioned for Pepper to sit at the table, draped with an elegant white tablecloth, with seven clipboards set like place mats, and deposited the wine in her kitchen without offering to pour a glass. A well-stocked brass bar cart stood in the corner of the dining room, dust frosting the bottles.

5

"I'm pleased you've decided to join us," Patricia said, wiping her hands against her thighs as though to clean off the evidence of absconding with the bottle. "We need more young people willing to stand up and represent the best interests of our storied building. It's a vital job that must not be taken for granted."

"Well, thank *you* for doing it. . . . How long have you been . . . ?" She didn't finish her question, fearing there was something unkind in asking it of such a spectacularly old woman.

"I've been president for twenty-two years. Before that, my husband, may he rest in peace, was president for fifteen."

"Sounds like a dynasty." Pepper raised her eyebrows.

"Don't you forget it," Patricia said with a mirthless laugh. "But to be serious for a moment, I care deeply about the Chelmsford Arms, and I am sure you will feel the same very soon." She flicked out a heavy cream-colored business card from a pristine white wallet. It read PATRICIA K. COOPER, PRESIDENT, CHELMSFORD ARMS CORPORATION. Her phone number was embossed underneath. "You'll find that I'm very easy to work with if you remember one thing: the Chelmsford Arms is a cooperative, which means we must all *co-operate*." That sounded like a threat.

"Do we all get business cards?" Pepper asked, finding the card a little silly. When would Patricia find occasion to use it, except to brag about her volunteer title?

Patricia narrowed her eyes. "You're a very funny young woman," she said, and left the room. Her Pomeranian trotted after her.

◄ ● ►

Pepper's friends had laughed when she told them that she was excited to join the co-op board at her new building. Everyone knew it was a thankless job mired in trivia, and the only people who joined those boards were retirees, cat ladies, and slimeballs angling for special favors. She didn't care. This was her first apartment that her parents weren't paying for, the place where she planned on raising her first child with Rick and where she would finally get her life on track, and she wanted to give herself some standing among her neighbors.

She had a good feeling about the building. The Chelmsford Arms had great bones, with high ceilings, elegant layouts, and generous floor plans, and there was very little turnover in the apartments, which meant residents liked it too much to leave. Also, she was falling in love with the neighborhood, Carnegie Hill. She'd grown up in Lenox Hill, also on the Upper East

Side but farther south, a neighborhood with better restaurants and bars and more life on the streets. She would have chosen to live there had it not been polluted by proximity to her mother. Rick had pulled for Yorkville, a stone's throw from the East River and a slightly faster commute to his office on Fifty-third Street, not to mention the promise of the Second Avenue subway line, which, if it ever opened, would improve real estate values. (She suspected that last item was the most appealing one for him.) Touring homes with their broker, though, she developed a special fondness for Carnegie Hill. It bordered Central Park and was within walking distance of several museums, including the Metropolitan Museum of Art—where she and Rick first met, at a holiday benefit for which her mother had bought a ticket but wasn't in the mood to attend. The leafy streets were quiet, the avenues stocked with charming little boutiques and cafés that were on no tourist's radar. Carnegie Hill was also renowned for being an excellent place to raise children, home to some of the best schools in the nation. Walking its streets, hope for her future ached within her.

She had another, more practical reason for joining the co-op board: it might lead to a job prospect that wasn't the same entry-level garbage she'd waded through for the first decade of her working life. Junior account coordinator. Editorial assistant. Legal assistant. Gallery assistant. After college, she'd gotten a job as a publicist for luxury handbag and jewelry brands, quitting six months in because her boss was the stupidest, most vapid woman she had ever met. Then she worked for three years as an assistant at *Vanity Fair*, garnering a spate of vicious performance reviews. When she followed orders, her boss told her to take initiative. When she took initiative, the woman called her insubordinate. Finally she realized she would never be promoted. The same well-bred last name that had landed her the job also painted her as too spoiled and stuck-up to deserve any real work. And the sad truth was, instead of weathering the abuse and fighting for more responsibility, she quit. No one but her cared if she didn't have a job. Her parents kept dropping suggestions to try volunteering. "If you're not paid, you can't be fired," her mother once said in her singsong way.

She made copies and organized files at her father's law firm for a few months, until she was certain she didn't want to go to law school. Then she answered the phone in her mother's friend's third-tier art gallery, specializing in photo-realistic oil paintings of the New York skyline, which to Pepper was basically pornography for tourists. She met Rick the day after she quit, which she took as a sign from the God she didn't believe in that she'd made the right decision.

For her next job, she was determined to find something that she loved, something that could become a career. But the fact was, she still didn't know what she wanted to be when she grew up. She had no marketable skills, unless you counted witty banter and the ability to walk normally in four-inch heels. She did have good taste, which sometimes helped land her a job and always helped her lose it. She didn't want to be one of those women whose identity was wholly composed of wifehood and motherhood, but at this point, if she could pull that off, it would be a come-from-behind victory.

In contrast, most of her friends were now "senior" this and "executive" that, or else their kids were already in school. Her best friend, Katt, ranked among the top hundred real estate brokers in the city. Maisie was an attorney and was married to an attorney, and any day now, a fleet of Rahul's mighty sperm would find their way to her eggs, which surely ranked among the plumpest, most fertile eggs in history. Pepper basically liked herself, but when she thought about her life as a whole, she felt like a complete failure. At least the co-op board was something to distract her from the black hole of her achievements.

The board "election" had been puzzling, though. When she and Rick moved into their apartment in July, he left it up to her to appeal to the board for permission to renovate. It was a simple process, once she'd gotten the plans from the architect, and despite her parents' warnings about having to dole out bribes to get anything done in New York, the approvals were granted promptly, months before the work was to begin. A few days after the renovation was approved, Patricia called her, explaining that a member of the board had stepped down "due to a health issue" and asking if she had any interest in "joining our little family." She agreed.

Fifteen minutes later, an email arrived from one Douglas McAllahan, "head of the nominating committee of the Chelmsford Arms Corporation," telling her she had been nominated to the position of board member. When she called him, asking how she should campaign, he laughed and said, "I wouldn't worry about it." She heard nothing for a few weeks and assumed she hadn't won. But then Patricia called to congratulate her.

"Don't tell me," Pepper said. "I was running against myself."

Patricia responded, "You were the best candidate for the job."

◄ ◆ ►

At 7:25 P.M. the doorbell rang, and Patricia's helper ushered in a short, frail gentleman in a brown tweed blazer and a Panama hat, which he removed upon entering. Wisps of white hair floated above his head like snow-fall, and he carried a dignified air as though he might drop it.

"Letitia, my friend!" the old man said, touching the black woman on the arm. "How has life been treating you?"

"The doctors say I have the heart of a teenager," Letitia replied with a forceful nod. "How are you? And how is lovely Carol?"

"I'm well. And who can really say with her? She's indestructible, impenetrable, inscrutable. But she'll be pleased that you asked."

"Always nice to see you, Francis," she said before sliding out of the room. Her bland, vaguely southern manner, and the fact that her sole purpose at this meeting was to open the front door and then vanish, seemed inexplicably hilarious to Pepper, and she snickered.

"What is it?" Francis asked, laughing as if he got the joke. "Did I say something funny?"

"No, it's . . . I can't explain it. I'm Pepper . . . I mean Penelope Bradford."

"Of course. I'm Francis Levy." They shook hands. "You come from quite a family."

"So I'm told," she muttered. Though she understood how lucky she was to have money and standing, she bristled when people fawned over her name. She didn't want to be a novelty, because people who saw her that way never took her seriously.

"I'm sorry if I sounded starstruck," Francis said. "What matters is that you're not a minion of the Czarina."

"I'm sorry?"

"Empress Pat. The Czarina. The Duchess of Carnegie Hill. Whatever you want to call her. She rules with an iron fist."

She smiled. "I like you already, Francis." She picked up a bottle of Hennessy from the bar cart and swirled the copper-colored liquid. "Do you think the Czarina will mind if I help myself?"

"That bar cart has been left out at every meeting, but in the thirty-seven years I have served on this board, none of us has been offered a single glass." He didn't bother whispering, which put Pepper on edge.

She put the bottle down, and the bar cart tottered, clinking amiably. "Anything else I should know before I come off looking like an idiot?" she asked quietly, scanning the room for a napkin to clean her hands of the sticky dust from the bottle. She resorted to rubbing the edge of the tablecloth between her fingers.

Francis hung his blazer over a chair and sat down. "You're a perceptive young woman. Let's see . . . Patricia Korngold Cooper's rules of order . . ."

"Korngold?"

"Her maiden name. We Jews are legion in this building, though some of us have, shall we say, redecorated our last names. So I take it upon myself to remind her." Again, he didn't lower his voice. "As for the rules: we are allowed in this room and the foyer, nowhere else. If you must go to the bathroom, use Letitia's, off the foyer."

"So she has to use a separate bathroom?" she whispered, glancing around to make sure no one else could hear.

Francis stifled a laugh. "It's not like that. Letitia can use whatever bathroom she wants. But she lives here—it's the bathroom closest to her bedroom."

"And what exactly is her role?"

"She's Patricia's maid."

"And she answers the door? Isn't that a little strange?"

Apparently, Francis didn't find it strange. "I'm sure if she didn't want to, she wouldn't have to. She's worked for the Coopers for her entire adult life—at least fifty years. At this point, she's practically family."

That made sense to Pepper, she supposed. Her parents had used the same housekeeper every week for most of Pepper's life, and though she didn't quite love Virginia, the woman did feel to Pepper like an aunt. She wondered, though, if Katt would have raised a stink about Patricia's maid answering the door. Pepper was raised not to discuss sensitive topics with strangers, but Katt called out injustice wherever she saw it, even if it wasn't there. She constantly posted outrage-inducing articles on Facebook and chaired fund-raisers for Amnesty International when she wasn't showing a town house to a sultan or a magnate.

When Pepper had told Katt that she was thinking of moving into the Chelmsford Arms, her friend had been a little surprised, because the building was known among real estate brokers for being the whitest co-op in Carnegie Hill. That hadn't seemed like a reason not to live there, though since she'd moved in, she had noticed that the only nonwhite people were the staff. Even in her family's small building on Seventy-first and Park, where she had lived the first thirty-two years of her life, there had been a black family, the Thompsons.

"What else?" Pepper asked.

Francis lifted the edge of the tablecloth, revealing a fine table covered in leather padding. "Board members must not write directly on the dining table, even with the protective padding. We write on the clipboards. Patricia's precious table was crafted by Duncan Phyfe himself and must never be touched by another human hand. You must never pet Helen of Troy—her obnoxious dog. We drink water from the tap, not her precious Mountain Valley Spring Water, the only kind that passes her lips. Oh, and we must always agree with her. But that goes without saying." He smiled giddily. "That's about it. The rest is in the bylaws. Be sure to read them, by the by. Those who know the bylaws hold all the cards." The thick pamphlet of the co-op's bylaws had been left on her doormat the day after she was elected to the board, and she had skimmed them and absorbed nothing. Maybe she would take another look.

"And if we break the rules?" she asked.

"You won't be nominated again when your term is over. She directs the nominating committee. In secret, of course."

"Is that what happened to my predecessor? Patricia said he had a 'health issue.'"

"No, Elizabeth had overian cancer, and she stepped down in July." Francis looked crestfallen, and Pepper apologized for crossing a line she hadn't known was there.

"The truth about the Chelmsford Arms is that we're an aging community, the oldest in Carnegie Hill," said Francis. "Our apartments are undervalued, because most wealthy people don't want to live in a NORC—a naturally occurring retirement community. Which is why everyone here is so excited that you've joined the board. We're hoping you can help attract young families to the building."

Suddenly her unopposed election to the board made sense. She didn't love being the token young person, and she wondered how she and Rick hadn't noticed that they were buying a home in a NORC in the middle of a neighborhood known for its young families. Already her dream of reinvention was beginning to tarnish. On the other hand, if attracting young families would bring more friends for her and Rick, and more children to play with her future children, that seemed worth her effort. Maybe the building, like their apartment, was a fixer-upper.

Patricia's gilded mantel clock chimed 7:30, and the doorbell rang a few seconds later. All four remaining board members flushed in, as if they had been huddled in the hallway, unwilling to spend an unnecessary second in Patricia's lair.

As Letitia filled seven water glasses, using, as Francis had promised, a separate green glass bottle for what had to be Patricia's seat at the head of the table, Pepper weathered a flurry of introductions and handshakes. Chess Kimball, secretary of the board, was a straight-backed financier in his sixties with a pink-and-brown bowtie and not a hair out of place, and who seemed to indicate pleasure by frowning and displeasure with a pained smile. Ardith Delano-Roux was a friendly golden-haired dame whose apparent plastic surgery addiction made it hard for Pepper to shake her hand or look her in the eye. The board treasurer, Dougie McAllahan, a stocky, bald real estate developer in a rumpled blue suit, had big lips like a duck's bill, a gray soul patch, a diamond stud in his left earlobe, and bulging eyes that made frequent pilgrimage to her breasts. Only after he sat down did she notice that the tendrils of hair encircling his gleaming scalp were gathered into a scraggly ponytail, at which point she understood that he was not married, because no woman would have let him get away with such an appalling hairstyle.

Birdie Hirsch, her next-door neighbor, greeted Pepper last with a sprightly kiss on each cheek. She was wearing an A-line Mondrian dress that suited her perfectly. Pepper couldn't think of any other sixty-something woman who could pull off such a short hemline, but Birdie possessed the spirit of a twenty-year-old. She was a tiny, sparrowlike woman—the nickname was apt—with the light twang of a French Canadian and boundless energy and an easy laugh. She was a phenomenal cook, unflappably cheerful: the consummate hostess. Her husband, George, was a gentle giant, with a brick of a jaw and more hair than a man in his sixties had any right to. The day after she and Rick moved in, George and Birdie showed up with an ethereal coconut cream pie and regaled them with memories of their years living in Montreal, the kind of memories Pepper was looking forward to creating with Rick.

"I'm getting a double dose of Birdie tonight," Pepper said, as they had dinner plans for after the meeting.

"I've been looking forward to it all day." Everything Birdie said was either an exclamation or a whispered confession; this was the latter.

At last Patricia returned from hiding, having made up her face and put in pearl earrings, and descended into her chair at the head of the table. Helen of Troy scrambled into her lap, spun around twice, and fell asleep.

"Welcome, all. I hope your Labor Days and whatnot were pleasant enough. Today I'm pleased to introduce our newest member, Ms. Penelope Bradford, daughter of Lewis Bradford, Jr., and Claudia Lindbergh Bradford. Needless to say, we are pleased that she and her fiancé chose to make their home together in our special little building."

Pepper smiled bashfully. The building was hardly "little"—it took up half the block, and there had to be at least a hundred apartments. But of course Patricia wasn't speaking literally.

"Welcome, Penelope!" said Ardith, reaching across the table with her liver-spotted hands and touching Pepper on the fingers. Pepper made an effort not to recoil. The woman looked like an alien: translucent skin, inflated lips, and deep-set cat eyes. "What a joy to have another young person on the board, not like these old farts." She laughed, and Pepper wondered if she considered herself young or if that was part of the joke.

"Our first order of business," Patricia said, reaching into her soft, faded leather briefcase to withdraw a greeting card, "is to honor Elizabeth, who lost her valiant battle with ovarian cancer last week. I bought this sympathy card for her family." She gave it to Chess to sign. "The funeral is on Friday, and I think it would be only right to send a bouquet of flowers. All in favor?"

Everybody raised their hands. Pepper, surprised that a vote could happen without warning or circumstance, and not positive she was allowed to weigh in before some kind of swearing-in ceremony, raised her hand last.

"Then I take it no one is opposed. I took the liberty of asking Dougie to look into floral pricing, assuming you would all be in agreement. Dougie, what did you find?"

He removed a folded paper from his pocket. "From Madison Florists, funeral arrangements start at three twenty-nine."

"They can't cut us a break, after all the business we've given them?" Patricia asked.

"They do the lobby arrangements," Birdie whispered to Pepper.

"They're ghastly," Ardith breathed. "The owner is certifiably colorblind."

"They're the premier florist in Carnegie Hill," Patricia said.

"That appraisal seems biased at best," grumbled Francis.

Dougie continued, "A website called ProFlowers could do the same bouquet for ninety-nine."

Patricia thought about this. "Why don't we spend something like one forty-nine at ProFlowers? We don't want to seem cheap. Especially since her funeral is at Campbell's."

"I was there in July for my ex-husband's ex-wife, and you could barely get in, those bouquets were so big," Ardith told Pepper. "When I got home, I found rose petals stuck to my derriere!"

Birdie and Dougie laughed, Chess and Patricia did not, and Francis stared at his clipboard with a show of patience. Pepper smiled, a compromise between laughing and not laughing, so as to alienate the fewest people, and raised her hand. "I'm sorry to interrupt, but my aunt owns a flower studio a block from Campbell's—it's called Floresce—and I can tell you, you're much better off with a local shop. Anything that needs to be sent through the mail is going to die before the funeral begins."

"Does this aunt of yours do funeral arrangements, Penelope?" Birdie asked as she signed the card.

"All the time," she said, happy to have found a way to contribute. "And she sources her flowers from an organic farm in Ecuador and designs each bouquet individually. It's guaranteed to be tasteful."

"Organic sounds nice," Birdie said.

"It's hard to argue with one forty-nine," said Chess, "especially since our main retail space is still empty."

"The woman died at forty-seven," Francis said. "She had intractable pain for the last three months of her life. And now her two teenage sons are going to grow up without a mother. So, please, let's not buy flowers that are going to wilt before the funeral."

"Francis, we know," Dougie said, gently.

Pepper took the card and wrote, "My heartfelt condolences for your loss" in small, tidy cursive in a tract of blank space. Then Francis took the card and began to write.

Smiling clearly did not come naturally to Patricia, and it made her look like a cross between a child and a madwoman. "Here's what I think. Ms. Bradford, if your aunt owns the shop, then it seems to me that you have a conflict of interest, and you should recuse yourself from this matter. Being a member of the board does not give you the right to hand out favors to family and friends. We are a serious organization with a strict ethical code."

A blistering heat billowed up into Pepper's face as shame tugged downward into her belly. It was the same impotent rage she often felt toward her mother, fury that ended in obedience as if she were restrained by a choke chain.

"Now, Francis," Patricia continued, "we will mark your objection. Unless anyone else objects, we will go with ProFlowers." She raised her eyebrows at everyone in turn, as if challenging them to object.

Dougie opened the card. "Christ, Francis, write a book, why don't you."

"What I had to say couldn't be reduced to a prepackaged sentiment," Francis said.

"All the good sayings are taken. 'Deepest sympathy.' 'My heartfelt condolences.' 'You are in my thoughts.' What the hell am I supposed to write?"

"'You're in my prayers'?" Ardith offered.

"But I'm an atheist."

"Atheists can pray, too." Her eyes widened, but the rest of her face remained dead. Pepper wasn't sure what expression she was attempting.

"How about, 'You are loved'?" Francis said.

"They'll think I'm some kind of fairy."

Francis stiffened. "You asked for suggestions."

"I've got it," Dougie said. "'She's in a better place now.'"

"I doubt her husband and children would agree with that," Francis said, examining his fingernails, which were clean and trim.

"'Everything happens for a reason'?" Birdie offered.

"You might as well tell them she deserved to die."

Pepper saw that Francis was right, if a little harsh.

Dougie thought for a moment longer and said, "'My *profound* condolences.' Wait, is it 'on your loss' or 'for your loss'? Or 'on the occasion of your loss'?"

"'For,' I think," said Chess.

He stuffed the card into the envelope and tossed it in front of Patricia. "Next time, I sign first."

Patricia put the card away and tightened both her robe and her squint. "Moving on. We have two applications for the purchase of apartments. Let's do the easier one first. This is from good old Cliff Barron in 6C. He wants to buy 6B from Mona Frickendorf, a three-bedroom for three-point-eight million. Cliff and Lorna are setting up a place for their children, who will be coming home from college within the next few years. He also put in a request to combine the two apartments once the sale goes through—the plans are enclosed. I thought you all might enjoy reviewing his current financials."

Patricia passed a three-ring binder to each board member. Dougie opened his first and guffawed. "No, I don't think it will be much of an issue. Prequalified!" This woke Helen of Troy, who hopped onto the table and pawed at the tablecloth until Patricia, by means of kissing sounds and hand motions, managed to coax it back into her lap.

Birdie shook her head as she flipped through her binder. "He's a serial CEO," she whispered to Pepper. "No one needs this much money."

"Are we going to let him combine apartments, just like that?" Francis asked. "I don't know if it's such a good idea, Patricia."

"We can't have too many five-and six-bedroom apartments," Chess said. "They attract the wealthy families that are coming to Carnegie Hill in droves."

"What happens if the economy turns again and those apartments go vacant?" Francis asked. "Who's going to be able to afford the maintenance on six bedrooms? What is that, twelve thousand a month?"

Finally, Pepper opened her binder. The first page of the application listed Mr. Barron's monthly net income, after projected maintenance fees and other expenses were taken out: $1.1 million. On the second page, his total assets: $184 million. Pepper felt as if she'd seen him naked. Was this how they'd talked about her and Rick when they sent in their board package? She flipped through the rest of the pages, past his tax returns, his bank statements, and dozens of pages of various other statements for all his holdings. It was like watching a vivisection. She desperately wanted a glass of wine and was no longer amused that Patricia hadn't opened the bottle she'd brought. She eyed the bar cart; maybe it would be okay to ask for a splash of something.

"The relevant numbers are in the first few pages," Patricia said to Pepper.

"I can see that," she snapped.

After everyone had digested the data, Patricia called a vote, and everyone, including Francis, approved the transaction. Pepper raised her hand, too, though she couldn't have cared less whether or not this sale went through. Lots of New Yorkers seemed to Pepper like overgrown children playing Monopoly. She'd gotten herself excited about the board, but now she wondered if her position should have been given to someone who worshipped money.

Patricia picked up another stack of binders. "Let's discuss the other applicant. A markedly different story. Tiffany White is a single woman of thirty-eight years, looking at 2H, a modest one-bedroom for one-point-six million."

Chess shivered. "The H line."

"It's north-facing," Dougie explained to Pepper. "Those lower floors are like a dungeon."

Pepper and Rick's apartment, 12G, faced northeast and swallowed oceans of light in the mornings but was dark the rest of the day. It occurred to her that people might shiver at that line, too.

"She does come with a glowing reference from none other than the Drs. Hightower, but I'll let the financials speak for themselves."

"The Hightowers are marquee shareholders in the building," Francis explained. "They're pediatric oncologists at Mount Sinai."

Chess frowned as he flipped pages. "What does this woman do?"

"She's a bookkeeper." A grin crept into Patricia's lips. "I believe she came into a small inheritance. And I do mean *small*."

"A bookkeeper!" Dougie shouted, red-faced. "What's next, a Walmart greeter?" Everyone laughed except Francis. This time, Pepper knew not to laugh.

"The Hightowers think she's God's gift to mankind," Chess observed. "I see she used to work for them."

"She has a dachshund," said Patricia as if she'd smelled something rancid.

"They have the most minuscule bladders," Ardith said. "That little rat dog will be doing its business all over the lobby rugs."

"Especially if she has to walk all the way from the H line!" Dougie said with a chortle that flung a worm of saliva onto the table.

"Who was in 2H before?" asked Birdie, flipping through the binder.

"It was Maria Ferrazzi," Francis replied. "Heart attack. Her family stopped talking to her after she refused to go into a home. Nobody found her until after she'd begun to decompose. The neighbors were complaining of the smell."

"Please, Francis," Chess said.

"I'm just giving you the facts."

Whether Francis loved death or hated it, it was a strange obsession, maybe a kind of thrill. Pepper had to be careful around unhappy people: she could pick up their misery like a cold.

She opened the binder reluctantly. The two magic numbers were Tiffany's $3,400 net monthly income and $2.5 million in assets, enough to buy the apartment in cash and have plenty left over, and more than Rick had in savings, to be honest. She flipped further into her board package, past the financial statements to the copious reference letters. Her pastor at an AME church, Crystal Burton, wrote in glowing terms about Tiffany's generosity and faith. So this woman was black. She also lived in Harlem. Maybe it was the presence of Patricia's maid, now dusting an urn in the living room—did the woman really have to clean at night?—or the way they were laughing about Tiffany, but Pepper understood that the absence of minorities in the building was no accident. Sitting around Patricia's table, letting this nasty shrew boss her around like her mother did, this evidence of unfairness bothered her in a way such things never had before.

"Do we even need to vote?" Dougie asked, smirking.

"She can easily afford the maintenance," Francis said. "I don't see what you're insinuating. I'd like to meet her."

"She's not secure," Patricia said. "We can't accept people who aren't sure bets."

"And why is she not secure?" Francis asked.

"Because her income isn't high enough. She'd spend almost half of it on maintenance."

"What's your income, Patricia?" Birdie asked.

Pepper nearly gasped at Birdie's boldness. Growing up, money was not discussed, along with politics and religion. But no one else around the table seemed alarmed. After a moment, Patricia said, "I assure you, I can afford to stay as long as I wish."

"Birdie," Chess said, "she doesn't make enough to live here."

"I think we should bring her in," Pepper said, mostly to defy Patricia. "You guys were saying you want younger people in this building. She seems ideal to me."

Patricia clapped twice to quiet the room; it felt like a personal reprimand. Helen of Troy stirred and nestled deeper into her lap. "We have a responsibility to our shareholders not to endanger the building's value. Her postclosing reserves are, to put it charitably, wanting. If our maintenance costs increase, or if, God forbid, we need to levy an assessment, she would be broke in no time. We must be conservative with our decisions. Although I'm sure she's a very nice person, I can't in good conscience recommend that we accept her."

"Can't we give her a little leeway, because she's, you know, African American?" Pepper asked.

Francis widened his eyes at her, either in surprise or warning.

"I don't see how that's relevant, dear," Patricia said, and Pepper felt as if she'd been slapped. "We make decisions strictly on numbers and reputation. It is patently illegal to discuss any protected class in this setting. Now, all in favor of accepting Ms. White's petition . . . based on her financials and references alone?"

Birdie and Pepper raised their hands. Francis smiled feebly at Pepper and raised his too.

"Francis, I thought better of you," Patricia said. "All opposed?"

The other hands went up.

"Four to three," Patricia said. "Sorry, Ms. White. Moving on—"

"So that's it?" Pepper asked. "No more discussion?"

Patricia slid her glasses down her nose and glared at Pepper. "I wouldn't have pegged you as a bleeding heart."

Bile lapped at Pepper's throat. "I'm not."

Patricia arched her eyebrows and glared at Pepper exactly as Claudia Bradford did in her cruelest moments. "Don't worry; we don't discriminate based on political inclination. We simply need to maintain hard heads when sorting through the applicants. I think I speak for all of us when I say we would like to improve our building's diversity. But that doesn't mean we can bring in just anyone off the street. We have a serious responsibility to our shareholders to keep our property values going up, Ms. Bradford."

Pepper understood that Patricia had no use for a Penelope, only a Ms. Bradford—"daughter of Lewis Bradford, Jr., and Claudia Lindbergh Bradford"—if she was to increase the building's value. She wondered if all of them, even Francis, saw her as a "marquee shareholder." She was being used, and she felt foolish for not seeing it before. Her anger made her hyper-aware of the untouchable table in front of her, penning her in, and the untouchable bar cart, leering from the corner. If she didn't get up, she thought she might burst.

Bearing the blunt gaze of the entire board, she pushed back her chair, took four long steps to the bar cart, picked up the bottle of Hennessy, and filled a glass to the top, splashing a little on the oriental rug. Francis grinned wickedly. Pepper sat down, crossed her legs, and took a dainty sip. The room was silent except for the ticking of Patricia's mantel clock. Inside Pepper's head, she was screaming.

◄●►

Pepper rushed out of Patricia's apartment the second the meeting ended. Unwilling to stand in the elevator with any of those monsters, she hurried down the stairs and through the lobby toward the back elevator bank. She didn't even want to talk to Birdie.

"Penelope!" Francis called, catching up to her as she waited for an elevator. "Just a moment!"

She spun toward him, dizzy from the alcohol. "What do you people want from me?" He recoiled like a street urchin, and she regretted snapping at him. He was, after all, a decent man.

"You were brilliant! I've been longing for that to happen for years."

"One more minute and I really think I would have stabbed her."

"It's all very funny, isn't it?"

"I didn't find it funny at all."

"You will. There's a certain comical repetition you'll grow to appreciate. Especially if you read Kafka."

"I'm sure there are plenty of other people who would have a great time being reprimanded by that horrible woman."

They stepped into the elevator. Francis pressed 5 for himself and 12 for her. She didn't like that all of them—maybe the entire building—knew where she lived. She felt nauseatingly visible.

"I know, she's monstrous," Francis said. "And Chess and Dougie, too. But you have to stay. It's vital that we build a constituency of real, feeling human beings, or else the building will fall to the plutocrats."

"I'm sorry, but the whole thing makes me sick."

The doors opened at Francis's floor, and he stood with one foot in the elevator, the other in the hall. "I'll put all my cards on the table. You can't breathe a word of this to anyone, but I am building a coalition to oust her. Elections are in January. Please say you'll stay until then. I need you."

He looked desperate. It would have been easy just to quit the board and avoid Patricia. But she didn't want to give up on a potentially meaningful role just because a venomous old biddy bossed her around. Her whole adult life, she'd dropped jobs and boyfriends the minute she faced the slightest obstacle. Here was a chance to see something through. "I'll think about it."

"Thank you!" His shaking hands reached halfway toward her, as though he wanted to embrace her but didn't have the courage. He stepped out, and the doors closed between them.

When she shut her eyes, the abrupt whirl from the cognac nearly thrust her to the floor. And still she had to rally through dinner with the Hirsches.

◄ ● ►

Pepper admired Rick's silhouetted profile as he drove through the long, tidy colonnade of prestige buildings on Park Avenue. She knew she was pretty enough to get by—she was slim with long, blond hair and big green eyes— but her friends agreed he was in a league unto himself. Part of her feared that he'd wise up and leave her, but he felt like her soul mate, to the extent that she believed in fated love. Birdie and George made marriage look easy; Pepper's parents, on the other hand, had never fought when Pepper was a child, but they divorced the minute Maisie graduated from college, as though they'd planned it for years and kept it secret. Mostly Pepper felt relief when she looked at Rick, that she had found the right person before she was too old to have children. Claudia had once let it drop that when you tried to have a baby after you turned thirty-five, doctors called it a "geriatric pregnancy." Pepper had wasted her most fertile years at rooftop parties, on vacations to trendy islands, and in a series of miserable jobs and four long-term relationships whose breakups were predictable to everyone but her. Even if she got pregnant on the honeymoon, she'd be thirty-four when she gave birth. That sounded old.

"How did the wine go over?" Rick asked.

"The president liked it so much she kept it," she said. "Maybe she thought it was some kind of bribe?"

"I'm sure she thought it was a gift," Birdie said from the backseat. "She thinks the world should be kissing her rump for the work she does."

"I did wonder how seven people were going to split one bottle," Pepper said. "I'd assumed everyone would bring something and we'd have a little picnic."

Birdie chuckled at that.

"Babe, you must have had *something*," Rick said, glancing at her. "I can smell it on you."

"I helped myself to some of her cognac." She hadn't meant to down the whole glass, but she'd needed to distract herself from her anger. "I think it may have upset Empress Pat." She giggled, finding it hard to stop.

"It was certainly bold," said Birdie, who clearly didn't approve of Pepper's appropriation of the bar cart.

"I don't get it," Rick said. "What happened?"

She twisted in her seat to address all of them at once. George couldn't fit in the back seat without having to hunch, in stark contrast to his wife, who could have ridden in his pocket. "There was a nice single lady who wanted to buy an apartment," Pepper said, "and everybody was pretending that they were deciding based on her 'financials,' but I'm pretty sure they rejected her because she's black."

"I'm not surprised," Rick said.

"Well, it surprised me," she said. "I mean, they were pretty bad."

"I assumed they were rejecting her because she was single," Birdie said. "But I agree with you, Penelope—I didn't like the way they were talking about her."

"Single people were always red flags," George said, staring out the window. He had served on the co-op board for decades; Birdie had recently taken his seat for a reason they didn't specify.

He'd been sullen all night; Pepper told herself that he was probably just a gloomy person, and that she wasn't to blame.

"With minorities, it was just that the few applicants we got were never good," he said.

Considering how Tiffany's application had been dismissed, Pepper wondered if some of the minority applicants weren't as bad as he thought.

"George, tell Penelope some of your stories about those buffoons," Birdie said. "Didn't one of Dougie McAllahan's friends-for-hire walk in on a meeting once?"

George grunted. "That was decades ago."

"Come on, George, you're such a wonderful storyteller. Tell us what happened."

He glared at her. "Why don't you tell that one, since you love it so much?"

She widened her eyes at Pepper, as if to say, "Look what I have to put up with," and Pepper realized that they had wandered into a fight. She turned to face forward in her seat.

"It was a college boy dressed up as a girl," Birdie said. "Dougie likes every dish in the buffet: boys that look like girls, girls that look like boys, boys on leashes, twins, you name it."

"Really?" Pepper asked. "He seemed so . . . conventional."

"We put up good appearances, don't we? Dougie was caught in bed with a fifteen-year-old girl once and nearly went to prison. But a few million dollars later, the girl's family forgot it ever happened. I'm not sure that girl ever forgot, though." She sighed.

"But as for the board meeting," Birdie continued, with a vehemence that implied a habit of forgetting to finish her stories, "this young hustler gets the time wrong for the appointment, and Dougie's chef thinks he's an intern, a girl intern, and sends him to the board meeting! The boy comes in and says in this squeaky voice, 'I'm looking for Sir Douglas?' And Dougie gently escorts him out and plays him off as a nephew. But here's the best part. When Patricia starts up the meeting again, the first thing out of her mouth is about not wanting to '*deviant* from the agenda'!" Everyone but George laughed. It gave Pepper some satisfaction to know that Dougie had been humiliated.

"I'm not sure it happened exactly like that," said George.

"Then why don't you tell it next time?" Birdie snapped.

They fell silent. Pepper watched Rick's big, confident hands turn the steering wheel onto Fifty-eighth Street and up to the curb of the restaurant. He gave the keys to the valet, slipping him a twenty and asking him to take special care of the car; he leased a new BMW every other year and was anxious about the slightest nick. Pepper got out of the car and wobbled upright, her vision swimming.

The restaurant took up three stories of a well-kept town house that could have been someone's home. There was no sign that it was a restaurant at all, not the name on the door or a menu in the window, and yet the city's gourmands had descended upon the place like cats hearing the can opener. Birdie had wanted to try it because it had received a three-star review in *The New York Times*—she had eaten at every three- and four-star restaurant in the city since 1988 and didn't want to break her streak. It had been nearly impossible to book a table, though; after six Mondays of calling at noon on the dot, she had only managed to squeeze them in at nine thirty on a Tuesday.

The interior was decorated like a farmhouse, with exposed raw-wood beams in the ceiling and bundles of twigs hanging from the walls and sprouting out of human-sized urns. A taxidermic bear head looked out, panic-stricken, on the dining room, above a hearth with a crackling fire. Servers in black T-shirts and jeans raced along the invisible grid between tables like well-mannered robots. Grandeur was passé, Pepper knew. Foodies didn't want marble columns or gilded chargers; they wanted to experience life on a farm—without having to till a field or birth a goat, of course.

"Welcome," the slender, motherly maître d' said with warmth but no enthusiasm, all alertness and control.

Their table wasn't ready, so they squeezed in at the bar, made from a tree trunk cut in half lengthwise and lacquered to a high shine. Birdie had been excited to try a cocktail with anise hyssop, lavender, and gin; George ordered a Tom Collins; Rick asked for a single-malt Scotch, neat; and Pepper, afraid to drink any more that night, ordered a Pellegrino.

While the bartender juggled bottle, shaker, and soda gun, Pepper's eye was drawn toward a sharply dressed black couple in their fifties who had just walked in. The man's mustache covered a wide upper lip, and the woman had long, straightened hair and wore sparkly green eye shadow. The man took off his trilby and, unbuttoning his coat, said to the maître d', "Two for dinner." He must not have realized that one couldn't just walk into a happening restaurant and expect to be served, even on a Tuesday night. Maybe they were tourists. Pepper moved closer so that she could hear.

The maître d' smiled empathically. "I'm sorry, but we have no availability at all tonight. We do leave our bar area open to walk-ins, and you're welcome to wait as long as you like, but I don't foresee anything opening up there, either. It tends to get even more crowded as the night goes on, un-fortunately."

The man looked around the restaurant. "I see open tables everywhere. Can't we sit at one of those? We'll be in and out."

"I'm afraid those are reserved for our ten and ten-thirty seatings," she said. "I'd be happy to recommend a few places nearby, if you'd like."

It bothered Pepper that not one other black person was in the restaurant, neither patron nor employee. The servers were all white, the busboys Hispanic. When she was a child, her mother had told her that minorities avoided this part of the Upper East Side because they wanted to live with "their own," and Pepper had passively believed that. But after sitting around Patricia's table and watching them reject a worthy black applicant, she felt complicit in something ugly.

The Cognac reached up to her brain and gave it a spin.

"We'll be leaving the bar in a minute," Pepper said to the black man. "I think you guys could squeeze in."

He looked at his wife, or maybe girlfriend, and shrugged. "Thank you," he said. "That's very kind."

She led them over to the bar, her hope draining away. The crowd was two and three people deep, and only three placemats were set out for diners, all of whom had their check. Even if the bartender served the couple, they'd be crowded the whole time. "Can we make some space for these folks?" she asked Rick. "They couldn't get a table."

"Uhh, sure," Rick said, stepping away from the bar with his Scotch and handing a slim glass of sparkling water to Pepper.

"You have to call Monday at noon, and keep trying until you reach some-one," Birdie told the black couple. "That's the only way."

"We didn't think it'd be a problem if we came late enough," the woman said, crossing her arms tightly. She made a helpless face at her husband.

As soon as George and Birdie evacuated the bar, others flooded in to take their places. Pepper couldn't very well stand there like Moses parting the Red Sea, but it upset her that these people wouldn't get to eat at the restaurant. The alcohol was rumbling in her belly and filling her head with squishy heat.

She approached the maître d'. "Hi, sorry to bother you, but I couldn't help overhearing that you couldn't seat these nice people. I know you have an extra table in there somewhere in case a VIP walks in, and probably two more because people ate faster than you expected. Can't you make an exception?"

If the maître d' was annoyed, she hid it expertly. She let out an art-gallery laugh. "My waiting list is twenty names long. If I squeezed in these fine citizens, it wouldn't be fair to any of the people who were here before." She addressed the black man, who now seemed anxious to leave. "If you show up at five sharp any day but Saturday, you'll very likely get a quiet meal at the bar. I regret that it's not possible tonight, but I hope you'll come back soon."

The couple approached the door and fastened their coats.

"Maybe I can convince our friends to give you our table," Pepper said.

"That's very kind," the man said, "but we couldn't accept that."

"Can I at least buy you a drink? They have really interesting cocktails."

The man's face held a combination of annoyance and fatigue. "Have a nice night." The two of them left.

She could feel Rick touching the small of her back, trying to help her through whatever disaster she'd cultivated. "You have a beautiful heart," he whispered.

The maître d' hugged four oversized menus to her chest. "Hirsch, party of four? Right this way." She pivoted and strode into the dining room.

They walked past diners regaling one another with stories, past plates of meat and fish, past the fire, its embers breathing light and dark, and Pepper began to cry. In came a familiar loneliness as old as she was, maybe older. Her mother scolding her for her curiosity. Her sister in her own world, incapable of understanding Pepper's mute sorrow. She hated herself for being so breakable.

The maître d' ushered them to a table in the center of the room, crowded with a precise topography of napkins, silverware, chargers, and glasses. She pulled out a chair for Birdie and helped her push it back in, then did the same for Pepper. She presented everyone an open menu and said, with her trademark smile that gave nothing away and let nothing in, "I do hope you enjoy our fall menu. Please let me know if there's anything else I can provide." Then she walked away, and Birdie raised her glass for the first toast of the night.

2

DAY OF ATONEMENT

Birdie placed the damp packet of filet in the refrigerator and tossed a pan of veal bones into the oven to roast. She and George adored filet mignon for its fork-tenderness and ability to meld with just about any sauce, from a béarnaise to *fruit des bois*, but the reason for its aphrodisiac power, she believed, was that it derived from the psoai, the long, narrow muscles flanking the erogenous area in cows and humans alike. It would be grotesque to remember the animal as one chewed its flesh, but she imagined that somewhere in those fibers lingered the meat's former purpose.

George was in the bedroom, sitting up in bed in a pair of plaid pajamas, watching an insipid dating show. The air smelled of his gas. It was difficult to look at him, decrepit and useless, his amorphous belly hanging to the side as though it were one of his possessions, like a briefcase or a hat. But she'd loved him so intensely and for so many years, her disgust couldn't extinguish her desire.

She opened the window. The buses on Madison Avenue grunted and sighed, and the sweet, yeasty odor from the boulangerie wafted in, clearing away his smell. "I'm making filet," she said, collecting a pair of socks and a dirty plate from the floor.

In the mid-eighties, on holiday at the George V in Paris, they'd ordered filets—Birdie followed Julia Child's dictum that everyone at the table must order the same dish, to prevent sharing—and the waiter dressed their steaks at the table with spoonfuls of demi-glace and a slab of soft butter. George pressed against her on the banquette and slid his hand up her thigh. While the starched waiters floated by with domed silver platters and enormous pepper grinders, he pleasured her to completion.

They'd made love almost daily well into their fifties, while their friends were dead tired from raising their impossible children, but now that the spigot had been shut off, she didn't know how to start it up again. If it was going to happen, she thought, it would happen after Yom Kippur dinner. After a good long fast, the future practically shimmered.

"I realized something in the middle of the night," he said, gazing at the ceiling. "I'm retired. I've been telling myself I'm just unemployed, but the fact is, no one will ever hire me again."

She sat next to him on the bed, right in a pile of crumpled tissues, which she brushed to the floor. "*We're* retired. Maybe we can make the best of it." She rubbed his leg.

In the corporate communications department at JolieBelle Cosmetics ("one word, two caps," he'd bellow to reporters), George had been instrumental in fashioning the company's sexy young image, in New York in the early 1970s, then in Montreal, and then, after an expansion in the mid-eighties, back in New York. She had worked as his secretary since they met. They'd dreamed about retiring for years, envisioning a grand send-off when he turned sixty-six, maybe seventy. But a few weeks before his forty-second service anniversary, when he was just sixty-three, the communications department was outsourced to a "dynamic media strategy" agency. If George wanted his golden parachute, he and Birdie had thirty minutes to pack up their office and leave. Six months of job hunting netted eight interviews and not a single job offer; Birdie suspected all of them balked when they saw his gray hair. He found some public-relations consulting work but was fired because he didn't have social media experience and spent too much time writing press releases, which, he was informed, nobody read anymore. News of the bloodletting at JolieBelle, including his termination, was covered in *The Wall Street Journal*; in George's eyes, this was tantamount to a public flogging. He wouldn't leave the apartment. She'd assumed he would buck up after a few weeks of lying low, but in this case, the tincture of time was revealed to be poison.

"Stop it." He pushed her hand away from his leg. "That doesn't feel good."

"I just wanted to give you a little massage," she said.

"You were hurting me."

"I'm sorry. I didn't mean to," she said, trying not to let his rejection upset her. "I'm heading out to the farmers market as soon as my bones are ready for stock. How's your fast going?"

He squinted at her. "*Today* is Yom Kippur? It's not even October yet."

"I didn't write the calendar."

He dropped his head on the pillow. "Birdie, I'm too old for this."

"I thought that word wasn't in your vocabulary."

"Then I'm too depressed. I'm too something."

"Will you fast for me? Sunset is at seven fifty. We'll be feasting before you know it."

"I can't pray to a God who would make me suffer like this."

"Who said anything about God?"

She couldn't tell if his stare held curiosity or revulsion.

"I love you, you know," she said.

"I know," he said, a tear forming in his eye. He knuckled it away.

"Do you think we might cuddle tonight?"

He closed his eyes. "I don't know. . . ."

She was surprised by a flare of anger. Not making love was bearable, but she couldn't stand asking and being rejected, time and again. "Forget it." She went to put the dish in the sink. Maybe he would change his mind after breaking the fast.

"Please don't leave."

Although she was cooking on deadline, she sat back down. She drew his head into her lap and combed his greasy nickel-colored hair with her fingers, smoothing out the ragged white hairs, thick as vermicelli, that had recently sprouted in all directions, and recreating the boyish part he used to wear.

"I want to try to be better to you," he said. "I want to be done with all this. Will you help me get better?"

"Let's fast together. It'll be good for you. For us. Dinner is going to be delicious."

He pulled her hand to his lips and kissed it, rubbing his bristly beard on her skin.

◄●►

She lingered in the Union Square Greenmarket, harvesting compliments on her reusable nylon shopping bags, one for each color of the rainbow. Tomatoes were still in season, just barely, and she bought a pint of Sun Golds—the only variety she could trust without an illicit sample—and a few knobby heirlooms in green, purple, and brown. At the mushroom stall, she sorted through the heap of shiitakes to find those whose caps hadn't begun to pale or fray. She picked a pound and a half of sour cherries, one by one. She filled her bags with handfuls of haricots verts, a vial of aged balsamic, a luxuriant bouquet of basil, a jar of local honey, a packet of Himalayan pink salt, a crusty loaf of artisanal rye, a wedge of soft, lumpy gorgonzola, a tub of Amish butter, and beeswax candles and a nosegay of lavender for the table. She could have spent the rest of her life orbiting the booths. Of everything in New York, the passion and bustle of the market reminded her most of Montreal. For that reason, it also made her melancholy.

She'd met George in 1973, when she took a job as his secretary in the public-relations department of JolieBelle's Montreal office. He'd been shipped in from the New York office to run the publicity unit and, driven by a preternatural zeal, was promptly promoted above his manager to vice president of the entire communications department. She enjoyed listening to him talk to journalists; the polished twang of his phone voice reminded her of classic movies. A week after they'd met, he asked her to dinner at a modest bistro, and before they knew it, they had fallen in love. She adored his childlike grin and his ironclad will, malleable only to her. Because dating within the office was forbidden, they shared only glances, controlling their appetites until nighttime, when their slender, youthful bodies collided in his twin bed.

In the months after they met, they couldn't afford airfare or fancy hotels, so they packed their bags, hopped into her rusty Peugeot, and took right and left turns on a whim. Somehow they always ended up in a charming village with a reasonably priced auberge, and they spent their holidays discovering hidden wonders and meeting friendly locals.

She missed those early days the most, back when they didn't have everything they wanted and still longed for Michelin-starred meals, Mediterranean cruises, a well-appointed country home. The anticipation was everything. Now, at sixty-two years old, she could spend all day preparing a meal only to lose her appetite after a single bite.

◄●►

Thinking she might try a new lipstick, Birdie stopped in at the nearby cosmetics shop, leaving her groceries at the register. Makeup did no favors to her petite features, and she rarely wore it—which had caused trouble for George at JolieBelle.

The girl who welcomed her had smudged eyeliner all around her eyes. Birdie had read about this makeup style while flipping through a beauty magazine at the doctor's office—smoky eye, it was called—but couldn't understand why anyone would want to look like a battered woman.

"I don't usually wear makeup," Birdie said, "but I'd like to see if I can take a few years off."

"No problem," Smoky Eyes said. She applied a sample of a clownish orangey-red to Birdie's lips.

Birdie stared at herself in the mirror, smiling and puckering, trying to make the lipstick appear natural on her pale face. She wondered if it was time to plump the area where her lips used to be, or fill out her deepening crow's feet. Or maybe to transition her jet-black hair, which was starting to look like a wig against her wrinkling forehead, to something lighter and more easily maintained. "It'll take some getting used to."

"It matches your coloring, and it's very trendy," Smoky Eyes said. Every sentence that spilled from her pouty mouth ended in a drawn-out syllable. "It totally transforms you."

"Doesn't it look a bit . . . deranged?" Birdie asked.

"To look young, you have to look daring," Smoky Eyes said, touching Birdie on the upper arm. "And you look daring."

Birdie asked for some time to think. When no one was looking, she put her hands on her cheeks and gently pulled upward and back to erase her lines. Now the lipstick looked right. She wasn't the type to care about face-lifts; she hadn't minded aging while George still desired her. But maybe a subtle nip and tuck wouldn't turn her into a freak show.

She headed to the cash register with the lipstick, scanning the JolieBelle shelves on the way. Her husband's company had launched a new line called Princess, with a drawing of a Cinderella look-alike on the glitter-coated display.

"You don't want that," Smoky Eyes said from behind her, startling her. "That's for kids."

"Kids?"

"Kids and tweens. It's our fastest-growing demo."

The idea horrified her. "But what use do children have for makeup?"

The girl shrugged. "Everyone wants to look beautiful. Hey, check this out." She produced a small white box.

Birdie turned the box over in her fingers. It was an "age-reversing serum with stem-cell technology."

"It's the most advanced antiaging technology on the market," the girl said. "My customers swear by it."

She wondered if Smoky Eyes hawked this to all the mature women who walked in, or if she reserved the recommendation for women who complained about their age.

"Pretty much all the products that claim to be stem-cell creams don't do anything, but this has actual human stem cells in it and is proven to work. There's, like, a ton of research on it."

"Where do they get the stem cells?" Birdie asked.

The girl laughed. "You don't want to know. Trust me."

Indeed, "human stem cells" was listed among the dozens of ingredients. She'd seen articles about these cells and their promise of eternal youth. "No, tell me. I want to know."

"I'm actually not allowed to tell you. People don't want it when they find out."

"How about I buy it, and then you tell me?"

"And you promise not to return it?"

"Promise." Birdie crossed her heart.

The serum cost three hundred dollars, more than she was supposed to be spending now that George wasn't working. But spending his money was satisfying, a subtle revenge. She put it, along with the lipstick, in her bag with the tubs and jars from the market. "Now you have to tell me."

The girl held her hand to the side of her mouth and whispered into Birdie's ear: "You know when they circumcise baby boys? Sometimes they don't, you know, throw it away." She stepped back, pursing her lips as if to stifle a grin.

"So, it's . . . foreskins?" Birdie whispered.

Smoky Eyes nodded slowly.

Birdie shivered. It didn't sound sanitary. And where on earth would they find so many? As soon as she exited the store, she dabbed a little onto her crow's feet. It smelled rubbery and sweet. She felt buoyed by a spurt of youthful energy.

◄ ● ►

Birdie held her groceries slightly behind her as she rushed past Francis Levy in the lobby of the Chelmsford Arms. Her neighbor, whose lengthy visits to the doormen smacked of loneliness, was sitting on the guest settee in a white button-down shirt, wrinkled khakis, and white sneakers, the bland uniform she often saw on Yom Kippur. She liked him—as much as good neighbors needed to. She supposed they could be called friends.

"Birdie!" Francis called, not getting up. "*Gut yontif.*"

"Francis, I didn't see you!" she exclaimed. "So wonderful to run into you. I would love to chat, but George is waiting for me upstairs. Happy Yom Kippur."

She realized her mistake in his pedantic wince. "It's not really meant to be a happy holiday," he said.

"Isn't there something happy in forgiving each other for our wrong-doings over the past year? For starting over with a clean slate?" The lobby was hardly the place for conversation, but Francis could be forgiven for wanting company. His wife took great pains to avoid him.

"It's not about forgiving each other, you see. It's about atoning for our offenses to God."

"Sounds like you know your stuff, Mr. Levy," said Ranesh, an irritatingly earnest porter who hadn't yet tired of Francis's lectures.

"What can I say? It's in my bones." He patted his rib cage.

"Speaking of bones," she interjected with a raised finger, "mine are waiting for me in the stockpot." She wasn't going to apologize for shopping or cooking on a holiday when shopping and cooking were almost as forbidden as eating and drinking. She wasn't even technically Jewish. George was the Jew in their relationship, which had caused a rift in both their families. But she liked the discipline of the ancient customs—and the fact that most of the holidays focused on the presence or absence of food and drink.

"What are you making?" Francis asked.

"I'm planning a special break-fast tonight. Filet mignon from Lobel's."

He raised his eyebrows. "Filet mignon after a fast? Isn't that a little rich?"

"George and I have a tradition of eating well after fasting all day."

"I thought he had terrible heartburn."

"One rich meal won't kill him."

"I prefer the tradition of eating simply after the fast," he said. "In the years after my father died, my brother and I would watch my mother wail and beat her chest for hours and say kaddish for my father with tears streaming down her cheeks. After a whole day of fasting and repentance, we would come home to a dinner of cold chicken and peas. It was peasant food, but we were happy, because for that night, my mother was present with us."

Francis's stories always implicated anyone who liked nice things. "That's a wonderful story," she said.

"Just be careful not to make a religion of the food. The power of the holiday has nothing to do with what you eat afterward. We become pure through sustained repentance."

She forced a smile. "I do need to get going. . . ."

"How is George? Did he start analysis?"

She didn't want Francis blabbing about George's depression to the staff and passersby. "I'll fill you in later." She stepped back a few paces.

"I'm worried about him, Birdie. Is he free now? Maybe I could cheer him up."

The last thing she wanted was Francis convincing George not to eat her filet or getting in the way of her efforts to seduce him. "I'm afraid today won't be good for a visit, George; he doesn't want to be disturbed during the holiday."

"*Gut yontif!*" Francis said to Patricia Cooper, the Jewish chairwoman of the co-op board, as she hobbled by with a menacing wave of her colorful enameled cane. Her nasty Pomeranian yipped at Birdie as they passed.

Seeing her chance to escape, Birdie raced past Patricia, past the fragrant lilies in giant glass cylinders, past the stairwell, past the elegant little mailroom. Only when she reached the elevator did she glance behind her. "*À bientôt!*" she called out with a friendly wave.

◀◆▶

Birdie didn't have much time left before sundown, but after setting the groceries down and checking on her stock, she dropped in on her neighbor Penelope for a quick hello. The girl was engaged to Rick Hunter, dashing and moneyed and sometimes quite amusing, and Birdie wanted to soak up some of Penelope's hope at starting her lifelong journey with him.

But Penelope was watching a zombie show on television and eating candy. The scene was made sadder by the apartment itself; its unspeakably awful previous owner had treated it like a halfway house.

"Don't you want to dress up the place a bit?" Birdie asked, perhaps too adamantly.

"All of this is going away," Penelope replied, waving her hand about loosely, "as soon as the stupid contractors can schedule us in."

That made sense, but still, the girl's indolence bothered Birdie. It was the path to unhappiness. She saw it in George and, years back, herself. "I find that I'm happiest when I'm cooking," she said, trying not to sound judgmental. "It's always an adventure, and it fills in the darker moments with hope and happiness. If you could find an avocation, you would leap out of bed in the mornings and keep a smile on your face until bedtime."

Penelope looked confused; perhaps the junk food was dulling her brilliant mind. "You sound like my mother. Don't worry, I'm looking for work."

"Maybe I can help. I'll give it some thought." She said goodbye, unable to tolerate another minute in that apartment.

When she returned to her kitchen, the veal bones had begun to surrender their musky essence. She pinched together a pâte brisée with flour and ice-cold butter on a chilled marble slab and adorned it with sour cherries, sugar, lemon juice, a splash of brandy, and extra dots of butter. She prepared the tomato salad, resisting the urge to suck the tomato seeds and slivers of basil off her dripping fingers. It was, after all, still Yom Kippur, and the magic of the holiday wouldn't work if she nibbled. She worked herself into a frenzy, giving herself the pleasure of not having to think. Every so often, she peeked into the bedroom, where George was producing a gut-wrenching snore. He'd be up half the night, but he could make his own decisions.

As the sun descended, she strained the veal stock, bewitched by its clean, masculine aroma. It saddened her that the demi-glace, the most delicious sauce in the French repertoire and best friend to all manner of beef, was extracted from the bones of baby cows. But the spirit of those calves made the sauce mellow and velvety. It was impossible not to be seduced by youth, she thought. Its presence and absence vibrated in everything.

Her knees buckled with hunger. In the synagogues, Jews would be wailing the final prayers, their voices desperate with exhaustion, begging to be inscribed in the Book of Life, the magical book that foretold who would live another year and who would die. It was one reason she avoided services on Yom Kippur; she had no desire to be reminded of her death.

◄●►

She had everything on the table before calling George. He had showered, shaved, and put on a clean dress shirt and slacks. "You've outdone yourself," he said, kissing her, arousing her with his smoky cologne. "Did a delivery come while I was sleeping?"

"Not that I'm aware of. Were you expecting something?"

"I was. . . . It should have gotten here by now." Shrugging, he picked up the spoon in the tomato salad. "May I serve?"

"We still have three minutes before the shofar is blown."

"God won't mind if we start a few minutes early."

She stared at her empty plate. "I want to wait." It would have been hard to defend her request. Here they were, about to tuck into nonkosher meat slathered in dairy, all purchased and cooked during the day of the year when it was most important not to do anything but beg God for forgiveness, and she was going to keep her husband from eating three minutes before the prescribed time. But she wanted to observe the holiday according to their tradition, and that meant hewing to the restriction. Was this making a religion of the food, as Francis had warned?

She got up to dress the filets with demi-glace, rosemary, and Gorgonzola. She freshened her lipstick and rubbed her new serum on her crow's feet. Upon her return, George was sniffing the lavender centerpiece. She wondered when it had become so difficult to talk to him. He'd been successful at JolieBelle because he knew how to fill a room with his voice, and now he barely spoke.

He sat back and examined her. She looked away. "You look beautiful," he said. "Did I get you that lipstick?"

"I bought it today."

"It's not JolieBelle, I hope."

She shook her head, smiling. "I would never."

"Well, you look beautiful," he repeated. "Just like when we first met."

She blushed. "Thank you. You look very handsome yourself."

"I clean up nice." He grinned, and she couldn't help laughing.

Staring into George's eyes in the candlelight and inhaling the cocktail of flavors made her weak with desire. They would enjoy the meal together, seasoned by their appetites, and then, she hoped, proceed to the bedroom. She wanted it desperately.

He cleared his throat. "It's not often we get a chance to appreciate how delicious and beautiful your food is before eating it," he said. "I forgot how much I liked Yom Kippur."

"I've missed you, George," she said.

"I'm sorry. I made an appointment with Dr. Clay to tweak my meds."

"You don't have to apologize."

"Sorry."

"I want . . ." Her voice faltered. The hunger was making her maudlin. "I want to move back to Montreal. I think we'll both be happier there."

"Those were magical years," he said.

"I want them back. We could buy one of those simple flat-roofed houses in Mile End, and I could go to the farmers market anytime I felt like it."

"And we could get bagels at St-Viateur every morning."

"And we could buy a spunky little Peugeot," she said, "like the one I drove when we met, and take weekend trips to the countryside, and stay in those horrible inns."

He chuckled. "We could do better than a Peugeot. And we could definitely do better than those moldy flea traps."

"I don't want to," she whispered.

"We could winter in Saint Martin."

"We could summer in Prince Edward Island."

He reached across the table and took her hands. His gaze was kind and strong. "Let's sell the apartment and go. I'll call the broker tomorrow."

The clock read 7:53. Yom Kippur had been over for a few minutes. But she didn't let go of his hands. She felt seen, more fully than she had in years.

He glanced out the window. It was dark outside except for the lights in the streetlamps and the windows of nearby buildings. The moon glowed resolutely. "Isn't it time yet?"

"Just another minute," she said.

He looked at his watch. "Didn't you say it was over at seven fifty? It's seven fifty-four."

"I'm sorry, I must have hallucinated from the hunger!" She laughed.

He plopped a filet onto his plate and spooned on extra sauce. She reached for the haricots verts and tomato salad, then forked her own piece of meat.

"*Baruch atah Adonai*, let's eat!" he shouted.

She gobbled down the food, her body quivering with relief. She couldn't remember the last time she'd felt so happy.

"Birdie, you've outdone yourself."

"Don't make me stop to speak!" she cried, catching a piece of tomato as it escaped her lips.

Within a few minutes, her belly felt distended, yet she didn't feel satisfied. Her stomach had shrunk from fasting: every year she knew it would happen, and every year she managed not to believe it. She put one last morsel of buttery filet in her mouth and forced herself to swallow, then leaned back in her chair and sipped her wine while George chewed.

"Remember when we used to get in the car and just drive?" she asked.

He nodded, swallowing. "Yeah, that was fun."

"It occurred to me today how miraculous it was that we always ended up somewhere wonderful. Did that ever occur to you, how charmed our lives were then?"

He looked puzzled. "Sweetheart, I always planned out those trips in advance. The left-right thing was a joke. How could you not know that?"

The wine soured in her mouth. "You told me it was serendipity."

"I assumed that a reasonably intelligent woman would have noticed that I stopped letting you pick the turns after a while, or, I don't know, that we always had a reservation wherever we went?"

She herded tomato seeds around her plate with her fork, trying to reconstitute a memory of knowing what was really going on. She felt idiotic for believing those trips had been magical. She watched him traffic food into his mouth, listened with revulsion to the slaps and snorts of his chewing, wondered how else her memories of their life together might be distorted. He ferried a second filet onto his plate and methodically devoured it. Embracing the bowl of golden tomato salad in one arm, he polished it off, piece by piece. Why hadn't his stomach shrunk, too? It seemed impossible that someone who'd fasted all day could eat so much.

She jerked upright. "You didn't fast."

He kept his gaze on the empty tomato bowl. "It doesn't mean I don't love you. I dressed up. I showered and shaved. Can't that be enough?"

Again she felt deceived, as though all their daydreaming about Montreal had been based on a lie. "It's our tradition. It's something we do together."

"Eating after a fast gives me a bad stomachache. You know that." He folded a slice of bread into his mouth.

"You promised you'd fast."

"I did not promise. I never promise anything."

She wanted to pluck the crooked gray hairs peeking out from his ears. She couldn't believe she would have considered making love with this ancient ogre just a few minutes earlier.

"Can we please just have dessert?" he asked.

"Dessert is for people who fasted."

He pushed his plate away and fiddled with the saltshaker. "I am trying to be better to you, Birdie," he said through clenched teeth, "but you are not making it easy."

She looked at the slope and hunch of his shoulders and at his belly, squeezed against the edge of the table. His deterioration was an affront. "Trying isn't good enough."

He plodded into the kitchen, unbuttoning his shirt. She followed him in and saw that he was heading for the tart.

"No!" she cried.

"Calm down, Birdie. Our neighbors are going to think I'm abusing you." He selected a knife from the silverware drawer and cut into the tart.

"You *are* abusing me." Before she could stop herself, she snatched away the tart and thrust it facedown into the garbage. It killed her to waste such a beautiful creation, but she couldn't stand that George might even get to taste it. She couldn't understand why she'd wanted to do anything nice for him. Her hunger had cast a strange spell.

He gaped into the trash can. "And you think I'm the sick one." He trudged into the spare bedroom and slammed the door.

The shattered pastry shell in the trash can looked like a scream. Her anger was unbearable, but she couldn't look away from the tart. She wanted to suffer if only to use it as a weapon against him.

A few minutes later, the doorbell rang. It was Ranesh, holding a bouquet of red roses and grinning. "Mrs. Hirsch? These are for you."

With the roses nestled in the crook of her arm, she opened the tiny envelope containing the card. It read:

> *Dear Birdie,*
> *You're the world to me. I know I haven't been easy to live with*
> *recently, but I'm going to try my best to deserve you.*
> *Love always,*
> *George*

"I hope this was a good time to bring these to you," Ranesh said as Birdie stared at the blossoms, dumbstruck. "Your holiday is finished, yes?"

She nodded.

"Oh, good. I know that you didn't want to be disturbed until the holiday was finished. I learned today that Jewish holidays end at sundown."

"These came earlier?" she managed to ask.

"Yes, a few hours ago," he said. "I kept them in the refrigerator room until you were ready to receive them."

She mumbled a thank-you, closed the door, and placed the bouquet on the console table. The blossoms, two dozen of them, were enormous, the petals velvety and crisp, the stems stripped of their thorns. It was excruciating to look at them. She didn't think she could go into the spare bedroom to apologize, but maybe he would come out, having heard the doorbell. She stared at the roses, trying to decide what to do. If she put them in a vase, she would certainly cry. She hoped they would survive the night without water.

She cleared the table, stacked the tubs of leftovers in the refrigerator, loaded the dishwasher, and wiped down the counters. Then she sat in the kitchen for a long time, listening to the hum of the refrigerator and the satisfied gurgle of the dishwasher.

3

THIRTY-THREE

Pepper wanted her wedding to be simple. No bridesmaids, no centerpieces, no priest, no band. No butlered hors d'oeuvres, no five-tier cake, no dessert buffet. No gift bags, no stylist, no veil, no rice. No limo, and certainly no cans rattling behind.

She and Rick would pick a date in the spring when a tolerable temperature could be relied upon and do their "I do"s in Central Park. Then everyone would hop in taxis to a low-key lunch at Patsy's or Pastis or Peter Luger. She'd wear a white lace cutout dress she'd found for twenty-nine dollars at Zara and pick up a box of cupcakes from Magnolia Bakery, where she and Rick often ate dessert for breakfast, the one meal of the day when he allowed himself sugar and fat. She'd email the invitations, maybe through Paperless Post to make sure her friends knew it wasn't a joke.

They might even be jealous. Her married friends had bemoaned their splashy weddings—one of which was so costly it might have played a role in the couple's divorce a year later—and when Pepper told her ninety-eight-year-old Grandma Phyllis that she was getting married, the wheelchair-bound dowager beckoned her close and uttered a single husky word: "Elope."

For his part, Rick's wedding vision took place in the grand ballroom of the Waldorf Astoria, but he deferred to her. "We can do it in our living room, if you want. As long as we do it. And do it. And do it."

"We'll do it to our heart's content," she had replied, nuzzling into his cheek. And without any warning or ceremony, they made love. After years of experiencing sex with other boyfriends as a tightrope between the amusing and the disgusting, it was a relief to feel at one with Rick's body, to put herself in his care and know that she was safe.

The simple wedding had another detail to recommend it: it would drive her mother mad. Claudia Lindbergh Bradford was a confection of galas and soirees, garden parties, fetes. The woman had given Pepper a subscription to *Elegant Bride* when she was fourteen. (Granted, it came free with a perfume purchase, but still. . . .) Pepper was allergic to Claudia's rigid social etiquette; she wanted the wedding to be about her love with Rick, not her mother's photo in *New York Social Diary*.

She hadn't found the courage to break all this to her parents, though. They hadn't even met Rick. In the past, Claudia had taken boyfriend introductions as permission to declare their unsuitability as husbands. Louie was successful and kind, and he would be a great father . . . but it really was best to partner with someone closer in age, wasn't it? Duvall was very well-spoken and intelligent . . . but one had to think about how the children would be treated. She liked Cornelius, she did, but he wasn't very quick, was he?—and after looks fade, one survives on wit. And Gabriel was an absolute catch . . . for some young gentleman.

The frustrating thing was that her mother was usually right, in a roundabout way. Pepper left Louie because people assumed that a woman her age couldn't be his intellectual peer—or that she was his daughter. It didn't help that he shared her father's narrow, chiseled face and dry laugh, and practically his name, Lewis. She broke up with Duvall because he was always calling her out on the smallest things: when she complimented his sister's thick, soft braids, expressed gratitude for the police, and referred (ironically, she'd thought) to the color of his cousin's skin as "caramel macchiato." Her affection for Cornelius soured when he admitted that he had never even heard of Virginia Woolf or Dorothy Parker, and it occurred to her that he might not know how to read. As for Gabriel, she ended it because they stopped having sex, and he was spending more and more time at the gym. Six weeks later, his Facebook wall announced that he was in a relationship with a man.

She already knew what her mother would say about Rick: his family had no standing. When he was sixteen, his father had been laid off from a tire factory in Akron, Ohio, after which his family moved to some depressed town along the Ohio River, outside of Cincinnati, where his parents got by picking up odd jobs until they retired. Rick had gone to public school. She could hear the twangy syllables of "Cincinnati" bouncing off Claudia's tongue.

But he was the smartest man she knew, wry and generous and handsome—he looked like Archie crossed with Superman. He knew her body in ways that she hadn't. And when he gazed at her, bearing the full weight of his attention upon her, she had never felt so alive. And didn't it mean something that he had risen from poverty to become an extremely successful wealth manager? She could feel her indignation rise.

So in November, when the likely wedding date was fourish months away, and when their apartment renovations were all set to go, she popped an Ativan and told her mother, then her father, that she was engaged. With enthusiasm that Pepper found hard to believe, they invited Pepper and Rick to a Thursday lunch in Lewis's West Chelsea apartment. Rick didn't love taking a two-hour lunch break, especially during one of the busiest months at his job, but Pepper had learned only to visit her parents immediately before going to therapy. That way she could sift through her upset with Dr. Riffler, mixing it with bits of understanding while it was still fresh, to keep it from hardening into depression.

She liked her father's new place. After her parents' bizarre, amicable divorce in 2004, Lewis rented a one-bedroom on the sixtieth floor of a pencil-thin skyscraper on West Fifty-seventh Street, so vertiginously high she couldn't look out the window without imagining her death. A few years later, he bought a two-bedroom duplex with a terrace that abutted the newly opened High Line park, a long, narrow walkway atop a disused railroad trestle.

Post divorce, Lewis liked to pretend that he and Claudia were sworn enemies, but that couldn't have been true. There had been no yelling, no battles over money or for the loyalty of their daughters, nothing remotely interesting except for Claudia's long-standing irritation at Lewis's humor. When the Chelsea apartment was finally ready to welcome guests (the bespoke Italian sofa was held up in customs for six months), Pepper was shocked to see vacation photos of their whole family, mother included, hanging in the stairwell. This was one more thing she would never understand about her parents. She was trying to accept that she would never understand anything about them.

◀ ◈ ▶

When Pepper and Rick stepped out of the private elevator into her father's foyer, a pair of birdlike women were assembling plates of cantaloupe, grapefruit, and raspberries with surgical precision. Her parents sat cross-legged on the well-traveled sofa, nursing Bloody Marys, and Maisie and Rahul were kneeling at the wrought-iron coffee table, flipping through a tome of baby pictures from Pepper's and Maisie's childhoods. Through the window, the High Line was squeezed with tourists like cattle being funneled toward slaughter.

Pepper sat in a comfy tufted armchair pushed up against a vase of birch branches, and Rick perched on the arm next to her. He wore a blazer and khakis, and she had chosen a silver lamé tank top with layered silver-thread necklaces, harem pants, and high-heeled boots: stylish but not too dressy, as she didn't want this first meeting to be too big a deal.

"Hello Lewis. Hello Claudia. Hello Maisie. Hello Rahul." At the same time as Pepper began introducing herself as Penelope, she had also started calling her parents by their first names, hoping they would treat her more like an adult if she treated them as equals. "You couldn't even cook brunch yourself?"

"It's lovely to see you too, Pepper," her mother said, extending her bony fingers, freshly manicured with nude polish, toward Rick. Her shoulder-length blond flip was freshly dyed. "I'm Claudia Bradford. You're even more handsome in person." Apparently she reverted back to her married name for special occasions.

"I bought a new face just for you," Rick said, taking her hand in both of his. "The plastic surgeons can do anything these days."

Claudia's smile puckered. Rick must not have realized that she'd treated herself to a face-lift after the divorce.

"We didn't want cooking to interfere with our conversation," Lewis finally explained to Pepper. "Lewis Bradford," he said to Rick. "We've heard great things about you."

"And I, you," Rick replied. He shook her father's hand, sandwiching it in both of his. She had dated so many men who came with disclaimers, it was a relief not to have to be Rick's publicist. Soon, they might like him more than they liked her—an exciting future that would bring its own familiar annoyance.

"Pepper tells us you're in finance?" her father said.

"Asset management," Rick said. "I find lucrative ways to invest people's money."

"He's extremely successful," Pepper said.

"So you help the rich get richer?" Maisie asked, stroking her belly. Pepper wondered if she was pregnant. She and Rahul were both drinking Pellegrino.

"Maisie," said Claudia, "you pretend you don't have a dollar to your name."

"I help them choose promising investments," Rick explained. "People forget that most of what Wall Street does is help companies grow." He rolled out a disarming smile.

"Just like people forget lawyers are in the business of seeking fairness and upholding our justice system," Lewis said.

"Right on!" Rick said. "I knew there was a reason I liked you."

Lewis laughed. "When you get to know me a little bit, you might change your mind."

The caterers brought in the fruit plates, and everyone took a tentative first bite. Each artistic melon pile was coated in honey and sprinkled with crunchy flakes of salt.

"Mr. Bradford, this is possibly the best fruit salad I've ever eaten," Rick said.

"The caterers are right there," Lewis replied, nodding toward the kitchen, "if you want to compliment them."

"Then here's a compliment that's just for you. Great tie!"

Lewis and Claudia laughed. Pepper was relieved that they appreciated his humor.

"We wanted to talk about the wedding," she said.

"Wonderful," Claudia said, sliding her half-finished plate onto the coffee table. "I inquired into availability at the Plaza, and there are still a few dates open in June."

Pepper took a deep breath. This wasn't going to be easy. "You don't have to help out, Mother. We're doing something small and informal."

"Meaning . . . ?" Claudia said.

"Meaning it's just going to be our immediate families and a few friends. A small service in the park, an informal lunch, and that's it."

Rick's finger traced circles on her lower back in silent support.

"I thought you always wanted to do it at Saint Thomas's."

She shook her head. "*You* wanted to do it at Saint Thomas's."

Claudia reached for her Bloody Mary.

"We go to church once a year," Pepper said. "Do you even believe in God?"

"Of course I do. Don't be ridiculous."

"Why don't we hash all this out later?" Lewis offered, giving Claudia's hand a squeeze. Pepper wished they wouldn't act like a married couple around her.

"We can't *hash it out later*," her mother said. "Later, she'll be married. Do you still want to wear Grandma Phyllis's wedding dress?"

"Mommy!" She realized she had slipped. "Claudia, I have never wanted to be married in that hideous dress. You can bury me in it if you like."

"Your grandmother has wanted you to wear that dress since you were born."

"It's butt-ugly," Maisie volunteered. "Sorry, Mommy."

"Maybe we could have it altered."

"I really don't want to have to fight about every little detail," Pepper snapped. "It's my wedding; I'm going to marry the man I love and move the fuck on with my life."

She hadn't meant to swear, and she saw in her mother's shocked expression the damage it had done. "Pepper, sweetheart, you misunderstand. I am not trying to start a fight. This is your wedding, and your decision. I simply needed a moment to scale back my expectations."

"I'm sorry. I'm sorry." She was near tears, regretting how angry she'd gotten at the woman for a viewpoint she might not have held in the first place. She hated that she couldn't talk to her without lashing out. Dr. Riffler had hypothesized that she fought with Claudia when she wanted both independence and care, but Pepper didn't want care from her horrible mother. Rick's arm touched down on her shoulders, reminding her to breathe.

"We love the idea, Pepper," Lewis said. "We'll use the money we would have spent on the wedding on a big present for the two of you."

"We will accept payment in fruit salad!" Rick announced. "And that tie."

"I'm sure we can do better than that," Lewis said, laughing heartily.

Pepper restrained herself from kissing Rick.

◀◆▶

On Monday, her mother invited her to lunch and asked that she not bring Rick. "We like him, honey, of course we do," Claudia said, "and of course we look forward to spending loads of time with him, but with him we can't be ourselves, not yet at least." Claudia only said "of course" when she meant the opposite, but Pepper couldn't believe they had a single criticism of Rick.

"Rick's not judgmental at all," Pepper said. "He really likes you guys, and I think he might feel left out if he's not invited." The second part wasn't true, and he was so busy at work, he probably would have had to bow out anyway. But she didn't like that they didn't want him there.

"Just do this for us, okay? It'll be like old times."

She didn't want to revert to old times, when her parents ran her life; she wanted to forge a new relationship with them as equals. But the anti-wedding was going to be difficult enough for them. She could yield on lunch. At least she was able to negotiate the meal away from either of her parents' homes and to Park Avenue Autumn; the formality of the restaurant would keep their barbarism in check.

Lewis and Claudia had almost finished a bottle of white wine when Pepper arrived at the table, ten minutes late: she'd waffled between wearing a form-fitting black dress or tailored pantsuit, ravishing daughter or hard-headed dealmaker, ultimately settling on the former. The restaurant was full but quiet, and she dodged a few servers while squeezing between tables. Logs hung from ropes along the ceiling, which felt autumnal without being literal, and she fleetingly wished her wedding could be artistic. But she knew better than to throw away a year of her life to sate a passing aesthetic hunger. She gave her parents bent-over hugs and sat down as a server tucked the chair in behind her, the genteel version of a trust fall.

"So, how is living with Rick?" Claudia asked, rapping her fingernails against the hard leather menu.

"Really well," she said. "It just feels so good to be in love." All her friends and Dr. Riffler had said it would take time to get used to living with a man, but Rick was tidy and considerate, and she was grateful not to have to take a cab to see him.

"He does seem very clean," Claudia said, as if that were the best compliment she could part with.

Lewis asked, "Did you hear about Maisie?"

"She's pregnant," Pepper guessed.

"Twelve weeks. Our first grandchild!"

Pepper worked to maintain her smile. She had always assumed her own children would be older than her younger sister's. She also wished Maisie had told her instead of letting the news filter through their parents, but that was the Bradford way: a dynasty of silence and distance.

The server, a pretty but plain actress type who was probably wasting her life trying to become a star, approached to ask if they had any questions about the menu.

Lewis squinted at the type, then put on his reading glasses and tried again. "Why do they put pomegranate in everything nowadays? What does it even taste like?"

"It's for texture," Claudia muttered. "Not everything is about taste."

"Do you know what you want, Mommy?" her father asked. They had always called each other Mommy and Daddy and never stopped, even after their split.

"I'll have the endive salad, without the Roquefort."

"Pepper?"

She hated salad; it was insane that a whole category of dish was based on lettuce, a vegetable that tasted like water. She ordered the hanger steak with whipped potatoes, and her father ordered the same. Without writing anything down, the server nodded and sauntered away.

"So, what did you think of Rick?" she asked. "He's hilarious, right?"

Her parents looked at each other as if deciding how honest to be.

"About Rick . . ." Lewis began.

Pepper panicked. She had lived this moment too many times before, the moment when her parents told her not to marry her fiancé. "You don't like him because he doesn't come from money?"

"Pepper . . ."

"Or is it because his parents didn't go to college? Or because they've never been to New York?"

"None of those things," Claudia said, exasperated. "I hope you don't think we're snobs. All we want is for you to be happy. We just don't think he's going to make you happy."

Pepper lost her appetite. If she hadn't been so confident about Rick's likability, she might have predicted this ambush. Maybe they were getting back at her for not wanting to get married in a church. "And why exactly is that?"

"He's dishonest, sweetheart."

"How could you possibly know whether he's honest or not?" she cried, trying not to let her mother's implications sink in. "You talked to him for all of an hour, and, okay, maybe he was nervous. You don't know how nervous you make people." She heard how loud she was being, and she could feel every eye in the room turning toward her. But when she looked to either side, no one seemed to be watching.

"We didn't have to talk to him, Pepper," Lewis said, keeping his voice down. "People like that, you know it the second you look them in the eye. He's a seducer. He's a snake. He's all shell and no core."

"Give me one example," she said. She willed herself not to cry. She did not want to give them that victory.

"It's not about examples," Claudia said. "It's about character."

"I knew you would do this," Pepper said. "I knew it."

"We wanted to like him, honey, we really did." Claudia reached for Pepper's hand on the table to console her, but Pepper crossed her arms, and Claudia's bony hand settled on her ex-husband's instead. "But as soon as you two walked in, your father and I had the same thought. He's like a used-car salesman. For that kind of person, a lie is the same as the truth."

Pepper was certain her mother had never bought a used car, much less met someone who sold them. And her parents lied to her all the time: for starters, they'd pretended to love each other for the first twenty-four years of her life. But she knew they wouldn't accept her arguments. They'd never taken her opinions seriously and wouldn't start now. "You didn't even try to get to know him," she said. "You just make these pronouncements, and you don't know the first thing about him."

"Do you know him?" Claudia asked. "How long ago did you meet?"

"Last December." She knew most couples waited more than seven months before moving in together, but they were in their thirties, and they'd known from day one that they were meant for each other. And her eggs wouldn't last forever.

"That seems awfully fast."

"We didn't need more time. We love each other. We make each other laugh. We like being together. I've never met anyone so right before." The more she insisted, the less credible she sounded to herself.

Now her eyeballs were floating in tears, and she held still to keep them from spilling over. She hated that she was thirty-three years old and couldn't control her emotions. *What would it mean if your parents didn't like him?* Dr. Riffler had asked. Now Pepper saw that their opinion mattered more than anything. She couldn't make it not matter. How would Dr. Riffler respond to that? She would acknowledge how much their opinion mattered, and Pepper would see that she could let it matter and still follow her heart.

Lewis walked around the table and folded over her, enveloping her in his body and kissing her on the temple. "You are good, Pepper. You deserve to find someone who will be good to you."

As soon as his fingers touched her arms, her sadness dissolved into anger. She couldn't stand that they would reject her relationship and then try to console her as if she were a little girl. It was disgusting, their sense of entitlement over her life. She squirmed out of his embrace; the tears stopped. "I *have* found someone who is good to me. You hate everyone I love. But Rick is good to me. He's honest to me. You don't like someone and you call it a character flaw. And guess what? I'm not taking marriage advice from you two. You failed at marriage. You're zero for one. Your opinion is worth shit."

She was so angry, she couldn't feel her arms or legs. She kicked back the heavy chair and grabbed her clutch.

"Pepper, wait," Claudia said. "Let's talk about this like adults."

She could have incinerated them with her gaze. "Yes, like adults. As in, I don't tell you what to do, so don't tell me what to do. You had no right to say what you said. I'll see you at my wedding." It took all her restraint not to tell them to rot in hell.

She pushed past the bewildered server and found herself on the sidewalk, enlivened by an indignation that soon gave way to a terrible ache.

◄●►

Back in her empty apartment, Pepper felt deserted. This adult persona she was constructing for herself now seemed false, and the thrill of embarking on a new life was replaced by a hollow agony, as if she'd ripped out the part of her that her parents still owned without knowing how to stanch the bleeding. She'd wanted to be immune to their disapproval for years, to fight back against them the way she had in the restaurant, but she hadn't been prepared for this pain, this feeling that something inside her was breaking, that she had severed her connection to them forever. She needed to talk to Dr. Riffler, but she'd seen her before going to lunch, foolishly thinking that a prophylactic session would suffice.

She scooped a handful of gourmet peanut butter cups out of the freezer and lay down with her laptop, scrolling through her Facebook feed with one hand while feeding herself with the other, plugging up her senses until she couldn't feel anything. She shouldn't have checked her email, because her father had sent her one.

> Dear Pepper,
> We're very sorry about what happened at the restaurant just now. We now see that it was wrong to spring our advice on you like that. Ultimately, you know Rick better than we do, and we shouldn't have come to a snap judgment, much less told you about it.
> We do have one request, however. Wait another year before marrying him. You will never really know who you're marrying, but you can learn a lot in two years. In the first year, the passion blinds you. A marriage is not about passion; it's about the love that remains after the passion fades. If you can wait another year for your wedding, we will give you our blessing. If not, I'm afraid we won't be in attendance.
> Love,
> Daddy and Mommy

She understood that he was attempting a reconciliation, but it didn't make her feel better, especially his last sentence, which was plain extortion. They still didn't have the right to tell her what to do. They'd seen something in all her previous boyfriends that she hadn't—and she'd been reluctantly grateful for the warning about Gabriel—but how often had they been right, and how often had they poisoned her against them? In every case, her relationship soured as soon as they lobbed their opinion. Problems she hadn't minded became intolerable, and a few fights later, she was single again, just as they had planned. None of her relationships had lasted longer than two years—which was one reason she didn't want to wait to marry Rick.

She didn't have to listen to them. They couldn't treat her like a child if their words didn't carry such weight with her. They certainly hadn't threatened Maisie with skipping her wedding, hadn't said a word about how their kids would be treated, even though Rahul was Indian. The difference was that Maisie didn't care what they thought. But Pepper didn't know how to free herself from their influence. Her love and hatred of them occupied the same place in her heart.

Rick came home late, giddy from a stock market surge. Hungry and exhausted, she fell into his arms. He was the same trustworthy man she'd fallen in love with; just feeling his soft skin against her lips and his muscular arms around her body proved her parents wrong. He whipped up a broccoli omelet for dinner and gave her half, and they ate and drank beers and laughed about his eccentric clients, one who wore a wide-brimmed hat inside to prevent the fluorescent light from aging her skin, and one whose sole mandate to Rick was to "invest in the future," spoken with the wide-eyed pluck of an Ayn Rand heroine. After dinner, he shimmied off her underwear, perched her on the back of his ugly herringbone sofa, and pressed his tongue between her legs.

It wasn't exactly untrustworthy, but it unsettled her, the connection between his work and his arousal. His entire client base comprised lonely widows and heiresses who handed over the keys to their fortunes in exchange for flattery. He worked hard to generate returns on their investments, but even he admitted that the key to his business was seduction. He'd never sleep with any of them, not just because he loved her but also because sex would break his hold on them. Still, she wished he didn't love the attention.

They migrated to the bedroom and finished; he had such control over his orgasm, they almost always came at the same time. Lying in his arms afterward, loving the peace of the moment, she decided it would be cruel to relay her parents' character assessment, and when, just before falling asleep, he asked how the lunch went, she instead told him that Maisie was pregnant. He understood her disappointment instinctively. "Our baby is going to be way cuter," he said.

"And smarter," she added.

"Her kid probably won't graduate from elementary school."

She laughed. "We're terrible."

He held her and kissed her until his muscles twitched from sleep. Then she slid out of his arms and ran like a madwoman through the hallways of her mind.

◄●►

She awoke to the sound of the front door closing. Rick had left for work. Anxiety jangled her into alertness as she remembered the aborted lunch with her parents. Rick had left a sticky note on her phone, wishing her a happy day and letting her know that he'd squeezed some orange juice for her and left it in the refrigerator. At the bottom, he drew some lips that said, "Mwah!"—which made her smile. She'd gotten three text messages from Katt to see if she wanted to go out to lunch, and she replied that she wasn't feeling well.

The sheets smelled musty, and she could almost hear her mother's admonishment about her slovenly housekeeping. All their other sheets were dirty: daily lovemaking took a toll on the linens. And Marta wouldn't be coming in for a few more days. So she stripped the bed, piled the sheets into the hamper, balanced the bottle of detergent on top, took a moment to tie her hair back, and rode the elevator to the basement.

She hadn't ventured into the laundry room since she and Rick toured the building in the spring, and then as now, she wondered why no one had made any effort to beautify the glaring white walls or the raw concrete floor. It must have been prime laundry time, as all twelve dryers were running and all six folding tables were occupied by black and Hispanic housekeepers . . . and Francis Levy, her mentor on the co-op board.

He apparently grew up poor, and on the board, he stood up for the little guy. When an ice cream truck began parking outside the building, annoying residents with its infernal jingle and luring tourists and children to an otherwise peaceful street, he fought to let it stay, because it made people happy, and the immigrant driver didn't have anywhere else to stop. He convinced the board to offer the smaller of their Madison Avenue storefronts to a hardware and home-goods store over a luxury handbag boutique. And he managed to prevent Patricia from letting one of the penthouse owners convert a room to a walk-in wine cellar, which would have required building a massive air-conditioning unit on the roof. He was so convincing that she didn't always know how she felt about the issues until he weighed in. She still didn't enjoy seeing Patricia every month and reading the tax returns of her future neighbors, but she liked hearing Francis's opinions and didn't want to disappoint him by quitting. Plus, she still had no other career prospects. The board was the only thing in her life that made her feel useful, and not very much, at that.

But when she spotted Francis in the laundry room, she felt the urge to hide: she didn't want him to think she did her own laundry. It was ridiculous, all her family's snobbery that she wanted to dispense with in her new life, a stain that would not be washed away.

"My friend Penelope!" he said. "Welcome to the Chelmsford Arms' storied laundry room."

She couldn't tell to what extent he was joking. "I'm honored to be here." She put her basket down on the floor and rubbed the creases in her fingers.

"As well you should. You stand on hallowed ground. When the burghers of Carnegie Hill become too much to stomach, I escape here. You can bet Patricia Cooper has never set foot in this noble chamber."

One of the housekeepers smiled at Pepper, and she had the feeling that she wasn't quite welcome.

"I'm just going to pop this into a washer and get going," Pepper said.

"Please, let me—I'm down here anyway."

"Thank you, but I've been trying to act more like an adult, and it would be insane if I let you do my laundry."

"You seem very adult to me," Francis said.

"Tell that to my parents." She studied the controls on the closest machine. It took a special card, and she had no idea where Marta kept it. She glanced around, looking for a machine that dispensed cards. "How does this all work?"

"You have to get a card, and then you go to a website to put money on it. The delicious twist is that the building manager hasn't had cards in years—I think the company stopped making them. I'm told they can be purchased for twenty dollars on eBay. But you can use mine." He produced the card from his pocket.

"Thank you. I can give you cash." She tapped on the front of her sweat-pants and realized she had forgotten to bring her wallet.

"It's on me. I can't tell you how much joy you brought me when you drank Patricia's precious cognac."

She rolled her eyes. "Thanks for reminding me."

"It was a stroke of brilliance! With that simple act, you modeled defiance and woke up the rest of the board to the necessity of ending her reign. After that meeting, Birdie told me that she would side with me in the next officer elections. All I have to do is convince Ardith, and I'll be the next president."

Pepper didn't love that everyone on the board was talking about her, but Francis was probably exaggerating things. She opened the lid of a washing machine and started stuffing in the sheets. "Ardith wouldn't vote for you?"

He sighed. "Patricia lets her host parties on the rooftop, which probably isn't even legal. But I'll work on her. The important thing is that we start making the Chelmsford Arms more moral."

"It's really crazy that we have a hundred apartments and no minority shareholders," she said.

"You're right; it's shameful. We can try to change the numbers in our building, but it's a systemic problem, not one you or I can fix. There are a lot of reasons we don't get high-quality African American applicants: part of it has to do with our idea about what makes a good co-op applicant, and the rest has to do with a system designed to keep money and power in the hands of the few. Besides, if you were black and could afford a junior four on the Upper East Side or a six-bedroom town house in Harlem, which would you choose?"

"The town house, I guess." It was sad, though. Maybe the Claudias of the world were right: maybe people wanted to live with their own.

"What we can fix," Francis said, "is the way the plutocrats rule our build-ing. We just have to be patient."

"It just feels like I'm wasting my time. Every time I start to say some-thing, Patricia shuts me down."

"Don't be discouraged. The rest of us want to hear your opinions. You have something none of us have: youth. And please don't take this as a crit-icism, but once you've been on the board a little longer, you'll see how to formulate your arguments in a way that appeals both to the capitalist mind and institutional security. Have you memorized the bylaws yet?"

She had tried, but the document resisted comprehension. It was basically twenty pages of obsessive nitpicking: no bicycles in the lobby, no more than two animals per apartment, no dog breeds with a dangerous reputation, no dishwashers over fifty decibels, no air conditioners on west-facing windows, etc., etc. A six-page section on protocol for board meetings, including a modified *Robert's Rules of Order* that no one followed, could have put a hummingbird to sleep mid-flight.

"A few times," she said. "I'm not sure how much I've retained, though."

"Memorize them. They'll help you understand how we think."

She decided to read them a few more times. She thanked him again, squeezed the last of her linens into the machine, and shut the lid.

"You might want to divide that up between two machines," he suggested. "Laundry likes to breathe."

He was trying to be helpful, but Pepper didn't want to be critiqued in a vulnerable moment. She hated that she was thirty-three and didn't know the right way to do the laundry. She didn't like cooking and cleaning, either. Nor was she much for working, apparently. She recognized her privilege in the meander of her adulthood, but there was a cost, too. A thirty-three-year-old woman who had no passion and only knew how to live off other people. A thirty-three-year-old woman whose parents thought they had the right to tell her not to marry the man she loved.

"What's on your mind?" Francis asked.

She realized she had been staring at her sheets in the washing machine with the porthole door still open. She knew she should tell Rick before blabbing to their neighbors, but she couldn't. It would hurt him too much.

"My parents don't want me to marry Rick," she murmured. "I know I shouldn't be surprised. I was just so sure they would love him."

He sighed. "Let's get your laundry going." She watched as he divided her linens between two machines, poured in detergent, locked the doors, and swiped his card.

"Thanks," she said. "You're a lifesaver."

"It's my pleasure." He motioned toward a row of chairs by the wall, and they sat. Pepper left one chair between them as a buffer. She watched the clothes rise and fall in the dryers. They seemed to be having fun.

"You know, Carol's parents hated me from the very beginning," he said. "They were very bourgeois, and they became quite wealthy from the stock market, and they hoped their daughter would use the money to marry up. And not only does she become a teacher, but she goes and digs up this impoverished yiddle with a dead father and a mother who cleaned houses.

They boycotted our wedding. We were estranged from them for years. Then Carol found out through her sister that her father had colon cancer. She wrote her parents a letter, explaining that they could hold their grudge forever or they could appreciate their daughter while they were still alive. And they reconciled. Not with me—I never saw them again—but Carol had a good relationship with them in their final years." He smiled. "You didn't ask for the spiel, and you got the whole megillah!"

"No, no, it's really interesting," she said, and meant it. "I guess you're saying it's okay if my parents don't like Rick."

"It's not just okay, it's necessary. Your parents don't like him because they love you," he said. "Now you have to find a way to ignore them out of love for yourself."

"And Carol's glad she married you, right? I'm sorry, that's insane—you don't have to answer that."

He shrugged. "We have our spats. The trick is not to let everything get to you. I promise your marriage is going to be very difficult at times. Everything that annoys you now is going to seem catastrophic. All you have to remember is that nobody's perfect, and that in the scheme of things, you're doing fine."

That wasn't the glorious declaration of love Pepper had been hoping for. But in another way, it was much better, because it let her off the hook to have a perfect marriage. If Francis and Carol's marriage was still intact after half a century, that seemed like success enough.

"No matter what," Francis said, "you'll be better off than the last couple who owned your apartment."

"You knew them?" Rick hadn't told her who had sold him the apartment, and she hadn't asked.

"Not well. But their story made the papers. And I believe they're making a TV movie out of it, too."

"Sounds juicy." If the story was so scandalous, it unnerved her that no one else had told her about them. Surely Birdie and George had known them. And Ardith—she knew everyone in the building. Also, wouldn't Rick have googled them? She hadn't gone with him to the closing; she'd assumed he bought the place from the estate of a dead lady.

"You decide." He smiled. "Roland Peterson was a well-known pastor and theological scholar, and his wife Deirdre was a bigwig corporate attorney. Roland had a faculty position at Harvard Divinity School and spent about half his time in an apartment in Somerville, Massachusetts. Don't ask me why they didn't move there, but I believe Deirdre didn't want to leave her job. One day, she gets a call from a woman in Somerville named Bethany Steel, who claims that she's been Roland's live-in girlfriend for ten years. The guy had a woman in both cities! And Bethany only found out about Deirdre because Roland was being audited, and he had listed his Somerville house as his primary residence to save on his taxes. When the accountant at the IRS called, he asked Bethany if she was Deirdre Peterson."

"That's insane," Pepper said. "So Deirdre kicked him out?"

"Nope. It gets more bizarre. Bethany and Deirdre meet, and they become friendly, and the next time he gets home to New York, they're both waiting in his living room—where you live now. And they tell him they're both leaving him. But then he confesses his love to Bethany, and right in front of Deirdre, gets down on one knee and proposes to her!"

"She said no, I hope."

"One would like to think so, right? Alas, Bethany said yes."

"Women are the worst."

"She got her comeuppance, though. Deirdre took him to the cleaners in the divorce, and she sold the apartment to you and bought a much bigger one in the Village. He had to put his house in Cambridge on the market, and then he commenced another affair with a woman in Boston. So Bethany left him, but she got nothing because they never did get married. This last part was just in the *Post* the other day."

"You read the *Post*?"

"Not really. The doormen keep a copy behind the lobby desk, and they tell me when there's something I should see." Francis rubbed his hands together.

She felt for both women in the story. They had trusted Roland, put their faith in him, and then years later, discovered that the foundation of their relationship was a lie. Her parents had advised her to wait another year before marrying Rick, but these women had been duped for a decade. Was it ever possible to know for sure that your husband has been faithful? Rick seemed honest, but maybe she was being naive.

One of the housekeepers was trying to get their attention: Francis's dryer had stopped. He collected his laundry, folded it, and said goodbye. It was just two towels. He had spent the morning in the laundry room to wash two towels.

◄ ◉ ►

Christmas was three weeks away, and Pepper decided not to go with her family to her grandmother's house in Vermont, as they had done every year since she was little and continued to do even after her parents' divorce. Rick was invited, but Pepper didn't want to pretend their veto of her marriage had never happened. If he came to Vermont, they would judge him whether or not they owned up to it.

"Don't punish yourself to make a point," Claudia said over the phone.

"I'm actually kind of disgusted with you right now."

"This isn't *Romeo and Juliet*. We just want you to be happy."

"That's what Mrs. Capulet said."

"All right, very funny. If you change your mind and want to come, there's room for two in the car. Maisie and Rahul are flying up." Pepper still hadn't congratulated her sister on the baby, because Maisie hadn't yet told her she was pregnant.

"Why are you even divorced?" Pepper asked. "You do everything together."

"Your father doesn't want to be married," Claudia replied after a pause.

"Don't you get a say?"

She laughed. "Have you met your father?"

It was a maddening rebuff, a nonanswer disguised as helplessness. And it dumped her right back into her childhood, when she was isolated by her parents' secrecy and left alone to sort out her fiery stew of emotions. Overwhelmed by anger and a loneliness that sucked the breath out of her, Pepper said goodbye and hung up.

Fortunately, Rick didn't know that Pepper had a Christmas tradition. And he didn't want to spend the holiday in Ohio, either. His parents celebrated in the usual way—ornaments, gifts, booze, ham, church, in that order—and the banality of it drove him nuts. So without having to explain to him that her parents thought he was a snake, they agreed to celebrate at home together, and not to bother parading their love for their families.

◄ ● ►

Sometimes Pepper wished her therapist would tell her she was making a mistake, but the beauty of the arrangement was that Dr. Riffler never intervened, just watched Pepper run headlong into disaster, then helped her figure out why she did it. When Pepper had told her about the awful lunch with her parents, Dr. Riffler said, "Parents don't always know what's best for their children." When she told her that she wasn't celebrating Christmas with her family, Dr. Riffler said, "That sounds like a big decision."

Pepper often didn't realize she was depressed until after the fact, but this time, with her therapist's help, she detected its signs. She declined multiple invitations from friends to go barhopping, ice-skating, or to Broadway shows because she was tired. She turned down lunch dates with Birdie because she didn't feel like eating more than cheese and crackers. She skipped Rick's work holiday party, even though she'd been looking forward to the spectacle since they'd met. And the damp December cold bothered her more than usual—it was the one downside of being thin—so she tried not to go outside. On the first anniversary of their meeting, Rick took her out to Masa, the notoriously expensive sushi restaurant in a glorified mall at Columbus Circle, and he moaned in pleasure over every bite while she could barely taste it.

She dreaded the icy clamp of winter, that interminable bodily siege, but worse was five months of renovations to the apartment, scheduled to begin the day after New Year's. Crashing in her family apartment—a loop of eight rooms that currently housed Claudia and her two clawless Siamese cats—was out of the question now. So she told Rick that her mother didn't want them living with her, and they found a furnished one-bedroom in a decent rental building on Eighty-sixth by the East River. They would move January 2. She hated to leave the Chelmsford Arms when she was getting to know her neighbors, but the renovation could not be postponed.

She had begun to dread the wedding too. The no-frills event had been predicated on a faulty assumption, that her parents would welcome Rick into the family. Previously, she didn't care whether they showed up, and she didn't want an overblown party to mark the minor transition to married life. But now their absence would be a painful repudiation, and the low-profile wedding felt too similar to not getting married at all. Also, if word got around that she and Rick had done it quietly and that he wasn't accepted by her family, suspicions would grow into rumors, and rumors would grow into news. Claudia often reminded her that their family was not invisible.

◄◆►

At three o'clock on Christmas Eve, Rick told her to pack an overnight bag and put on something fancy. She didn't feel like celebrating but decided to do it for his sake. After disappearing for an hour, he called to tell her he was waiting outside. On the way out the front door, Ty, the muscular black doorman whose friendliness Pepper had originally enjoyed and now resisted, winked and said, "You're a lucky lady, Ms. Bradford."

"She doesn't know how lucky she is," Rick said.

A horse-drawn carriage waited out front, and Rick sat on the purple velvet upholstery, fixing the lapel of his tuxedo.

Didn't he know that those carriage horses were worked to death in miserable conditions? But the white horse did look majestic in the lamplight, with an ostrich plume fluttering atop its head, and she supposed she was touched by the grand gesture. And maybe the activists were overstating things; it was hard to know what to believe. She climbed in and kissed him. He gave the go-ahead to the Eastern European coachman, and the carriage lurched into motion.

Inside Central Park, they headed west, and she lay against Rick's shoulder, barren branches sliding across her vision. She wondered if they were headed to the Mandarin Oriental, Rick's favorite hotel. She doubted he'd cross the park for a restaurant, as the Upper West Side was a food desert for fine dining. They'd be better off riding that carriage to Queens.

They passed an empty playground, a team of high school athletes huffing by in sweats, and Francis's wife, Carol, smoking a cigarette on a bench, huddled to stay warm. They curved around the Great Lawn and passed Belvedere Castle, a human construction that helped frame and beautify the wilderness.

They emerged from the park near the Museum of Natural History and pulled up to a tall, narrow apartment building with a pale stone exterior and large mirrored windows. Rick thanked the driver with a chunk of bills and led Pepper inside, where a lone doorman escorted them into an elevator, inserted a key in the control panel, and hit the button for PH 2, the second-highest of three penthouses. The doors opened out onto a private landing, and Rick slid the oversize brushed-steel apartment door to the side.

When he flipped the light switch, Pepper was blinded by white: high-gloss walls, empty except for three pop-art paintings of cherry lips; a seamless acrylic floor; a modular sofa that could have seated ten; and a limestone bathtub in the center of the enormous living room. The far wall was one big window that took in all of Central Park, a murky rectangle fractured by ghostly lighted paths.

"What is this?" Pepper asked.

"Heaven." He laughed. "Just kidding, it's my friend Barry's bachelor pad. Not bad, right?"

She ran her fingers along the smooth, cold lip of the tub. She wasn't a bath person, but she'd make an exception for such a sculptural wonder. "I guess he likes to take baths?"

"Only when he has company, I think." Rick stepped toward the glass wall, huffed on it and drew a smiley face in the condensation. "You know what's crazy? He's got a wife and four kids in Saddle River, and they don't know about this place. He comes here about once a month and gets all his fantasies taken care of. Then he goes back to his family. His wife says he's a great dad."

The casual tone of Rick's story disquieted her, as did the enormous lips on the walls, which, in the context of Barry's infidelity, seemed degrading. Pepper remembered poor Deirdre Peterson and her two-woman man. If the story had been in the news, Rick had probably heard it, right? And he must have seen Deirdre's name on the apartment contract. Then why wouldn't he have told Pepper what happened? Maybe Francis had exaggerated the story's reach.

"He doesn't sound like a great dad if he's screwing around," she said.

"I just think not everyone is wired for monogamy, and if a guy can get what he needs safely and discreetly, everyone wins."

"Except his wife."

He laughed and kissed her. "Babe, I don't know what you think I'm saying. I want it to be just us, okay? I just think it's crazy when families get ripped apart because a guy isn't able to be monogamous."

"I'm with you in theory. But Barry sounds like a real shithead, if he's lying to his wife and risking contracting some STD. And breaking the law, too."

He studied her. "How about we try out the bathtub before dinner?" He turned the knobs, and a wide ribbon of water cascaded into the tub.

Sometimes Rick was as perfect as a prince; other times he could be vulgar and morally suspect. Was he both of those things, or was the perfect side of him an act? And how much of the latter side could be chalked up to his gender and forgiven? She wondered if she would be so critical if her parents hadn't told her he was a liar. They knew how to dismantle a relationship from the inside; she had to try to see her fiancé without the tint of their judgment. Still, there was no way she was getting in that tub. Rick was right: the world did put a lot of weight on fidelity. But she didn't want to share him with anyone else.

He pulled her tight and kissed her forehead. "I love you, sweetheart."

"I love you too." She said it mechanically, though it wasn't untrue. He'd probably gone to some trouble to get this apartment, and she really wanted to enjoy it, for his sake.

She felt a tickle on her back and realized that he was unzipping her dress. She hated to spurn his romantic gesture, so she let him slip her dress to the floor, undo her bra, and kiss her breasts. She was getting less and less in the mood.

"You turn me on so hard," he mumbled, switching breasts.

She closed her eyes to think. He hadn't done anything wrong, not seriously, at least. But to take her to this sickening place where his sleazy friend went to cheat on his wife, and to think she'd be aroused by that? She felt ill to think that her parents might have been right about him. But this wasn't evidence of dishonesty, just poor judgment.

He slipped his fingers under her lacy briefs.

"I'm sorry," she said, crossing her arms over her breasts, "but can we go home? I really don't like it here."

He stepped back, and she began to dress. "Really? I wanted this to be a special night."

"It's special because we're together, sweetie," she said, adding the pet name as a conciliatory gesture. "I appreciate that you went to all this trouble, but right now all I want is to go home and get delivery and watch a movie. That's kind of how I imagined our Christmas would go."

He pursed his lips. For some reason, he didn't want to go home, and she was getting frustrated.

"Okay, I understand why you don't want to stay here," he said. "In retrospect, I feel a little dumb for thinking you'd like it. But can we go to a hotel? Our place is in such bad shape, it'll be more romantic for me if we can take a break from it."

She suspected he wasn't telling her the real reason he didn't want to go home, but this was a compromise she could make. He took out his cell phone to call the Mandarin Oriental.

It hadn't occurred to either of them that on Christmas Eve, every nice hotel in New York would be full. She grew increasingly annoyed as he called his favorite hotels—the Peninsula, the Four Seasons, the Soho Grand, the Carlyle, the Greenwich, the Standard—and grimaced as he listened to the inevitable decree. He tried an American Express concierge, and the best the woman could offer him was a Doubletree in Midtown.

"We could try Atlantic City," he suggested.

She didn't want to stand in that apartment another moment. "I'm sorry, but can we please just go home?"

"We can't go home, okay? I have a surprise planned, and it won't be ready until tomorrow morning."

She felt terrible for making him reveal that. She didn't want a surprise, though.

"What about your dad's apartment?" he asked. "He's not home, right?"

She didn't want to take anything from Lewis during their standoff—didn't want to need him in any way—but she also didn't have to tell him. He'd given her a key and told her she could come over at any time. "Yeah, that works. Let's go there."

At least Rick was willing to change his plans for her. She was grateful for that.

◄ ● ►

Their ill-fated excursion improved from there. Safely inside her father's apartment, they ordered Chinese food and watched a dumb romantic comedy while snuggling on his spacious sofa, which seemed to have been designed for it. In the morning, they turned on both rain showerheads and the horizontal massage jets for some truly excellent sex. They packed their overnight bags and breakfasted at a twenty-four-hour diner, one of the few spots open on Christmas morning. Her pancakes were sludgy, the syrup gummy, and the coffee flat and bitter, but the change in routine was romantic, if a little sad, because it bumped up against the absence of Pepper's family tradition. A call came in from her mother's cell; she didn't take it.

"I have a present for you," she told him, as she stacked individual-size jelly tubs into a pyramid. "When do you want to exchange gifts?" She'd bought him a pink shirt and matching tie, and the luxuriantly sideburned salesman had convinced her that it wasn't the most generic gift ever given to a fiancé. Since her parents had criticized her for not knowing Rick well enough, she could hear them inside her brain every time she didn't know him perfectly. At least she knew his shirt size. The salesman didn't believe that a guy with a seventeen-inch neck could fit into a slim shirt, but it was true: Rick's gym body defied the laws of proportion.

"My present is at home," he said. "I think you're going to love it." He floated two twenties onto the table, gulped the last of his coffee, and called an Uber on his phone. She wished he would kiss her.

◄ ● ►

Sergei was on door duty when they got back home; she recalled hearing that he was married, maybe with kids, and wondered why he'd volunteered to work on Christmas. He was talking with Caleb, the new porter, and both of them were smiling. "Glad to see you're making friends, Caleb," she said, which caused both of them to stiffen. Maybe Nikolas, the manager, had been on their case about chatting during work hours.

Rick wore a goofy, open-mouthed grin on the elevator ride and held it while she fumbled in her bag's zippered pocket for the key. Their landing smelled piney, and when she opened the door, the scent wafted around her. The air inside their apartment was crisp, almost rural, as if the windows had been opened. She shot Rick a puzzled smile; still grinning, he gestured toward the bedroom. Inside, the pine scent flooded her nostrils. She found herself in a forest.

A grove of Christmas trees, maybe a dozen, had been set up around the bed. The Egyptian-cotton damask bedspread, a housewarming gift from Katt, was covered in fir needles. Once the shock had subsided, she grasped what he had done: since she hadn't wanted to spend Christmas with her family in Vermont, he had recreated Vermont inside their home, using Christmas trees. No wonder he hadn't wanted to come home last night. This must have taken a team of workers several hours.

His frozen smile verged on the maniacal as he awaited her response. She laughed a little at that. But in truth, she wished he hadn't done this. It stung to be reminded of the Vermont wilderness that she was missing, and by extension, her family. The point of staying in the city was to avoid thinking about her holiday tradition, which her engagement to Rick prevented her from enjoying. She'd wanted intimacy, and he'd given her spectacle. Maybe her parents were right about him. Maybe he was all shell and no core. Maybe something was wrong with her, and she had no ability to judge men, and she would never find real love with anyone, and she would live out her days with her mother, hoarding cats and letting her mind dribble away. Despairing, she began to cry.

"Are these tears happy or sad?" he asked, taking her hand in both of his.

She shook her head. She didn't know how to explain without hurting him. And she didn't want to hurt him. She already felt terrible for failing to appreciate everything he'd planned.

He hugged her from behind. "I've been feeling this distance between us, babe, and I love you so much, and I sensed, I don't know, I sensed that you needed me to prove it to you."

"I know you love me," she said. "I love you too. It's just . . . this. . ." She waved her hands around, trying to think of something kind to say.

"You hate it."

She freed herself from his embrace. "I don't hate it! You were so sweet to want to give me such a nice gift. But it's . . . it's not for me. I'm sorry, I know how much thought you put into this, but I just wanted our Christmas to be a chance to be together, just us, not trying to make it into some event."

He took measured breaths, weathering this criticism. "I'm sorry, I messed up. I got so excited about the idea, I didn't think about what you really needed. It's obvious now. I'll call the guys up and have them take it down. Man, do I feel stupid."

"No, no—let's keep it up," she said. Now that she felt heard—and saw that he was capable of hearing her—her upset had subsided. She still felt a knot of sadness, the part of her that wanted to unite with her family, but she could bear it. "It's beautiful. I'm really kind of blown away. I just want you to know that you don't need to do things like this to impress me. You don't need to put on a show for me. I'm marrying you because I love you, not because of the things you can give me."

"That's why I'm marrying you, too. You know that, right?"

"Of course."

"And your parents? They don't think I'm some social climber?"

"No; they don't care about that."

She scooted backward onto the bed and lay faceup. A needle pricked her back: they were sharper than they looked. He lay beside her, holding her hand. Then he rolled toward her, propped himself on an elbow, and gazed down at her.

"Listen, Pepper," he said. "Whatever happened between you and your parents, you can give it time to settle down before we get married. We don't have to do it right away."

She wanted to tell him what they thought of him, because she didn't want to keep secrets. But it would be cruel to say it. A secret had to be okay if it was kept out of kindness, right?

"Or if you just want to be together without getting married, that's fine, too," he continued. "I'm not going anywhere. I just want you to be happy. That's the only thing I want."

His permission felt like a gift, and she was tempted to wait another year to marry him. But if she followed her parents' advice, they would take credit for her happy marriage. She didn't want them to factor into her marriage at all. And she still wanted to get pregnant before she turned thirty-four. Of course they could have a child without being married, but what would be the point in waiting? "I do want to get married to you, and I don't want to wait. But thank you for saying that."

Taking in Rick and the forest he had conjured, an idea clicked into place.

The same Christmas trees that had overwhelmed her and brought her to the edge of despair now inspired her, and for the first time, she wanted to plan a beautiful wedding. With a little effort, the celebration of their union could be gravid with awe.

"What is it?" asked Rick, holding a wobbly smile as if trying to figure out how to respond.

She inhaled the scent of the firs and soaked in the majesty of the scene. She would remember this moment forever. "I just had the most incredible idea."

4

CALEB'S FIRST DAY

TWO WEEKS EARLIER

On his first day as a porter at the Chelmsford Arms, Caleb Franklin fell in love.

The M3 bus had jerked to a stop at Eighty-eighth and Fifth, twenty minutes before his first shift, as the sunrise lit up the sky. The December air crackled with cold.

He never felt so black as when he found himself in Carnegie Hill, the epicenter of Upper East Side privilege. Even this early, the place was crawling with white people, whose rigid backs and calm stares projected wealth and belonging. And straightness. Two doughy, proportioned guys jogged by in designer workout clothes. A doorman helped a fur-coated woman into a cab. Caleb said hi to a blond lady picking up her husky's dog doo with a tiny plastic bag. She smiled apologetically.

The Chelmsford Arms was a handsome building, its lower floors sheathed in limestone, its upper floors in almond-colored brick; along the cornice, a bas relief of angels and wreaths. Caleb considered himself lucky to have gotten a job here: it wasn't the nicest building in Carnegie Hill, not by far, but it was known for its caring service. The residents were lucky, too, but most rich people took their comforts for granted.

He introduced himself to the night doorman, Oscar, a stout, square-faced Hispanic man wearing a visored cap and a long wool coat with fringed epaulets. Nikolas Lykandros, the resident manager, was on vacation, Oscar told him, but Ranesh, the other porter, would arrive by seven to show him around. Unsure of what else to do, Caleb sat on the white leather settee in the foyer to wait, blowing on his hands to keep them warm.

The Chelmsford Arms was only twenty-four blocks south of the fourth-floor walk-up where he had lived all twenty-three years of his life, on 112th and Lenox, with his family of four (now three, since Freddie got married and moved to Buffalo). But the differences were startling.

In Caleb's building, aspirationally named Lenox Manor, the front door was a popular target for scratchiti, and the linoleum-clad lobby and creaky rubberized staircase always smelled like french fries. They were clean, at least, because he and Freddie, and now just Caleb, had swept and mopped the floors every Saturday morning since longer than he could remember. His parents were positive people: they saw no reason to rail at the overworked super when they could maintain the place themselves. A carved wooden sign above their kitchen sink read STAY POSITIVE, and they really lived it. His father and mother even seemed at peace with the fact that the Lenox Manor was going to be torn down in a year to make space for a luxury condo high-rise. With the modest payout they'd get for giving up their lease, plus their retirement savings, they would buy a condo in a gated community in Florida. But Caleb would have to move to Washington Heights or the Bronx, because white people were taking over Harlem.

His father had been an English teacher and track coach at Frederick Douglass Academy, and his mother had been a medical records clerk at Mount Sinai, but they still couldn't afford college for their sons, and Caleb didn't want to take out loans when people across the country were losing their jobs and homes. "You owe them; they own you," his father often quipped. He felt proud of his financial judiciousness: he didn't want to be in debt his whole life. Whereas Freddie had gone to LIU full-time, only to take a job where he was working before, at the Associated Supermarket, and was now so deeply in debt that no bank would give him a mortgage. At least in Buffalo, he could afford the rent.

So Caleb had worked as a porter at a smallish building in Gramercy and taken night classes at Hunter when he had the money and energy. The job at the Chelmsford Arms paid better and would cut his commute by fifteen minutes. Someday he hoped to be a social worker, but at this rate, he'd be forty before he got his master's, a fact so discouraging that he sometimes wanted to quit. But, as his father might say, "Would you rather be forty without a master's?"

"We're not supposed to sit," Oscar said. Caleb jumped up just in time: an old white guy in a faded button-down, loose khakis, and a Yankees cap strolled into the foyer from within the building. He was almost a head shorter than Caleb, who was six one.

"Morning, Francis," Oscar said.

"Good morning, Oscar."

Caleb was surprised when the man also tipped his cap to him. "Good morning," Caleb said. He didn't think he was supposed to address the tenants by first name, so he threw in a belated "sir."

"You must be Caleb," the man said, reaching for a handshake.

Caleb's dad had instilled in him the importance of a firm handshake— but Caleb squeezed too hard, bundling the old man's finger bones in his grasp. He mumbled an apology.

"I'm Francis Levy," the man said, opening and closing his hand as if to make sure he hadn't broken any bones, at which point Caleb noticed a tear in his sleeve, near the cuff. "I'm the unofficial welcoming committee. You're early! That bodes well for your tenure here."

"Thank you, sir," Caleb said.

"Please, call me Francis. I'm no 'sir,' just a regular fellow."

"Francis, then."

"Now, I hope you'll stop by my apartment for a cup of coffee when you have a minute," Francis said.

That was beyond strange. In his five years of working as a porter, no resident had ever invited him for coffee. He wasn't supposed to enter their apartments, not to open a stuck window or check out a ceiling leak or anything. That was the handyman's job. One of his fellow porters at his last job in Gramercy would unpack people's luggage or groceries for extra tips; when one lady's ballistic Chihuahua broke a porcelain figurine, she blamed it on him, and he was fired.

"Don't worry," Francis said, "I've cleared it with Nikolas. At the Chelmsford Arms, we consider the staff part of our family."

Caleb glanced at Oscar for guidance; the doorman was on the phone.

"Carol and I are in 5H," Francis said. "So you'll come?"

Caleb's father was always saying, "Go-getters aren't 'no'-givers." Someday, after he got established in the building, he might be able to decline strange invitations. For now, he'd be a yes-man. "Yes, thank you."

"We like Francis," Oscar said once the old guy had returned to his apartment. "You'd be smart to do what he asks. He's on the board here. If any of those people have it in for you, you're in trouble."

So he'd made the right decision. He would do what Francis asked.

◄ ● ►

Soon, the rest of the morning shift arrived in uniform. Ranesh, the other porter, offered Caleb a tour of the back of the house to show him his responsibilities. But then another doorman appeared and snared Caleb in his gaze.

The doorman, probably in his mid-to-late thirties, had boyishly mussed blond hair, round oceanic eyes, and a tense little mouth. His cheeks, chin, and nose were cherubic mounds, but his face wasn't fat, nor was his barrel-shaped torso, practically shrink-wrapped in his shirt.

He introduced himself as Sergei. Straight men didn't meet your eyes, much less jump in and go swimming. Time ground to a halt, as ribbons of electricity sliced through Caleb's limbs.

"I have to, um . . . ," Caleb mumbled. He pointed toward the back of the building. "He's taking me on a . . ."

"A tour," Ranesh said, sounding irritated.

"A tour," Caleb repeated.

Ranesh looked from Caleb to Sergei, unaware that the floor was seesawing and that the air had turned to soup. "In truth, I have things that need seeing to right away. I see the poinsettias need watering, and I need to check if there was water damage from the rainstorm. Could you get him changed and teach him how to bag the garbage? I can take over in an hour."

"I could show him the ropes," Sergei said. The guttural twang of his Russian accent was an incredible turn-on. But he was no longer pouring that delicious stare into Caleb's thirsty eyes. "I was porter for five years before they made me doorman," he said to Caleb.

"Marvelous," Ranesh said flatly, glaring at Sergei. He walked through the lobby and disappeared into a small hallway.

"Don't mind him," Sergei said under his breath. "He is mad at everyone because José got promoted to doorman instead of him. He'll get over it. Now let's get you suited up." Sergei opened a door to an old marble stairway, which they took to the basement.

The elegance ended downstairs, where Caleb took care not to hit his head on one of the colorful pipes clustered overhead, as he followed Sergei down a narrow, tortuous corridor. Behind a heavy, unmarked door were two rows of lockers with benches on either side, and a bathroom with shower, toilet, and sink at the back. He pointed to one of the lockers where *Caleb Franklin* was written in red Sharpie on a HELLO, MY NAME IS sticker, which covered layers of similar stickers for past employees. Three gray-and-blue porter's uniforms hung in the locker, the vests monogrammed with *Caleb* in gold cursive.

Sergei explained: "You are expected to get them dry-cleaned before they make a smell; you give your receipts to Gloria in Mr. Lykandros's office. In the future, you can change here or change at home. But if you are getting them cleaned, it is probably most easy to change at home."

"Should I change now?" Caleb asked.

Sergei nodded, still watching him.

Caleb draped one uniform over the bench, and slowly, with his heart in his throat, he unbuttoned his shirt and removed it. He could feel himself getting an erection, and as much as he wanted Sergei to see it, maybe touch it and take it into his mouth, he faced the locker as he unzipped his khakis and pushed them down his legs. He was not going to come on to anyone at work, especially not on his first day. As his dad loved to say, "Don't shit where you eat. Or else you'll be eating shit."

The room was silent except for the clinking sound of his belt and his noisy, shallow breathing. He could hear Sergei's breath, too.

The door opened. Out of the corner of his eye, Caleb saw Sergei jerk toward the door. It was Oscar. Caleb yanked on the uniform pants before the other doorman could see his bare legs or the tent in his briefs. He felt guilty, though he'd done nothing wrong.

"Hello, fine sir," Sergei said, louder than necessary, as if trying to erase the intimate silence they'd just shared.

Oscar laughed as he unlocked his locker. "Don't 'fine sir' me. I'm off the clock." He grabbed a black nylon satchel from his locker. "My knees are killing me, and I'm sick of kissing ass for those Christmas tips. I'm getting the hell out of Dodge."

"Oh, but you must not corrupt our young porter on his first day," Sergei said with a smile. "We all love the Chelmsford Arms."

"Hail to the Chelmsford Fuckin' Arms," Oscar muttered.

◄●►

The refuse room smelled more like plastic bags and engine grease than actual trash. Everybody in the building dropped their trash down one of three chutes into a compactor that funneled it into giant contractor bags, which had to be switched out a few times a day. Since recycling hadn't been invented when the Chelmsford Arms was built, he and Ranesh had to pick that up floor by floor twice a week.

Sergei explained that the compactor was persnickety and had to be switched off and on every time it conked out, which was just about every time anyone tried to use it.

"She is like a wife," Sergei said, and kicked the compactor. "A royal pain in the ass, but if you are good to her, she will behave."

That caught Caleb off guard. Was he speaking from personal experience? He hadn't imagined this Slavic god could be married. But there, on Sergei's left ring finger, was a thick gold wedding band. Caleb despaired. He couldn't have misinterpreted that stare. Was it possible Sergei had a wife at home and fooled around with guys on the side? Caleb didn't want to ruin the doorman's marriage. But his longing was physically painful.

As Sergei led him around the rest of the building with a spray bottle and rag from the janitorial closet, pointing out all the wainscoting, brass rails, elevator buttons, and door handles that gathered fingerprints, Caleb was studying him, desperate for hope. Sergei's mannerisms were butch, but Caleb had slept with tons of guys who passed—construction workers, bouncers, and personal trainers with wives and girlfriends and sometimes babies at home. Or maybe that penetrating stare had been a meaningless look from a straight guy who didn't know the power of his eyes.

And this was good news, wasn't it? Caleb wasn't supposed to fall for anyone in the building. But every time he looked at Sergei, he was swallowed up in hormones. Sergei's face seemed designed to set Caleb's whole body on fire. Caleb was free-falling through fantasies of living together, making sweaty love half the night, and waking up naked, the covers bundled at their intertwined feet. He did fall for guys easily, but he had never been so impaled by someone he hadn't even kissed.

Back at the doorman station in the lobby, Caleb had decided not to say anything to Sergei. He didn't have to chase every hot piece of ass who glanced his way. He'd let this attraction fade. Dating at work had "wrong" written all over it.

Sergei opened the door into the storage room, stuffed to bursting with boxes and padded envelopes. He explained that more than a hundred packages came in every day in the last two weeks before Christmas. If Caleb had time after his maintenance duties, he was to take each one up to the correct apartment. It was like a hoarder's living room, and the porters and doormen were supposed to clear it out every day.

"The weekend staff did not do their job," Sergei grumbled, tipping some of the boxes to read the names. When he squinted, he looked as if he smelled something bad. There. Whatever had come over Caleb was already subsiding. "I think there was a fill-in guy—they are always a waste of space."

"Should I get started on this now?"

"Not yet—I want to show you one more thing. You are going to love it," Sergei said. Again he met Caleb's eyes for an excruciating instant, and all his resolve evaporated. Sergei pulled open a heavy metal door that led into a walk-in refrigerator lined with textured steel.

"They just put this in last year," Sergei said, letting the door close behind them with a clack. Now they were alone. Caleb could hardly breathe. "We store shareholders' groceries here when they are not home. In the summer, we take breaks in here to cool off." He winked.

Now the slim possibility that they would fall in love seemed worth the risk of being wrong. The worst-case scenario was that Sergei said no, right? Was that enough to get him fired?

Caleb wasn't ballsy enough to flat-out ask Sergei on a date. Asking if he wanted to "grab a drink after work" wasn't idiotic, except Caleb didn't drink: alcohol gave him headaches. He thought about kissing Sergei and trusting that it would end well—but if he was wrong, his life as a porter would be over.

"Hey," Caleb began, pushing into Sergei's chest with two fingers. "Do you want to hang out sometime? Like, outside of work?"

He held his breath. His heartbeat knocked against his skull. Sergei stared at the door. Had he not heard the question?

"Do you want to hang out sometime?" he asked again, this time in a deeper, less friendly voice.

Sergei shushed him fiercely. Then he swung the door open and walked out.

Caleb stared in mute disbelief as the door clicked shut. This was the worst-case scenario. Sergei would probably report him. He could pretend he was just trying to network, but he might be fired anyway.

Now he noticed how cold the room was, and he shivered horribly. Still he couldn't bring himself to leave. He didn't see how he could face Sergei ever again.

◄●►

Caleb would have given anything to spend the day packing up garbage or mopping the semiprivate landings on each floor, anything to avoid Sergei, but package delivery was sorely needed. Caleb and Ranesh each commandeered one freight elevator, while Sergei sorted the packages and Thomas, the oldest doorman at the Chelmsford Arms, watched the door, which meant that Caleb passed his new enemy at least ten times over the next six hours. He kept his eyes low and tried to think positively.

Ranesh let him deliver all the packages addressed to members of the co-op board, to begin to ingratiate himself with them. Caleb started with a Tyvek pouch of pills for Patricia Cooper, board president. An elderly black woman answered the door and introduced herself as Letitia. In extremely white places like this one, it was a relief to see another black person. She was wearing jeans and holding a paperback mystery, keeping her place with one finger. "Delivery for Mrs. Cooper," he said.

"I can sign for this." She took the package and started to say something else, then went silent when an ancient white lady hobbled over on a cane. The president of the board smiled and mumbled a lot of thank-yous and welcomes through clenched teeth, and Letitia nodded and walked off.

In 14A, Ardith Delano-Roux asked him to pull down a cut-crystal punch bowl and eight matching glasses from the top shelf of her cabinet. Caleb knew better, but he didn't want to alienate a board member, and the truth was, he'd rather do manual labor for an old lady than have to go back to the lobby and see Sergei. He climbed onto a chair and very carefully brought each item down.

Next, she had him reaching for a paper-towel roll at the top of her closet and dragging a fifty-pound statuette from the parlor room into the den. All the while, she went on about the beauty of brown skin. "Don't you think very dark skin, almost black, is utterly breathtaking?" He smiled and reminded himself to stay positive, because she surely thought she was being kind. You couldn't let white people get to you, or else you'd die from the paper cuts. You couldn't fight back, either, because they'd never understand.

◄◆►

Caleb stopped by Francis's apartment later that morning, once the mountain of deliveries had been cleared.

Francis set a large lacquered tray with coffee service down on the table. The glass container of coffee looked like some kind of beaker, and the sugar bowl and tiny pitcher of milk seemed handmade. While Caleb fixed a cup, Francis sat back and crossed his legs in a figure four.

"Do you have any questions about the building or your role in it?" Francis asked.

Caleb shook his head. He sipped the coffee: watery but good.

"I think you're going to like working here. You said in the interview that you're going to college?"

"Yeah, at Hunter." He didn't want his employers to think he was about to jump ship, so he added, "It's probably going to take me six or seven more years to finish."

His face lit up. "Carol and I taught at Hunter High School for thirty-five years."

For a second he couldn't breathe; he smiled reflexively. This white man in this fancy-ass building had been a teacher just like Caleb's father, who had lived in the same shitty rent-controlled apartment for almost forty years—and now they were being evicted because people like Francis wanted to build more luxury apartments for white people on their land. Public-school teachers got paid the same; Francis must have come from a wealthy family. Caleb hated the unfairness of it.

"You're smiling," Francis said. "Did I say something funny?"

"No, no, it's just that my father was a teacher, too," he managed to say. "At Frederick Douglass Academy in Harlem."

"That's wonderful! I knew we had a lot in common. I can tell you're eager to learn."

"Yes, sir."

"What are you studying?" Francis asked.

"Psychology."

"Ah." Francis raised his eyebrows. "Have you read Kafka?"

"No."

"You must!" he exclaimed. "He understood the human condition better than anyone." He hoisted himself to standing, pulled out a paperback book from the shelf, and handed it to Caleb. It was a yellowed copy of *The Metamorphosis*. "It's about the inhumanity of the modern world. All of Kafka is about inhumanity, I suppose. When you've read it, come back and we'll talk about it. Only if you want to, of course."

Caleb flipped through the book. He was supposed to be studying for his final exams, but he'd have to kiss some serious ass if Sergei let on what had happened in the cold room. Besides, the book was pretty short.

"Thank you, Mr. Levy," Caleb said, clutching the book to his chest. "I mean, Francis."

◄ ● ►

Next, Francis took Caleb to meet his best friends in the building, George and Birdie Hirsch in 12F. Mrs. Hirsch was a small, bony white lady with dyed black hair who moved her head a lot, like a cat. Everything in their apartment looked like high-gloss plastic, not from any furniture store he'd ever been in.

"Welcome, Caleb, welcome!" Birdie exclaimed. She brought them into her uber-fancy kitchen, with shiny black cabinets with little windows in them and a backsplash made of white subway tile and a border of tubular yellow glass like mustard on a sandwich. They stood around a center island admiring a cake—tall, yellowish-white, and expertly frosted, perched atop a porcelain stand on the black stone countertop. It looked like a computer rendering of a cake.

"Can I interest either of you in a slice of pistachio cardamom cake?" Birdie asked. "I was up half the night baking." The laugh that followed sounded forced.

"You know I can't," Francis said, touching his stomach.

She gave Caleb a piercing look. "Caleb?"

It was only 11:15, though he had been a big proponent of cake for breakfast since he was a kid. Still, he didn't know if he was supposed to be inside this apartment much less eat this lady's cake.

"Thank you, but I should get back to work," he said. "It was really nice meeting you."

"Don't be silly," she said. "You'll wear yourself out if you go racing around all day without relaxing a little. My George was always go, go, go, and now he doesn't know what to do with himself."

"Is he feeling any better?" Francis asked.

"Don't ask." She glanced at Caleb, as if deciding whether he could be trusted with the answer. "The psychiatrist changed up his 'cocktail,' as everyone apparently calls it, and maybe he's a tiny bit happier, but he's still not exercising. Then last week he was diagnosed with sleep apnea, so he wears this mask all night that makes his breathing sound like Darth Vader. I don't think he's sleeping much at all."

"That doesn't sound good," Francis said.

"Frankly, I think the whole problem could be fixed if he lost a little weight. Then he wouldn't need the Darth Vader machine, and he probably could go off some of the antidepressants too."

"I fear the problem may be deeper than that."

She flashed Francis a fake smile. "Let's get you that cake, Caleb." She pulled out a small gleaming plate from a cabinet, a fork and knife from a drawer, and a linen placemat and matching cloth napkin from the hall closet, then arranged all this into a table setting on the center island. When she picked up a cake knife, Caleb interrupted.

"You don't have to cut into that cake just for me, Mrs. Hirsch."

"Caleb, my dear, what would you do in my place?" she asked, pointing the knife at him. "I love to bake but I hardly eat sweets. Francis here eats nothing but eggs and toast, Carol is lactose intolerant, Ardith is gluten free, and I haven't seen Penelope in months. And George should hardly be eating this much fat."

"Why did you bake it if you didn't want George to eat it?" Francis asked.

With a little grunt, she cut into the cake, rinsing the knife and wiping it dry with a tea towel after each cut. At the end of this ritual, she withdrew a hearty slice with the knife and washed it again. In truth, he was relieved that something that day was going right. He didn't like pistachio-flavored anything, but this was really good. Soft as a pillow but dense like a mattress. Sweet, tangy, buttery, and just a little nutty.

With parted lips, Birdie watched him eat the entire slice, press his fork into the crumbs, and eat those too. "You have no idea how much pleasure it gives me to watch you eat."

"It does look delicious," Francis observed.

Her husband plodded in from one of the bedrooms, in a navy-blue bathrobe and slippers. George was a very big man, well over six feet, and broad in the shoulders; he seemed even more imposing next to Francis, who was short, thin, and hunched, and Birdie, who was even shorter. Despite his potbelly and mussed hair, George wasn't a bad-looking guy, maybe sixty years old and with a face like a news anchor, plus a few days' stubble. His sleepy eyes didn't seem to open all the way.

At the sight of him, Birdie's face hardened. "George," said Birdie, "this is Caleb. He's the new porter, replacing José."

"José left?"

"He was promoted to doorman," Francis said. "Malcolm left. Good to see you up and about, by the way."

"I thought I heard clinking," George said, peering at the cake. "Is it cake time?"

"You can have a sliver after lunch," said Birdie.

"What, so you give it to the porter and not me?"

Caleb didn't like the way he spat out the word "porter." "I need to get going," he said.

She reached for the cake knife; the overhead lights glinted off the metal. "You won't stay and have another slice?"

He did want more of that cake. His mother had packed him a ham sandwich, but she always bought the cheapest ham, which he swore was half rubber. But he didn't want to be a pawn in this couple's argument. "No, thank you," he said. "It was delicious."

"Don't be silly. Of course you want more. Look at you. You could probably eat the whole thing and not gain an ounce. I'll just give you a little piece."

"He doesn't want more," George said.

She cut a piece 10 percent smaller than the last, again washing and wiping the knife, and placed the slice on a clean plate.

"You don't have to eat it," Francis told Caleb.

He glanced at all of them and tried to figure out what to do. Oscar, Sergei, and Ranesh all had told him how important it was to please the board members. Birdie and Francis were on the board; George was not. Caleb had already messed up with Sergei. He didn't want to mess up twice on his first day. Besides, she'd already cut the slice.

He enjoyed the first few bites, but the cake was very rich, and soon he was full. As he chipped away at it, all of them were staring at him in a way he didn't like. Now he realized that he had made the wrong choice for the second time that day. The cake felt like a bowling ball in his stomach, and sweat from his armpits soaked into his shirt and vest.

"He has a marvelous appetite," Birdie observed.

"You could probably take some home with you, Caleb," said Francis.

He finished the piece and gulped down the glass of milk Mrs. Hirsch poured for him. He wiped his mouth and excused himself, fighting the urge to puke.

"Can I tempt you with one more piece?" Birdie asked, brandishing the cake knife.

"For Christ's sake," George said. He glared at Caleb. "It's not your place to encourage her." Then he went back into the bedroom and slammed the door.

"George!" Francis called after him. "I was hoping to chat with you a moment."

"It was wonderful to meet you, Caleb!" Birdie exclaimed, ushering him out. "Come back for another slice anytime you like."

Caleb's automatic smile lasted until Birdie had closed the door.

◀◆▶

Before he left work for the day, Caleb tried to apologize to Sergei for being inappropriate, but the doorman said, "Not now," and walked away.

So although he'd promised some high school friends he'd go ice-skating with them in Central Park that afternoon, he texted them that he wasn't feeling well and headed home. His whole body hurt, and he wanted to curl up and sleep until morning. His schoolwork could wait. He tried to stay positive, but all he could think was that he had to go back to that hellhole the next morning and the morning after that, on and on for the rest of his life, probably. He wished he didn't have to work for a building full of petty, entitled white people and a doorman who already hated him, and besides, he was freezing his ass off. Where was global warming when you needed it?

While climbing out of the 6 train station at 110th and Lexington, someone tapped him on the shoulder. "Hey," came a familiar voice. He spun around and came face to face with Sergei, wearing a puffy down coat over his uniform. With a hot sense of dread, Caleb understood that he'd been followed. He had been stupid, and now he was getting his punishment.

"So you like me, do you?" Sergei asked, his little mouth curling into a hint of a smile. "Or do you go around hitting on all the doormen?"

He was too tired and cold to listen to Sergei's villain monologue. He just wanted to go home, smoke a joint, and fall asleep. "Get the fuck away from me."

Sergei took a step back. "But I thought you wanted to, you know, hang out."

"Quit fooling with me, man."

"I am not 'fooling.' What happened before, I'm sorry. It's just, I do not want anyone to know what I am. Those people have nothing better to do than gossip."

It took Caleb a moment to understand what Sergei was saying, then a few more to believe it. Then all he could do was stare into Sergei's round blue eyes, feeling suspended in his gaze. He leaned in for a kiss, but Sergei stepped back.

"Not in public," the doorman whispered, glancing around. "Do you have your own place?"

Who exactly did Sergei think was going to see them? The three women smoking in front of the Mexican bakery, the couple talking inside the bougie coffee shop, or the people in the taxis crawling down Lexington Avenue?

Caleb shook his head. "I live with my folks."

"I have my own place. But it's not close to here."

Caleb's fatigue had been replaced by jittery anticipation. He'd already told his parents he wouldn't be home for dinner. Sergei and Caleb caught the downtown 6 train and switched to the 4, then the Q.

On the ride, Caleb talked about his relentlessly crappy day, which now didn't seem so bad. Sergei told him about the shareholders with mistresses and the ones who hired prostitutes. "Mr. McAllahan likes boys and girls," he said with a snicker. "I am sure they are all eighteen years, but they do not look like it."

Ms. Delano-Roux had three different gentleman callers of varying ages. Chess Kimball, another board member, invited his "niece" over every time his wife was out of town. Everything Sergei said excited Caleb.

Sergei knew who had a drug problem, who had been arrested, and which of the building's teenagers were gay before their parents knew. On that note, he made Caleb promise not to touch him while they were in public. Caleb didn't want to date someone who was paranoid-level closeted, but he understood why the doorman, who knew everyone's secrets, feared that any stranger might out him. And it was actually kind of hot, knowing they'd have their own secret.

Because of a stalled train up ahead, the train sat on the Manhattan Bridge for an eternity. But the train wasn't crowded, and the view of the East River and the Statue of Liberty was kind of romantic. Caleb enjoyed the pressure of Sergei's knee against his. Caleb thought, as he often did when meeting someone new, that this might be the last first date of his life.

When they ran out of small talk, the conversation veered into the past. Sergei talked about his upbringing outside of Moscow, about the privations of a childhood behind the Iron Curtain—though at the time, that life was all he knew. "Some of our neighbors were arrested by the KGB," Sergei said, "but they would never go after regular people like us. Still, you always wondered whether someone was watching, especially when you were doing private things in your bed."

After the Soviet Union fell, they would go without fresh fruits and vegetables for months at a time, and they couldn't go out after dark for fear of being attacked. Still it was extremely difficult to leave Russia, because they couldn't be classified as refugees. Fortunately, Jewish agencies were adept at securing visas for Russian Jews to emigrate to Israel, Germany, and the United States, and though his family was fully secular, his mother had been born Jewish. In 1995, when Sergei was twenty years old, his family moved to

Brighton Beach. His father became an electrician, and his mother waited tables at a restaurant on the boardwalk.

Russia had been a homophobic place, and Sergei's parents still believed that being gay was against nature. When they saw him going out at night, dressed in tight acid-washed jeans and brightly colored T-shirts, they must have been suspicious. The day after one of these nights out, his mother took him aside. "If you have anything you are wanting to tell us, please, I beg you, do not. It will kill your father. He will never speak to you again." And that was that. When Sergei finished trade school, he moved into his own place, but it wasn't far enough away. His landlord was friendly with his father, so if anyone in the building saw him getting too close with another man, he would be reported for sure.

Caleb could relate to that fear. Harlem was a close-knit community, and back when he was in the closet, he didn't feel safe being himself north of 110th Street. But outside the neighborhood, he was protected by the anonymity of New York. "Why didn't you move farther away?" he asked. "Or, like, into a building where your dad doesn't know your landlord?"

"You think it is so easy?" Sergei replied. "Nowhere else can I find a nice apartment for so cheap. Six hundred dollars a month—wait until you see it. And south Brooklyn is where all my family and friends live. I cannot move away."

Caleb was suspicious of that argument, but in truth, he had never wanted to live outside of Harlem, and had someone given him an apartment in the Chelmsford Arms, he probably wouldn't have taken it.

They got off the subway in Sheepshead Bay, a few blocks from Brighton Beach. Caleb could smell the salt in the cold sea air, and the light seemed brighter, too. On the walk from the station, Sergei kept his distance and said little. He lived in a tall slate-colored building with no doorman, and he asked Caleb to wait in a nearby deli for a few minutes before buzzing his apartment number, just in case the super was watching the closed-circuit cameras. Caleb did as he was told, amused by the charade but sensing that he shouldn't be. Only when Sergei locked his apartment door behind them did he reach for Caleb's face and kiss him.

5

A SIMPLE WEDDING

For her wedding, Pepper envisioned a forest of pine trees ensconcing the Temple of Dendur at the Metropolitan Museum of Art, in the resplendent atrium where she and Rick had first met. They would invite maybe a hundred people, a few close friends and family extended only as far as first cousins, for a rustic picnic on the forest floor. She had no idea what things cost, and she knew erecting a forest inside the Met would not be cheap, maybe not even possible, but she was still willing to do without most trappings of the typical wedding. No need for an elaborate meal, and certainly no hors d'oeuvres. They'd forgo table settings, flower arrangements, a band, and gift bags. The inexpensive white dress remained unworn in her closet, and she could handwrite the invitations on plain card stock.

She couldn't have pinpointed when that plan began to evolve, but it must have started after Lewis and Claudia didn't respond to her emailed save-the-date, for the Saturday in late June when they were able to book the atrium. Aside from the occasional email exchange with her father, she had communicated with them exclusively through Maisie, who said the subject was being elegantly avoided. When, upon Pepper's urging, Maisie asked flat out if they were coming, Claudia warned her not to get involved with her sister's childish grievances.

Pepper had never before felt such rage at her parents as she did in the weeks after Maisie delivered that news. Dr. Riffler asked her why it was so important that her parents show up, and she didn't have a therapeutically useful answer, except that everybody's parents showed up to their child's wedding. Skipping her wedding would be unforgivable.

When she couldn't stand being angry any longer, she composed a polite email explaining how much their attendance would mean, that two seats would be saved for them, and that if they decided not to show, their absence would be acknowledged during the ceremony. She tried to be nice about it, but not even a cheering squad of emoji could mask her resentment. She reminded herself that this was not her fault. Even if her parents didn't like their future son-in-law, the least they could do was fake it for one day.

She reread the email draft. It wasn't convincing enough, somehow. She saw that she had embarrassingly little sway in whether they came or not. So she added, after the word "ceremony" a subordinate clause: "which will be attended by multiple reporters and editors," even though she hadn't invited anyone of the sort. Claudia would do anything to prevent a scandal, even if it meant smiling for the cameras at her daughter's wedding. Pepper sent the email and felt a little better.

Days passed with no response, and Pepper grew angrier and more upset. She didn't want a whole bunch of news outlets at her wedding, but she didn't *not* want them there, so she decided to reinforce her position. She had lunch with Louisa Crispin, a friend of Katt's who maintained a well-read blog about real estate and society, and told her about the wedding. Louisa was overjoyed and promised to bring her camera. She also offered to reach out to her contact at *Town & Country* to see if they wanted the official photos.

Now that she had media coming, she saw that her wedding, as planned, needed to be more of an event. She'd never cared what strangers thought of her, but when she imagined Louisa eating a cold chicken-breast sandwich under a tree, she cringed. When she imagined her parents judging her based on the resultant story, she panicked.

So although the contract with the caterer had been signed and the trees had been ordered, she retained an event designer who had planned a wedding for a duchess and a birthday party for Bruce Springsteen, and the character of the wedding changed.

The event designer tried to work with her vision and proposed long farmhouse tables cutting through the pine forest and a menu created by a chef couple who had run a gourmet destination in rural Virginia, where the food was styled to resemble dirt and weeds. He also suggested increasing the number of guests to at least 250. Any fewer than that and the crowd would look sparse, he said. Pepper decided to invite 350 in hopes of getting

300. Now that she saw the whole thing diagrammed out, she was excited at the prospect of a big wedding.

Rick was willing to pay for whatever, but he hated party planning, and she tried not to antagonize him with questions. But it saddened her to imagine a wedding alien to his taste—and she didn't want him to be surprised by the ballooning cost—so she ran every decision by him. His responses were supportive but curt. Around the same time, he began working late, and at home he spent more time with his phone than with her. He replied to Facebook messages during meals, idled an hour at a time in the bathroom, checked his email in elevators and on cab rides with her, kept his earbuds in when they were relaxing together, and, after turning out the lights at bedtime, when her skin was anticipating his touch, flicked his screen on and watched highlights from ESPN or *Saturday Night Live*.

Every time he looked at that phone, she felt pushed aside. She tried to joke about it without being a nag: "Your mistress is calling," she would say if she spotted his phone ringing on the table. Or, "Can it just be us tonight, without our third wheel?" And he would say something like, "I have a demanding mistress," before skulking into the other room with the phone and closing the door.

At times she wished they had stuck with the anti-wedding, or at least the picnic idea, but she was afraid to admit it to Rick for fear that he would want to scrap all her planning and disinvite everyone. Then it would really look as though she were ashamed of him. Especially because the tabloids had already gotten wind of the event. If she canceled the wedding, they would eviscerate her.

◄●►

Pepper had joined the co-op board partly to make positive change in the building, but through four monthly meetings, the bloc of Francis, Birdie, and her had been outvoted on nearly every measure, from approving minority tenants to requiring benefits for domestic help to hiring a decent florist for the lobby arrangements. It was like Congress: with few exceptions—unanimously banning tap dancing, for example, after one shareholder's daughter took it up—each member voted along party lines. So far, the only change she had instituted was the custom of bringing refreshments to the meetings. After that impossible first meeting, when she realized that Patricia wasn't going to serve her guests anything, Pepper brought two open bottles of wine, thereby forcing Patricia to put them on the table. The following month, Francis arrived with scones, and Ardith brought cheese and crackers. After that, everyone except Patricia contributed something.

But snacks at board meetings made a negligible improvement in the building, and represented a sad fall from the idealism of her youth, when she hazily believed that she could make a difference. Maybe things would change when Francis became president. Hope for a post-Patricia era was the main thing keeping her from quitting. And when the January meeting rolled around, as she waited with Birdie for Letitia to answer the door, Pepper found herself smiling, imagining the look on Patricia's face when she lost her precious presidency. Like the Wicked Witch of the West, she'd probably melt on the spot.

Francis arrived with Ardith a few minutes late, looking angry. The closest thing to anger she'd ever seen in him was patient disapproval. She told herself he was just tense with election nerves. They took their seats, and Pepper poured them both some wine, not wanting to ask Letitia for anything, since it still seemed wrong that she had to work at night. Francis kept his eyes low.

"You are an emissary from heaven," Ardith told her. The dowager raised her glass and took a sip.

"St. Peter wanted me to tell you to drink more wine," Pepper said.

"Let's not waste any more time," Patricia cut in—she seemed to interrupt no one but Pepper. "We have a lot to cover, including finalizing the budget and an interview with the Szymanski family at eight o'clock."

"Is that the family with all those children?" Birdie asked, her nose wrinkling.

"They have about twenty, don't they?" Ardith said. "Maybe we should ask them their views on birth control."

"I'm not getting any younger," Patricia scolded. Claudia was fond of saying that, generally when Pepper didn't jump at her every summons. Thinking of her mother, Pepper felt the familiar rage. She wasn't going to obsess about the wedding, not tonight.

"Clearly," Ardith muttered.

"Our first order of business is an easy one," Patricia said. "Board elections. Douglas is again running for treasurer. All in favor?"

Everybody but Dougie raised their hands. Pepper didn't like voting for him, but she didn't want to oversee the co-op's finances, and as Francis told it, the board used to go door-to-door, begging for a treasurer each year until Dougie took on the role.

Patricia smiled. "Congratulations, Douglas. Next, Chess is running for secretary. All in favor?"

Again, every hand except the nominee's went up. Maybe in a year or two, when she got to know the building a bit better, Pepper would run for secretary. In her mother's building, where she grew up, the secretary of the board published an entertaining quarterly newsletter that combined financial reports with building news and an interview with a shareholder. All Chess did was email a page of sloppy meeting minutes.

"Excellent," Patricia said. "Lastly, I am running for president. All in favor?"

Every voter, even Francis, raised a hand. Pepper felt disoriented, as if just waking up from a nap, and didn't raise hers. Had she misheard? "You're running unopposed," she said, hoping to be corrected.

"Does that surprise you, Ms. Bradford?" Patricia asked, removing her glasses as if to get a better look at Pepper.

"No, I just wanted to make sure."

Francis mouthed, "I'm sorry." He had promised he would beat Patricia, and now he was voting for her.

She wanted to quit right then: she couldn't imagine twelve more meetings in Patricia's dining room, the horrible crone cutting her off every time she tried to speak. But she refused to submit. She would not let herself be bullied ever again.

"Were you planning on voting?" Patricia asked Pepper with a wincing smile. "There aren't any other candidates."

Abstaining wouldn't accomplish anything. Still, she didn't raise her hand. Her body refused to help Patricia win. "You won the election. There's no need for me to vote."

"Are you saying that you don't think I should be president for another year?" Her eye twitched.

Pepper smiled, feeling a hint of power over Patricia. "I'm not saying that. I just think the effort to raise my hand is unnecessary. Congratulations, you win."

Francis widened his eyes at her. Birdie stifled a smile.

"Fine, save your energy," Patricia said.

"Would you like me to mark you as having voted for her or having abstained?" asked Chess, his pen poised above the day's minutes.

"Abstained," Pepper said. "But not for any ideological reason."

Ardith emitted a husky giggle. "I didn't realize we were dealing with ideologies here."

Patricia shrugged, and Helen of Troy leaped off Patricia's lap and bounded into the kitchen, its fluffy pantaloons bouncing up and down. "You are a strange girl. Very well. Thank you all—or most of you, at any rate—for entrusting me to lead the building once more. We serve all the shareholders of the Chelmsford Arms, and I serve you. So I hope you'll let me know how I can better serve you."

"Can we move on, please?" Francis snapped.

"For once, Francis wants to hurry the meeting up!" Patricia's dig garnered a laugh. "Very well, then. Next on the agenda . . . I have received an anonymous complaint about certain residents lingering in the lobby, occupying the doormen with chatter. As we all know, our doormen have a job to do in keeping us safe. It is not easy work, and they do it very well. They are cordial as a courtesy to us, but we must not abuse that friendliness. Without naming any names, I would simply like to remind everyone that the lobby's function is a place for welcoming guests, not a venue for social hour." Everyone must have known she was addressing Francis, as he spent mornings talking with the doormen.

"Who complained, Patricia?" Francis asked, no less angry than before.

"The complaint was anonymous. We are not naming any names—"

"Oh, come off it. Coyness doesn't become you. It's not a crime to talk to the doormen, and of course I recede when they need to focus on their work."

"I thought you wanted to speed this meeting up, Francis," said Patricia with mock surprise. "But while we're on the topic of inappropriate relationships with staff members, I would like to remind everyone here—and particularly you—that, except in the case of handymen for minor repairs, we do not invite staff members into our homes. The liabilities are staggering."

"Nothing untoward was going to happen," Francis said. "We simply had coffee." Pepper didn't know what he was talking about, and from the look on the other faces around the table, no one else knew, either. Except Ardith, who shrugged giddily like a woman in a yogurt commercial.

"Are we referring to that scrumptious new porter?" Ardith asked. "I couldn't take my eyes off his perky little derriere. I kept inventing chores just to watch him work."

So Francis had been having coffee with Caleb. It was unusual, but not worth making a stink over. Pepper glanced at Letitia, standing a few feet away, wiping down glassware in Patricia's dining-room hutch. She wondered how Patricia's housekeeper felt about Ardith objectifying Caleb. Of course, Letitia didn't flinch.

"I'm frankly disappointed in both of you," Patricia said. "If I may quote from the bylaws: 'Shareholders are not to engage in any relationship, whether personal or financial, with anyone employed by or contracted with the Chelmsford Arms Corporation. This includes, but is not limited to, romantic entanglements and business dealings.'" Pepper was impressed that she had rattled all that off from memory.

Ardith raised her glass. "There is nothing so life-affirming as a romantic entanglement with a working man—preferably one that brings mutual satisfaction."

Birdie and Dougie laughed at what had to be a joke, as Pepper couldn't imagine Ardith making love to anyone, much less a reasonably attractive young man. Maybe it had happened a few decades ago.

"It is extremely risky to enter into any kind of relationship with someone you have the power to terminate," Patricia continued, ignoring Ardith's joke, "and we must not permit even the appearance of these relationships."

"We get it," Francis said.

"I'm not emphasizing these things for my own health, Francis. But fine, I won't belabor the point. Next on the agenda is a request by our very own Ms. Penelope Bradford," Patricia said with raised eyebrows. Pepper had submitted the agenda item in advance, hoping to sidestep Patricia's inevitable objections. And she'd hoped it wouldn't be discussed until after Francis had become president. Now that she'd gone and irritated the old witch, she dreaded what punishment awaited her. "Something about our preferred vendors?"

"Yes," Pepper began, quelling a sudden pulse of nerves. She began her practiced speech. "As you all know, we're required to use the building's preferred vendors when we renovate. I see the wisdom in this: I wouldn't want someone coming into our building for weeks or months without a careful vetting process. But as someone whose renovation has recently begun, and who has seen firsthand the limitations of having only three contractors compete for our business . . ."

"I know what you're going to propose, Ms. Bradford, and the answer is no."

She coughed, feeling as if Patricia had reached across the table and grabbed her by the throat. "How do you know what I'm going to say?"

"You want to expand the list of preferred vendors, and I'm telling you it's not our place. We hire a managing agent to run our building, and we do our level best to get out of their way. They have selected a diversity of companies who are known to do good work in our building at a fair price, and we must defer to their expertise. Do you or I know who the best contractor in New York City might be? Of course not. But they do. They are the experts, not we, so I would suggest you not waste our time second-guessing them."

Once again, Pepper's attempt at making positive change was being snuffed out by this gorgon. She made fists of her hands under the table, trying to dispel her rage. Francis looked sympathetic but said nothing. "I don't know the best one, but I'm pretty sure the three we're stuck with are close to the worst. Can't we ask the managing agent to review a few more, using input from the shareholders? They work for us, not the other way around." She heard herself begging but didn't know how to regain her authority.

Fatigue softened Patricia's features, a look that Claudia often adopted, making Pepper feel like an annoying child. "Ms. Bradford, what is it you're really asking? You want us to change the rules so you can use a different contractor. I've said it before, and I'll say it again: your election to our board does not grant you preferred status in the building. That is not why you are here. You are here to maintain the value and prestige of the Chelmsford Arms. You are here to help residents cohabitate peacefully. You are not here to wheedle special favors. That is what we call corruption, and if you possess half the intelligence you pretend to, you will stop trying to appeal to the board for your personal gain. Do I make myself clear?"

"I am trying to help my neighbors by giving them reasonable contractors for their renovations," Pepper said through gritted teeth. "That will help increase the value of the building." She wanted to kick her chair back and leave. But she sat there as Patricia changed the subject and the meeting lumbered on. She couldn't decide whether that reflected a great deal of maturity or a great deal of cowardice.

◀ ◆ ▶

She managed to hide her upset with Rick until an afternoon in mid-February, at the stationery showroom in Chelsea. She and Rick were talking over calligraphic font families with the invitation designer, a plump woman in her fifties with a chest tattoo and a nose ring. Pepper wanted something strong but airy, stately but accessible. She loved Eurydice, with slender crossbars and serifs that looked like Doric capitals. Rick pointed to his favorites and resumed writing text messages.

"Can't you save that for later?" she asked.

"Sweetheart," he said, without any sweetness, "it is literally impossible for me to care less about the font family of our invitations. You could write our names in Sanskrit using goat's blood, and I would be perfectly happy."

"I'll be right back," the designer said, tidying the stack of samples before leaving the showroom for the letterpress studio in the basement, to run an errand whose sole purpose must have been to leave the bickering couple to themselves.

"You have an opinion," she said. "You knew you liked Whisperwind better than Catalpa. You're just digging your heels in. What's going on?" She understood why couples fought over their weddings: the stress of presenting their relationship to the world was almost unbearable. It saddened her that she and Rick weren't impervious to it.

He stuck his jaw forward thoughtfully. "It just feels like this wedding is some kind of stratagem, like you're trying to prove something to the world."

"You like spectacle," she said. "What was the forest in our bedroom all about if not showing off? Or the hooker apartment?"

He grimaced at the latter memory. "Yeah, I like spectacle, but just for us. Private spectacle. It seems like you care more about what *Town & Country* wants than what would really be nice. I love that you don't give a shit about what other people think. Or at least I thought you didn't."

She paced the white-painted floorboards of the showroom. "I'm sorry, but this is an exception. I really want this to go well. We're only getting married once; why not make it something really creative and memorable?"

He stepped in her path, and she walked into his embrace and rested her head on his shoulder. "Okay, babe. I'll try harder to be on board with all this. Something about it feels mean-spirited, that's all. Maybe I'm reading into it."

When the meeting resumed, they chose Whisperwind, a fresh take on Papyrus, for their names, and Furrier, a squat, bold typeface, for the details, debossed on a soft, heavy card stock. They weren't Pepper's favorites, but she wanted Rick's taste to be visible.

On the ride home, his words still stuck with her. He was right: it was mean to shame her parents into coming. She wished she hadn't pressured them to come with the threat of the tabloids. But in the course of obsessing over what would make guests happy and massaging every detail into perfection, she had begun to feel less angry at them. She still would be miserable if they didn't show, but now the wedding wasn't just a reaction to their cruelty: it was a work of art that she and Rick were birthing together and sharing with the world. Did it really matter if this beautiful celebration had been born partly of resentment?

◄ ◆ ►

In May, six weeks out, she and Rick had 217 yeses out of 350 invitations. Half of the out-of-towners declined, and most of her cousins were only sending an emissary to "represent" each family. She and Rick elevated 75 names from the B list—former coworkers, second cousins, college friends, professional hobnobbers—but the last-minuteness must have given away their second-tier status, because only 32 of them said yes, and, meanwhile, a dozen confirmed guests canceled. She worried that her parents had waged a war against her wedding, calling up everyone they knew to decline the invitation. But her Aunt Beth, Claudia's favorite sister and the first woman she would have summoned to her aid, was coming with her husband and all four of her children "with bells on."

Three weeks out, she realized that if anyone found out how many extra people she was inviting, the press might paint her as desperate. Her solution was to proffer invites to people in the building, neighbors who wouldn't have expected to be invited but who were interested enough in her to show up. Just a few more friendly faces in the crowd would make a big difference. Birdie and George were already a yes, but she could invite the rest of the board, even Patricia. Anything to fill seats.

She met Francis for coffee at his favorite bakery on Ninety-second and Madison. She was still irritated with him for not running against Patricia in January; he told her afterward that Ardith would not budge on her support for Patricia, and he didn't want to arouse Patricia's ire with a failed bid against her. He was optimistic about the regime change happening next January. Pepper was less optimistic, as the only members coming up for re-election in December were Francis and Birdie. Maybe, with a lot more therapy, she would one day get used to the harridan-in-chief.

Francis ordered a small coffee with foamed milk; before sipping it he stuck his pinkie in and asked that it be microwaved. "I have not been served a sufficiently hot drink in years," he lamented. "This world is terrified of lawsuits."

She couldn't decide if she needed more caffeine or less to calm her wedding nerves. Finally she decided on a chai latte and a triple-berry scone. She placed the scone nearish to the middle of the table and offered him some, but he shook his head: he couldn't eat rich food.

As she squished the crumbs into hillocks and lifted them to her mouth, the way she had eaten muffins as a child, she told him about the wedding and asked if he and Carol could be there. He said they'd love to attend, though without enough excitement or gratitude to assuage her fear that he didn't actually want to come. A few months of wedding planning had eroded what little emotional sturdiness she'd developed in the first thirty-three years of her life.

"You don't have to come if you don't want," she said.

"I just said that we wanted to come."

She apologized for sounding paranoid and told him about Rick's frustration over the wedding and her parents' refusal to RSVP. He wasn't getting indignant on her behalf, which made her wonder if she sounded vindictive or histrionic. She stopped midway through the tirade and said, "What do you think?"

He looked tired, maybe disappointed. "It sounds like it's going to be a lovely party," he said, seeming to emphasize that it was only a party. He probably sided with her parents.

"It does seem pretty hateful of them not to come to their daughter's wedding," she said, pressing a finger into the crumbs.

He sipped his coffee. "I can see how much you want them there. But the thing to remember is that your parents are separate from you. The wedding is about you and Rick. If you make it about them, they'll give you reasons to be unhappy."

She didn't like his implication that she didn't have a right to be mad at them. Had he said this to Carol when her parents hadn't come to their wedding? But Dr. Riffler had said something similar: "Are you trying to prove to your parents that your marriage is good, or are you trying to prove it to yourself?" She'd been so upset, she nearly walked out of the session. Now she tried to absorb the lesson. Her parents were separate from her. If only *they* would have accepted that before trying to break up her marriage!

◀●▶

She walked back with Francis to the Chelmsford Arms to check on the progress of the renovation. Despite the voluble promises of the Greek contractor, the first five months had brought about little improvement—and after six months, Rick and Pepper would have to pay a thousand-dollar fine for every week it continued. This time, however, she saw that the place was beginning to take shape. The floors had been laid—wide limed-oak planks in the living room, textured Scottish wool carpeting in the bedrooms, creamy Carrara marble in the bathrooms, and black slate in the kitchen. The built-ins had been stained and finished, the dentil moldings had been installed but not painted, and the stainless-steel appliances huddled in the center of the kitchen like seditious dinner-party guests.

Rick's hideous loveseat, acquired for free off Craigslist in the late nineties, remained in the middle of the empty living room. It was Rick's favorite place to make love. They'd left it in the apartment (after laundering the cushion covers) to give the contractors a place to sit, provided that they would dispose of it once they were done. Eyeing its stained herringbone upholstery, scarred by clumsily sewn-up tears, she couldn't wait until the apartment was finished and the awful thing was out of their lives forever.

◄●►

Once she had finished surveying the apartment, she knocked on her neighbors' door to invite them to lunch. Birdie answered the door and squealed, then exchanged cheek kisses in the French way. She said that George was sleeping but that she would love to come to lunch.

"He sleeps a lot, doesn't he?" Pepper observed. He'd been sleeping or otherwise occupied the last few times she'd stopped in. It had occurred to her that maybe he just didn't like her.

"Well, he's up all night, so, yes, he sleeps much of the day."

"How do you sleep if he's awake? Even the light from Rick's phone keeps me awake."

Birdie closed the door behind her and pressed the elevator call button. "I sleep like a log."

Pepper sensed that she didn't want to keep talking about George, but Birdie hadn't answered her unstated question. She mustered her resolve and stated it as politely as she could. "Is everything all right with him?"

"Of course, dear." Without taking a breath, she said, "Listen, I've been meaning to try a new patisserie in the high seventies. Would you mind if we skipped lunch and made a beeline for dessert?"

An ancient sadness ballooned in her chest and squeezed her belly, the loneliness of being outside a secret. The "secrecy reflex," as Dr. Riffler called it, came on strongest when she asked a question and was ignored or rebuffed. It had started happening in her twenties, but Pepper knew its causes dated back to her early childhood, living with parents who shared almost nothing with her. That was the way with all her anxieties: the childhood armor that had protected her wore off when she became an adult.

"Dessert sounds great," Pepper said. She chose not to take Birdie's request as a ploy to minimize their time together. Planning a wedding left her feeling rejected at least ten times a day, especially by older women.

The elevator was taking its time. Pepper glanced back at her own apartment door and remembered Francis's wild story about the Petersons. Birdie must have witnessed the drama play out. Why hadn't she mentioned it? "Were you friends with the people who lived in our apartment before we did?"

Birdie nodded toward the door as if acknowledging someone standing there. "A little bit, yes. Not as close as you and I are, mind you."

"Francis said the husband was living with another woman in Massachusetts."

Birdie laughed. "Yes, yes, it was all quite sordid."

"Did you not want to tell us?" she asked, trying not to sound confrontational.

"I don't like to spread tales," Birdie added, stepping into the elevator.

Again, Pepper was gut-punched by her secrecy reflex, and she couldn't respond. Fortunately, she didn't have to. In the cramped elevator, one had to face forward to keep from smelling the other's breath.

Outside, the early afternoon sun beat down, and Birdie donned a wide-brimmed straw hat.

"It's fine that you didn't tell us—about the Petersons," Pepper said.

"I simply didn't want to jinx things between you and Rick," Birdie said.

"How would it jinx anything?"

"A betrayal like that, it lingers in a place like an angry spirit." She laughed. "You must think I'm a superstitious kook!"

"No, no, of course not," she said, though she didn't believe in the supernatural.

Birdie laughed again. "Anyway, I thought it best not to trouble you."

It seemed controlling of Birdie to keep something from her because she didn't want it to worry her. "It wouldn't have troubled me."

"So, your wedding—tell me everything," Birdie said, clasping her hands like a child begging for presents. "It sounds utterly magical."

Pepper wished her other guests had been so excited. She told Birdie about the Temple of Dendur, the forest, the long, weathered farmhouse tables—then heard how much she was talking and stopped. "What about you? What was your wedding like?"

"George and I eloped: his parents didn't want him marrying this shiksa"—Birdie pointed a thumb to her chest—"and mine didn't precisely cotton to the idea of my marrying a New York Jew."

"Mine aren't thrilled about my marriage, either."

She chirped out a laugh. "None are, dear. If your parents were one hundred percent in favor of your marriage, then you'd know to break off the engagement *tout de suite!*"

"I'm really glad we're talking," Pepper said, overcome with relief and another wave of sadness. "It's been very hard to plan a wedding that my parents might not come to."

"I understand completely. Oh, have I been there! Here's one thing I know: you are very brave to follow your heart. Not everyone is strong enough to do it, and yet what is the point of having a heart if you don't listen to it?"

"I'm starting to wish I didn't have one."

"Now I know you're not being honest," Birdie said.

Over salted chocolate tartlets with jasmine tea, they talked for more than an hour about their families and the wedding. The Hirsches and the Levys had faced similar rejection from their parents, but unlike Francis, Birdie made Pepper feel talented and considerate, not self-centered or misguided, for planning such a dazzling event. She also seemed confident, perhaps more so than Pepper herself, that Rick was her perfect match.

◄ ● ►

Rick and Pepper still went out to the theater and art openings, weekended in Boston and Montauk, picked out minor furnishings and artworks for the apartment, and made love in gymnastic configurations. But it all began to feel routine; he had stopped finding ways to surprise her. And her own creativity was drained by the wedding, as every box she'd checked became unchecked: the cake designer was oversubscribed that weekend, the travel agent had booked the wrong cruise, and the bridesmaid dresses fit no one. Pepper began to fear the chirp of her cell phone. Her friends assured her that wedding planning strained every relationship, as did watching their home's haphazard transformation by a contractor of questionable fastidiousness, and if she and Rick were still together after both of those trials, their marriage would feel like an eternal honeymoon.

So maybe she could blame their fight that morning in June, a week before the wedding, on those stresses. Pepper was sitting in the kitchen of the temporary apartment after a 6:30 A.M. spin class, sifting through a stack of wedding magazines over breakfast to decide if any of them were worth saving, when she heard an insistent buzz. It was Rick's phone, charging on the kitchen counter, going haywire with message alerts. It was normal for him to get messages on the weekends, though not ten at a time. There couldn't have been a stock-market crash or IPO on a weekend, but something was wrong. Maybe his father had died. Or Ben Bernanke. She got up to look.

They were Facebook messages, an agonizing scroll of them on his home screen, from someone named Molly Radiance. It was probably one of Rick's clients; most of them used absurd pseudonyms on the internet to hide from financial predators. "I'm freaking out, Rick." "I need to see you." "Don't shut me out." Another shouldered in while Pepper was looking at the screen: "Please."

She turned the phone off and poured herself a second cup of coffee. Why was this nutjob so desperate to see him? It was probably nothing to worry about, just another example of the madness of the super wealthy. But assuming this woman wasn't completely off her rocker, she must have known he was engaged to be married in a week . . . or maybe he told his clients that he was single.

Her mother's voice seeped into her mind: *He's dishonest, sweetheart.*

She leafed through the magazines, absorbing nothing. She sipped the coffee; her hands were shaking from the caffeine. There was an unspoken history in the messages, of intimacy and conflict. The woman might have just been crazy, but she also might have been a full-fledged girlfriend—though where would he have found the time? He had been working late a lot; maybe he'd been seeing her in the evenings. But he didn't smell like another woman, and he was home every night, never on business trips.

She poured out her coffee and scooped dried hibiscus into the teapot filter basket. While the water was heating up, she took an Ativan. She knew she should get out of the apartment, to calm down before confronting him.

Again she heard her mother's voice: *For that kind of person, a lie is the same as the truth.* Molly seemed like a woman who had been toyed with, but how much? Pepper took in a slow breath; she didn't need to unravel over a suspicion. She had no reason not to trust him, except for her parents' warning. But weren't those messages evidence of untrustworthy behavior?

Her thoughts froze her in place. A few minutes or possibly an hour later, he appeared in his boxer briefs, his hair in his face, and poured himself a mug of coffee. He struggled with the refrigerator door; it was a Sub-Zero and you practically had to pry it open with a crowbar.

"Who's Molly?" she asked, a little too loud as he sat at the table.

"Molly . . ." he said, as though trying to place the name, as though stalling to cobble together a lie.

"She's been messaging you all morning," Pepper said. "I wouldn't have looked, but your phone was buzzing like crazy. I thought it was a flood warning. 'I need to see you.' 'I'm freaking out.'"

"Christ," he said. He grabbed his phone and turned it back on. "She's that crazy client I was telling you about. She's really lonely—her husband died six months ago and left her ten million—but I've let it go too far. I'll hand her off to a junior associate." He started texting at full speed. She hated that phone. When she'd joked that it was his mistress, maybe she'd known something that she hadn't let herself believe.

"Just tell me you didn't sleep with her," she said with a dry laugh. She said it to be able to dispel her paranoia, the way she would with Dr. Riffler. But now that it had been said, it had entered the realm of possibility.

"Of course not. Why would you say that? It hurts my feelings that you'd even think that." He kissed her on the cheek.

The familiar knot tightened in her stomach, and she could hardly breathe. Whether or not he had slept with her, he had to be hiding something. "I was just kidding. But you must have done something that made her text you these things."

He tapped some buttons on the side of his phone. She wished he would look at her. She thought she could forgive anything if he would just look at her. "She got really attached to me, and I was enjoying the flattery, and I didn't realize that she was mentally ill. But nothing happened. I mean, do you really think I'd cheat on you? Why are we getting married if you think I'm a scumbag?" Now he looked at her, and she couldn't bear it. She dropped her gaze to a spread of wedding dresses. She hated the whole wedding industry, built on the ridiculous conceit that beauty could make you happy. One week from their wedding, and it seemed they were dancing toward a breakup, all based on a suspicion planted by her parents. She hated how much power they had over her, that they might have destroyed her marriage with a single conversation. She hated even more the possibility that they were right.

And she couldn't fathom moving back into her childhood bedroom. If she left Rick, she might as well jump into the East River and let the current take her.

His phone vibrated. "Will you please turn that off?" she said.

"I'll tell her not to contact me again."

The phone buzzed three more times.

"Turn off the fucking phone!" Pepper shrieked, slapping the table and spilling crimson tea onto the magazine. "I'm sorry, I'm so sorry. But why are you being such an idiot?"

"It's a phone, Pepper. It rings."

"My mother said she wasn't going to watch her daughter marry a used-car salesman. She said you couldn't be trusted. Was she right?"

She couldn't look at him but could feel him staring at her. She hated herself for spreading her parents' venom, for letting it poison their relationship.

"I didn't realize I was marrying your mother," he said. He stood up, pushed in the chair, pocketed his phone, and walked out. She heard the front door close. She was grateful that he didn't slam it shut.

◄●►

Pepper ate half a bag of frozen peanut-butter cups and binge-watched a new courtroom comedy on Netflix. The show was mindlessly unfunny, but it had the desired effect. By the time Rick came home, her mood had improved.

"I gave my phone to my assistant," he said, standing at the threshold of the living room, holding a bouquet of roses. "She's going to take my calls for the next three weeks. I'm on vacation."

She couldn't remember the last time either of them had gone a day without their phones, much less three weeks, but she didn't question her good luck. She paused the show and crossed her legs on the couch, giving him space to sit down. "Thank you," she said.

"I'm sorry I prioritized work over you," he said, handing her the roses and kneeling in front of her. "And I'm sorry I gave you a reason to think I was unfaithful. I won't do it again."

"I'm sorry I didn't trust you," she said. "And I'm sorry I told you what my mother said."

"A used-car salesman?" he said, grinning. "That's not a compliment?" It didn't sound so bad, coming from him. "You could have told me that before. You don't have to keep things from me."

"It was just—I wanted so much for them to like you. I was afraid to tell you that they didn't."

"Pepper, I knew they didn't like me from the second I met them. You weren't hiding anything from me. I didn't even realize you were trying to."

They kissed, first sweetly and then messily and then ravenously, and it awoke in her a memory of her love for him, buried by meaningless anxieties and second-guessing.

◄◆►

The rehearsal dinner was at Eleven Madison Park, a restaurant inside an old bank building, which was as close to perfection as anything on earth. Friends and family from across time and space appeared as if by magic to wish her well. Those months of planning were coming to fruition in the best way, and she didn't care about the other details that had kept her up nights all spring.

Except for one: her parents never RSVPed. Maisie had promised that they would be there, but when she noticed two empty seats beside Rick's stiff, bedazzled parents, she hurried out of the building to keep her guests from seeing her cry.

She crossed the street into Madison Square Park, where mobs of young office workers in tight clothes milled about, soaking in the greenery and the evening sunlight. She knew she would have to come to terms with her parents' absence or else ruin what was meant to be the happiest day of her life. She willed herself not to need them anymore and laughed at the impossibility of it.

Rick followed her out, weaved his arms through hers, and held her while she cried into his warm chest. "They still love you," he said, for the tenth time that week. "It's okay if they don't love me."

She stepped back and gazed at all six feet of him, from his glossy sweep of hair to his patent-leather wing tips.

"I love you," he said, "more than you could ever know. I've never loved anyone else."

"I love you too, the most, the most," she said. "And I believe you."

He took her hand, and they walked back inside. She couldn't be sure he'd never stray, but if she wasn't going to call off the wedding, she had to trust him. Somehow, letting herself love him without reservations lessened the sting of her parents' absence.

When she sat down again, she looked around the room and saw her parents sitting in their seats, chatting gamely with Rick's parents as if they'd been there the whole time. She nearly cried with relief. Lewis caught her eye and winked.

◄◆►

She remembered her wedding day in fragments, crystalline moments outside time:

The sculptural organza layers of her McQueen dress billow with each step.

Pepper's bridesmaids and Rick's groomsmen surprise her with a choreographed dance.

Maisie brings over her cell phone. Grandma Phyllis is on the line from Brattleboro, offering congratulations.

Birdie hands Pepper a caviar blini on a napkin. "If you only have time to eat one thing today," Birdie says, "eat this." To Pepper's relief, the caviar is delicious.

Ardith introduces Pepper and Rick to a handsome bearded man, young enough to be her son, who is mooning at her. "You are a natural-born event planner, Mrs. Hunter!" Ardith says. "Nothing impresses me anymore, but you, my darling, have stirred me to the core. We *must* conscript you into planning the Beacon of Hope benefit. Today is your day, but we will soon put you to work!" As Ardith laughs, a sturdiness arises from within Pepper, the unfamiliar knowledge that she has talent and could find in it a career, that her life up until now could amount to something useful to the world. This moment makes her even happier than those ecstatic promises at the altar, because although being loved has changed her, finding her purpose has changed her in a way that is all her own.

Lewis stands to give a toast, swinging his champagne flute like a conductor's baton. "Thank you, Rick, for marrying my sweet Pepperoni," he says. "We were this close to arranging a marriage ourselves, so you can all imagine our delight that Rick walked into her life. Welcome to the family." She is able to believe him.

In her toast, after regaling the audience with embarrassing childhood memories of Pepper, Katt mentions a serendipitous occurrence: just three days ago, the Defense of Marriage Act was struck down, allowing gays and lesbians to marry. She says she is proud to live in a country where weddings do not have to be reminders of inequality. Claudia whispers to Pepper that she is appalled that Katt has brought politics into the occasion, but Pepper is glad she did. It reminds her how much cruelty she doesn't see until she is confronted with it, and it makes her more grateful for her wedding, knowing that others had to fight for theirs.

She had read in a wedding magazine that a disastrous wedding is good luck for a marriage. Suddenly it unsettles her that the wedding has been perfect. She regrets thinking that when a server drops a chocolate truffle on her, marking her bodice with a cocoa tail.

Lastly, they arrive in the hotel suite. There's a bottle of champagne in an ice bucket, a tray of chocolate-dipped strawberries the size of tennis balls, purple orchids floating in a lavender bath, and waffle-weave bathrobes stretched out on the bedspread. She extricates herself from her dress and collapses onto the bed, too tired to eat though she is famished, too tired to make love though she longs for her husband's touch. Rick is kissing her temple, then her jaw. She anticipates the next kiss, fighting to stay awake, wondering where it will land, but she never feels it.

6

CRAZY

TWO WEEKS EARLIER

She messaged him first. Even after everything, Rick could still cling to this.

Her Facebook name was Molly Radiance. Thirty-six years old, from Brooklyn. She was a bone-thin brunette with an expectant heart-shaped face, and he probably would have ignored her if she hadn't "liked" a bunch of his photos and written, "Your pictures are inspiring!" in her message.

She had just fifty-four "friends," compared with Rick's eighteen hundred. Their one mutual friend was a nice-enough girl Rick had taken home from a night of drinks at The Campbell Apartment and never saw again. This was before he met Pepper and fell in love, before they bought a classic six in Carnegie Hill for just shy of $3 million and embarked on an endless renovation whose costs continued to rise, and before Pepper mutated into a bridezilla who vaporized all his free time into questions of meal choices and party rentals. Should the invitations be embossed or debossed? Did Pepper look better with a scooped back and a sweetheart neckline or a scooped neck and a high back? Was this or that friend invited to the rehearsal dinner or just the Sunday brunch? Did they want to give the photo exclusive to *Town & Country Weddings* or *Martha Stewart Weddings*? The Pepper he'd fallen in love with would have scorned the Penelope she'd become. Rick hoped her insanity was temporary.

In the first days of their engagement, Pepper dreamed up the most relaxed wedding in Wasp history: a ceremony in Central Park followed by a pizza party. Her parents even seemed to be on board. But then she'd gotten into a fight with them and seemed to be planning the most extravagant wedding on earth to spite them. He had no choice but to bankroll her revenge fantasy, and he cringed every time an estimate floated in. Sixteen thousand for hors d'oeuvres. Seven thousand for a cake. Twelve thousand for hair and makeup. Eighteen thousand for photography.

So even though it was almost midnight and he had a long list of hedge funds to spec for his clients, he messaged Molly back. "Thx. Your pics are nice, too."

She sent a friend request, and he accepted, intrigued by this fresh excitement.

"Congratulations on getting married," she wrote. "I'm so happy for you!!!"

Indeed, "Engaged to Penelope Bradford" was in his public profile. "Thx. It's good to be reminded how great it's going to be." Smiling emoji.

"Why would you need reminding? It's your special day. And you're doing it at the Met! I could just die!"

Pepper had been interviewed for *New York Social Diary* about their wedding plans, but it was still unsettling that Molly had looked this up. "I'll just be glad when we're married and we can focus on each other again," he wrote. She didn't respond right away, so he added, "ru seeing anyone?"

"Not right now. I've had a lot of bad luck with a lot of manipulative jerks. I'm soooo ready to fall in love again. I wish I could be with someone like you." Blushing emoji.

Exactly what was she angling for? Of course he wasn't stupid enough to ruin his and Pepper's lives for a roll in the sack. Plus, in all likelihood, she was a catfish: some flabby-armed housewife hiding behind pictures she found online.

"When ur ready," he wrote, "you'll find the right guy for u." He added a winking emoji and instantly regretted it.

◄ ● ►

Richie, the name he went by as a child, hadn't given much thought to sex until he was fourteen, at a Catholic sleepaway camp on Lake Erie. The place was austere, but his father, a foreman in a tire factory, had to borrow money from his union to afford the tuition, even at the "scholarship rate," which was reserved for black kids and him. His bunkmate, Artie, an Irish boy with an upturned nose and an aw-shucks smile, bet he could sleep with two girls from their sister camp by the end of the summer. He made it to three. Richie, still four foot eight and asthmatic, had never even kissed a girl.

After that summer, he rebuked himself for waiting so long to get into the sex game. It seemed that if he didn't play his v-card by high school graduation, women would shun him forever. What adult woman would sleep with a virgin? He read every book he could find about seducing women, became a legend in high school for his muscle-melting shoulder massages, and once tied one of his mother's bras to her Tempur-Pedic pillow to practice undoing the clasp. He waited tables at the local Olive Garden twenty hours a week to save up for a used Audi convertible, which he bought the day he got his driver's license. He wore Ray-Bans everywhere, even indoors. He started going by Rick, a sexier name than Richie, he thought. When he closed his eyes, he saw an annotated map of the female anatomy. Still, it took until his freshman year at Princeton, with a married teaching assistant who didn't know that it was Rick's first time.

The sex was better than he'd hoped, and all that preparation had been put to good use, but something was missing. He assumed it was a problem of chemistry, that if he found the right girl, he'd know it by the way he felt in the morning. But future girlfriends and one-night stands left him feeling just as empty, no matter how strong the attraction or how masterful his technique. By his late twenties, he could have his pick of the bar crowd for the price of two eighteen-dollar martinis. Those women adored him, but his postcoital glow didn't last: by noon he'd be ready to go back on the prowl, toss off a few compliments, and watch another woman spread her legs for him. It was soul-sucking work.

Then he fell in love with Pepper, and he knew it was love, and he was sure he'd never love anyone more than her, and the sex was better than anything he'd had, and he proposed, deciding that he'd just have to live with that elusive, buried feeling of always wanting more.

◄ ◆ ►

"This one isn't bad," Pepper said about the hors d'oeuvre she'd just eaten, the "seared tuna on rice crisp with wasabi crème." "I like the crunch."

"It's our most popular choice," said Ronald P., the Met's catering manager, an essentially masculine guy despite the fact that he was constantly declaring everything *superb*. "We even sell them to the steak-and-potatoes crowd." Apparently everything caterers served was categorized by whether or not the highly influential steak-and-potatoes crowd would deign to consume it.

Eight of each hors d'oeuvre had been brought out on a bathroom tile, a chalkboard, or a painter's palette, as though something as boring as a plate might offend the engaged couple. "I like it," he said. "It's like sushi." If low-grade sushi cost eight bucks apiece, he didn't say.

He'd been thinking a lot about money recently. Well, he'd always thought a lot about money; after his father was laid off from the factory, he'd vowed that, once he left home, he would never again have to suffer the indignities of being poor. He wasn't the smartest person on earth, but with his near-perfect memory and ferocious work ethic, he got straight A's in school and 5's on eleven AP tests—a school record. Among the colleges that offered him full rides, he'd picked Princeton because it was known for producing wealthy alumni. After a few years on Wall Street, he got the knack of making money, and for a while he was happy.

It wasn't that money couldn't make you happy; he'd proved that it could. The problem was, you habituated to it really quickly, and no amount was ever enough to erase the fear of losing it all. It was like sex in that way: if you didn't have it when you were younger, you could never get enough of it as an adult to satisfy you. Especially when you were spending it by the wheelbarrow.

Between buying the apartment and renovating it and renting the temporary apartment and financing the uber-wedding, his mind had been colonized by a massive spreadsheet. Pepper considered it low-class to discuss money, which made it doubly hard to stop obsessing over expenses, because he had to hold all the worry himself.

The fifty grand for renting the Temple of Dendur was the one wedding line item he approved of, as he'd met Pepper at a benefit there a year and a half earlier. He'd initially hoped to poach her as a client, but his affection for her took him by surprise. She meant what she said, was extremely intelligent (and endearingly snobbish), didn't laugh at her jokes, and didn't try to impress anyone. She wasn't vain, either, although she had a body that defied gravity, iridescent green eyes, and a pouty little mouth. He wasn't crazy about her forehead—her hairline was a smidge high, giving him unnerving insight into the shape of her skull—but the rest of her more than made up for it. That first night, he dared her to pull a penny from the reflecting pool. She presented it to him, the sleeve of her four-thousand-dollar Chanel dress dripping wet, her grinning face childlike and sweet. They went to his place and talked until dawn. He drove her home after breakfast, grateful that they hadn't fucked. After going out almost every night over the next three months—they didn't need the "Are we exclusive?" conversation because there was no time to see anyone else—they realized almost at the same moment that they'd fallen in love. As they were both in their thirties, they started apartment hunting immediately. Pepper's biological clock ticked louder than a jackhammer.

"It's great that you like it," she said patiently, surveying all the hors d'oeuvres they'd been offered thus far, "but you have to not like something so we can decide."

His phone buzzed with a message from Molly: "Do you have time to talk? I really need you."

He held his phone against his chest to hide the text from Pepper. "Shit, I need to . . . there's a work emergency."

"We'll be done in two minutes," Pepper said.

"Just a sec, babe." He texted, "What's up?"

Ronald P. excused himself to fetch more food.

"A close friend just blocked me," Molly wrote. "He said he can't talk to me anymore."

Pepper glanced toward the kitchen doors. "Why does everything taste like it came from the freezer aisle of a Trader Joe's?"

"But I thought every dish was 'crafted from scratch' in their 'world-class kitchens,'" Rick replied, quickly texting, "Why?"

"I told him I loved him," came Molly's text. "I really thought I did, really."

He wondered if she'd ever met this "close friend" outside of Facebook. "He doesn't deserve u," he wrote.

"Could you just tell me which ones you like best?" Pepper asked. "I don't want our wedding to be 'The Penelope Show.'"

"Definitely this tuna thing," Rick said. "And the mushroom cup, the micro steak on toast, and the caviar potato eyeball." It wasn't a real eyeball; it just looked like it should be served on Halloween.

"Ew, not the caviar," Pepper said, wrinkling her nose.

"I'm in so much pain," Molly wrote. "I feel like I want to hurt myself."

"Don't do that," he wrote, cringing at how stupid it sounded.

"Earth to Rick," Pepper said. "Why are you defending the salted bug paste they're calling caviar?"

"If we don't have caviar," he explained with condescension that wasn't entirely ironic, "your friends will not know we spent a third of a million dollars on this wedding."

"And if we serve this mealy shit," Pepper replied, "the entire world will think we have no taste."

Another text from Molly: "I just fall so hard in love sometimes that it scares me."

"Could you put that down for two seconds?" Pepper asked. "The stock market isn't even open today."

"It's a new client. She needs a lot of attention."

His phone buzzed again. "It's really good to be able to talk to you," Molly's text read. "You're a great listener and a great friend."

Rick texted, "Got 2 go. At a tasting," as Ronald returned holding a miniature Viking ship with lamb chops as passengers.

◄●►

Molly arrived at their little lunch date a few days later in a too-tight skirt suit made of nubby yellow tweed. She'd gained a few pounds, she already had gray hairs, and her forehead was carved with worry, but she really was the girl from the photos. He'd partly agreed to see her just to prove that she existed, but of course she did; he'd googled her. When he typed in "Molly Radiance," he discovered that Radiance1987@hotmail.com was an email address for one Molly Susan Weintraub, a performing-arts teacher at a private school in Brooklyn Heights. Molly had placed first in a spelling bee in Brooklyn in the late nineties. Her Goodreads list was heavy on Jane Austen and Dorothy Parker. She'd camped out with Occupy Wall Street. Her father was a life coach.

She held the initial hug longer than he did, the first step of an awkward dance.

"Just an FYI: you're *extremely* handsome," she said with a raised index finger. "Sorry."

He couldn't say he wasn't flattered. "Apology denied," he said, sitting down. "Your punishment will be a spanking."

"I hope you'll be gentle with me," she said with a manufactured laugh.

"I'm *very* gentle." He pushed the platter of oysters toward her. "Want one?"

She inspected one, sipped the brine, then went bottoms up, making a crunching noise. Was it possible she'd never eaten an oyster before?

"The shell's not edible," he said, suppressing a smile. He liked the feeling of having something to teach her. Pepper never admitted to ignorance; if she had a gap in her knowledge, she would pretend it wasn't worth knowing. He tried not to think about her. He could manage not to feel terrible about what he was doing if he forgot that he was getting married in a week.

He sipped his wine and studied her. He couldn't believe he had let their flirtation go this far, but she had pushed for a meeting, and he told himself it would be harmless. After they made the date, she started sending him messages about feeling his muscular arms and tasting his lips, which he'd dismissed as jokes. Now, as he watched her listening to him and laughing and touching her face, he understood that they were going to have sex. He had seduced women for so many years, he could predict every moment leading up to their orgasms and was powerless to stop it. He wasn't even interested in her: he was being dragged toward her by the unloved boy of his past. It seemed that if he married Pepper before sleeping with Molly—or *someone*—he would regret it forever. The question was, why was he trying to destroy his life? And why wasn't he more afraid of doing it?

He swallowed. "Molly, you're a great girl. But I have to be honest with you. This has to be a one-time thing. I shouldn't even be doing this now. Can I trust that you'll be able to handle a clean break?"

"I guess I'll have to." Out came her desperate laugh.

"How about we go to the Soho Grand? Their sheets are incredible, and you can spend the whole night there if you like."

"Is that a hotel?" She sucked through her teeth. "No offense, but doesn't that seem a little . . . tawdry?"

"It's a really nice hotel."

"I don't know. It's not really what I had in mind."

"Sure, fine, I get it. Where do you live?"

She winced. "My roommates don't allow guests."

He cocked his head. "Then how were you thinking . . . ?"

"I was hoping we could go to your place?"

"Molly," he said, glancing around before taking her hands. "My fiancée is home."

"Oh, God, we shouldn't do this." She tore her hands away and placed them in her lap.

"You're right. Let's just forget it." He called for the check, and they finished their drinks without meeting eyes, though he could tell Molly was sneaking glances at him. He was relieved to be done with her, relieved that, when he proved to lack all self-control and decency, fate had intervened.

When the check came, she got out her credit card.

"Don't," he said.

"I'll pay next time," she said, tucking her card back into her wallet.

Pepper called. Without apologizing or asking permission, he picked up. "Hey babe, what's up?"

"Sweetie, *none* of the bridesmaid dresses fit. It's like they picked measurements out of a hat. We're at an emergency fitting at the atelier, and the owner is saying that we're the ones who got the measurements wrong."

"I'm sorry, babe. That sounds shitty. Hey, why don't we go back to the idea of everyone wearing something they already own? I'm sure everyone has a gray dress."

She moaned. "I wish we could. I know how crazy things have been for you lately, but could you swing by the Chelmsford Arms and pick up the receipts? They're in the rattan box in the bedroom closet."

"Babe, they're working on the bedroom right now. Last time I checked, there was a huge roll of carpeting blocking the closet."

"No, they're done with all the flooring. I called the contractor to see if one of the workers could bring it over, and he said they're taking a few days off until the fixtures are delivered."

He watched Molly, rummaging through a canvas tote whose print reminded him that it wasn't a plastic bag, and rode out a sickening thrill. "So no one is there?"

"It would mean so much if you could bring it. I really need to see you right now."

"I'm finishing up with a client downtown. . . . Will you still be there in an hour?"

"We'll wait for you. Thank you, thank you, thank you. I love you."

"Love you too."

"I wish you'd refer to me as your friend," Molly said after he put his phone back into his pocket.

His blood fizzed in his veins, and he pinched the bridge of his nose. He didn't want to talk himself out of this. "Let's go."

"Where?"

He swigged the rest of his wine, then his water. "To my apartment. You're getting your wish after all."

◀◉▶

After they moved into the apartment at the Chelmsford Arms, Rick and Pepper discovered that the rear elevators, where their apartment was located, was the least prestigious of the three elevator banks, and the apartments were worth 20 percent less. The one benefit was accessibility through the back entrance: Rick could come home without parading through the lobby and jerry-rigging a smile for the doormen. He couldn't live without them but wished he could walk through the lobby just once without worrying what they thought of him. He brought Molly in through this rear entrance, blocking the camera's view of her until the doorman buzzed them in.

But he cringed to see Birdie Hirsch, his perky French-Canadian neighbor, getting into the elevator. They nodded at each other. Molly said hi, then sat on the vestigial elevator-operator seat and ran her fingers along the ridged brass rail. "What floor, madam?" she asked with a stiff nod.

"Have we met?" Birdie asked Molly.

"Oh, this is Molly," Rick said. "She's . . ."

"I'm his ex-girlfriend," Molly said, shaking Birdie's hand. "Pleasure to meet you."

"Oh," Birdie said, her mouth open as though ready to emit whatever response would surely come to her.

"We dated all through college. Rick proposed to me, but my family didn't approve, because he wasn't Jewish. By the time I came to my senses, he was engaged to Penelope."

"My husband and I had the exact same problem with our families," confided Birdie. "We eloped."

The elevator stopped, and they stood by their respective front doors like guards waiting for their shift to end.

"She's my cousin," Rick said, searching for his key. "She's just being funny."

"*Enchanté*, Molly, whoever you are."

"Are you crazy?" Rick asked once he'd closed the door and checked to make sure no one else was inside. "She's my neighbor! She talks to Penelope all the time."

"Maybe you deserve to be found out." She slapped his ass.

He kissed her. Her mouth was soft and her tongue followed his lead. It was exciting to be kissing someone other than Pepper, and a little sad.

"Would you have a drink with me?" she asked, eyeing the sofa mistrustfully. He'd gotten it right after college—decorating his first apartment entirely with freebies—and had been proud of how stately it had looked, almost too good for him. Over the years, it had soaked up splashes of punch and beer, and it had been torn in the fury of half-clothed lovemaking by a stiletto heel. Now it was outclassed by the lavish apartment that surrounded it, and it looked as though it understood that when the renovation was finished and the last traces of Rick's unpolished life had been eradicated, it would have to die, too, so that Rick might be happy.

She plopped down on the couch. "This is such a nice couch. Everything you have is so amazing. I just have to say, my heart is beating *extremely* rapidly."

"How about an Ativan?"

She nodded, but only when he walked into the bathroom did he remember that all of Pepper's medications were in their temporary apartment.

There was a box in the second bedroom marked "toiletries," but the only pills in there were over-the-counter painkillers and vitamins. When he finally returned to the living room with an open bottle of Pinot Gris, anxious about all the time he'd wasted and hoping she hadn't stolen anything, she was kneeling in front of a box of books.

"Sorry, we don't have any good pills," he said, taking a swig from the bottle and handing it to her.

"You have an amazing library. I love how passionate you are about feminism." She gulped down half the bottle.

"Those are my fiancée's. She's not that much of a feminist." He couldn't blame Pepper for banishing Rick's business-advice manuals and political screeds to their storage facility in Queens: her books were hardbound editions in pristine condition, while his scrappy, dog-eared paperbacks mostly derived from stoop sales or waterlogged giveaway boxes dragged out with the garbage. Yet he wished he'd kept some of those books in the apartment, maybe to tuck behind Pepper's when they filled up the new bookshelves, just to have them close. He felt a pang, as though he had already lost her. He didn't want to start their life together by cheating on her. But a parallel voice in his head told him he would never forgive himself for backing down.

"She seems wonderful," Molly said.

"I have an idea—why don't we not talk about her?"

She looked around, taking in the new dentil moldings along the edge of the ceiling and the new commercial-grade kitchen, and nodded brusquely. "I guess this is how the one percent lives."

"We're not so different from you." He thought of his bewilderment in his first months with Pepper, at her amusing snobbery and ignorance of financial realities. "Or at least I'm not." He reached for her again, and she stepped out of his grasp.

"What exactly do you do?" she asked, rubbing the spines of Pepper's books. "I mean, I googled you. I know it's an investment banking thing."

"It's asset management. Helping high-net-worth individuals invest. I'm an adviser, not a banker." People had a tendency to lump all careers in the financial industry into one fork-tailed monster, but he'd had nothing to do with subprime mortgages, bank bailouts, or any other left-wing shibboleth. He invested in green energy and B Corps as much as he could, too. But he wasn't going to defend himself to this woman.

"Like hedge funds and stuff?"

"I work with hedge-fund managers, but I've never managed a fund myself."

"I've never thought it right that people who spend their lives playing with money should get to take home so much of it." Her sneer gave her a menacing squint.

"Hate me if you want, but the fact is, I take a lot of shit from a lot of people, and there's never a moment when I'm not trying to attract new clients. Anyone could make the same money, if they wanted to."

"I wouldn't do it," she said with a shrug.

"Then you really can't complain." It came out harsher than he intended. He smiled at her, which made it worse.

"I read in *The New Yorker* that the reason we had the financial crisis was because bankers are rewarded for lying," she said.

"We don't have a lot of time."

"Oh—sorry. I'm sorry."

He finished the wine and took her by the hand to his trusty sofa, then undid the buttons on her blazer and blouse with one hand while kissing her neck and ears. Her skirt resisted unzipping but soon gave way. A flick of his fingers and the bra fell open. Sometimes he used to enjoy undressing women more than the sex itself. But now the process felt rote, like making an espresso or taking out the trash.

"You have a beautiful body," he whispered, running his fingers over the bumps of her rib cage.

She held her arm over her breasts. Standing beside her, Rick put his hand on her belly and felt it tighten, then relax. He pried her lips open with his and melted his tongue toward hers.

"Do you mind if I put my bra back on?" she asked, wiping her mouth. "I think I'll be more relaxed."

"I do mind," he said, pushing her arm out of the way. "Your breasts are too beautiful to cover up."

She took a deep, loud breath. They sat on the couch and he lapped at her nipples. They tasted like rose-scented lotion.

"Oh, Rick," she moaned. "Will you say my name?"

"Shh." He kissed her on the mouth and began rubbing her clammy inner thighs. He was ready to be done.

"Do you think Penelope might walk in on us?" she asked as he unrolled a condom.

"Don't worry, I locked the door chain."

"Could we maybe . . . unlock it?"

He stopped stroking her. "Why would you want my fiancée to catch me in bed with you?"

"Then I could have you all to myself." She laughed.

He plucked off the condom. "This is insane."

"I wan't being serious! It was just a fantasy, to restore your honor by marrying you. Of course I know you love Penelope, not me. I would never dream of taking you from her."

He teased his underwear from his pants, pulled them on, and tucked his rapidly deflating erection beneath the waistband. "I think you should leave."

"Just forget I said that, okay?" She laughed again. "I say a lot of things I don't mean."

"I'll show you out."

He turned the light on—it was a caged bulb hanging from a wire—and waited for her to dress. After practically pushing Molly out the back entrance, he sprayed Pepper's perfume over the couch, opened the shades, scrubbed his face and hands, found the bridesmaid dress receipts, took one last look at the sad old couch, silent witness to his infidelity, and cabbed over to the atelier, feeling as though his life had been spared.

◄ ● ►

"Who's 'Molly'?" Pepper asked Rick as he walked into the kitchen that Saturday morning, desperate for coffee.

The shock of hearing Pepper speak her name took a moment to penetrate his fog. He drew an even breath. "Molly . . ."

She looked up from a wedding magazine, one of about twenty in her collection. It was weird to be looking at that thing a week before the wedding, he thought. Was she planning on adding to the spectacle? "She's been messaging you all morning. I wouldn't have looked, but your phone was buzzing like crazy. I thought it was a flood warning. 'I need to see you.' 'I'm freaking out.'"

Now he was awake. "Christ," he said, snatching his phone from the charging station on the counter and trying to gauge how lethal the truth—or a cleaned-up version that ended in the restaurant—would be. "She's that crazy client I was telling you about. She's really lonely—her husband died six months ago and left her ten million—but I've let it go too far. I'll hand her off to a junior associate." He texted, "What's wrong?"

"Just tell me you didn't sleep with her," she said with a withering laugh.

"Of course not," he said. Had she seen him with Molly? Had Birdie told her about their elevator run-in? It wasn't likely; she probably hadn't seen Birdie since they'd moved to the temporary apartment. Either way, he wasn't lying: he hadn't slept with Molly, by the grace of God or some mischievous deity named Dumb Luck. If the goal was to be 100 percent honest, and he was able to get 90 percent of the way there, that was pretty good, right? Especially when he'd never make this mistake again—Molly had cured him. "Why would you say that? It hurts my feelings that you'd even think that." He kissed her, then stuffed a forkful of goat cheese omelet into his mouth and forced himself to swallow.

She examined him. "I was just kidding. But you must have done something that made her text you these things."

"She got really attached to me, and I was enjoying the flattery, and I didn't realize that she was mentally ill. But nothing happened. I mean, do you really think I'd cheat on you? Why are we getting married if you think I'm a scumbag?" He looked at her, feeling annoyed, and she looked at her magazine, at a big photograph of a woman in a wedding dress. Suddenly the whole idea of a wedding dress seemed insane. It looked nice and all, but what did the bride do if she had to take a shit?

His phone buzzed. It was Molly: "I'm at Grand Central. Meet me by the clock in fifteen minutes. I have something to tell you." He had to admit, he still got excited to hear from her. But for the sake of his marriage, he had to stop this once and for all.

"Will you please turn that off?" Pepper asked without looking up.

"I'll tell her not to contact me again."

The phone buzzed again: "Don't shut me out." Then, "I'm going crazy here." Then, "I don't trust myself to be alone."

"Turn off the fucking phone!" Pepper shrieked, slamming her hands on the table, sloshing her tea onto the magazine. "I'm sorry, I'm so sorry. But why are you being such an idiot?"

"It's a phone, Pepper. It rings." He held down the power button, frustrated at how long the phone took to respond. He wished he'd never replied to Molly that first night. He wished he could go back in time and convince himself to shut down his computer and go home to the woman he loved.

"My mother said she wasn't going to watch her daughter marry a used-car salesman," she muttered. "She said you couldn't be trusted. Was she right?"

He wiped his face with a sixty-dollar napkin, a recent wedding gift, and he thought, *Who would pay sixty dollars for a napkin?* He'd known it would be risky to marry into a family of snobs, but he'd thought Pepper only acted that way as a joke. "I didn't realize I was marrying your mother," he said. He'd meant it as a bit of levity, but it sounded like a jab.

◄●►

"Okay, what is it?" he asked Molly when he found her at Grand Central, amid weekend travelers beelining in all directions. She was wearing a deep V-neck T-shirt that showed, as one of his college friends had put it, ABN: All But Nipple. On anyone else, it would have been sexy.

"I miss you, Rick," she said, taking his hand and running her fingers down his forearm. "Let's go to Beacon and have a day together. There's this little café by a waterfall that you're going to fall in love with."

He snatched his hand away. "Molly, we're not going anywhere."

"Oh, Rick, you don't mean that." She reached for him again, and he leaped back.

"Molly, listen to me." He enunciated every syllable. "There is something grossly wrong with you. We are never going to speak again. Do you understand?" It was satisfying to force her to see her madness, to shame her for wanting him.

"You think I don't know that something's wrong with me? You think people haven't been telling me my whole life? That doesn't give you the right to be cruel."

"If I've been cruel, it was in leading you on in the first place. It's over."

"Come on, Rick, let's talk about this like adults."

"I'm leaving now." He decided against telling her he'd remember her fondly. It would have been a lie, anyway—and he was trying not to lie anymore. "I hope you find a way to be happy."

He walked off into the throng of travelers. A recorded announcement over the loudspeaker that began "Don't fall for it!" struck him like a personal reprimand. He opened Facebook on his phone to block her. It relieved him that he had never given her his phone number or email address. Maybe he wouldn't hear from her again.

Pepper had texted him: "I feel awful about what I said. Will you come back so we can talk?"

"If you didn't even *like* me, why did you try to *sleep* with me?" Molly called after him. "Cheater!" He could feel everyone around him turning to watch. She was probably basking in the attention.

If it wasn't worth the half a million it ultimately cost, the wedding was still the happiest day of Rick and Pepper's lives. Any lingering resentment from the Molly debacle was swaddled in the euphoria of the best party of their lives. Those two hundred pine trees looked majestic, Pepper was a goddess in ivory, and her father raised a glass and welcomed him into the family. He was relieved that Molly did not appear. It seemed that all her rage would burn itself out inside the fun house of her mind.

Although he and Pepper occasionally ventured outside their honeymoon stateroom and took in the splendors of the cities along the Rhine, they spent most of the trip in bed, a picked-over room-service tray languishing on the coffee table. Upon their return, they were consumed by writing thank-you notes, choosing photos, and moving back into their apartment—which, after eight long months, was finally renovated—and Rick barely thought of Molly. When he did, his mind traveled along the same track. First he wondered if he should have gone ahead and done it, because now that he was married, he'd never get to fool around again. Then he thought actual sex would have caused Molly to lose her mind. Then he wondered how she was faring, which of her second-degree Facebook friends she was terrorizing, and whether he had helped her come to terms with her madness. Then he thought about something else.

◄ ◉ ►

When they were filling the new built-ins with Pepper's books, she noticed that all her Virginia Woolf novels were missing. "Did I lend them to someone?" she asked.

"Maybe they'll turn up," Rick said. But he already knew what had happened.

Lots of other things were missing, too: Pepper's perfume, their Viking range owner's manual, a copy of the wedding video, and a two-thousand-dollar bottle from Rick's wine refrigerator. Then Pepper noticed that someone had eaten almost half of the overpriced wedding cake they were freezing for their first anniversary. "I think that's all that was left over," he said. They changed the locks.

One morning, the blond, stern Russian doorman, Sergei Avilov, handed him a note in a sealed envelope. "Your cousin dropped this off."

"My cousin?"

"Lady who comes to water your plants?" Sergei asked. "She is not your cousin?"

"We don't have plants," Rick said, tearing open the envelope.

Dear Rick,

I hope this note finds you well. I honestly hope you are happy being married to Penelope now, and that you are no longer angry with me. I have been thinking and growing a lot since we last talked, and I think we should give each other another shot as friends. I have moved into my own place in Spanish Harlem; my phone number and the address are below. I hope you'll come visit me someday, and we can start a new chapter in our friendship.

Love,
Molly

"I am truly, truly sorry," Sergei said. "She had the key, so we just assumed . . ."

"If she comes back, don't let her in," he said, then went into the apartment and burned the note on the stove—though not before memorizing her street address. She'd moved less than a mile from the Chelmsford Arms.

He created a new email account and wrote her at the Radiance1987 address. "This is the last time I will contact you. If you break into my apartment again, I will have you arrested. If you ever try to contact me again, I will get a restraining order." It pleased him to be blunt with her.

He checked the email account for a reply every day for a week, then every few days for a month. He was surprised to feel the slightest disappointment that she hadn't written him again.

And then one morning in October, Rick received an envelope in the mail with no return address. No note was inside, just the key to their apartment. Molly had given it back.

At first he was relieved, as it seemed he would be finished with her forever. But the whole thing still felt unfinished. It irked him that Molly had stayed in their apartment and stolen their things, and now she was pretending to take the high road and washing her hands of the whole affair. He knew he should leave it alone. Nothing would be gained by telling Molly off again, and reopening that Pandora's box could wreck things with Pepper for good. Yet he found himself repeating Molly's address like a mantra. He accidentally typed it into a work email, and it echoed in his head when he woke up at night. He thought he might never be able to let it go if he didn't get to say his piece and put an end to the whole crazy mess.

◄●►

Molly lived on the fifth floor of a rickety walk-up above a Mexican sandwich joint. Rick pressed buttons on the buzzer panel until a neighbor let him in, then climbed to her apartment, his shoes clacking on the grimy, metal-edged stairs. He caught his breath, fixed his hair, and banged on the door.

She opened the door wearing duck-print pajamas and holding a remote control. Her hair had further grayed in the almost four months since he'd last seen her. "Oh, Lord," she said. "What do *you* want?"

"Maybe an apology? For breaking into my apartment?"

"I didn't 'break into your apartment.' You gave me a key, and now you have it back."

"I did not give you a key. You stole a key."

She raised her eyebrows and shrugged as if to say, "Semantics."

"Listen, Molly, you aren't right in the head, and if I see you anywhere near my building, I'm calling the police."

"I'm the crazy one? You're the stalker who came rushing over here after I returned your dumb key. You're right, I do start to lose it when guys play with my emotions. I told you that very clearly and you still tried to fuck me. But it's over, Rick Hunter. I'm surprised you're still chasing after me."

Her revisionist history was so full of delusion, he didn't know where to begin. "Molly. I am not 'chasing after' you. You can't tell the difference between someone wanting to get close to you and someone wanting to get away from you."

"From my end, it doesn't look like you're trying very hard to get away."

"You knew what you were doing when you sent me that key."

"You know," she continued, as if he hadn't said anything, "I used to be jealous of you and Penelope, for having zillions of dollars and living like royalty, but now I see that you're just as horrible and miserable as everyone else." She slammed the door.

"You're a fucking lunatic!" Rick shouted. He kicked the door, then kicked it again for good measure. She'd probably planned the whole thing: get him riled up enough to knock on her door, then barrage him with all the things she'd been wanting to say since the beginning, before she sent that first Facebook message, things she'd wanted to say to all the shit boyfriends who had screwed her up in the first place. She couldn't stand being told that she was mentally ill and had to throw it back in his face. Well, fine. Just because she had the last word didn't mean she was right.

A small, tired Hispanic woman was pulling a baby stroller up the stairs toward him, jouncing it at each step. A little girl with a bow in her hair sat in the stroller, staring at him with wide, curious eyes.

"Let me help you with that," he said.

Without looking up, the mother continued to muscle the stroller upward, one stair at a time. He hoped she didn't understand English.

◄ ● ►

He kept expecting to pack up the madness with Molly and slot it into his memory, let it mellow into an anecdote he could tell at parties, maybe adjusting the chronology to exculpate himself, but the upset didn't fold up neatly, and weeks later, he was still annoyed without quite knowing why. Part of him wished he had fucked her, not stirred her up and fled the scene with blue balls. He imagined returning to her apartment and getting it over with, but that seemed very rapey—not to mention that Pepper would have grounds for divorce.

While stuck at the office, writing reports that should have been done before the wedding, Rick googled Artie, his summer-camp bunkmate. From the guy's wedding announcements and Facebook wall, Rick saw that he'd had four children from three failed marriages. It felt like a comeuppance for the extravagant bounty of his youth. Since summer camp, Artie's face had flattened, his mischievous little nose now red and fleshy.

He submitted a friend request on Facebook; to his surprise, Artie accepted immediately.

Rick wrote, "Long time no talk!" Smiling emoji.

Artie wrote, "You grew up!"

"How's everything going?"

"It was my daughter's birthday today. So blessed that I got to spend it with her." Angel emoji. "You?"

"I got married this summer. It was awesome."

"Congratulations!" Smiley emoji with hearts in place of eyes. It was strange, but encouraging, to receive that emoji from a man.

"I still think a lot about our summer-camp days—we were so different then!"

"Yeah, totally," Artie responded. "That place was the best."

"U certainly had ur share of the girls."

A ghostly ellipsis informed Rick that Artie was typing, but no message came. He clicked through Artie's photos, mostly selfies taken with one or more of his kids, at a beach, at a bowling alley, at a baseball game. The guy looked at peace, though you couldn't always tell that sort of thing from a photo. Sometimes Rick thought that if he had gotten to have sex with just one of Artie's girls at summer camp, he wouldn't still crave the approval of so many women. That just one teenage roll in the hay would have sealed up the crack inside him through which his sense of attractiveness still leaked out.

Finally Artie finished his response: "I think I had more fun than they did."

"No way; you were a legend!" Then Rick took a deep breath and added, "Hey, I know this is going to sound weird, but I could really use your advice on something. I always felt like I missed out on an important rite of passage by never getting laid as a teenager. I'm happily married, but I still feel as unfuckable as I did way back then. Do you think sex as a teenager helped you feel more secure as an adult? Did I miss a developmental milestone, or am I making that up? Ease my mind here, bro." He read it aloud twice before taking a deep breath and tapping SEND.

Artie wouldn't mind answering that, Rick thought. He'd probably like reminiscing about when he was the alpha dog and pondering how it shaped him. If Artie would just tell him that he hadn't been deprived of any fundamental life step, that it wasn't too late to fix his baked-in sense of unattractiveness, maybe he could let go of his teenage loneliness and avoid the next Molly that came along.

Artie didn't respond. Maybe he didn't get what Rick was talking about; after all, as a former teenage stud, he'd never had to think about this. Rick tried to make it simpler. "Like, was banging Melinda or Brianna different from sex now?" He sent that. Then, to flatter Artie even more, he added, "I would have given my left nut to fuck even one of those girls." He sent a winking emoji, then a devil emoji.

He busied himself with email for a few minutes. Artie didn't reply. He tried to work on a report. Still nothing. And now Artie's Facebook page was gone. Rick refreshed the page, wondering if the internet connection had gone wonky. Then he realized with a stab of humiliation that Artie had blocked him.

PART TWO

7

THE DIAGNOSIS

As the perishables in his grocery bags doubtless began to spoil, Francis trawled the aisles of the CVS in search of a card for Carol's seventy-fifth birthday. The joke cards witlessly poked fun at aging, and the "poetic" cards made him ill. He settled on a jaunty illustration of a dog and a cat embracing, thinking it droll that animals from warring species might fall in love.

He was going to surprise her with the most extravagant gift he'd ever given: three weeks in London and Paris. Carol visited friends in London every few years, but Francis had never come along. He hated living out of a suitcase, getting lost in unknown neighborhoods, and—worst of all—dining in restaurants of questionable sanitation. But for a milestone birthday, he couldn't think of a more generous gift.

Sandwiched between two women shouting into their phones on a crosstown bus whose air-conditioning left much to be desired, he scribbled a birthday greeting. *London + Paris + me + you = your happiest dream come true. Yours forever—Francis.* He smiled at his little rhyme.

His mood plummeted, however, when he set his groceries down in the kitchen, famished from the day, and the only food on the Formica countertop was a scattering of graham-cracker crumbs from Carol's nibbling. It was her night to prepare dinner. Even after fifty-two years of marriage, she still couldn't understand, and refused to indulge, his desolation upon coming home to an empty kitchen. It shouldn't have been a mystery: his father had died of food poisoning from a restaurant when Francis was seven, and his mother was forced to work twelve-hour days, leaving Francis to cook for his younger brother. The ordeal had instilled in him a love of the kitchen (reinforced by the terror of eating outside the home) but also left him wretched when nothing was simmering on the stove.

He tucked the card into his desk drawer and collapsed onto the white wool sofa in the living room, letting his panama hat tumble to the floor. He'd felt hollowed out for the past few weeks, even now that he was sleeping seven hours a night with the Lunesta that Dr. Feigenbaum had prescribed. He hoped he wasn't getting sick. Age was a curse no one deserved.

Fifteen minutes later, Carol wandered in from a walk, her face glistening, her eyes glassy, her chrome-colored hair whipped into a tumbleweed. She hung her threadbare purse over the back of a dining chair and plopped down on the brown corduroy sofa. "God help me," she whispered.

"God isn't here right now," he said, trying to make his upset palatable to her. "May I take a message?"

"Francis, quit it," she said, her lips stiffening.

"It occurred to me just now that dinner on Wednesday is your only responsibility in our marriage."

"Call an ambulance! Francis is hungry!"

"If you called an ambulance, at least I'd know you were thinking of me."

She squinched up her face and shuffled into the kitchen, returning a moment later to toss the pint of Fairway potato salad that he had just purchased, along with a teaspoon, onto the coffee table. The polypropylene container slid onto the floor with a thud as the spoon rattled to a stop. "*Bon appétit*," she muttered, then sank into her couch, closed her eyes, and massaged her temples.

He knew better than to ask for a napkin. Clearly she was upset, but so was he. How was he expected to take care of her when she couldn't take care of him?

A few bites of potato salad perked him up, and he cobbled together a humble dinner, stretching a leftover beef stew with orzo, bliss potatoes, and a three-bean salad. A stack of day-old seedless rye from Zabar's, stale but serviceable, rounded out the meal. Tasty and hearty yet bland enough for his sensitive stomach. He was rather proud of it.

He sat back down on the white sofa and smiled feebly. "Dinner's ready."

She didn't look up from her *New Yorker*. "I'm not hungry."

"I'm sorry I tried to pick a fight."

She sighed, dropping the magazine to her chest. "It's just . . . when you're hungry, nobody else is allowed to be hurting."

"Couldn't you have put out a plate of crackers or something? I just want to know that I'm not alone."

"Francis, look here." She stuck out her tongue and curled it upward.

He peered around in her mouth. Over the years, her breath had become bitter and dull; this odor, distinctive to Carol, soothed him. "What is it? What am I looking at?"

"There's something on the bottom of my tongue. It feels prickly."

He looked again. A brown splotch, like a mole, had taken up residence in the buttress that connected the tongue to the floor of the mouth. He shivered. "What is it? Did you go to the doctor?"

"I just noticed it today. I have an appointment with Dr. Sharpe tomorrow afternoon."

"Can I come with you?"

"You absolutely may not. You'll just make everything worse with your . . . dog-and-pony show."

He put his hand on her shoulder. "Carol, you don't want to see him alone, not for this. Let me be there for you."

She shut her eyes and nodded. "You're right; I don't want to go alone. I just wanted to pretend it's not a big deal."

"Whether it's a big deal or not, we need to know."

"Maybe I don't want to know." She burrowed into his chest, and, holding her tight, he kissed the top of her head.

◄●►

Francis had never met Dr. Sharpe, as Carol wanted separation in their lives: their bank accounts, their friends, and especially their doctors. He was a short, hunched man with white hair, big fleshy ears, and a warm smile, and he wore a plain collared shirt and navy-blue tie underneath his monogrammed lab coat. Francis appreciated that the examining room had glass jars of tongue depressors and cotton balls, and an old physician's scale standing in the corner like an English butler.

Francis put his panama hat on his chair and shook Dr. Sharpe's hand. He had worn a tie and corduroy blazer for the appointment, his uniform throughout his years as a high school English teacher. He tried not to be annoyed at Carol for visiting a Park Avenue doctor's office in a stained WNYC T-shirt and shorts that she had made by taking a pair of scissors to a pair of sweatpants. "Dr. Sharpe, I'm Dr. Levy." He rarely introduced himself using his doctoral honorific, nor did he correct people for calling him Mr. Levy, but he found his Ph.D. to be helpful in certain circumstances. "I can't tell you how glad I am to meet you today. Thank you for being so conscientious with Carol all these years."

Dr. Sharpe nodded. "You're very welcome. It's kind of you to say."

"Thanks for the introduction, professor," Carol said to Francis. "I can take it from here."

The doctor chuckled.

"There's a spot on my tongue." She leaned across the desk and opened her mouth like a bullfrog. Francis cringed. She'd been raised by bourgeois parents in a bourgeois building in Brooklyn Heights, which gave her the privilege of not having to care how people perceived her. After Francis's father died, and after his truncated family moved off the Grand Concourse into a one-bedroom apartment with cracked windows and sloping floors, it was essential to keep up appearances, to hide their poverty from the outside world, because if they could convince others that they were okay, they could almost believe it themselves. And so she couldn't understand his consternation when she lunged at the doctor with her open mouth, or welcomed guests barefoot (or worse, with holes in her stockings), or wore her cleverly altered clothes out to dinner, or left dirty dishes in the sink or her mail on the coffee table, or forgot to wipe down the stove after frying eggs, or chewed with her mouth open, or slurped through a straw, or piled her dirty clothes on the bedroom floor, or crammed her closet with dozens of surplus wire hangers from the dry cleaner. He recognized how rigid he could be, but she knew the rules of etiquette and flouted them as if to upset him deliberately.

While Carol's jaw remained open, Dr. Sharpe retrieved his flashlight pen from a drawer, pulled on latex gloves, and selected a tongue depressor from the jar. He examined her mouth, grazing her cheek with the fourth and fifth fingers from his right hand. Francis could almost feel those paternal fingers on his own cheek, soothing him. The doctor peeled off the gloves and dropped them into an empty trash can, then sat back in his maroon leather chair. "Have you been smoking?"

Carol seemed alarmed by the question. She shook her head.

An understanding jarred Francis. *Have you been smoking?* not *Do you smoke?* or *Have you ever smoked?* No wonder she didn't want Francis at the appointment. He stared at her, astonished. What other secrets was she keeping?

Dr. Sharpe made a steeple with his index fingers. "I don't want to make any assumptions, Dr. and Mrs. Levy, but I don't think you have anything to worry about."

Francis trembled. His father had been told the same thing four hours before his death, and his mother's doctor had used those words thirty years later, squinting at her chest X-ray. Whether doctors were trained to cover up the truth or Francis was just cursed, there was always something to worry about.

"Whatever it is, you'll need to get it biopsied," Dr. Sharpe continued. "I know a fine ENT surgeon at Mount Sinai. He's usually booked a month out, but I'll have Judith call him to see if he can squeeze you in tomorrow or Monday. Any questions?"

It couldn't be nothing to worry about if Dr. Sharpe wanted the biopsy the next day. Panic roiled Francis, but he resisted asking the doomsday questions echoing in his mind. This wasn't his doctor. This wasn't his crisis. But he couldn't help envisioning himself alone in their apartment, roasting a chicken and potatoes and setting the table for one. He didn't know how he'd cope with such forbidding silence.

She picked up her purse and slid her chair back. "No, thanks."

He was astonished by her negligence.

"Dr. Sharpe," Francis whispered, as Carol waited in the hallway, "perhaps you could give me some more insight into what we might be dealing with here?"

"It could be a mouth cancer. But it's most likely a benign growth," the doctor repeated, loud enough for Carol to hear.

Perspiration trickled into Francis's elbow. "Surely you know the statistics on this sort of thing. Surely you've seen hundreds, if not thousands, of growths like this." He loosened his tie. His throat could barely take in enough air. He needed air.

"Francis, I'm leaving," Carol said. "Don't miss the choo-choo train."

The doctor looked at him sleepily. "I would advise you not to worry about it. But based on its size and shape, I'd say there's an eighty, no, seventy percent chance it's benign."

Carol hurried back to the waiting room, leaving Francis behind, clutching his belly with both hands.

◄◆►

"I knew I shouldn't have let you come," Carol said, clomping down Park Avenue, tucking her hair behind her right ear every few steps. The city air was sludgy and stank of Camembert, and the Wasps of Carnegie Hill had swarmed to the Hamptons, but Park Avenue was still frantic with taxis. "He said he didn't want us worrying about it. Now we're worrying."

"My father died because not one person worried about him," Francis said, panting to keep up, saliva thick in his throat. "They sent him home from the hospital and told him to take Pepto-fucking-Bismol."

She stopped and faced him. "Worrying about me is not the same as caring for me."

"Then tell me how I can care for you."

"Right now? By leaving me alone. This is my problem, not yours."

"So you getting sick has nothing to do with me, is that it? It won't affect me at all?"

She rubbed her eyes. "I'm going to the park."

He stopped himself from asking her if she was going to smoke. It wouldn't be right, not then. Of course she was going to smoke. On some level, he'd known she was smoking all along.

She crossed the street and walked toward Fifth Avenue, looking back every few steps in irritation. But he couldn't stop watching her. He wanted to take her in while he could. With his luck, she'd be dead by Yom Kippur.

◄ ● ►

Carol was already asleep when Francis took his pills and climbed into bed. In their years together, he couldn't remember more than a handful of times when she had trouble falling asleep. It seemed to be the benefit of willful ignorance, of her ability to enter that Xanadu where nothing could penetrate her pleasure dome. Some days, she barely lived in the real world at all.

She had been disappearing like this longer than he'd known her. When she was a teenager, her parents never allowed her out after dark and grilled her about her schoolwork, her friends, and the few boys who called. Her caviling mother routinely cleaned her room, discarding photographs of celebrities, record albums, makeup, and gossipy notes from her friends. After the usual screaming match, Carol would slam the front door, ride the subway into Manhattan, and wander Central Park for hours, cadging cigarettes.

When she met Francis, she sheepishly told him about the habit, and, fearing for her health, he begged her to stop. They didn't speak of it again. Even when he occasionally smelled smoke on her, he didn't ask her about it so that she wouldn't have to lie. Now he wished he had confronted her years ago.

The sleeping pill was taking its time. He stared at the ceiling, imagining his mother's portly doctor telling Carol that the cancer had spread and was no longer treatable, imagining shoveling dirt onto her coffin with the back of the shovel, imagining going to sleep in an empty bed. He was six years older than her. They'd always assumed he would die first.

He dragged himself out of bed, brewed a pot of chamomile, and read his favorite Kafka story, "A Country Doctor," in low light on the white sofa, to the buzz of the dimmer switch and the steady exhale of the air conditioner. In the story, a doctor visits the home of a sick boy and fails to notice a deep gash in the boy's side. The horror of the doctor's negligence twisted inside Francis, and the doctor's punishment, being undressed and shoved into the bed up against the boy's festering wound, satisfied Francis like a scream. And yet the intimacy between doctor and patient soothed him, too: he hated and loved doctors, feared them and needed them. They were ghosts of his father, powerfully alluring but always disappointing.

He was asleep within minutes.

◄ ● ►

In the morning, he called Dr. Feigenbaum to tell him about his fatigue and his nerves. He wished the doctor would ask questions, but the conversation lasted less than a minute. He had long come to terms with the impossibility of finding the perfect doctor in New York. Perhaps it was no accident that it had been easier when many of them were still older than him.

Dr. Feigenbaum phoned in a prescription for Valium at the Duane Reade, and Francis reluctantly swallowed one. A votary of classical analysis, he didn't trust drugs that affected the mind, especially when they might compromise his vigilance, but he feared the worry and poor sleep would evolve into something much worse. The Valium made him soupy, and he floundered about the apartment the rest of the day, botching a chicken soup with too much salt and rereading the same paragraph ten times in *The Basic Kafka*. He took a Lunesta that night and by morning felt drained of blood.

◄ ● ►

That afternoon, Francis was expecting Caleb Franklin, the porter, on his day off. Patricia disapproved of Francis inviting Caleb into his home, but he didn't need her permission, so long as no cash exchanged hands. He rather enjoyed disobeying her prohibition.

Francis liked most of the staff, salt-of-the-earth types who had to earn their living—unlike most of the shareholders who lived off inheritances, investments, and undeserved salaries—but he was particularly fond of Caleb, perhaps because the diffident porter was putting himself through college, as Francis himself had done sixty years earlier, or because Caleb's parents had been high school teachers, Francis's own noble profession. Or perhaps he liked him simply because he detected a spark of life in the porter's eye, a deep, inexpressible sensitivity that spread to his entire way of being in the world. He carried his lanky body softly; with him, Francis felt safe.

Caleb's one shortcoming, Francis thought, was that he was guarded: he submitted to Francis's attempts to teach him but did not chase the knowledge. To wit: though this would be Caleb's fourth visit since he was hired in December, he still hadn't read Kafka's *Metamorphosis*, even though his spring semester had ended in mid-May. Letting go of his favorite books for too long made Francis anxious, and he was considering asking for it back. But he was afraid that might push Caleb away, and he couldn't afford that, since Penelope, his other refuge in the building, heiress to a shipbuilding fortune and daughter of one of the most prominent corporate litigators in New York, was still living across town while her apartment was being renovated. Like Caleb, Penelope's eyes also housed a spark, but of an entirely different kind. Where Caleb was sensitive and closed off, Penelope could be insensitive but was possessed of a breathtaking openness, a yearning that most people extinguished when they became fully adult, because it was of no material use, or worse than that, a weakness that could be exploited. Both his neighbor and the porter made Francis feel at home in the barbarous land of Carnegie Hill, and as he rarely saw Penelope these days, he was doubly looking forward to seeing the porter, despite his crippling exhaustion.

To Francis's surprise, Caleb arrived with *The Metamorphosis* in his hands. They discussed the book over coffee and social teas, cookies that Francis had loved since childhood but whose blandness seemed to unnerve his young friend. Caleb said he had enjoyed the book, though he found it unrealistic that a cockroach would have such a soft exoskeleton—soft enough that one of the apples his father throws embeds in his flesh and ultimately kills him. "We've had roaches my whole life," he said, "and those things are hardy!"

Francis explained that "cockroach" was a poor translation of the German, which described Gregor Samsa more generally as a monstrous insect. "Regardless of what he was, I think Kafka knew that insects have hard exoskeletons. Why do you think Gregor's is so soft?"

"Maybe his shell never hardened," Caleb said.

"I agree completely, and I would go one step further. I think he has a deep sensitivity that others don't understand, and they hate it. They hate his sensitivity so much they would rather destroy him than understand it." Francis hoped this would resonate with Caleb.

"Ohhh," Caleb said, studying Francis more intently than felt comfortable. "Now I get it. He's different, and his family hates him for it."

"Exactly."

"So it's about being gay."

Francis had heard that reading before. He supposed that in this era when gay and lesbian rights were at the forefront of the national consciousness, it would be the easiest one to grasp, even if it limited the scope and power of the allegory. "That's a valid way to see it. Tell me more. Where do you see gay subtext?"

Caleb considered this as he flipped through the book, not stopping on any of the pages. "Well, in the last scene, his sister becomes this sexual object who's ready for a man. But Gregor doesn't get to have that. Everyone is disgusted with him."

"Very perceptive."

Caleb furrowed his brow. "I don't know, Mr. Levy. Being gay doesn't make you a cockroach—or bug, or whatever. I think Gregor didn't try hard enough to tell his family who he really was. This is more like fear than reality."

Francis sensed Caleb's frustration, about what, he couldn't tell. He tried to defuse the tension. "I'm not quite grasping. . . . Could you say more?"

Caleb scowled. "People think that if they tell their family who they really are, they'll be seen as some kind of monster, but it's not true. Not in this day and age, at least. It's just fear that keeps people in the closet."

"Something tells me we're not talking about the book anymore," said Francis with a tentative smile. Was Caleb coming out to him? He wouldn't have guessed the porter was gay, but he supposed he had picked up on it anyway, admiring his sensitivity.

Caleb tossed the book into Francis's lap, startling him. "I don't think he's a bug at all. He just thinks he's a bug, and so people treat him like one."

"Do you . . . do you think you're a bug?"

"No, but someone I know thinks he is." He looked into his coffee cup.

They changed the subject, to Francis's relief. He told Caleb about his childhood in the Bronx, hoping that the porter would see that he wasn't like his neighbors. Caleb sat patiently while Francis talked. When he needed to leave, Francis gave him a copy of *Indignation* by Philip Roth—a book that reminded Francis of his own upbringing and the anti-Semitism he'd faced in college. "It's considered a minor Roth novel," he explained, "but I believe it will someday be known as one of his greatest. It's a distillation of his vision, of what it means to be different in America." It was, of course, about Jewish experience, but he hoped that it would speak to black experience as well, or gay experience, if that was what Caleb was trying to tell him. He saw himself in Caleb and hoped that the feeling of alienation would translate across their differences.

◄●►

On Sunday, while Carol was walking in the park, Birdie Hirsch dropped by on her way to the farmers market with her collection of chic nylon reusable bags. She offered to get him something small: a wedge of cheese, a few tomatoes, or a jar of honey. If she hadn't emphasized that it had to be small, he might have taken her up on the offer. But he didn't want to be made to feel burdensome when she was the one offering in the first place.

"How is Carol?" she asked, sipping a cup of coffee he had prepared. "It sounds like she's having quite a scare."

All weekend, he had watched Carol glide from room to room in her haze, departing every ninety minutes for a stroll around the Great Lawn.

"She won't admit how scared she is," Francis replied.

"I'm sure everything will turn out fine."

Her glib reassurance annoyed him. People couldn't let others' unhappiness stand; they had to tie it up with advice or brush all worries away. "It must be nice to be able to see into the future," he said, smiling.

"It has its downsides," she replied with a laugh.

"What does the future hold for George?"

She closed her eyes and rubbed an imaginary crystal ball. "Let's see . . . he will be miserable . . . forever!"

He liked Birdie, but it irked him how flippant she could be about her husband's depression. She took his life-threatening illness as a personal slight. "Would it help if I found him a recommendation for an analyst?"

"He's already seeing a psychiatrist every other week on top of all his other doctors. I don't think he has time for analysis!" She laughed.

"Birdie, this isn't a joke. My cousin took his own life because he didn't get the help he needed."

"I'm sorry, of course you're right," Birdie said. "It's just that I had been so looking forward to all the things we could do once we didn't have to work ten hours a day. And now we do even less than we did before we were retired. If you can get him someone good, by all means." She looked at her watch. "Oh—I have to get going. Lovely to see you!"

He stopped her as she marched toward his front door. "Wait, don't go. I'm hoping you can help me with something. I'm worried—I don't know how to say this—I'm worried that Carol has been smoking. I'm wondering if she's ever mentioned it, or if you've seen her doing it. I don't want to be a policeman—that's the last thing I want—but the thought of it, especially given the current mess, is making me very scared."

She laughed, cruelly, he thought. "Of course she smokes."

"What do you mean, 'Of course she smokes'?"

"You can smell it on her. And your bathroom, the one down the hall there, reeks of cigarette smoke."

After Birdie left, he stepped inside Carol's bathroom and inhaled carefully. He'd always told himself the bitter smell came from the scouring powder he used on the tub. "Carol!" he shouted to no one. How could she smoke, knowing that his mother died of lung cancer? It wasn't fair to tell her how to live, but it wasn't fair of her to live without any regard for him. He took a Valium and lay on the white sofa, flipping channels on the television, only to turn it off a minute later. Nausea trickled up his throat.

He decided to pay George a visit. Friendly conversation was no substitute for good psychotherapy, but it couldn't hurt, either. He scanned his collection of opera CDs and picked out *Tosca*, a crowd pleaser. He rode the elevator up to the twelfth floor and rang Birdie and George's doorbell.

Heavy metal music was playing in Penelope and Rick Hunter's apartment next door—apparently the contractors were still not done with the renovation. Francis missed Penelope. She and her husband had been gone almost eight months now, and when he saw her at the monthly board meetings, she'd seemed more and more anxious. She wanted guidance in her life, and her therapist didn't seem to be helping. He decided to make more of an effort to help her, not just wait until he ran into her at board meetings and in the laundry room.

After Francis rang the bell a second time, George opened the door in his bathrobe and slippers, days of stubble colonizing his cheeks. He looked groggy.

"Francis, my man," he said. "Always a pleasure."

"I hope I didn't wake you. I could come back. . . ."

"No, come in. I shouldn't be sleeping anyway. Some of my new meds make me pretty tired."

"Mine too," Francis said, following him into the kitchen, where they sat at the injection-molded plastic table that Birdie had once admitted cost thirty thousand dollars. "But I never feel rested."

"I think they drug us to keep us old fogies down," George said. "Imagine what we could do if we had any energy at all. Can I get you a glass of something?" He heaved himself up and opened the refrigerator. "We have goat milk, tonic water, and Chardonnay. I could make you a cocktail. I'm sure it's very fashionable in Brooklyn." He laughed. Maybe he wasn't as depressed as Birdie made him out to be.

"I'll just have water, thank you."

"Want a slice of chocolate lavender cake? Birdie made it last night. I know she's angry with me when she bakes after midnight. Last week she made five kinds of macarons. There might be some left over." He rummaged through the refrigerator, inspecting a few plastic containers. "Nope, all gone." He took out a chilled water bottle and set it on the table, then gave Francis a cube-shaped glass.

"Why is she angry with you?"

He sighed and sat back down. "She wants me to go with her to all these museums and shows and restaurants, and it's hard enough for me to get out of bed. Last week she was mad because I wouldn't schlep all the way to Red Hook for a ten P.M. reservation at one of those warehouse restaurants—hence the macarons. She didn't used to be like this. She seems to think it would be a tragedy if she died without trying every restaurant in the tri-state area."

At the mention of Birdie's death, he worried anew about Carol. Francis supposed he should be grateful that she wasn't dragging him around the city, avoiding thoughts of death by sheer velocity. But her defense against the gravity of the situation, to pretend it didn't matter and affected no one, was hardly better, because that left Francis holding all of the worry.

"Maybe there's a middle ground," Francis suggested. "If you gave her one or two outings a week, that might get her off your case."

"Believe me, I've tried. She's insatiable."

"Can she go out with friends?"

"You're it, buddy," George said. "And a few others in the building. We've always spent so much time together, neither of us had much time for friends."

"Nobody tells you how hard it is to be retired," Francis mused. "In the span of one day, you lose the respect of your colleagues, and you have to invent new reasons to get out of bed every morning. I've been retired almost twenty years, but I still remember the shock of it. It took me months to cobble together enough rituals and bits of pleasantness to fill my days."

"I get the sense there's a moral to this story," said George.

"Just that it's not too late to take up a hobby or volunteer. I'm not saying there isn't a place for good psychotherapy—and if you're open to it, I'd like to refer you to someone good—but it's good to stay active, too."

"I'll try," he said, seeming unconvinced. "It's just, you don't know how it felt to be fired the way I was. It was humiliating. Without me, that company would be dead in the water, and it took them all of five minutes to take me out back and shoot me. And then Birdie tosses me out of her bed when I actually have some feelings about the whole fiasco."

"What do you mean? She doesn't let you sleep in the same bed?"

"I'm surprised she hasn't told you, but that's my Birdie. Yep, I sleep in the guest room now. It's not so bad, though—we both get more sleep."

That didn't seem like the way to help George get well. "You're a good man, George."

Francis decided against giving George the *Tosca* recording. George had insisted at Penelope's wedding that he had never wanted to harm himself; still, he didn't want to give him an opera that climaxed with a suicide. "Remember that."

◄●►

Carol still wasn't home when Francis returned to the apartment. He sniffed once more in the guest bathroom and decided that, yes, she had smoked in there. He told himself that it was her right to smoke, and that she probably didn't have cancer. In this way, he managed to calm himself.

But when she wandered in, dazed, eating a brownie from a greasy brown paper bag and a piece calved off onto the floor, the house of calm he had constructed washed away as if made of salt.

"Crumbs, Carol." He walked past her to get her a plate. She smelled a little smoky. Maybe.

"Sorry, just feeding the mice." She picked up the piece, inspected it, and tossed it into her mouth. "Ten-second rule."

"I noticed an odd smell in the guest bathroom. You know my sense of smell isn't what it once was. Would you mind lending me your nose?"

She looked at him through narrowed eyes. "Sure."

In the bathroom, she sniffed and declared that it smelled fine.

"You don't smell anything at all?" he asked.

"Francis, what do you want from me?" she asked, arms akimbo.

"Birdie thought it smelled like smoke."

"Doesn't Birdie have her own bathroom?"

"She came by to ask after you."

"And then to sniff around in the bathroom?"

"Do you smoke?"

She set her jaw.

"It's the one thing I asked when we got married," he said. "The one thing."

"Right, the one and only thing you asked." She threw up her hands, rattling the remainder of the brownie in the bag. "Just like the one thing you ask is for food to be set out when you come home. And the only thing you ask is that I carry my cell phone and check my email every five minutes and call you if I'm going to be home more than thirty seconds late. And the one thing you ask is to come to my doctor's appointments, in case I don't bully the doctor into telling me that I'm going to drop dead. The one thing you ask is that I don't drink more than half a sip of wine with dinner. The one and only thing you ask is that I read your mind every minute of every day and do everything your horrible mother didn't do for you!"

He found the doorjamb with his hand and backed out of the bathroom. He had to proceed carefully when she blew up like this. Of course she would be upset; she was less than twenty-four hours from a biopsy that could foretell her end. He would have to pack away his upset and take care of her. "I want you not to smoke for your sake, not for mine."

"Baloney," she said. "Now close the door. I have to pee. And maybe"—she wiggled her fingers at him—"smoke a cigarette!"

The Valium label said to take one every three to four hours as needed, and not to exceed five in a day. Francis had swallowed one forty-five minutes earlier, but he was sure Dr. Feigenbaum would tell him to take another if the anxiety persisted. He compromised with half a pill and lay on the bed. He was feeling light-headed but still raw. He couldn't bear having a wife who smoked, couldn't bear to bury her the way he buried his mother. Any reasonable person would have taken this cancer scare and resolved to quit. But with her mortality spread before her as clearly as a map, it seemed she was smoking more than ever. He cringed at the thought of her entreating strange men for cigarettes, of those men stepping close in with a lighter, their fingers brushing her cheek.

He got up to take the other half of the Valium. Calm descended like snowfall, and he settled into a light snooze.

◄◆►

He awoke in the dark, alert but unable to move. He found that he wasn't anxious about this. He wondered if he was dying or if he'd already died. He could feel ants crawling over his skin, taking little bites with their venomous mandibles, but this didn't perturb him, either. He could hear Carol snoring next to him, the noise painting silvery curlicues and flowers in the air. It reminded him of the rococo wallpaper in the apartment his family rented while his father was still alive. It was the last time they had lived respectably.

At a point, he decided he should do something about his condition. He tried to call to Carol but only drooled on the sheets. The saliva burned his cheek.

The next thing he knew, a rhombus of sunlight from the window was pressing into the bed. His body ached, but his trance had broken. He pushed himself to standing and tottered into the kitchen, where he was unsurprised to find no coffee on the stove, no toast on the counter, and no Carol in the apartment. He fought through the familiar despair and brewed a double-strength French press pot, sipping it while he left a message for Dr. Feigenbaum, requesting the soonest possible appointment.

"This is not a brain tumor," he told himself, as he propped his head up on one hand and tried to manage the Sunday *Times* crossword puzzle, left over from the previous day, as a test of his faculties. He couldn't break into a single word grid, but then again, even as a lifelong reader and English teacher, he had never been a match for the Sunday crossword.

When Carol came in from her morning constitutional, it took focused effort not to ask if she'd smoked. She needed to be calm for her procedure. "How are you feeling?" he asked.

"Hungry."

"Let's get pizza at the Sinai cafeteria afterward." He was in no mood to deal with the hazards of restaurant food, but the hospital cafeteria was relatively safe, and he liked watching the attendings hold court with their flocks of eager residents.

"We're going to eat at the hospital?" She sounded annoyed.

"Well, I don't mean the mountain! You like it there, too, I thought."

"Are we going somewhere nicer for dinner?"

"It's going to be a very long day, and frankly, I've been feeling far more tired than usual. A very strange thing happened to me last night: I was wide awake, but I couldn't move."

"Then forget it. We can eat at home." She sat down and started filling in the crossword with a pen.

She could be forgiven for not asking him about his locked-in experience; this was a stressful day for her. But a moment later, he caught a whiff of cigarette smoke. "You smoked on the morning of your biopsy?" He tried to say it gently.

She snorted out a sigh. "I'm addicted, okay? Is that what you want me to say? I'm a hopeless junkie. Believe it or not, I've been trying to quit."

It would be kindest not to continue. He held her hand, which had probably pinched a borrowed cigarette not thirty minutes before, and looked into her eyes. For once, she was present with him.

She laughed. "What am I going to do with you, Francis?" She shook his hand wildly and kissed it.

◄●►

Even though the biopsy was scheduled for 9:00 A.M., they were still waiting at ten thirty. Francis's head throbbed, and the stentorian receptionist, broadcasting her phone calls to the ENT waiting room, wasn't helping. He sipped from a miniature bottle of Poland Spring and nibbled on some Lorna Doones he'd packed in a Ziploc bag. He tried to hide his eating from Carol, but she insisted that she didn't care.

She rebuffed his attempts to keep her spirits up. She had every right to be grumpy, but he wished she would realize that another person was in the room, hurt by her coldness. Twice she brought up their planned lunch at the Sinai cafeteria sneeringly.

"Where would you prefer to go?" he hissed, the second time she mentioned it. "Le Bernardin? Café Boulud? We could go to a four-star restaurant in your hospital gown! Maybe Jean-Georges offers a Mount Sinai discount."

She snapped open her *New Yorker.*

"Fine, we won't go out, since you've suddenly decided you're too good for pizza. I'll make scrambled eggs and toast."

She widened her eyes, staring at the pages.

◄●►

Carol was napping in her chair when her name was finally called, almost two and a half hours after the scheduled appointment. Her eyes opened a crack, and she wiped a spot of drool off the corner of her mouth.

"It's go time," he said, smiling sadly.

She nodded and he helped her up. He found he was barely strong enough to stand. "See you on the other side," she said.

A nurse led her through a door to the side of the reception desk. He saluted goodbye. But as she walked away from him, he was gripped by a suffocating, indecipherable panic. White spotlights pierced his vision, and a headache bit into the back of his neck. Then he felt himself toppling, and everything went black.

◄●►

The silver rococo grew behind his eyelids, and he felt his body jerking back and forth, washing his vision with ripples of pearlescent light. Something was lifting him, and he seemed to be flapping like a fish. An ambulance siren wailed. Then a cold light blinked on, and he woke up in a hospital bed, his forearm stinging and his head crackling with pain. He heard beeping, hushed conversations, and footsteps.

Carol's face hovered above him. "Francis," she repeated, snapping her fingers. "Oh, my God, he's awake."

"Where am I?" he asked. His throat felt like sandpaper, and his jaw ached.

"We're in the emergency room. Dr. Feigenbaum's here to check on you. He thinks you overdosed on pills." She raised her eyebrows and grinned. "Looks like I'm not the only addict in the family."

Overdose? It didn't seem possible.

Dr. Feigenbaum's bald, bespectacled face appeared. "Mr. Levy, it's good to have you with us," he said with a big smile. "We were worried there for a minute."

"What does she mean, I overdosed?" Francis asked.

"How often are you taking the Lunesta?"

"Just one per night."

"And the Valium?"

"Not very many. I think I took two yesterday."

The doctor tapped Francis's shin. "I'd guess that the sleeping pills and the Valium were amplifying the effects of your blood-pressure medication. You whipped up quite the cocktail!" He laughed, but Francis didn't find it funny. All his medications had been prescribed. The labels for the Valium and Lunesta said to take as needed.

"What did I do wrong?"

"You did nothing wrong. But I would lay off the sleep aid for a few weeks. It's really not meant to be used on a nightly basis. It doesn't give you a high-quality rest."

Francis stiffened. "You couldn't have mentioned that before? I could have died!"

"It's okay, Mr. Levy. You're going to be okay."

"It is not okay, doctor. It is definitely not okay. You are in charge of your patients' lives, and you guffed it."

"Francis, calm down," Carol said. She shook her head. "Somehow I knew you'd find a way to upstage me today."

"Carol, if you think I fainted on purpose . . ."

"I'm just kidding! Jeez Louise, you were much more pleasant when you were asleep."

◄ ● ►

In New York, you either waited three months to see a specialist, or you were "squeezed in." Francis appreciated the efforts of doctors to squeeze him in, but sometimes all the squeezing left him wrung out. When Dr. Rothschild, his forty-something cardiologist, offered him a squeeze-in after he'd spent the entire day in the hospital, shuttling from the emergency room to the "imaging suite" and back, Francis's instinct was to turn him down.

Here was the problem: after Carol had left for her biopsy—for the second time—Dr. Feigenbaum discovered a slight arrhythmia in his heartbeat, which the emergency-room doctor hadn't noticed. It was probably nothing, really very slight, Feigenbaum insisted, but it may have contributed to the fainting spell, and it was important to have a CT scan done immediately. Francis wanted to scream.

"How are you doing?" Dr. Rothschild asked. "I heard you had a rough day."

"Don't ask," Francis muttered.

"I'm sorry to hear that." Something in Dr. Rothschild's patient stare told Francis that he was about to make things worse. "I wish I had good news for you, but I'm sorry to say there's something to be concerned about. We found a midsize aneurysm in your aorta. Do you know what that is?"

Francis's breath crashed around his skull. He leaned forward, trying to pay attention.

The doctor sketched a diagram on his notepad, starting with a heart, drawn like a valentine, not the organ, then adding what looked like a shepherd's crook sprouting from the top and descending down the page. "This is your aorta," he said, pointing to the shepherd's crook. "It's the artery that leads directly out of the heart, carrying a tremendous quantity of blood to the body."

The phone rang; Dr. Rothschild paid it no attention. Which worried Francis even more. The doctor always glanced at the phone when it rang.

"Sometimes, for reasons we don't fully understand, the walls of the aorta weaken, and they balloon out slightly." The doctor drew parentheses around the middle of the aorta. "This is called an aneurysm. It's like a bubble."

Then he drew a line across the aorta and whiskers coming out of the aneurysm and used words Francis didn't understand: thoracoabdominal, dissection, stent, renal arteries. Something about a trauma, something about dilation. Dr. Rothschild slowed down and repeated himself, waiting until Francis understood, but Francis was distracted by his pounding heart;

surely this couldn't be good for whatever condition he was now afflicted with. He desperately wished Carol were with him. "Do you understand?" the doctor asked.

Francis nodded. He didn't want the doctor to know he hadn't been listening.

"The good news is that you're not in imminent danger. I measured your aneurysm at five centimeters. We start to worry when an aneurysm reaches six centimeters."

Five centimeters sounded awfully close to six. "What happens when it reaches six centimeters?" Francis asked, worrying that the doctor had said "inches" and that Francis's inattention would be exposed.

"Sometimes nothing. Some people walk around with these things for years and don't even know it. But we've found six centimeters to be a tipping point for most people. When it gets bigger than that, it expands rapidly until it ruptures."

The door opened and a nurse leaned in. The doctor shook his head almost imperceptibly, and she disappeared.

"Is there anything I can do?" Francis asked. "To keep it from, you know . . ."

Dr. Rothschild tore off the sheet and handed it to Francis. "I'm happy to help you find a second opinion, but personally, I'd recommend you live your life and forget all about it."

"Why did you tell me all this if you want me to forget about it?" Francis asked, crossing his legs to project less anxiety. It seemed important not to let the doctor think Francis was worried. He wished he could take a Valium. But he didn't want to faint again.

The doctor chuckled at a joke Francis hadn't made. "You don't have to worry about it, but you should make sure your estate is in order."

"I'm sorry, doctor, but I seem to have missed something."

Dr. Rothschild studied him with sadness in his eyes. "This is fatal, Francis."

Somehow that piece had eluded him. It hadn't occurred to him that a ruptured aorta meant death. But of course it did. He imagined his chest bursting open and spraying the contents of his body all over Carol.

"But I mean it when I say you don't have to think about it," Dr. Rothschild added. "Continue to limit your salt intake, keep taking those beta-blockers, try to stay out of stressful situations, don't go running any marathons, and come back in six months for another scan, but otherwise, go and live your life. You might have several years left." He put his hands on his desk, smiled, and breathed in as though about to stand. This signaled the end of the appointment.

Francis had dozens of questions, none of which could be put into words. He folded the diagram carefully in quarters, pinched off the fringes, and tucked it into his breast pocket. He looked around for his panama hat until he realized he was wearing it. When he stood, his head sloshed about like a fishbowl. He sat back down. "I think I might like to sit for a while."

Dr. Rothschild looked at Francis, then at the door, then back at him. He leaned back in his chair. "Take your time. There's no rush." It was a lie, of course, but it was immensely relieving to hear. The phone rang and the doctor didn't pick it up. The phone rang again.

◄●►

Carol was sleeping when Francis got home that evening. He collapsed into bed next to her and fell asleep. When he woke at five in the morning, Carol was up and about, but he was too tired to get out of bed. He awoke again at nine, still crippled with grogginess, to find a bowl of warm oatmeal with sliced apple on his bedside table. He took a few bites, relishing the moist warmth in his throat, and fell back asleep.

He finally struggled out of bed at noon. Carol was sipping a glass of milk and staring at the television on mute.

He sat down next to her and rested his hand on her thigh. "Thank you for taking care of me."

She grunted.

"I don't think I've ever slept so well in my life. I couldn't even tell you what day it is."

"Apparently," Carol said.

"What's that supposed to mean?"

"It's benign," she said. "Dr. Sharpe just called."

It took him a moment to realize she was talking about the spot under her tongue. He embraced her, kissing her temple. "That's wonderful news! Let's celebrate."

She nodded, limp in his arms. "You forgot my birthday."

He sat back, stunned by his memory lapse, trying to recall if he'd thought anything was off about scheduling her biopsy that day. No wonder she hadn't wanted to eat in the Sinai cafeteria. At least he'd bought the card. He padded into their study and found it in his desk drawer.

London + Paris + me + you = your happiest dream come true, it read. He envied the Francis who had written that, a man who would consider flying across the Atlantic, who didn't know that his heart might rupture at any minute, who didn't know how afraid he had to be. *Yours forever*, the card said, but it wasn't true. It was the furthest thing from the truth.

He returned to the living room empty-handed. "I'm so sorry, Carol. I was going to get you something, and I completely forgot. I promise I'll get you a gift this week. Happy birthday. For what it's worth."

She grunted and stared at the television. "It seems it's not going to be my last. Knock on wood." She knocked on her skull.

"You know I love you," he said.

"Of course I know," she said, smiling sadly. "And I love you too. This is going to sound crazy, but a part of me was disappointed that it wasn't cancer. I guess I wanted to be taken care of without feeling like I'd have to pay it back with interest."

"Carol, you don't even want me at your doctor's appointments."

"That's not what I mean. What about you? Did they find anything in that CT scan?"

He studied her. She was still an attractive woman at seventy-five. He wondered if she would have married him if she were starting her life over and knew him as she did now. It saddened him that he couldn't be sure of the answer. "Nothing," he said. "Turns out I'm perfectly healthy." For her birthday, he'd give her the gift of shielding her from his pain. He would find a way to bear it alone.

"All that worry for nothing." She kissed him on the lips.

Carol turned up the volume on the television, and he drifted into the kitchen to fix a snack. He craved a Valium: he liked how it held him. Maybe, he thought, as he poured the pills into the garbage and mashed them around with the coffee grounds, an addict was just someone who needed to be cared for more desperately than himself.

8

PALACE OF BEAUTY

A blankly cheerful nurse appeared at the glass door to the examination rooms. The folded violet paper gown in her hand looked like a cyclamen petal, silken and fragile. "You're here for an antiaging consult?"

"A consult, yes," Birdie said, clinging to the word for dear life. "I'm not sure I'm going to have anything done."

Ardith had warned her about Dr. Rosen. "Every time I set foot in his 'palace of beauty,'" she'd said, freighting every other word with exasperation, "I spend five thousand without blinking!" Maybe Birdie would allow herself one indulgence—a squirt of something to fill out her lips or crow's-feet, perhaps. She wouldn't go further than that. She wouldn't lose her head.

The nurse touched Birdie on the upper arm. "Dr. Rosen is very good, Ms. Hirsch." She ushered her into a cramped, icy examining room and handed her the gown. "Take everything off and put this on, open toward the front."

Birdie found it admirable that medical procedure was followed in a beauty clinic, but she wasn't taking off her clothes. "Oh—I'm just here for my face."

The nurse closed the door behind her with an emphatic click.

Birdie tossed the gown on the examining table and sat on an acrylic chair in the corner. She had gotten a cut and color the day before and applied her stem-cell serum that morning. Now that she thought about it, all this primping probably had more to do with Ardith's other warning about the doctor: "He's a shameless flirt."

◄●►

Dr. Rosen was a soft man in his fifties with a sweet, bland face. The absence of a wedding ring excited her in a small way. George hadn't worn his since gaining twenty pounds over the summer. He refused to resize it and didn't want her meddling, so she measured his finger with a string while he was sleeping and took the ring to a jeweler. Resenting her for fixing it, he wouldn't wear it. Now, whenever she saw his fat, naked hand, she seethed.

"Sorry to keep you waiting, Marie," Dr. Rosen said, descending onto a low stool without breaking his gaze. He positioned an orange plastic clipboard on his knee.

"Oh, it's Birdie. You can call me Birdie." George had given her the nickname when they'd first met. Now, after so many years, George had begun crying out her old name during his daytime nightmares. Each time it bewildered her: it was hard to feel that "Marie" was really her.

"Got it. Birdie. What brings you here today?"

"I'm really just here for a consultation—I'm not sure if I want to have anything done. . . ."

He smiled, warmly or smarmily she couldn't decide. "You look stunning."

She crossed her legs the other way and smoothed her skirt. "Thank you, but I was told you could make me look better."

He studied her. "You have a natural expressiveness, and your skin is radiant. I can make you look younger, but I can't make you more beautiful."

It sounded like flirting. Was he going to erode her defenses with flattery, then spring thousands of dollars' worth of treatments on her? "Maybe I wouldn't mind looking younger," she said. "Everyone in my building gets Botox."

"What building is that?" he asked, marking something on his clipboard.

"The Chelmsford Arms, on Eighty-eighth and Madison?"

He laughed. "Your neighbors have been very good to me."

"Ardith Delano-Roux said you were the best."

He cocked his head. "Do you know you remind me of my first girlfriend?"

"I did know that," she said, feeling her crow's feet articulate themselves as she laughed at her little joke.

"I thought I was going to marry her. She broke up with me the night before our high school graduation."

"I'm sorry to hear that" didn't seem appropriate for such ancient history.

"Anyway," he continued, "I wouldn't recommend Botox for you. Botox is really meant for the forehead. It can make crow's-feet look like gills. But I have a great laser resurfacing treatment for you. It'll tighten up your face much more naturally than a facelift."

"Resurfacing" sounded like something one might do to a driveway. Maybe because he'd complimented her so thoroughly, she was disappointed that he recommended any treatment at all—though of course he'd be insane not to. And yet his reticence with Botox felt like a different kind of rejection.

"Let's not do anything today. Read this, think about it, and if you're interested, make another appointment." He opened a drawer and selected a pamphlet on which a woman named Linda R., fifty-four (actual patient, photo not retouched) said, "Look as young as you feel!"

"I'm booked solid through the first of the year," he continued, "but tell my secretary you're a priority patient." As he gave her the pamphlet, he took her hand.

"When was your last skin-cancer screening?" he asked, gliding the fingers of his other hand down her forearm.

"Oh, I don't have skin cancer," she said, hearing how stupid she sounded. It had been a few years since her last screening. "I mean, no one in my family has ever had it."

"You do have beauty marks that need to be checked. I have time now, if you like."

Considering that she had waited a month for the appointment, it seemed fishy that he suddenly had time for an impromptu inspection of her nude body.

He left her alone in the examining room, the fluorescents buzzing. She undressed, keeping her jewelry on, and slid her arms into the paper gown, then lay on the table and waited. Her toes began to hurt from the cold. Maybe Dr. Rosen was seeing another patient at the same time. Maybe that was how he could fit in a spur-of-the-moment cancer check. Ardith had said he was extremely busy. George had been busy, too, back when he was working. She'd always hated those long hours, but in retrospect, she preferred that to her current plight, laboring over meals that he as often as not gulped down in bed, or cleaning up dishes and take-out containers from the floor of his room while the TV yammered on. Perhaps she could have borne the unhappiness with a martyr's resignation had she seen it coming, had she and George not been perfectly entwined for the first thirty-nine years of their marriage.

The door swung open and closed. Dr. Rosen didn't apologize, didn't say anything, just nudged the gown open and touched her clavicle with his ungloved fingers. Her skin tingled with relief. She hadn't been touched so tenderly in months. He ran a tickly stick through her hair, a few inches as a time, to inspect her scalp. As he moved down her arm, pausing at each mole, she squinted up at him, the light stinging her eyes.

He nudged the gown open farther, exposing a nipple. She closed her eyes and absorbed his masculine gaze and the warmth of his hip, pressing into her arm.

"Susan," he said. "That was her name. I think she ruined me for love."

His fingers touched her lower rib cage, and she imagined him taking a breast into his mouth. She did not allow her pelvis to rock. Then he tugged the gown closed and examined her legs. She shivered as the cold traveled up her limbs and warmth spread inside her lower abdomen. She rolled onto her belly when he told her to; leaving her robe atop her like a blanket, she soaked in the caress of her arms on her bare torso.

He uncovered one section at a time, touching and looking, looking and touching. Doctors never studied her so closely. As his fingers reached her thigh, then her buttock, she became aware of her wedding band. Could he be looking at it, wishing she weren't married? She closed her hand into a fist.

"She became a painter and moved to California," he said. "After my divorce, I found her on Facebook. She married one guy and stuck with him, twenty-five years next May. She invited me to visit, but I don't think I could."

He was taking a long time with one spot at her waist. The cold air settled on her buttocks, and she wondered how far the gown was open. She spread her legs a bit. She saw him select a handheld microscope that resembled a high-end camera lens. He rubbed some oil on the spot and peered at it through the microscope. Was he really still studying her for medical reasons?

"You really look just like her," he said, rubbing in tiny circles.

She wanted to tell him that her wedding ring didn't mean anything anymore, that if he wanted her to be his Susan, she would. A respectable doctor would never make advances on a patient; it was up to the patient to take the first step. He was flirting with her, wasn't he? It was impossible to tell.

"I'm probably going to leave my husband," she said. She'd never spoken those words before, never even thought them. Her bond with George had been a fortress, even without children to hold them together, and now it seemed as flimsy as her paper gown. But now that she'd said it, she realized how much she wanted to be free. It excited her, the idea that she needn't live in his gloomy shadow, that her happy past didn't demand of her an un-happy future.

Dr. Rosen took his hand away. "I'm sorry to hear that," he said after a pause.

She cringed at her stupidity. "No, it's a good thing. I needed to tell some-one. I thought . . ."

He pressed hard into her lower back. "I don't like the look of this mole. I'm going to take a biopsy. It'll sting a bit."

Her breath caught as the novocaine burned small and deep, like punish-ment for her confession. Then she felt another burn, more muted, then a third. Then he was fiddling with the spot.

"What are you doing?" she asked, her voice lost in her throat.

"Scraping off some of the mole to have it tested."

It scared her that he could cut her without causing pain, that a piece of her body, even something possibly malignant, could be taken from her with-out her feeling it. Sadness blanketed her, and she wanted to go home. Not home to George, home to Montreal, where she and George first fell in love.

"I'll call in two days with the results," he said. "You can get dressed now."

When, two days later, he told her over the phone that he had found a precancerous mole, that it was nothing to worry about but would require scooping a teaspoon of flesh out of her lower back, her first thought, before throbs of anxiety and relief collided in her heart, was that she wished this pompous jerk hadn't been the first to know that she was going to leave George.

9

PRIVACY

Pepper discovered the hole at the back of the bottom bookshelf in the living room a few days after resettling in the apartment. The fucking contractors probably drilled it on purpose. She could hear peaceful jabbering, like an NPR broadcast. When she reached her head into the empty shelf and awkwardly positioned her ear over the centimeter-wide hole, the voices became louder. With further maneuvering, she managed to hold her eye up to the hole—and was astounded to see a pair of legs in pajamas. Could she have been imagining it? She switched back to listening and could just make out a conversation.

". . . only going to go up in value . . ."

". . . ready to face a Montreal winter . . ."

". . . don't have the energy for packing . . ."

It was George and Birdie next door. They seemed to be performing a play, albeit one with dreadful acoustics and an obstructed view. Her skin tingled. What were the chances, in a triple-mint building on Madison Avenue, that two apartments might be connected by a peephole?

◀ ● ▶

The wealth-management division of the bank where Rick worked was throwing a "Black Friday" party, inspired by the pseudo-holiday / shopping orgy the day after Thanksgiving, when stores traditionally began to turn a profit for the year. The private bank had beaten its financial projections for the year in mid-October—that very day, in fact, hence the party. But Pepper was far more interested in the dinner party Birdie was hosting for Francis and Carol Levy. Birdie and Francis were closer to each other than to Pepper, and she was looking forward to hearing the comments and casual intimacies she wasn't privy to at the co-op board meetings or when each of them occasionally met her for coffee.

"You might feel better if you came," Rick said, glancing in the mirror as he toweled off from a shower. "I always love how your ass feels in that slinky red dress." He climbed onto the bed and kissed her, nudging her tablet off her lap and resting a hand on her belly. His skin was cool and soft and smelled of his musky body wash, and she felt herself melting into him, but she noticed that, as usual, she preserved a small separation, the space between two puzzle pieces that don't quite fit. Marriage was like an eternal slumber party, thrilling and somehow terrifying that her parents wouldn't come get her in the morning. She'd wake up at night and watch him, sometimes for more than an hour, wondering if they had been right.

She picked up her tablet and returned to her email. She was on the host committee for the fall gala for Beacon of Hope, a nonprofit connecting impoverished women to housing and health care, thanks to Ardith Delano-Roux. It was exactly the kind of opportunity she had hoped for when she joined the co-op board, and she was loving the work. The cochairs took her ideas seriously and gave her autonomy, as long as she hewed to the budget. But while observing her neighbors over the past few days, she'd fallen two hundred messages behind.

"Will you come if I say pretty please?" Rick said, kneeling on the bed like a puppy, nudging her hip with his nose. "They're spending a quarter of a million on this thing."

"As much as I've been looking forward to watching a bunch of middle-aged frat boys getting shit-faced while you flirt with everything in heels, I think I'll pass." She'd meant it to be funny, but it sounded harsh.

"It's just client relations. I'm not interested in anyone but you."

"Was Molly just client relations?" She'd promised herself she'd stop bringing Molly up—he swore up and down he didn't do anything inappropriate with her, and she believed him—yet something in her needed to punish him.

"Molly was insane." He tore the cellophane off a pink dress shirt and plucked out the pins. "You really don't want to come? I'll miss you."

"I'll miss you too," she said, moving a swath of unread emails to a subfolder, assuming they had already been dealt with and hoping she wasn't missing something vital.

He studied her. "I'm worried about you, babe. Have you left the apartment all week?"

In truth, she'd only been outside a few times: for a girls' night out at a restaurant in Bushwick where everything on the menu was cooked in liquid nitrogen, for a standing monthly hair appointment, to visit Francis's apartment to talk about board politics, and to buy a green juice and some raw ginger cookies from one of the four juice bars within walking distance.

"I'm just swamped from this gala. Go have fun."

He started to say something, then said, "I'm here for you, okay?"

Once he left, she knelt down at the bookcase and pulled out the books from the bottom shelf. The delicious odor of roasting meat wafted in. A knot in her neck pinched as she pressed her ear up to the hole.

"What's wrong?" she heard George ask.

"I can't look at you now?" Birdie said.

"You're squinting at me."

"I just didn't realize sweatpants were appropriate dress for a dinner party."

"These are dress sweatpants," he mumbled. "You can wear them for any occasion."

"As long as it doesn't involve other people."

"But my slacks don't fit."

"Please, George, don't you have anything else?"

Pepper imagined that the swish she heard was of George's sweatpants falling to his ankles. She smiled.

"How's this?" he asked.

"If you're not going to wear pants," Birdie said, "at least find a pair of underwear without holes."

"As you wish, madame."

The Hirsches' doorbell rang and she heard quick thudding footsteps. She switched from listening to looking just as a pair of legs sliced through her vision.

"Greetings! *Bienvenue!*" Birdie hollered. "It's marvelous to see you!" She made loud kissing sounds. "We were just talking about how we should do this more often. Allow me to take your coats. Can I fetch you an aperitif? I've opened a Chenin Blanc, and we have a craft lager from Brooklyn. I visited the brewery just last week. No one else there was over thirty years old."

"I'll have the wine," said Carol.

"Just water for me," Francis said. "My pal George! Good to see you."

"And you," came George's somber voice.

"How were your High Holidays?"

"Low."

"George . . ." Birdie began, a knot of pleasantry, exasperation, and warning coiled inside that syllable.

"I'm with you, George," Carol said, dispelling the awkwardness. "To me, it's not a holiday if it doesn't have food."

"Apparently the ancient traditions of our people aren't convenient enough for Carol," Francis joked. "We emailed the forefathers to see if they would make an exception, but it must have gotten lost in their spam folder."

"Fortunately, I asked the fore-mothers," said Carol, "and they said not to trust rules written entirely by men."

It was like bad community theater. Birdie and Francis in particular seemed intent on masking their annoyance with enthusiasm.

After half an hour of cocktails, chair legs scraped the floor: it seemed that the four of them were sitting down to dinner. Pepper imagined a roast turkey with all manner of trimmings, maybe brussels sprouts and a crispy chestnut stuffing, served on white bone china.

She pulled away from the hole to massage the crick in her neck, then leaned back in. It was harder to hear them in the Hirsches' dining room, but she could make out some of the conversation. Francis and Carol had endured a series of medical scares, fainting spells for him and cancer for her. To their great relief, both were just scares. Pepper noted that he hadn't mentioned this at any of the board meetings or in their private conversations. It saddened her that the best friend she'd made remained mostly a stranger. In the Chelmsford Arms, she and Rick had been promised a community of residents, yet most of her neighbors kept to themselves.

At nine thirty, Francis made an excuse about not wanting to keep them awake all night, and the guests left. As soon as the door closed, Pepper heard a loud fart.

"George!" Birdie groaned.

"It's a biological function," George said, "and don't I get credit for holding it in for all of dinner?"

Pepper smiled. Listening to the dinner party had been diverting, but it was the private banter that excited her most. She'd never felt that kind of bawdy intimacy in her childhood home or in her current one. She wasn't sure she wanted it, and she wasn't sure she didn't.

◄●►

A key turned in the lock, and Pepper woke with her head in the bookshelf and her body sprawled on the floor. She didn't have time to shove the books back into the shelf before Rick appeared, cradling a crystal award and a gift bag in one arm while prizing the key out of the lock.

"Rearranging the bookshelves, are we?" he asked, dumping his bounty on the console table and yanking off his tie.

"How was the party?" she asked, pushing herself up to standing. She leaned against the bookshelf until the blood reached her head. Her neck was stiff and painful.

"It was okay. I did the vodka luge with my SVP. And one of the junior analysts barfed into the punch fountain. There's a video going around on Facebook, if you want to see."

"I'm good."

"I missed you the whole time, you know." He whipped off his belt and tossed it onto the sofa, then started unbuttoning his shirt.

"You mean the whole time you were groping women in the bathroom?" It seemed that joking about it would prevent him from cheating on her, if he was really considering it.

"The only one I want to grope is you." He grabbed a fistful of her ass, knelt down, and kissed it. "I want to make a baby with you."

"I do too. I was just kidding." Try as they might, she hadn't yet conceived. But now she was having second thoughts. Once she bridged the space between them, she thought she'd be ready.

She pushed him playfully away and glanced at the bottom bookshelf. Would it be safer to wait until Rick left the room to put the books back or to do it now? She couldn't tell which would seem more suspicious. "I'm sorry I didn't come. I just like you best when we're alone."

"So you don't like me when we're in public?"

She felt a familiar panic, of having told him unironically how she felt and wishing she could take it back. It seemed she could ruin their marriage just by being honest in a sensitive moment. Now she would have to back-pedal until she undid the damage of that stray truth. How long did it take for a relationship to set, the way her neighbors' had? "I like you all the time, but the Rick I fell in love with is the one who's not trying to charm everyone."

He looked wounded. "I thought you loved my charm."

"I do—I love you, period. But I feel closer to you when it's just us."

He stepped out of his pants and boxer briefs in one motion and embraced her, his penis nodding awake. "Is this close enough?"

She sucked through her teeth. She liked his penis more than anyone else's she'd ever seen—it was long and slender and professionally groomed—but it could be a ravenous little snake, a reminder that she wasn't generous enough with her body. "I'm sorry, but I'm exhausted."

"You don't have to make excuses," he said, letting go of her. "If you don't want to have sex with me, just say so. I'm just telling you that I want to. Consider it an open invitation." He pulled his underwear back on.

"Let's do it tomorrow. I'll take a bath before you get home."

"Appointment scheduled!"

She hugged him and kissed along the well-trod pathway from his ear to his shoulder. She ran a knuckle over his left nipple. She liked the smooth skin of his chest, but who was he waxing it for?

He froze except for his eyes. "Do you hear that?"

She glanced at the hole, wondering how he would respond if she showed it to him. Maybe he'd get excited and want to spy with her. Or he might help her figure out what attracted her to their neighbors' lives. Both futures were impossible, of course. He'd be disgusted by her snooping. He'd ask why she was more interested in her neighbors' marriage than her own. He'd spackle it shut and never mention it again.

"Three million and the walls are thin as paper," he muttered. "We should have bought that town house in Yorkville." He picked up his clothes and went to bed.

Pepper replaced the books in the shelf before following him to the bedroom.

◄ ● ►

Dr. Riffler found Pepper's interest in the hole reminiscent of The Locked Door. When she had nightmares as a girl, she would creep into her parents' bedroom and snuggle between them. One night, when she crawled into their bed, her father was absent. Pepper never found out where her father had gone or why, but after that night, her parents locked their bedroom door. Sometimes, when she was having nightmares, she'd sleep on the gray carpeting outside their bedroom. Her parents never scolded her for doing so, never mentioned it at all. In the mornings, they would step over her on their way to the kitchen, and her nanny would fetch her when it was time to get ready for school.

"You probably think I'm crazy for not telling Rick about the hole."

Dr. Riffler sipped a mug of brown liquid. Pepper was fascinated by that beverage, but even after almost four years of therapy, she still didn't know, and was afraid of asking, what it was.

"I don't want him to take away the one exciting part of my life," Pepper said. "He doesn't understand things like that. Deeper needs . . . I don't know what you'd call it. He's really straightforward and practical and . . ."

"And?"

Pepper stared into her lap. She wasn't ready to talk about Rick in the vicious, consuming way she'd complained about her parents. Her marriage was so new, maybe it wasn't strong enough to survive a ransacking. She didn't know how strong a marriage had to be to endure like Birdie and George's. It comforted Pepper that despite their frustrations with each other, they were still together after forty years, that resentments and bickering didn't doom their bond. It gave her permission not to have a perfect marriage. Her parents, on the other hand, had rarely disagreed before their marriage dissolved with no notice and little fanfare.

"I don't know," Pepper said. "I'm not sure I really know him. I'm not sure he's ever shown me who he really is."

"The Locked Door locks from both sides," Dr. Riffler said with the subtlest lift of her eyebrows.

◄ ● ►

Rick came home late that night, leaving a large Williams-Sonoma box, a belated wedding gift, in the foyer. He made himself a pot of coffee and skimmed a stack of mutual-fund performance reports at the kitchen table. He'd drunk coffee almost every day since he was eleven years old, and now he could down three cups at nine at night and be asleep by eleven. Pepper couldn't even glance at a Diet Coke past noon.

She sat down across from him and watched him work. She was shaking with nerves. "I figured out why we can hear our neighbors so easily," she said, barely able to hear her voice over her breath and thumping pulse.

"Why is that?"

"Want to come see?"

In the living room, she pulled the books aside. "In there," she whispered.

He kneeled and looked through the hole. "Do you think they're spying on us?"

The truth was, it hadn't occurred to her that they might be spying on her. It seemed unlikely: in the nearly two weeks of watching them through the hole, she'd never encountered either of them peeking from the other side. "Of course not. I think it was the contractor's idea of a joke. Thanks, Paramus."

"Passaic."

"Whatever." She screwed up her courage and said, "I kind of can't stop looking through it."

He smiled in his sexual way. "A peephole—is that a turn-on for you?"

She should have known he'd make it about sex. They'd had good sex three nights ago, but every time they did, it felt as if she were paying him back for all the times she wasn't in the mood. "Not everyone loves sex as much as you do."

"You don't have to be so literal. I just wanted to know if watching was a turn-on for you."

"I'll tell you what's not a turn-on. Asking me every five seconds if I'll sleep with you."

He crossed his arms. "Maybe if you ever asked me, I wouldn't have to ask you so much."

She could feel herself wanting to destroy her marriage with all the things she'd been too scared to put into words, these strange cruelties banging around inside of her that she didn't know if she believed. She wanted to incinerate the thing they'd built if only to see what could withstand her honesty. "Did you ever think that maybe you don't know who you married? That you never knew? Because I'm still wondering if you're just a con artist who tricked me into thinking you were some magical Prince Charming."

◄●►

When Caleb dropped off another wedding gift the next morning, he asked how she and Mr. Hunter were doing, as he always did. Pepper said they were doing well, and though it wasn't true, she and Rick had stepped back from the precipice they'd reached the previous night. He seemed to have believed Pepper's desperate retraction before she cocooned herself in the comforter and pretended to fall asleep, and in the morning, he made omelets and citrus salad and acted exceptionally agreeable, which made her feel awful.

◄●►

"So your mind is made up?" George said through the hole a few days later. The desperate voices of a black-and-white movie twanged in the background.

"Yes and no," Birdie said. "I need to be alone for a while. It doesn't mean I've given up on you."

"Then what does it mean?"

"It means I can't take care of you anymore. I'm too tired, George."

The room tilted, and Pepper rested her forehead on the floor to even it out. Her stomach tightened, making it hard to breathe. She prayed there was some context in which this exchange didn't mean they were separating. If Birdie and George were breaking up after forty years, how could she and Rick survive?

She could still faintly hear their voices.

"You'll kill me if you go."

"That's why you're going, too," Birdie said.

"What do you . . ."

"You need to start living again. And this apartment—this marriage—is suffocating you."

Pepper crammed her books back into the shelf, slid the chain into the lock on the front door, and lay on the sofa, trying to calm down. She wished she'd never found the hole in the first place. She vowed never to look through it again. But she knew she couldn't trust herself not to.

Finally she put on a pair of designer jeans and a ruffled blouse, pocketed her keys, fixed her hair in the mirror, and left the apartment. She knocked on the Hirsches' door, chewing her lip until she tasted blood.

"Penelope! So lovely to see you." Birdie opened her arms, and they embraced. The movie was off, George was gone, and the sweet waft of baking calmed the air. Had she imagined the whole thing? "What brings you here?"

In fact, Pepper had no idea what she was doing. She certainly wasn't going to convince Birdie to take her husband back. "I was feeling a little lonely," she said, "and I thought maybe we could talk. Is this a bad time?"

"No, please come in. You're welcome anytime."

Pepper had seen the Hirsches' apartment a few times, but Birdie's bold, brilliant taste never failed to astound her: an amorphous lemon-yellow sofa, a white marble coffee table with lusciously photographed cookbooks, and glossy black curio cabinets filled with wooden puppets. Pepper sat on a blob-like ottoman that revealed itself to be inhospitably firm. She glanced along the baseboard behind her, looking for the hole. Maybe it was under the sofa.

"Would you like a cookie?" Birdie asked. "I made cornmeal lime snickerdoodles."

"I would love one. They smell amazing."

"I'll give you a plate of them. That way Rick can taste them—or you can have them all to yourself. I won't tell!" Somehow Birdie could laugh at her own jokes without seeming foolish.

Pepper followed Birdie into the open-plan kitchen and stood by the gaping farmhouse sink, a relic amid futuristic appliances. "How is George doing?" She tried to steady her voice.

"He's getting along," Birdie replied, scooping cookies off a cooling rack and onto a plate on the black limestone countertop. "We were just talking about how we'd like to have you and Rick over for dinner sometime soon. Once you taste my chocolate soufflé, you'll be ruined for other desserts."

"That sounds wonderful," Pepper said, thinking it actually sounded sad. She leaned against the countertop. It was ice cold. "But is everything all right? I have time to talk." She couldn't tolerate hearing that everything was fine when it wasn't, especially from a woman she'd come to know so intimately through the hole. She was desperate for the truth.

She looked up at Pepper and smiled stiffly. "Yes, of course everything is fine. Here you go."

Pepper bit into a warm cornmeal cookie and let it soften on her tongue, exuding a sharp sweetness. "Oh, my fucking God, this is amazing."

"I hope I haven't ruined cookies for you!" She laughed.

"You totally have. And it was worth it."

"Well, come over whenever you like. I can ruin all sorts of things for you. These days, I do nothing but bake."

"Francis told me you were moving to Montreal," she blurted out.

Birdie cocked her head. "I wonder why Francis would tell you that. We're not moving anywhere."

"That's a relief. We like having you as neighbors. But Francis was sure you were moving." She thought if she let go of the countertop, she'd collapse on the floor.

Birdie put down the spatula and crossed her arms. "Penelope, I don't like gossip. I don't know why Francis is spreading rumors about us, but I must insist that it end here."

"I'm sorry, I didn't mean to pry." She dropped her gaze to the plate of cookies, heat crawling up her neck and into her cheeks.

"Tell me, how is Rick's cousin faring? I used to chat with her all the time while you were renovating, but since you've come back, she hasn't dropped by." With a dead-eyed smile, Birdie slid the plate toward Pepper so forcefully that two cookies tumbled off.

Pepper ran down a list of Rick's cousins in her head, but all of them lived in Ohio or Wisconsin, and none had visited.

"Molly, was it?" Birdie continued. "Very nice girl. Strange, but nice. Between you and me, she didn't look much like Rick, but cousins don't always look alike, do they? Can I offer you a glass of milk?"

Pepper's face burned, but she fought to keep her expression calm. Molly, Rick's crazy "client," in her apartment . . . ! What else hadn't Rick told her? "Oh, Molly!" she said, trying not to let her nausea show. "Right, he mentioned that she might be stopping in while we were gone. I didn't realize she'd actually come."

"You should keep better tabs on who's coming and going in your home." Birdie cackled, as if she'd just made a joke.

"Speaking of which, I should get going," Pepper said, standing up. "We're just a few weeks out from the Beacon of Hope gala, and everyone's in a tizzy." She fumbled her way toward the front door.

◄●►

Dizzy with rage, Pepper rummaged through all the pockets of the jackets and pants hanging in Rick's closet. In the inside pocket of a blazer, her fingers curled around condoms. And in his old summer camp trunk, among his baseball cards and video games, she found a box of ten. Ribbed—had Molly asked for those? Had he fucked Molly while Pepper was in East Hampton for her bachelorette party? Had he fucked her after their honeymoon? Was he still fucking her? How could Rick come home after sex with Molly and look her in the eye and tell her he loved her? She'd wanted badly for her parents to be wrong about him, but she'd known from the minute she met him, when his eyes trickled down her body as he offered to get her a martini, that he loved to seduce women. She'd known, and she'd told herself it didn't matter.

◄●►

For dinner, Rick brought home a big tray of sashimi. With sick disinterest, she watched him pop the tray open and arrange the bits of fish, dotted with various piquant sauces, on plates. "Hermione Crabtree signed on with me today. Almost a hundred million in assets. We're not going to know what to do with the commission on *that*. Where do you want our summer home? East Hampton or Montauk? Or maybe a cottage in the Hamptons and a chalet in Aspen?"

"Will you have to fuck her to get it? Or have you already?" Her anger dissolved him in her vision as she threw the snake of condoms on the kitchen table. "Why did I find these in your blazer?"

"What?"

"Did I not say that in English? Why do you need them? Is it Molly? Or this Crabtree woman? Or someone else? Tell me the truth."

He put down the ginger and sucked his fingers, staring vacantly as if inventing a lie. "I'll tell you," he said. "I promise I've never slept with Molly or anyone else since I met you. I carry condoms because I'm afraid I might, and if I do, I want to do it safely."

"You're afraid you might? Like you might trip on a crack in the sidewalk and your dick might land in someone's vagina?"

He took a breath and ran a hand through his hair, and she realized she was terrified that he might tell her something she didn't want to know. No, she was terrified he was going to tell her anything. "Remember that picture of me right before my prom, and how you said I looked like a cancer patient?"

She nodded, unsure how this was relevant.

"Well, I was utterly unfuckable. I was convinced that I would die a virgin. I worked really hard on becoming more attractive to women, and I built some muscle and got a better haircut, and when I moved to New York, women were throwing themselves at me left and right. But I realized that even if I slept with a different woman every night for the rest of my life, I would still always believe deep down that I was unfuckable. Even now, although I love you like crazy and I know you love me, I need a lot of sex to quiet that voice in me that says I'm not attractive. And when you don't want to have sex with me, I feel so ugly that I would do anything to get sex, and that's when I'm afraid I'll lose control."

She saw it with terrible clarity: she had married a sex addict.

A number of mysteries about him now made sense: his ability to convince just about any woman to invest with him, the acting she sensed in the opening moves of making love. But she was too angry to calm down. She didn't want to be responsible for his ability to be faithful. "So you're saying your cheating will be my fault, because I don't want to have sex five times a day."

He shook his head. His hand, which had kept running through his hair, stopped, his fingers now clutching his skull. "That's not what I'm saying at all. This is a problem with me, and I'm trying to fix it. It's really shitty to always feel desperate."

"I'm sorry your life is so hard, not being able to fuck everything in heels. My heart really goes out to you."

"I'm trying to be honest with you," he snapped. "Can you quit it with the sarcasm for one fucking minute?"

She despised his perfect face and his bedroom eyes and his sterile, manicured body. She couldn't understand how she'd promised her life to a horny Ken doll. "You couldn't have been honest about this *before* we got married?"

He sat backward on a chair across the table from her, looking as though he might spring up at any moment. "I want to be open with you, Pepper, but you keep sending these signals that you don't want to know anything about me."

"That's not true. I want to know about you. I feel like I don't know who you really are."

"Why don't you ask? You're not the only one with feelings in this relationship. Whenever I start to tell you something, you either freeze like I'm about to yell at you or you come out with some snarky bullshit that completely shuts me down."

She scanned her memory for moments when she'd shut him down. Maybe she'd done it just now with his sex addiction, or whatever he'd call it, but that didn't count. "Tell me something. I'll try to listen."

"Here's something: I love you. I have never loved anyone but you. But I'm afraid I'm losing you, and I don't know how to stop that from happening."

She was blindsided by sadness, a deep tendril of affection wrapped in miles of regret. Her anger was suddenly gone, and she felt naked without it. She tried to take his hands but only reached his fingertips. "I hear you," she said, "and I'm sorry."

They stared at the table between them, at the uneaten sashimi and the beer he had thoughtfully placed in front of her without her realizing it. She hadn't washed the empty coffee cups from that morning. Boxes of wedding gifts were stacked in the corner of the kitchen, waiting to be welcomed into their lives. Rick was probably sick of her, moping around the apartment.

"Now will you tell me something?" he asked. "Something about how you're feeling?"

She put her hands back in her lap. She didn't want to ruin their marriage, but she could only think of one thing to say, and she didn't know if it was true, but the more she tried to ignore it, the more obstinate it became. "I don't know if I love you."

His eyes widened, then blinked out tears. "Oh," he whispered.

She reached toward him again as if to physically take it back. "I'm sorry. I'm so sorry. I think I love you. I just don't know."

"How could you not know?" He shook his head. "I mean, you either know or you don't, right? I mean, you say it to me all the time. I mean, we got *married*, for Christ's sake."

"Maybe I want it to be true so badly that I've never let myself find out."

She'd said it, and he was still there. She couldn't believe he hadn't yelled or stormed out. But maybe she'd ended it anyway.

"Do you think Dr. Riffler would see us together?" he asked. "Maybe we should try, you know, couples therapy."

The sadness burrowed through her, the regret fanning outward. "Not Dr. Riffler—I need her to myself—but I would love to see someone with you."

He nodded, inhaling a ragged breath. "Do you think I could hold you? Just for a minute?"

She still couldn't feel her anger, but it held its shape in the atmosphere, like trails of smoke after fireworks. She shook her head, and he nodded in pained understanding. She wanted to keep her body separate, at least until she had recovered from his betrayal, and Birdie's. And maybe her parents'. She didn't know if she would ever recover from that.

10

BONDS: GUARANTEED

Pepper was not proud that her first thought upon seeing that Dr. Dixon was black (or was it better to say African American?) was whether they had the right place. Then again, it didn't help that his office was on the twenty-first floor of a residential building, one of those former commercial megaliths off Wall Street that had been chopped up into Tetris-shaped condos after 9/11. It was as though his office had tried existing as a home and then thought better of it. Frankly, the dark, narrow space would have been more functional as a bowling alley.

The office had homey touches: an indigo batik rug, a tall brass lamp, heavy blue curtains. Maybe that was to help couples relax. She tried to let the furniture relax her. But every time she thought about Birdie's impending divorce from George, she felt a convulsion of panic.

Dr. Dixon tossed off questions she and Rick could agree on: whether they had trouble making it past the doorman (no), who referred them (Dr. Riffler), how unfortunate it was that the days were getting so short (we'll survive), and how long they'd been together (two years come December).

Staring into the middle distance, Dr. Dixon performed a brief calculation. "So you got married in December 2011?"

"No," Rick said, laughing nervously, "that's when we met. We got married in June. Four months ago."

Pepper laughed too. There was something funny about that. Funny and shameful.

Dr. Dixon raised his thin eyebrows as if surprised that their marital skiff had run aground so quickly, but said, "Congratulations. Where did you folks get married?" And they talked about the wedding, about all those pine trees and their friends and family flying in from San Francisco and Chicago and Chicago and Melbourne and the photos in *Town & Country Weddings*, though the magazine wasn't out yet. It was sad to think that their marriage might end before the photos were published. Dr. Riffler hardly even blinked in session, but Dr. Dixon was always fidgeting: adjusting his bronze steampunk glasses, touching his finger to his lips before speaking, and crossing and uncrossing his legs.

Rick asked how many sessions Dr. Dixon thought it would take. He must have realized it was a dumb question before he finished.

"Some couples just come for three or four sessions for a tune-up," said Dr. Dixon. "I've seen great things happen really fast. If you're open to it, though, I wouldn't put a cap on it. I have one couple who has come in once a week for ten years, and they are terrifically happy with their marriage."

"We'll do whatever," Rick said. Pepper resented that he answered for her.

Dr. Dixon encouraged them to speak in "I feel" statements and try not to assign blame. Pepper did her best, and no one interrupted her. She glanced out the window as she talked, at an old painted sign, barely legible, on the upper left corner of the tan brick building across the alley. GOVERNMENT BONDS: GUARANTEED RETURNS, it read in a heavy, slab-serif typeface, but the edges were faded, making BONDS: GUARANTEED more prominent. She found the promise vaguely reassuring.

Next came Rick's no-blame accusations. He opened a note on his phone and read from it. It surprised her that he had prepared something. "I have a very strong sex drive, and I am not getting enough sex. When I ask for it, Pepper belittles me. . . ."

"Try addressing her, not me," Dr. Dixon said.

Rick nodded, resolute, and turned to Pepper. "I work very hard, and when I walk in the door at night, I don't think I'm asking too much for you to look up from your book. Instead I feel a chill as soon as I walk in that tells me I'm not welcome. It's like . . . it feels like I'm being punished for cheating when I haven't."

He was right: she had been cold toward him. "You must have done something," Pepper muttered, "or Molly wouldn't have been camping out in our apartment."

"Molly was a crazy client of mine," he explained to Dr. Dixon. "She wanted to see our apartment, and I thought it would be harmless to bring her by. A few months later, we find out through our neighbor that she was going there while we were waiting out our renovation in a rental."

It annoyed her that he would talk to Dr. Dixon to avoid giving her an explanation. He couldn't have been as innocent as he pretended, especially because of the condoms in his blazer pocket. But as angry as she was, and as much as she wanted to blurt that out in their session, she was also afraid that the truth was as bad as she feared (i.e., that she had married a sex addict or a sexual predator), and so she let the question stew inside her. Dr. Riffler had suggested that part of her preferred remaining in the dark. "I find your story hard to believe," she said.

"Can I interrupt?" Dr. Dixon interrupted. "Penelope—or would you prefer Pepper?"

"Penelope is fine."

"I hear that your trust has been shaken. And Rick, I hear that you are frustrated that you are not being taken at your word. In our time together, I'm hoping we can examine this conflict, to figure out what's really going on and to see if we can find ways to bring insight to what's happening."

She knew they had to talk about Molly. But for now she was content to let Dr. Dixon steer the conversation toward other times she hadn't trusted someone or hadn't been trusted, especially as a child or in past relationships. After almost four years of individual therapy with Dr. Riffler, she was practiced at braiding strands of her past into a narrative, and she talked about things Rick already knew: her parents' secretive divorce and that awful lunch when they warned her that Rick was untrustworthy and told her not to marry him. She was a little bored, still complaining about them. Maybe the secret to therapy wasn't to reach some miraculous epiphany but simply to rehash the past until you couldn't stand talking about it anymore.

And then their time was up.

"Marriage lasts a long time," Dr. Dixon said in conclusion, "and questions of trust and fidelity come up again and again in almost every coupling. Rick, given Penelope's history, I can't stress enough how essential it will be to be one hundred percent honest with her. And Penelope, your struggle will be to stay receptive to Rick's honesty. I believe you can learn to trust him."

He probably said that to all the couples who walked through his door.

"I want that very much," Pepper said.

Dr. Dixon gave them homework. Every night before they fell asleep, they would each say three things they appreciated about the other person, and one thing the other person had done that day that disappointed them. Pepper liked the idea of being forced to talk about their relationship every night—she couldn't imagine her parents doing that.

"I've counseled couples for a long time," Dr. Dixon said, "and I can usually tell from the first session when it's too late to save a marriage. But I have a lot of hope for your relationship."

The words were heartening to hear, whether or not they were true. After months of worrying that she shouldn't have married Rick, she wanted hope.

They stood. She had the urge to kiss Rick, to show him how much she wanted to make their marriage work, but she waited until they reached the elevators to give him a peck on the cheek.

"Thanks, babe," he said, avoiding her gaze. It hurt that he didn't kiss her back.

◄ ● ►

"Has it gotten any easier to be honest about disappointment?" Dr. Dixon asked at the start of their fourth session, after they settled into their chairs and reviewed their homework.

"It isn't always easy," Rick replied, "but I think it's good for us."

Pepper had thought the homework would get more complicated as the sessions went on, but each week, the assignment was to keep doing the "three appreciations and a disappointment" every night—which felt remedial. They had done the exercise faithfully, even if both of them always tied on a disclaimer, like "I felt this when we texted today and I'm not feeling it anymore . . ." or "I really don't have anything substantial to say, but . . ." Still, the conversations were helping. For example, she'd always hated texting, tapping out messages letter by letter, and was irritated when Rick volleyed five or six messages in a row: a photo of his lunch, a reminder of when he'd be home, a "thinking of u" and sometimes an emoji without context, maybe a cat with its tongue out or a dropsical smiley face. But after hearing how hurt he felt when she ignored them, she made a special effort to respond. And he sent fewer of them. Also, he stopped pushing to make love every night, which left her the space to ask for it.

At first she waited to talk until their nightly check-in, mainly so that she would have something to say, but after a while, she started telling him in the moment. And through the alchemy of shared honesty, she began to look forward to his homecoming each night.

In the sessions they still evaded the Molly question. Dr. Dixon insisted that they would talk more about Molly, but that it would be more helpful to explore his unmet need for validation. "Sometimes when one person in a relationship wants more sex than the other person does, we read that as a plea for more intimacy," Dr. Dixon said. "Sometimes, it means two people are wired differently, and that's a different conversation." He had a way of speaking that seemed profound but didn't quite land, which annoyed her. Another thing that annoyed her: she got the feeling that their therapist was siding with Rick.

"I think we might be wired differently," Rick said. "Just speaking hypothetically, what's the conversation if that's the case?"

Maybe we need to fix your wiring, Pepper didn't say.

"I can't answer that for you," said Dr. Dixon, "but I will say this: Hollywood leads us to believe that only one kind of marriage can work, and I'm not just talking about monogamy, which is what appears to be on the table right now. Couples are expected to be having regular sex throughout their lives, but this is a relatively new phenomenon in the history of marriage. I've seen happy couples who stopped having sex, and they're doing just fine. Hollywood puts a lot of pressure on couples, and part of what we're doing in this room is creating a unique vision for your marriage together."

Despite all the verbal foliage Dr. Dixon planted around it, Pepper understood this to be a conversation about open marriages. Now she was sure he was taking Rick's side. He had led them here, hadn't he?

Dr. Dixon nodded at Rick. "Why don't you ask Penelope for what you want?"

"Because I don't think it's okay to want what I want," he said, interrupting a study of his fingernails with the occasional glance at Pepper.

"I agree," Pepper said, crossing her arms and tightening the cross of her legs until she felt twisted like a rope.

"A desire is different than a demand," Dr. Dixon said. He peered at Pepper over the top of his glasses. "Penelope, it's important that this be a safe space for you both to work out how to forge a marriage that fulfills both of you. Just because we talk about something in here doesn't mean either of you have to agree to it. It's important to be able to express your desires to each other and be open to the possibility that those desires won't be met. Rick, do you want to say more about what you want?"

"Pepper . . ." Rick stared at the floor as if it were painful to meet her eyes. "I don't want to do this if you don't want to, babe, but I feel really frustrated when you don't want to have sex with me. I don't want an open relationship. What I want is . . ." He looked at her. "I want it to be just us, and I will really try to keep it that way, but I want to know that I could be forgiven if I slip up."

"So you want an open relationship," Pepper said.

"I don't want permission," Rick said, "I want forgiveness."

"You want forgiveness in advance. Which is permission."

"I want forgiveness if it happens, but I don't want it to happen."

She couldn't hide her anger. Had he proposed couple's therapy to legitimize having sex with other women? Back when Pepper was working in magazine publishing, a spacey production manager named Cassidy had been in an open relationship with her husband. They "played together" and "played separately," and if Pepper was interested in exploring *any* of her fantasies, Cassidy wanted to know. Pepper wasn't morally opposed to an open relationship; she just got sick at the thought of being in one.

Dr. Dixon looked at Pepper. "Penelope, I can hear that Rick's request is upsetting to you. Do you want to say more about what you're feeling?"

"I'm feeling betrayed. By you, Dr. Dixon. It's like you're trying to convince me to agree to an open relationship. Like, oh, 'Let's just fuck other people and then all our problems will be solved.' I mean, why did you even bring it up?"

"I'm not trying to convince you to agree to anything, Penelope. I'm merely surfacing what Rick has been trying to talk about since we started our work together, so that you can talk about it together, explicitly. I've noticed you adopt a sarcastic tone that has a way of ending conversations. Our work here is about starting conversations and seeing them through to resolution."

"So I'm the villain here, because I don't want my husband to cheat on me?" She was beginning to cry, and she looked out the window to compose herself. The BONDS: GUARANTEED sign felt like a big fat lie.

"No one here is a villain," said Dr. Dixon.

"Do we have to use the word 'cheat?'" Rick asked. "It's sounds mean."

"Maybe that's because cheating is mean." Pepper pulled at the hem of her skirt to make it cover more of her legs. "Have you ever thought that maybe you don't 'need' as much sex as you think you do? I mean, doesn't your whole sex drive boil down to wanting more women to admire you? No, let me rephrase that: Doesn't your whole life boil down to wanting more women to admire you?" She knew she was being cruel, but it seemed idiotic to talk about an open relationship when he hadn't worked through his issues.

Rick gave her an anguished look.

Dr. Dixon sucked his lips into his mouth. "Rick, tell Penelope how that makes you feel."

"It hurts," he said.

"Penelope, I can sense how much anger you're feeling about Rick's desire for more forgiveness in your relationship," Dr. Dixon said in the gentlest, most infuriating tone. "It's important to be able to express your anger with each other. Can you be specific about which of Rick's behaviors have hurt you and why?"

"I'm sorry, but I can't fucking do this right now," she said. She looked Rick in the eye. "This whole drama played out with Molly—she lived in our apartment!—and you wouldn't have even told me about her if you could have gotten away with it. And the more I think about it, the more I'm sure you fucked her. So I really don't want to broach the subject of an open marriage, or what hurts me or doesn't hurt me, until I know exactly what you did." She felt exhilarated for standing up for herself, for approaching a secret that could undo their marriage and flinging the door wide open.

After an airless silence, Dr. Dixon said, "I hear that this is a crucial piece for you, Penelope. Tell Rick what you need from him."

"Rick," she said, trying to even out her breath, "I need you to tell me what happened with Molly."

Fidgeting with something in his pocket, Rick looked at her. His gaze was painful to bear. "You're right. Molly wasn't a client. She found me on Facebook."

She felt as if the room had become a vacuum, sucking her apart, disintegrating every limb, organ, and droplet of blood. She had known this about Molly and believed herself paranoid for suspecting him.

"I think the fact that I was getting married turned her on," Rick continued. "We flirted for days, just a constant stream of chatting. It seemed harmless, and she worshiped me. And I felt like the wedding was pushing us apart—"

"It's not the wedding's fault," Pepper snapped.

"You're right," he said, nodding, mussing his hair with both hands. "I wanted to have an affair. Not because I didn't love you. It was just some black desire in me that I couldn't shake. When I was a kid, all my friends were having sex, and no girl would touch me. I thought I was disgusting, and I never got over that feeling. I used to feel better by going out to a bar and having sex with a stranger, and when I met you, I thought I didn't need that anymore. But then I did. Or I thought I did. I know this isn't an excuse, but it seemed less bad to me because we weren't married yet. I really want to be faithful to you, Pepper. I really, really do. And I can. I didn't have sex with her, and I don't want to do it with anyone else."

It was bad, though not quite as bad in context. They were both working through their childhood scars. His were more destructive than hers, but she could make sense of them.

"So what did you do?" she managed to ask. "I think I need to know."

"We met for lunch, and we agreed to have sex like it was a business deal," Rick said, and again Pepper felt sick and wished she hadn't asked. "I wanted to get a hotel room, but she insisted on our apartment. I know that should have been a red flag, but I wanted so much to get it over with, I didn't see it."

This isn't about how crazy she was—it's about how crazy you are! She stopped herself from saying it, because she didn't want Dr. Dixon to silence her.

"You called with some wedding emergency," he said, "and it came out that the contractors had left the apartment for the day, and of course I wouldn't have done it in our bed—well, our bedroom wasn't done yet, but you get the point—but I thought we could do it on my grungy old couch that we were going to get rid of anyway, and we kissed, and we took our clothes off. . . ."

Pepper almost retched. She remembered that day: the bridesmaid dresses didn't fit anyone, and she had asked Rick to meet her at the atelier with the list of measurements. The thing was, she remembered him arriving with the wedding binder a few minutes later. She remembered being grateful that her superhero fiancé had dropped everything to come to her rescue. How had he fucked Molly, or whatever they did, without bending time?

"I'll stop," he said, looking fearful as he met her eyes. "We didn't go through with it; that's all you have to know."

She didn't want him telling her what she did not have to know. "Please finish. Tell me everything."

He nodded. "It was taking me a while to get hard."

She looked at Dr. Dixon to keep from imagining Rick shuttling a hand over his dick in front of a naked Molly.

"After a minute she said she wanted me to unlock the door. She had a fantasy about you walking in on us having sex, and then she would get to rescue me from the disgrace by marrying me. When she said that, I knew she was sick, and that I was just as sick, maybe worse. I saw that I was betraying you in the worst way, and I hated myself for it. I kicked her out."

"And that's when she started texting you?"

He nodded.

"So you didn't give her the key to our apartment?" she asked.

"Definitely not. She stole it when she came over, I think. I realized that she was breaking into our apartment when we moved back in, and that's why we changed the locks. I don't see how she could have come over more than a few times—I mean, the contractors never mentioned her, and we were there pretty often, too."

She saw the connection between the missing wedding cake, books, and perfume and Molly's presence in their apartment. She felt retroactively exposed. But maybe Birdie had exaggerated.

"Let me just say I'm profoundly impressed," Dr. Dixon said, shifting forward in his seat. That ended their moment of honesty, and now Dr. Dixon was looking at it in retrospect.

Pepper was relieved at having dismantled an impasse that they had created. She felt sturdier, and it was easier to breathe. She could imagine forgiving Rick at some point in the future. But if she forgave him, that didn't mean what he did was forgivable. Because it was cheating, whether or not they'd been married yet and whether or not he'd slept with Molly.

"What happens if another crazy person contacts you on Facebook and begs you to screw her?" she asked.

"I really think that was a one-time thing," Rick said.

"Maybe Molly put you on a registry. 'Married men who stray.'"

"I've learned my lesson. I mean, I still fantasize about having an affair sometimes, but I know now that it won't fix anything."

"That's not reassuring."

"I know. But if I'm tempted again, maybe if I just tell you, I won't feel the urge to act on it?"

Now she understood why that couple had been seeing Dr. Dixon for ten years. Unfaithful men didn't change overnight.

"I hate to stop you, but it's past time," Dr. Dixon said. "But let me say again that I am extremely proud of both of you. This radical honesty that I witnessed today is powerful. Pepper, you were able to express your need for Rick's honesty, and Rick, you were able to give it to her. How do you feel?"

"Better," Rick said, wiping his face with a monogrammed handkerchief.

"Excellent," said Dr. Dixon. "I look forward to continuing our conversation next week."

She could barely stand. She was worn ragged, because asking him to tell the truth and listening to the answer might have been the hardest thing she'd ever done.

◄●►

As they left the office, she felt as if they were walking away from a house they had burned to the ground. Pepper looked back at Dr. Dixon's door and shuddered. Now that she was outside of it, she didn't see how she could ever go back in.

"That was good, right?" Rick said as the elevator doors closed. "I mean, hard, but good, too, right?"

She nodded. "I'm glad we got through that."

"And we'll do it again," he said with a nervous laugh, as if he sensed what she was thinking. "That was the best three hundred dollars I've ever spent." He fixed his hair, checking his blurry reflection in the steel elevator doors, then pulled on his calfskin gloves.

She knew that the session had been liberating for their relationship, and yet talking about Molly had felt so nauseating, so vile, that the thought of exposing more secrets with Dr. Dixon made her stomach spasm. Rick's confessions about Molly had to be enough. She made an apologetic grimace. "I can't go back."

"But babe, we were just getting to be open with each other. I feel so good! And hopeful!"

As she watched his grin fade, she glimpsed how his face would look when they were older. His eyes would recede, and the edges of his lips would fall into a permanent frown. Someday she would love him enough not to care how he looked. The thought comforted her. "I need some time to digest . . . all of it." She stepped out of the elevator and hurried through the lobby. She didn't want the doorman to hear their conversation. She pushed through the revolving door into the windy November afternoon.

"Pepper, wait up," Rick said, chasing her down the narrow sidewalk. "I don't get it—this was so great. I feel like I'm learning so much about myself—"

"Then maybe it's time to get your own therapist," she called behind her. He had unloaded on her about Molly for much of the past hour; it had to be okay to ask for space. She tightened the belt of her jacket to protect herself from the wind whipping off the East River and gusting down the skyscrapers. The whole Financial District was blustery and stark, and she couldn't imagine why anyone would want to work there, much less live there. Rick worked on Fifty-third Street, in the infamous Lipstick Building where Bernie Madoff's offices used to be, but when they met he had worked on Wall Street, and at that time the neighborhood had seemed quaint and romantic. She missed those days—and the version of herself who had loved him single-mindedly.

"The garage is the other way," he said.

She stopped, took a deep breath, and turned around. Cloaked in a protracted, tentative silence, they went to retrieve the car.

11

TIPPING SEASON

Two weeks before Thanksgiving, a Christmas tree appeared in the lobby of the Chelmsford Arms, trimmed with the usual plastic rubbish. The sconces and chandelier candles were topped with plaid lampshades, potted poinsettias replaced the autumn flower arrangements, and orchestral versions of Christmas songs tinkled on repeat from hidden speakers. In a perfunctory nod to the Jews in the building, a plastic light-up menorah had been placed on a console table by the front elevators, cottony fake snow concealing its electrical cord.

It was that time of year again, Francis realized with a shudder. Tipping season.

Lots of things were tipping these days, apparently. Dr. Rothschild had said the bubble in his chest was approaching a tipping point. (Francis abhorred the term "aneurysm"; it sounded like a parasitic species feeding on his heart.) Five centimeters, or was it six or eight? When would it pop? When would Francis's life be tipping into the grave? It was too frightening to consider, so he put it out of his mind.

That night, a full-color photographic staff listing, comprising five pages and twenty-two names, was slipped under the Levys' front door. Francis read the first one to Carol while she lay on the couch, either emerging from or treading into a nap.

"Sergei Avilov has served as a doorman with the Chelmsford Arms for nine years. When he's not ensuring the safety of our shareholders, he enjoys weightlifting and soccer. Every Christmas, he takes his wife on a horse-and-carriage ride through Central Park."

"Sounds like he's having more fun than we are," Carol said.

"I suppose the tip will defray the cost of the horse-and-carriage ride?" Francis mused. "Or is it for the gym membership?"

Francis was closer to the staff than most of the upper-crust tenants in the building, which was why he knew that Sergei was not married, and that he lied about it to increase his tips. And because he had spent hours talking with Sergei over the years, helping him open up about his childhood in the crumbling USSR, tipping gave their genuine relationship a mercenary tang. Francis still saw himself as a fatherless Jewish boy from the Bronx, scanning the sidewalk for pennies, not a retiree in the godless Upper East Side, doling out thousands in bonuses to the staff. He and Carol couldn't even have afforded to live there had her grandmother not bequeathed them the apartment.

Then there was the problem of how much to tip. He never kept track from year to year and was sure the amounts fluctuated wildly. Was it twenty for the porters, forty for the doormen, and sixty for the managers? Or double that? The staff never seemed offended, but that didn't mean he was free of their judgment.

Carol put on a CD of jazz Christmas standards—which, in light of Francis's hatred of the stuff, seemed aggressive—while he flipped through the spurious employee listing. Caleb would indeed use the tips for tuition at Hunter, but Francis doubted that Ty Joseph, the most distractible of the doormen, was really going to take his mother on a trip to build houses in Mexico.

But the white lies hardly mattered when held up against the bald greed of Nikolas Lykandros, the resident manager, with his greasy hair and thuggish smirk. His $95,000 salary came with a free apartment, easily worth $100,000 in rent, plus the fattest tips of all the staff and a $12,000 bonus from the board. All told, it was three times what Francis had made as a teacher. Rumor had it that Nikolas also collected a kickback from the preferred vendors the building required for renovations. It was a sticking point for Francis that no one could say if the kickbacks existed or how much Nikolas skimmed off the top. Enough for a second home in the Greek Isles, at least.

"What happens if we just tip the ones who helped us this year?" he asked Carol. "Last week I came in buried under groceries, and Ty was too busy chatting up some pretty young thing on the sidewalk to notice me."

"He's always friendly with me."

"My point exactly. You know, the Jews only give gifts in December because the goyim do. I'll bet you that none of the staff knows the first thing about Hanukkah. Maybe we should give everyone jelly donuts and a menorah."

"Give it up!" Carol exclaimed, and they both laughed.

In Francis's favorite Kafka short story, the narrator, lost in an unfamiliar city, asks a policeman for directions. Laughing, the policeman tells him to "Give it up!" Only the bewildering cruelty of Kafka's world could help Francis bear the madness of his own.

◄●►

The chichi haberdashery on Madison Avenue seemed to have sprung up overnight, and although Francis was glad to see a store with classic, well-made suits in the window, it distressed him that he couldn't remember what had occupied that space before. New York's capitalist engine could wipe clean entire histories, and his faltering memory seemed capable of the same. When he was gone, too, erased by the bubble that grew as the days flickered past, how long would he be remembered? Who would notice his absence?

The store wasn't busy, and the young Rubenesque, tightly coiffed saleswoman latched on to him the moment he entered. Her lipstick looked like chocolate syrup.

"I'm looking for a gift for my brother," Francis said. "Something small but tasteful. Maybe cuff links or a wallet?"

Jacob had invited Francis and Carol to a "Thanksbirthukkah" celebration in honor of all three events—Thanksgiving, the first day of Hanukkah and Jacob's seventy-fifth birthday. Apparently this triple coincidence would never again occur, even after the earth crumbled into dust. Francis didn't approve of the flippant merging of a religious holiday with a secular pig-out, but he had been trying to spend more time with his brother, and besides, he and Carol had not been invited anywhere else.

The invitation had included the phrase, "Your presence is present enough"—one of those modern verbal confections that made Francis gag—but he wasn't going to risk showing up empty-handed. It was a shame that every act of generosity in this world had to come with a price tag, but just this once, Francis wanted to be above reproach.

But the simplest wallet in the store cost $450, and the silver cuff links Francis liked were $1,200. He fled one price tag only to find another even more bemusing. He wished he could tell the saleswoman that these prices were absurd. He and Carol, living off teachers' pensions and the remains of her inheritance, were not nearly as wealthy as their neighbors, but because they lived thriftily, they could afford the occasional extravagance. Even so, Francis could not live with himself if he spent $1,200 on two bits of silver.

Finally he found a $170 tie clip on sale for $60. It was an elegant piece of architecture, angles without adornment. Would he have spent $170 on it? He thought so.

"This is a lovely little thing," the saleswoman said. "Paired with a tie, it'd make an ideal gift." The ties started at $280.

"No, thank you. I couldn't presume to guess my brother's taste."

"What's his favorite color?" Apparently this woman could not even hear the word "no."

Francis gave it some thought. When Jacob was six, his favorite color had been green, but that couldn't still be true. He had driven a red sports car for a few years in his fifties, he often wore gold jewelry, and his house was sky blue. None of these seemed likely as candidates. "I couldn't say. . . ."

"If you're brothers, you probably have similar taste. Why don't you pick out your favorite, and then he can always exchange it?" She smiled blandly.

He would have had a better shot at pleasing Jacob by buying the ugliest tie in the store. But he wasn't going to get anywhere explaining that to this woman. In fact, he couldn't manage to say anything, fearing that his every word would be seized upon to increase her take.

"How about this one?" she offered, holding up a navy tie embroidered with tiny white anchors. "You can't go wrong with blue."

"I really wouldn't feel comfortable choosing for him."

"No worries at all." She was ready for this deflection. She strutted over to the register and retrieved a business card, which she deposited in Francis's hand. "We have an online gift site. You can prepay for the tie, and he'll be sent an email that links to a microsite without any pricing information. All he has to do is click on his favorite tie, and it'll be shipped to him within two business days. We have a really great functionality where he can upload a picture of himself and see how the tie looks on him before he buys."

He didn't know how to respond to this techno-gibberish. "Just the tie clip, thank you!"

"Of course," she said, calm as a swamp, and proceeded to bury the clip in yards of tissue paper and an enormous textured box. Then she placed the box in a large glossy bag with ribbon handles and stuffed that with tissue paper, too.

Despite its tomb of frippery, it would be a lovely gift, he thought, once he'd escaped that ridiculous shop, carrying the bag by the bottom so as not to disturb the tissue paper. It was simple and refined. Everything Jacob owned was flashy: the six-bedroom house in Short Hills, the membership at a country club that had excluded Jews until the seventies, and the Mercedes sedan with vibrating heated seats and a British robot in the center console who could make dinner reservations. Francis wanted to show him, in this subtle way, that simplicity was the key to sophistication, that simplicity was the Jewish way.

◄ ● ►

Francis arrived early to the November co-op board meeting to watch Patricia Cooper safeguard her home from her guests. Mrs. Cooper, who had practically inherited the presidency in the 1990s from her late husband, unfolded protective leather pads onto her heirloom dining table, as she, or more commonly Letitia, had before every meeting for as long as Francis had served on the board. He helped her put down the usual tablecloth, then gave her the wax paper bag of scones he'd procured at half price from the nearby carriage-trade bakery an hour before closing.

Everyone else trickled in, bearing snacks, and sat down. Helen of Troy circled on Patricia's lap before plopping down and falling asleep. While Penelope poured the wine and the others passed around the snacks, Patricia distributed nomination forms for new board members. "Francis's and Birdie's seats are up for reelection," she said through her Long Island lockjaw, "and if you know anyone who would like to run, simply fill out the form and leave it at the front desk for Douglas to pick up. As usual, nominations will be announced at the next meeting."

The bylaws of the Chelmsford Arms were as confusing as they were undemocratic. Board elections were held by buildingwide ballot at the end of December, separate from the annual meeting open to all the shareholders in May—which meant that tenants who were away for the holidays had to submit a proxy vote, which few bothered to do. That, combined with the fact that most residents didn't care who was on the board, meant it only took about fifteen votes to win a seat; if Patricia's candidate wasn't winning, she would phone a few vacationing friends and convince them to mail in their votes.

Also, to prevent the mentally unstable from running for a board position— and that was a real concern—an "impartial" nominating committee had to approve the applicants before they were added to the ballot. It wasn't impartial, of course, because the board president selected the nominating committee and then phoned said committee with a list of her approved nominees.

And of late, Patricia had always chosen Dougie McAllahan as chair and Chess Kimball as vice-chair. Unbelievably, both were board members—they were already treasurer and secretary, respectively—and every third year, when their terms expired, they were called upon to nominate themselves. Not once had they disobeyed Patricia. Francis wasn't power-hungry, nor did he want to shoulder the workload of the board president, but he had long dreamed of unseating Patricia, to bring fairness into building oversight. His first act as president would be to end the closed-door meetings that Patricia was so fond of, to let air into the arcane workings of the board. Officers were decided every January, and if he were to run, he could only count on the votes of Penelope and Birdie. Ardith agreed with Francis on most issues, but she had been friends with Patricia for more than fifty years and would not betray her, no matter how autocratic her actions. So, despite promising Penelope that he would run for president, he never did, not wanting to give Patricia another reason to dislike him.

"Francis," Patricia said, "do you wish to run again?"

"I do."

"Very well. And Birdie?"

"I'm going to step down," she said with a demure nod.

"Oh, shame!" Ardith said, holding her hands to her heart. "That simply will not do."

Francis couldn't believe it. Birdie had shown no sign of wanting to quit the board. If she were replaced by another of Patricia's cronies, he'd have no chance of knocking Patricia off her throne.

"I'm very sorry to hear that," Patricia said. "Very well, then. Douglas and Chess, please take all this into consideration. Next month, we will announce the nominations. Any questions? Wonderful. Now let's approve the holiday bonuses for the management."

She distributed a one-page memo that laid out the bonuses. Assistant managers would be given $5,000. The chief engineer would get $10,000. And Nikolas, the resident manager, would be showered with $20,000. Francis had nothing against bonuses, but it seemed immoral to give so much to Nikolas, who didn't need it, when most of the staff received nothing but tips.

"This represents a significant increase over last year," Patricia explained, "but it came to my attention that we hadn't improved upon these bonuses since 1993, and we had fallen out of line with other triple-mint buildings in Carnegie Hill. Does anyone have any objections, or shall we proceed?"

"Looks fine to me," Dougie said. These bonuses must have been peanuts to him. He developed luxury eyesores in Midtown, then sold them floor by floor to foreign investors, who sold them to other investors and so on until they tripled in price. If all the empty condos in Manhattan were suddenly put on the market, prices would plummet and—God forbid—decent people could actually afford to buy a home.

Penelope smiled, nudging the paper away.

Francis raised his hand. "This is not an objection—if this is what professionals in their line of work earn, then far be it from me to risk them finding more remunerative employment elsewhere. But in the name of transparency, I think it only fair to report these figures to all the shareholders in the building before they decide how much to tip."

Patricia glared at him over the transom of her progressive glasses, calling to mind his mother in her later years, after a lifetime of scrubbing the houses of gentiles had turned every remnant of softness bony and brittle. "They are already laid out in the annual budget. And it would be no surprise to any of our shareholders that we pay Mr. Lykandros—who, by the way, is one of the most esteemed building managers in New York—a holiday bonus commensurate with his position."

The Pomeranian growled in its sleep.

"I would guess," he said, "that our shareholders do not realize that he receives a holiday bonus from the board, much less twenty thousand dollars."

"Our job as the board of directors," Patricia said, even more condescendingly, "is to handle the details that our shareholders do not frankly care about."

"Patricia's right, Francis," Birdie said. "You're making a big deal out of nothing."

"At least let's vote on it," Francis pleaded. "Penelope?"

Penelope grimaced. "What if we gave everyone on the staff a bonus? Not a huge amount, but it does seem unfair to favor the managers."

"You seem to think this building is made of money," Patricia said.

"This building *is* made of money," Ardith said with a dry laugh.

"I'm just advocating for transparency," said Francis.

Patricia shot Francis a look of such unfiltered disgust that he wondered if she had a deeper reason for not making a fuss over the bonuses. "I assume the rest of you are in favor of the proposed bonuses? Then I will collect the memos, and we can move on."

When Patricia wasn't looking, Francis slipped his copy into his pocket.

"While we're on the topic of holiday bonuses," Francis said, "why don't we talk about the possibility of setting a recommended tip? We're all in the dark this time of year, and for all we know, we could be stiffing the people who serve us so faithfully."

Silence took root, which surprised Francis not at all. When he'd asked Birdie how much she gave, she pretended not to have heard.

"I think the staff profits handsomely by keeping us in the dark," Ardith said. "I'm certain I give way too much."

"How much do you give?" Francis asked. "Then we could figure out if it's too much."

"A lady never tells." She giggled.

"I'm sure a recommended tip would only increase the amount the staff gets," Francis said.

"My dear Francis," Patricia said, "you are trying my patience."

"At least put it to a vote!" he cried.

"Very well." She sighed. "Since you seem intent on wasting all our time. Raise your hands if you would like us to offer tipping recommendations—though I don't know how we could possibly settle on such figures!"

Francis and Penelope raised their hands. He suspected that she cared not at all about the subject, but he appreciated that she voted with him anyway.

"Birdie?" he asked.

"It's not my place to vote, I think," she said, swirling her glass of the juice she had brought to mix the kale pulp with the clear liquid, "since I'm leaving the board." She apologized to Francis with her eyes.

Her reasoning made no sense—there was no such thing as a lame-duck board member—but maybe she knew something he didn't.

"There we have it," Patricia said, repressing a smile. "Now Francis, let's not hear another peep out of you!"

He detected a knowing flicker in her eyes, and it hit him as decisively as a grenade: he was not going to be nominated for another term. He couldn't believe he hadn't seen it coming. He was a gadfly to the board, fighting for morality amid cruelty and greed, and Patricia had finally had enough.

He said little for the rest of the meeting. When it ended and Patricia began shooing everyone out, he still couldn't move. The co-op would be overrun by plutocrats, and he was powerless to stop it.

◄ ● ►

Jacob's Thanksbirthukkah party was as awful as Francis had feared. The turkey dinner was smothered in a bitter brown sauce, and the soggy latkes were topped with strange compotes in neon hues. Despite the prohibition against gifts, a table in the back was piled high with boxes from Bergdorf Goodman and Neiman Marcus. Francis decided to give his modest gift to his brother in person. But when Jacob placed his hands on the back of Francis's and Carol's chairs and asked, "How are you enjoying your meal?" as impersonally as a waiter, Francis decided to mail it in the morning.

"It's quite nice, thanks," Francis replied.

"Scrumptious," Carol said with her mouth full.

"You've barely touched your turkey," Jacob said to Francis. "It's really good, I promise. Bobbi and I eat here all the time."

His non-Jewish wife, hearing her name, raised her eyebrows from the other end of the table.

Francis smiled. "It's very good quality. But you know I have a delicate stomach."

"Jesus, Frankie, if you've made it this far, a little mole sauce isn't going to kill you."

The truth was, Francis didn't know what could kill him. Whereas he knew what foods his stomach could and could not handle, he had been given no such guidance for his heart, except to avoid salt and too much exertion. For all he knew, this turkey coated with brown sludge might be his last meal.

"I'd prefer not to take chances," was all he said.

"Suit yourself." Jacob banged the back of Francis's chair and nodded proprietarily toward the next pair of guests. That was all the time he had for his brother.

"Wait, Jacob," Francis said, pushing his chair back and presenting him with the gift bag. "I brought a gift for you."

"You didn't have to," Jacob said.

"It's a big day!" Francis replied, playing along. "I wanted to get you something."

Jacob sifted through the tissue paper, opened the box, and rotated the tie clip in his fingers. In his meaty hand, the sleek little clip seemed paltry.

"It's a tie clip," Francis said. "Quite tasteful, I thought."

"Right, of course. It's great. Thank you." He put it back in the box and embraced Francis. "I love you, Frankie."

Francis gasped for breath in the bear hug. He felt the knowledge welling up in him: despite their differences, despite the fact that Francis had opted for a career in education while Jacob had made a fortune in vinyl siding, despite the fact that they hadn't talked about anything in decades except travel plans and the weather, this was his brother, his flesh and blood. This was the only person in the world who understood where he came from. This knowledge—this love—didn't have to be expressed; it lived in their breath and in the deepening lines of their faces.

"I love you too," Francis said.

◄ ◆ ►

While Carol took in the holiday displays along Fifth Avenue, window-shopped at the bazaar in Bryant Park, and admired the tree at Rockefeller Center, Francis stayed home, waiting for the holidays to pack up and leave. Even that word, "holidays," was just a cover for Christmas. There was nothing Jewish about this annual glut of materialism, when New York City was overthrown by shopping and parties. The humanity and morality of Judaism was drowned out by mandatory tips and twenty-thousand-dollar bonuses, not to mention rigged board elections designed to silence opposition.

Carol insisted that he sit down with Patricia and talk about his nomination. But she didn't understand that the board president was not honorable and could not be reasoned with. In his decades of service, he had ensured fairness among the tenants and fought for the rights of the staff, while safeguarding the building's grand traditions from the flashy and new. Now, without the chance to defend himself, Francis was being dismissed simply because he annoyed Empress Pat. His lack of proof made it worse.

He stopped by the Hirsches' apartment. Birdie was close with Ardith, who would certainly know something about Patricia's motives. Those two fed on gossip.

"I'm running out in a minute for a hair appointment," Birdie said upon opening the door.

"Your hair looks very good," he told her, honestly. Her boy's haircut was dyed black, and she was militant about keeping her roots from showing.

"Well, I'm not going to wait until it looks bad!" Cackling, she tapped Francis playfully on the shoulder.

The door to George's bedroom was closed. "How's George?"

"He sleeps half the day and then complains that he's bored all night," Birdie said. When she attempted an eye roll, her whole head traced a circle in the air. "But if I have the gall to wake him for lunch, I'm a harpy who doesn't respect his need for sleep."

Francis thought of his mother, who had no patience for her sons' emotional needs. The death of their father went wholly undiscussed at home. When Francis felt sad, she barked at him to stop feeling sorry for himself. "He's going through a lot, isn't he," he said.

Birdie smiled. "I really do have to get going."

"I'll just take a minute of your time, then," he said. "I've received some disturbing news, and I'm wondering if you were dealt the same judgment."

"I'm not sure what judgment you're referring to, but I haven't been dealt much of anything." She beckoned him inside, and they stood in the foyer. "What's wrong?"

"It's about the board. You don't know what I'm talking about?"

"Is this about your tipping crusade? Honestly, you need to let it go. It's unseemly to be squabbling about a few hundred dollars this way and that."

Francis took a moment to compose himself. "I've found out that, for no reason she will admit, Patricia will not be nominating me for another term." It was an assumption, not a lie, and besides, he wasn't going to learn anything unless he offered some bait.

"How dreadful! She didn't say why?"

It wasn't dreadful; it was malicious. But he didn't want to correct her. "I can only assume it's because she wants to get rid of me. Because I stand up to her. She can't tolerate that, I know. After I found out, I began wondering about your reasons for stepping down. Are you really doing it of your own volition, or were you forced out, too?"

"Me? No, it's my choice." She opened the closet and sifted through the coats.

"May I ask why? You know I wanted to run for president this year."

"You say that every year. I can't wait any longer, Francis. Someday I'll learn to stop waiting for men to fulfill their promises." He didn't like being lumped in with George as source of her frustration.

"Do you feel that your voice isn't being heard? If we're not vigilant, Patricia is going to cover the walls in McDonald's advertisements."

"Francis, it's all a bunch of sound and fury over nothing. Name one thing you've accomplished since you've started on the board."

There were so many things, he didn't know where to begin. "I've saved Thomas's job, for one." Years back, Patricia had tried to fire the staff's most senior doorman when he yelled at an intoxicated tenant, and Francis had intervened.

"Have you ever done anything that wasn't just blocking Patricia's terrible idea?"

He thought about this. It was true: most of what he'd done was to prevent moneyed interests from influencing the co-op. "I got the employees a third uniform."

"Thirty years on the co-op board for one extra uniform? You've proven my point. Nothing real gets accomplished—it's just a dysfunctional family acting out their frustrations on one another. I won't be a part of it anymore." Before he could rebut her argument, she looked at her wrist where she usually wore a watch. "I really must be going. I'm late as it is."

"So you've heard nothing about my dismissal."

"Not a whisper." She opened the door for him and undid their conversation with a broad smile. "Thanks for stopping by!"

◄●►

Since he was already on Penelope's landing, Francis rang her doorbell. She'd never invited him over, but she had come to his and Carol's apartment for tea here and there. To his relief, she welcomed him in.

He admired her industrial espresso machine and accepted her offer to make him a latte—extra-light, of course. She ground some coffee, packed the filter basket, and latched it into the machine. While the twin threads of coppery espresso streamed into the mug, she foamed a tiny steel pitcher of milk. He couldn't help smiling. It was like watching a ballet.

"I appreciated your support the other day," he said, as they sat in the kitchen with their mugs. The silken beverage was delicious.

"Sure, anytime. I mean, I have a weird block about the money stuff. But until I get past that and, you know, figure things out for myself, my rule of thumb is basically to vote against anything Patricia wants."

"My rule of thumb exactly," he said, though he didn't understand what "things" she was referring to. "We really have to get rid of her, don't we?" He felt a buzz of delight and feared he was imbibing too much caffeine for his flawed heart. But it was the best latte he'd had in years.

"Are you going to run against her in January?"

"I will if I'm still on the board. But I have a hunch that Patricia isn't going to nominate me for another term."

"Is it her decision?"

"Unfortunately, it is." He explained how the corrupt process worked, which seemed to surprise her. He rarely met a young person so attentive, so eager to learn. Most people, young or old, didn't care to listen, as though it were important not to let anyone else's point of view seep in. Even young Caleb, who loyally visited for coffee each month, remained suspicious of his kindness. Penelope was ravenous for opinions.

"I guess I'm wondering . . . you've been on the board for, what, thirty, forty years?" she asked, getting up to rinse out her cup. "Why would she want to kick you out now?"

"We have reached a kind of gridlock. Everything I want, her cronies block, and everything she wants, you and I and Birdie manage to block. Now that Birdie is stepping down, all she needs to do is get rid of me, and then she can deliver the building to the plutocrats."

"Then why hasn't she gotten rid of me?"

"Because you're useful to her. She needs young people"—he thought better than to say "of good breeding"—"to make the building seem relevant. And although you wisely oppose her legislative efforts, you haven't given her the trouble that I have."

"I'd like to be that person, to help make good changes around here, make the building more diverse, and better for families with children, you know? I mean, we still reject basically all people of color, and there's no playroom or stroller parking or anything. But I never know if what I believe is really thought through. Every time I open my mouth, Patricia tears me a new one."

"You've memorized the bylaws, I hope?"

"I've tried," she said unconvincingly. "I'll try again."

"Good. Patricia breaks the rules constantly. If you see when it's happening, you'll have a much better shot at outfoxing her. But most of all, trust your instincts. You have good ones—I knew it the second you drank from her bar cart."

She blushed. "You don't have to keep bringing that up."

◄●►

The one person who would surely know Patricia's scheme was Dougie, head of the nominating committee. Francis couldn't risk such a delicate question to a phone call—he could get tongue-tied on the phone—so with great deliberation, he composed an email:

> Dear Dougie,
> I still fondly remember your generosity when you helped Carol's sister find an apartment last year. I know we don't see eye to eye on every issue as relates to the board, but I hope you'll agree that a variety of opinions are needed to keep our "S.S. *Chelmsford Arms*" sailing mightily forth year after year.
> Now for a bit of "unpleasantness" (Patricia's word): It has come to my attention that Patricia was considering rescinding my nomination for another term. It appalls me that she can do this, but she herself (re)wrote the rules. The role of commander in chief suits her well, don't you think?

Ay, here's the rub: Another volunteer opportunity has come up, and
I need to know sooner rather than later if I will be continuing on with
the board. Would you please let me know at your earliest convenience
if you will be nominating me?

Sincerely yours,

Dr. Francis Levy

He liked the sly, chummy tone and the way he subtly invited Dougie
to ally with him against Patricia. Also, he hadn't lied. He really believed
Patricia was going to rescind his nomination, and he did have another
volunteer opportunity, at a Harlem soup kitchen, albeit one that had been
offered to him years earlier and that he hadn't had time to take on.

For about an hour after he sent the email, Francis felt confident that
Dougie would be swayed by the email and disclose Patricia's plot—though
he did worry that he shouldn't have included the first sentence, that a year
ago to a businessman like him was ancient history, and besides, his admiration of the man, exaggerated or not, was neither here nor there. He waited,
refreshing his inbox, puzzled, then frustrated, that Dougie didn't reply right
away. He had gone back and forth on whether to use an exclamation point
at the end of the first paragraph, ultimately deciding not to diminish the
seriousness of the message for a smidgen more levity, but in retrospect he
worried that he should have done it, because the finished email suffered
from a dearth of urgency and friendliness, which an exclamation point might
have remedied.

When he realized he had gotten no new messages for over an hour, he
called Verizon to check that his internet was working, and the "customer
service representative" on the other end insinuated that he was an idiot.

As dusk fell, he began to regret sending the email in the first place. If by
chance Patricia wasn't planning on kicking him off the board, Dougie
might think she was sending the message through Francis!

Then he realized he'd made a terrible mistake of a different order. Of
course Dougie wouldn't tell him the truth—he resided securely in Patricia's
pocket. Dougie would snitch on him in a second. He was no more honorable
than Patricia.

He got up to start on dinner—anything to stop imagining Dougie showing Patricia his email and laughing. *This moron thinks I'm his friend! He's
been a nuisance ever since he started. The way he goes on about bonuses and tipping, you'd think we were living in a tenement! What is he doing in Carnegie Hill?
Ship him back to Eastern Europe.*

At dinner, while Carol was off in her own world, her jaw making slow circles as the food went down untasted, Francis left his iPhone on the table with the email program open, refreshing the new messages every time the screen dimmed. Maybe all his conjectures were wrong, and Dougie would confirm that he was receiving the nomination, and that would be that. But nothing came except an impersonal email from Jacob thanking all thirty guests for coming to his party.

"Are you expecting a message from the queen of England?" Carol asked.

Francis handed her the phone. "I'm sorry, I'm being rude. Don't let me look at this until after dinner," he said. She put it in her pocket, then resumed the mindless attrition of her meal.

All his suspicions and fears seemed more real in the middle of the night. He tossed and turned, imagining what devious agreements Patricia might push through after kicking him off the board. Around four in the morning, he woke up worrying that the email had gone into Dougie's spam folder. He typed, but did not send, a second email, asking if Dougie had gotten the first one. His heart was in no shape to weather this anxiety, he knew. He needed to calm down but didn't know how. He wished he hadn't thrown away the Valium Dr. Feigenbaum had prescribed that summer.

Come sunrise, Francis drafted a third email telling Dougie to ignore the original. But if he had indeed received the original, he must have chosen not to reply. After all, what kind of man wouldn't respond promptly to such a sensitive request? Francis saved the email to his drafts folder and reached for *The Basic Kafka*, trying to distract himself with a short story.

He settled on the central Kafka parable, "Before the Law." In it, a man waits at the door to the Law, begging for admittance. But the doorkeeper continues to refuse him. The man waits his entire life without receiving permission. With his dying breath, he asks the doorkeeper why no one else has ever approached the door to the Law. The doorkeeper responds that the doorway was never intended for anyone but him, then shuts it.

Francis thought he might send a xeroxed copy of the story to Patricia as a Hanukkah gift.

A few minutes later, when he opened his sent-items folder to reread the original email, he saw that he had sent the third email after all. He bent forward as the knowledge burned through his stomach and pummeled his vulnerable heart. He had to get away from his computer, but first he frantically tapped out yet another email, explaining that he would in truth love to hear back from Dougie about his nomination. After tinkering with it nearly an hour, he deleted it and shut down the computer.

A possible truth dawned on him: Dougie, along with Patricia and surely Chess, maybe the rest of the board, too, were in league to get rid of him. Maybe it was Dougie's idea, not Patricia's. Like Josef K. in *The Trial*, Francis had been accused without probable cause and would be convicted without due process or a fair trial. Perhaps that explained why Birdie was stepping down: she refused to take part in the vendetta against him. The more he retraced the lines of the conspiracy, the more real it seemed.

He sat back in bed and waited for Carol to wake up. When she stirred at quarter past nine, he embraced her and wailed.

"What is it?" Carol asked.

He described the look Patricia gave him at the meeting and Birdie's silence on the matter, then showed her his unanswered emails to Dougie.

"Jeez Louise, you need to take it easy with the Kafka," she said.

"What do you mean?"

"The guy was a professional victim. He's perceptive about how awful the world is, but he completely ignores his protagonists' role in their undoing. Whether or not the co-op board really is ganging up on you, I guarantee you're making things worse."

"I don't see how you can blame me for this."

"What on earth is going on with you? You've been on some sort of crusade for months. It's like you're looking for people to get mad at."

"Carol, you don't understand how these people work," he said. "They're completely unscrupulous. There is no low too low for them. They're only on the board to ensure that their apartments go up in value, no matter whom they destroy in the process."

She made a megaphone with her hands and shouted, "Give it up!"

"Oh, for God's sake," he said, getting up to retrieve his coat.

◄●►

Sometimes Francis needed to escape Carnegie Hill. These people had taken everything material, every aspect of life that didn't matter in the slightest, and found a way to worship it.

He tightened his overcoat and pulled down his plain knit cap and trudged north to the edge of Spanish Harlem, where the pristine canvas awnings of Carnegie Hill gave way to simpler painted signs and light-up plastic lettering. Francis sometimes considered buying a studio apartment on Lexington Avenue in the low hundreds, a refuge where he could live modestly and without pretension, where he could luxuriate in the memory of singlehood, but he knew Carol would take it the wrong way, and besides, he was not blind to the irony of spending fifteen hundred a month on the fantasy of being poor.

He wandered into a small grocery store on 100th Street. Despite the narrow aisles, the dirty and mismatched linoleum, the harsh yellow light, and the warring odors of cleaning fluid and sour meat, Francis was fond of the place. He liked the sacks of rice and gallons of corn oil, bulk provisions meant for families with limited income. He flipped through the circular, crammed with deep discounts on foods that he loved and that gourmets like Birdie would never stoop to buy: Friendship cottage cheese, Nabisco Wheat Thins, Birds Eye frozen vegetables.

As he moved into the aisle, his eyes fell upon the canned vegetables, lined up in tall columns like soldiers in green camouflage. Next came the red army of tomato products. Contadina tomato paste was just fifty-nine cents a can, a good deal, and good quality. But their cupboard was already filled with cans of Contadina tomato paste, Green Giant corn, Le Sueur peas, and Goya beans. Their cupboard was as full as his mother's had been empty, and there was no way to justify the difference. His mother had made poor wages, and he had made a decent salary, and people like Dougie McAllahan raked in unconscionable sums. He hated the Chelmsford Arms—its existence jeered at the value of a dollar—but Carol had wanted to live near the park and it would have been selfish to prevent her from accepting the apartment from her grandmother.

Del Monte canned peaches were on sale, ten for ten dollars. He picked up a can and cradled it in his hands. His mother had bought him a can of those peaches on his eighth birthday, the year after his father died. It was all she could afford as a birthday gift, and he had been terribly grateful, savoring those sweet orange hemispheres in his mouth before biting into the tender flesh. At two years old, Jacob didn't like the peaches but greedily drank the syrup. Young Francis devoured every peach in the can and ran his finger along the bottom to lick up every drop of juice. He went to bed with a stomachache but had never felt so content. He hadn't wanted any more of the world than canned peaches and his mother's love.

He pressed the can of peaches to his lips. He wanted to kiss it. His mother was gone and so were all his uncles and aunts, Irv the peddler and Preston the shop clerk and Sheldon and Ruth who ran their parents' dressmaking store and Sadie and Vivian who became schoolteachers, and all his grandparents and great uncles and aunts. Jacob was alive but had saved nothing from the past, and Francis hardly recognized himself. Everything wonderful and horrible about their childhood had been erased by money, and when he died, his family history would die with him.

He was crying now, and he had gotten the label wet with his tears, and for a disoriented moment he was struck with guilt, worrying that he couldn't afford to buy it.

"Excuse me," someone said. It was a middle-aged Hispanic woman in yoga pants and a puffy down jacket, with two doe-eyed sons trailing her. The older child was playing a video game as he walked, and the younger one was eating M&M's one at a time from a small package of them. There was no way to let them by, as the aisle was plugged up by two other shoppers.

"There's nowhere for me to go," Francis said.

"Are you lost, honey?" the woman asked, pulling out her pink earbuds. She took his free hand with both of hers. "I'm a nurse."

He wanted to fall into her arms, let her run her fingers through his hair, but he remembered that he looked like an old man, and he needed to show her that he wasn't senile. "No, no, I was just reminiscing. I used to love these peaches. My mother got them for me on special occasions."

Smiling, she took a step back. Her boys were staring at him. "Del Monte peaches? I haven't thought about those in years. I loved them when I was a kid, too. I can't eat them now—my doctor would kill me. But they were *good*."

"They're on sale, a dollar each," Francis said. "It's a very good price. Get 'em while they're hot!" He laughed. Could she tell that he was not the type of person to say something like that?

She picked one off the shelf, glanced at the nutrition facts, and put the can into her basket. "Talk about memory lane. I bet my grandkids will like them."

"Those are your grandchildren? You look so young!"

"Aren't you sweet? Truth is, I'll be fifty-five in June. I was feeling sorry for myself, but you just made my day."

The aisle was now clear, and he said goodbye to the nurse and bought the can of peaches with the damp label.

◄ ❖ ►

A few days later, Francis was sitting on the settee in the lobby, listening to Sergei complain about his parents in Brighton Beach, when Thomas walked in from the package room. "I've got a juicy tidbit for you," Thomas whispered, and Sergei slipped outside as if to stand guard. "You didn't hear it from me, but Ranesh said Nikolas wrote a check out to Mrs. Cooper for fifteen grand."

Francis nearly gasped. "How did Ranesh find out?"

"He saw it in Nikolas's desk drawer."

"What was Ranesh doing in his . . ."

"I didn't hear anything." Thomas grinned. He handed Francis a folded piece of paper. "And I didn't give this to you." It was a color printout of a photograph of the check in question.

Francis thought he might faint from giddiness. Whether it was a bribe or a kickback, he had what he needed to take down the esteemed President Cooper.

"You'd think with all that money coming in, she could afford to tip the staff," Thomas grumbled.

"She doesn't tip?"

Thomas waved at a shareholder on the sidewalk, waiting for her toy poodle to finish urinating. "You didn't hear it from me. But since Mr. Cooper died, she hasn't given any of us a cent."

◄●►

"We might as well get right to it, as we have two seats to fill," Patricia said in lieu of a welcome at the December board meeting. Birdie had not shown up. "I will now cede the floor to Dougie to share with you the nominations."

Dougie swigged the Cabernet Franc Penelope had brought. Francis didn't want to upset his already knotted stomach with wine. "Our first nomination is Marilyn Devine," Dougie said.

Francis wondered why he wouldn't mention Francis's nomination first, since he was the incumbent. He sensed it wasn't an accident but willed himself to reserve his judgment. He ate a piece of his scone and arranged a constellation of crumbs on Patricia's tablecloth in quiet resistance.

Dougie reached into his pants to adjust himself, then wiped his hand on his shirt. "I'm sure everyone here knows of her work, if they don't know her personally."

"Who is that?" Penelope asked.

"You don't know Marilyn Devine?" Ardith asked, astonished. "The Divine Miss Devine? Have you not seen *The Man from Huxley Hollow*? Or *Wounded Love*? Oh, my child, where is your education?"

"Are they on Netflix?"

"With any luck, the reels were destroyed," Chess said. "She should never have had an acting career. Whenever she's on TCM, I can't take my eyes off her because I'm afraid she's going to forget a line."

"She was a goddess of the silver screen," Ardith said.

Patricia cleared her throat.

"We therefore endorse Ms. Devine with our nomination," Dougie said. "Our next nomination is Mr. Eugene Pozzo, a celebrated figure in the city's literary community." He lifted a typed piece of paper to his face and squinted at it. "Mr. Pozzo is the editor of *Argument*, a magazine that has been described as *Vanity Fair* crossed with *The New Yorker*. He is also the author of a very important book, according to *The New York Times*: *The Science of Fitting In*."

"Fitting in is a lost art," Patricia said, bringing her hand to her mouth as if surprised at her impertinence.

"We therefore endorse Mr. Pozzo with our nomination," Dougie said. "And that concludes our nominations."

After fearing its approach for a month of days and nights, the understanding that Francis hadn't been imagining things, that Patricia really was kicking him off the board, brought momentary relief. But where terror left a vacuum, anger flooded in—at the other board members, none of whom seemed surprised, and at Patricia, who had orchestrated his downfall. She looked at him over the rim of her glasses and delivered a squinty smile.

He could hardly remain upright. "And where is my nomination? You must recall that I intended to run again."

Patricia glanced at Dougie. "Is Francis among the nominations?"

Dougie shook his head.

"I'm sorry, Francis," she said, "but you were not chosen."

"On what grounds?" Francis asked.

"I don't know. The deliberations of the nominating committee are confidential."

"Oh, come on," Penelope said. "This makes no sense. He said he wanted to run."

"I don't make the rules, dear," Patricia said with fatigued pedantry.

Francis felt shaky and feverish as he rose from his seat. "Ms. Korngold," he spat, employing her maiden name, "I have loyally served on this board for nearly four decades, and I volunteered on committees for many years before that. The least you can tell me is why you want me off the board."

"Francis, I don't know what you're talking about. I'm sorry you weren't nominated. All I can say is the committee reviewed all the applicants thoroughly, and they must have had good reason to leave you out. Now please let us get on with the rest of the meeting."

"Do you think I'm stupid? Am I supposed to believe it was a coincidence that neither Birdie nor I will be reelected for another term?"

Ardith smirked. "Birdie's leaving the building. She's getting a divorce."

Francis tried to stifle his surprise. How could she not have told him about her divorce? There was only one explanation: she was leaving George because he was depressed. Shame on her. It was unconscionable to discard him when he most needed care.

"What?" Ardith asked, looking around the table. "I assumed everyone already knew."

"I would never have predicted that one," said Chess. "Not in a million years."

"I knew," Penelope said. Francis couldn't believe Birdie had told Penelope and not him. When had he been anything but kind to her?

"Are we finished with our little gossip party?" Patricia asked.

Francis felt himself losing control of the moment. He clenched his fists and stared Patricia down. "Have you or have you not accepted fifteen thousand dollars from Nikolas to keep quiet about kickbacks from the preferred vendors?"

Her expression darkened. "You've lost your mind."

"That's not what Nikolas said," Francis sang. "And that's not what the police investigation will find, I'm afraid."

"This is vastly entertaining," Ardith said, in between prim bites of a toffee hazelnut cookie.

A vein bulged in Patricia's forehead. "We do not and have never allowed kickbacks in this building. What you're saying is preposterous. And those who live in glass houses should think carefully before throwing stones, Francis. I know you've been 'entertaining' that porter in your home since he joined the staff. If that's not an inappropriate relationship, then I don't know what is."

"There is nothing inappropriate about my treating a staff member with kindness. You've been president so long, you can't see that you're utterly corrupt."

"'Corrupt' is a strong word, Francis," Chess said, holding out a cautionary hand.

"You can't tell me you or Dougie have any say in the nomination process. It's all her, all transacted in hideous secrecy. Do any of us really have a say? Has her will ever been challenged? I for one have smelled something fishy with our preferred vendors for years, and this proves I was right." Francis walked around the table, showing each board member the printout that Thomas had given him, saving Patricia for last. Penelope glanced at the paper and averted her gaze. Chess didn't even look.

Helen of Troy hopped down from Patricia's lap and nipped at Francis's feet, barking. It was all Francis could do not to kick the fox-faced monster.

Patricia took off her glasses and rubbed her eyes. She seemed more tired than upset. "Francis, since you're such a champion of transparency, I'll tell you what that check was for. I'm subletting my apartment this summer to Nikolas's mother. She is paying for it, but for tax reasons, the money has to go through him."

"No matter how you spin it, you have entered into a business arrangement with someone you have the power to terminate, less than a month after practically doubling his Christmas bonus," Francis said, still standing. "And on top of that, the board never approved this sublet. A profound violation of our bylaws. This is very bad, Ms. Korngold."

"Cooper," Patricia corrected.

He turned to face the other board members. His heart was thudding out of control. This was exactly the type of stress Dr. Rothschild warned him about. Was this where he would die? Would his blood stain Patricia's Duncan Phyfe table? Would it splash into Ardith's Parmesan artichoke dip? Would he remain conscious long enough to watch it happen? "I motion to impeach our 'beloved' president and to demand her resignation."

"You should know better than to rent him your apartment," Chess said.

The dog did not stop barking, and Patricia did nothing to calm it. "Could someone shut that thing up?" Francis demanded.

"Just one minute, before you destroy our building's future," said Patricia, walking around the table to retrieve her frantic pet. "I see now that it was wrong to open my home to the mother of an employee. I do regret that. But let me be clear about what my resignation would bring about. Running this building is a demanding, thankless task. You all show up and vote, but it is I who gather, who file, who make sure this building continues to operate at the highest quality for the benefit of our shareholders. This would be nearly a full-time position for a high-level administrator, yet I do it for free. Are any of you prepared to take on this mantle? And if not, who will?"

"I will. Gladly," Francis said, raising his hand. "I vote to impeach. All in favor?"

He glanced around the table. The other board members, except Patricia and Ardith, stared at their agendas like scolded children. Penelope sipped her wine.

"You mustn't take yourself so seriously, Francis," Ardith said. "It's bad for the wrinkles."

"Penelope?" Francis asked. "You haven't been absorbed into this corrupt system. Wouldn't you like to see honest management of our building?"

"I would," Penelope whispered, sounding afraid. "But you really need to calm down."

He couldn't bring himself to continue right away. If Penelope thought he was crazy and Carol thought he was crazy, maybe he had to listen to them. But he could hardly back down now. "And the rest of you, by your silence, am I right to assume that you approve of a president who accepts bribes?" he asked. "You approve of a regime of corruption and decay? One in which one person makes all the decisions single-handedly, clearing the way for her personal wealth and power?"

Dougie rolled his eyes. Chess cracked his knuckles. Ardith closed her eyes and breathed audibly.

He thought of "The Emperor," a short Kafka piece about a man who doubted that the emperor was descended from the gods, and he made as much of a stir as a droplet flung from the sea. Francis's efforts to unseat Patricia had merely splashed onto an arid beach. But maybe Carol was right; maybe Kafka's perspective was skewed. Maybe there was a better way to defeat the emperor than roiling the tide.

"For heaven's sake, Francis," Patricia said, "you're blowing things all out of proportion. If you're really so desperate to be on this board, we can nominate you too."

Give it up! he could hear Carol saying, as clear as if she were in the room.

"Thank you." He straightened the lapels of his blazer and sat down. "I appreciate that."

◄●►

After the meeting, Dougie squeezed into the elevator with him. "Christ, Francis, you really put on a show."

Francis smiled, watching the floor numbers decrease. He admitted to himself that he might have confused the nominating committee with all those emails, and that Patricia might not have been conspiring against him. Or maybe she had—and was making nice to shut him up about the illegal sublet. Either way, if he was reelected to the board, he would run against her in January. Maybe the sublet would push a few votes in his direction.

"I'm surprised you didn't know about Pat's sublet," Dougie said. "She's been doing it for years. You can't follow every rule in this city. It'll drive you nuts."

"It seems pretty illegal to me," Francis said.

"You've got to cut her some slack. She's broke, you know. Her husband gambled away their savings before he died. Now she's burned through a reverse mortgage, and she's got a shitload of credit-card debt."

"She has a *maid*, Dougie."

"Letitia? She was just working during board meetings, you know, to keep up appearances. But Patricia can't even afford that anymore—I assume Letitia's going to move out any day now. I don't know how Patricia pays her maintenance; I think her kids must pay it because it's cheaper than a nursing home. I buy her dog food. And Ardith buys her Depends."

Francis was flabbergasted. No wonder Patricia never offered anyone a glass of Scotch. She probably hadn't bought a new bottle in decades. "That's very generous of you."

"Poor old lady tried to kill herself last year," Dougie went on, shaking his head. "Too bad she's built like a truck. Stomach of iron. Threw up the pills and woke up the next morning."

"If I had known . . . ," Francis began, but he didn't know what he would have done. He didn't trust himself to say anything further.

The elevator doors opened at the lobby, and they stood next to a cluster of poinsettias. Francis didn't consider them to be a suitable flower arrangement, as they were leaves, not flowers, and poisonous ones at that. But you had to pick your battles.

"I'm glad you're sticking with the board," Dougie said, heading toward the front elevators. "Just do me a favor. Don't ever send me another one of those crazy fucking emails. Patricia thinks you need to go to the funny farm." He let out a throaty laugh, slapped Francis on the shoulder, and sauntered away.

◄◆►

Jacob called a few days later, during the first big snowfall of the year.

"Frankie," he said, "I'm sorry it took me so long to thank you personally for coming to my party."

"It's quite all right," Francis said, taking the cordless phone into the bedroom. He needed to concentrate when talking to his brother. It seemed things could easily go wrong. "Thank you for having us. We had a lovely time."

"You don't have to bullshit me. I know you hate parties, and I know you hate restaurants. That's why I'm grateful you came."

"I'm not *bullshitting* you." He said the word with difficulty. Peering through the window, he stared at the parked cars with tall white hats and a cluster of children scooping up loose snowballs with their bare fingers and flinging them gleefully.

"I also wanted to thank you for the tie clip," Jacob said. "I mean, I haven't worn a tie since I retired, but my brother shouldn't be expected to know that."

He'd seen Jacob in a tie so many times, it seemed impossible that he hadn't worn one in—how long had he been retired for—ten years? But memory was a tricky devil. "I'm sorry, I didn't realize. . . ."

"Just one thing about that. Do you have the receipt? I wanted to exchange it for something that was more, you know, my style."

As a sale item, it wasn't returnable. Francis scrambled for a way out. "I'm sorry, I don't think I still have it. But listen, why don't we go shopping together to buy something you want?"

"Ah, forget it."

"Jacob, I'd like to get you a gift that suits you."

"It's fine, Frankie. You bought the thing on clearance and you don't want me to know. I get it."

"It was the nicest thing they had," Francis said evenly. "I wanted to find you something simple and beautiful. People don't appreciate simplicity anymore."

"Be honest with me. Did you buy the thing on clearance? Did you go in and look for the cheapest goddamn thing in the store?"

He should have known that Jacob would want to know how much Francis had paid for his gift. Someday he would resign himself to the fact that gifts in this modern, godless world were only cash in a more palatable form. He imagined sending Jacob a hundred thousand pennies, since his brother cared so much about money.

"I assumed that the invitation made it clear you didn't have to get me anything," Jacob said. "We put that in there specifically for you, after you pulled that stunt at my grandson's bar mitzvah. But since you did go to the trouble of getting me something, and since you know that your Depression mentality drives me bonkers, at least you could have gotten me something that wasn't on clearance."

"I thought it was tasteful," Francis repeated, trying to remember what he was thinking when he bought the tie clip in the first place, whether the sale price had been an attraction or a deterrent. Somehow he'd known that he wouldn't be able to keep the price a secret. He was ashamed that he'd wanted to. The whole world was polluted with secrecy and lies, and everyone played along. Only his friend Franz Kafka could see through it.

"Why can't you accept that we have different tastes, Frankie? Why are you always insinuating that there's something wrong with me?"

In the nights after their father had died, Jacob wouldn't stop crying, even after their meager dinners, and their mother often locked herself in her room with her pain. Francis would tiptoe into the kitchen and take from the next day's meals to feed his brother. When their mother caught him, she beat Francis with a stick until he bled. Francis never told Jacob about that beating or why there was a dark stain on their bedsheet or why, until her death, their mother often referred to Francis as "my little thief." This was the gift he'd given to his brother, for his seventy-fifth birthday and every one before that: the gift of bearing their impossible history by himself.

An idea occurred to him. Maybe he still could give Jacob something that he'd like. Penelope's wondrous espresso machine must have cost thousands, but how much money did Francis need?

"Jacob, I'm sorry. You're right. The truth is, I didn't know what you would like. But I did . . . I do want to give you something. Keep an eye out for a package in the next few days."

After a pause, Jacob said, "Thanks."

Francis hung up, feeling magnanimous. Maybe the holiday spirit had gotten to him. He opened his desk drawer and picked up the stack of envelopes filled with tips for the staff. Every year, to Carol's great annoyance, he delayed until Christmas Eve to hand them out. This year, he was relieved that he hadn't distributed them yet. He'd stuff them full. He'd be whispered about in the offices and basement corridors as the most generous fool in Carnegie Hill.

When he opened the top envelope, to Sergei Avilov, to remind himself how much he'd tipped, the amount was double what he remembered. Maybe he hadn't been so stingy after all. He opened the next envelope and the next, his repeated surprise turning to suspicion. He knew he'd given a twenty-dollar bill to each of the porters, but there were two twenties in those envelopes. Carol must have added to all of them.

Give it up! he could hear her saying, as he tucked the envelopes back in the drawer, feeling spared by her foresight. "Give it up!" he said to himself, grateful to be married to someone so levelheaded and humane.

12

BEING KNOWN

For the past year, Caleb's whole relationship had played out in Sergei's one-bedroom apartment on the eighth floor of the bland high-rise in Sheepshead Bay, whose view of the ocean was blocked by the backs of the rust-colored apartment complexes of Brighton Beach, buildings that Caleb now despised. To be Sergei's boyfriend meant hewing to his restrictions, which amounted to one annihilating rule: they could only love each other inside the two rooms of this apartment, when the lights were off or the venetian blinds flipped shut; outside, they had to pretend to be strangers. No touching and precious little smiling or talking. On nights when Caleb was staying over, now three or four a week (Sergei had never been inside Caleb's apartment), Sergei got a head start of fifteen minutes before Caleb was allowed to follow him to Sheepshead Bay, and he left fifteen minutes before Caleb for work, so that they only rode the same train when the system was so backed up that fifteen minutes didn't make a difference. Even then, Sergei would sit in a different car.

They had never gone out to a restaurant or a gay club or church on Sunday or whatever the hell normal couples did, except for a blissful week in Palm Springs for Caleb's twenty-fourth birthday, because they agreed that no Brooklyn Russians or Chelmsford Arms residents—the two populations it was most important to hide from—would ever go there. Rarely they went to a movie, as long as they walked in and left separately and sat in the back row. Sometimes during these movies Sergei would give him a peck on the cheek, a display of affection so meager, Caleb wished he'd kept his lips to himself.

At work, it was torture to be in the same room with Sergei and not be allowed to speak sweetly or make eye contact. Sergei thought it romantic to play out their forbidden love in secret; for Caleb, the fun had worn off after about a week. Before he met Sergei, he'd hooked up with plenty of hot, built guys who hated their nature and would use Caleb's body as long as he left before their girlfriends got home. He had a sixth sense for closeted men.

Caleb stayed in the relationship because he loved Sergei and couldn't imagine being with anyone else. He loved the way Sergei's shoulders hunched when he laughed; the way, when they finally made it inside the apartment and locked the door with the bolt and chain, Sergei always kissed his forehead and nose before meeting his lips; the way his accent sounded, messy and sluggish; the way Sergei spooned him, lifting him with both powerful arms and pressing their naked bodies together with a perfect seal. He loved hearing about Sergei's past, an innocent childhood in his Russian village, a world Caleb had learned about in history class but could never quite picture. And Sergei's thick, strong body was a miracle, his chest hair heart-shaped, his arms and legs furry, his hands muscular and callused. Yet none of that described the real reason Caleb loved him—a chemical magnetism he couldn't explain.

But the night before their first anniversary, it struck Caleb that they had been hiding for a whole year without moving an inch toward openness. He'd been trying to stay positive and move at Sergei's pace, but the fact that it had been a whole year, a year of his brief life hiding for the sake of fear, was suddenly intolerable. Letting it slide even one more day seemed too self-obliterating to bear. He understood if Sergei needed more time to tell his parents, but at work? Once Sergei felt the freedom of being out to a few people, Caleb was sure he'd come out the rest of the way.

They were lying together in Sergei's queen-size bed with the lights off, half watching a rerun of *The Golden Girls* on his lo-res box TV from the 1990s. While Sergei absentmindedly played with himself, going alternately hard and soft as if doing a party trick, Caleb peered around at the sea-blue walls, the chromosome-shaped fissure in the ceiling from which water sometimes dribbled, and the cluttered IKEA dresser and side tables, the adornments of his cage.

"Can we talk?" he asked.

Sergei muted the TV and lit a cigarette. "Sure. What's up, my little munchkin?" He rubbed the top of Caleb's faux hawk.

"Our anniversary is tomorrow."

"I know that." Sergei sounded hurt. "I was going to make you dinner."

"I want to go out."

"You mean like to a restaurant?"

"Sure, a restaurant—that's how normal people celebrate their anniversaries. Or a skating rink, or a Broadway show. Or a walk on the boardwalk. Or a Starbucks. Just something . . . public."

"You know I cannot do that," he said, then reconsidered. "Maybe Philadelphia. We could take the same train."

"But sit in different cars?"

"A lot of Russians ride those trains."

Caleb felt trapped inside his skin. "I don't want to go to Philadelphia. Let's go out in Brooklyn. It doesn't have to be near anyone you know."

Caleb was wearing briefs and a tank top, and Sergei didn't bother putting on his boxers. It was weird to argue while he was naked.

"I love you, my Caleb. I love you to insanity. I would do anything for you. But you know the consequences if I am found out."

Of course Caleb knew: it was Sergei's finishing move in all their arguments. His family would never speak to him again. His parents would tell his landlord, or vice versa, and he'd lose his apartment with its unheard-of six-hundred-dollar rent—less than a resident of the Chelmsford Arms paid for a parking space. He also was sure he'd lose his job, despite their union and the labor laws that protected gay people: his coworkers wouldn't trust him, he'd be accused of something, and the building would let him go. Even when he admitted he probably wouldn't lose his job, he was sure he'd never be promoted again, and his holiday tip income would shrink. He even forbade Caleb from coming out, because it would incriminate Sergei by association. "They have to like us," he'd once said, "and I know for a fact that a lot of them are not comfortable with the gays." Finally Caleb had come out to Francis, mostly but not entirely by accident, so that he wouldn't have to go twenty-four hours without seeing someone besides Sergei who knew that he was gay. Francis didn't dance him around his apartment singing "It's Raining Men," but the revelation didn't faze him, either.

But Caleb knew there was no arguing with fear. When he had come out to his family at sixteen, his father hadn't beaten him, disowned him, or sent him to conversion therapy, but he had warned that their extended family and the folks at church would judge him while smiling to his face. And then no one had batted an eye. Much to his father's chagrin, he'd worn earrings and a pink Beyoncé tank top to a family barbecue in Morningside Park, and his conservative grandmother and a roided-out second cousin who'd been a professional boxer had both chatted with him as if nothing had changed. But for years, Caleb's father was sure they gossiped behind his back about how Caleb was going to hell. The complete lack of evidence couldn't convince him otherwise: his faith in his perceptions extended to his craziest ideas. After years of worrying that his parents would discover his sexuality by accident, Caleb didn't have the mental space for paranoia.

At the same time, when Caleb did "gay it up," he felt uneasy, like he was disappointing his father. He'd always listened to and respected his parents, and coming out to them had been the first time he realized he couldn't be exactly what they wanted. After that, his father had been less affectionate. And though he knew it wasn't wrong to dress and act how he wanted, he did feel more relaxed when he passed. But there was a difference between that and outright lying to everyone you knew.

"What about the consequences of hiding?" Caleb asked. "What about trying to have a real relationship with someone? I mean, I'm not saying you need to come out to your parents, but can't you relax a little outside of that? Because I can't do this secrecy shit much longer." It was what his father would have called "a penultimatum: an ultimatum with a back door."

"I am hearing you," Sergei said. "I will try." He held out his arms, and Caleb let himself be hugged. He still had a smoking-hot boyfriend, even if no one else would ever know. Maybe there was something sexy about that, in the abstract: a secret life of passion, protected from the rest of the world. Maybe.

They dropped the conversation there. Caleb lay on the bed and asked for sex to end the awkwardness between them. He wanted to take in his boyfriend passively, to force Sergei to prove his love for him. Sergei positioned Caleb's calves into the valleys of his shoulders as if strapping on a backpack, and they made love with *The Golden Girls* on mute and Sergei's cigarette smoldering in a plastic ashtray. A few minutes in, though, he found himself wishing that Sergei would overcome his fear of being penetrated and let Caleb top him.

Afterward, he rolled over and gazed out the window. The stars weren't visible, just those Brighton Beach monoliths where Sergei's parents lived, families communing behind a scatter of lighted windows, earthbound galaxies with their terrible gravity.

◄◆►

Of all the shareholders of the Chelmsford Arms, Caleb liked Francis the best. He liked sitting down with the old guy and being treated like a human, not an employee; he liked having a relationship with an older man that had nothing to do with sex, and he appreciated Francis's attempts to round out his literary education. Their friendship, if you could call it that, was one-sided: Francis invited Caleb up, served the coffee, and assigned the books. But after months of stopping by in his free time, Caleb felt assured that the old man had no ulterior motives, and he was starting to trust him.

He also really liked Mrs. Hunter. Whereas Francis talked to him like a teacher, she talked to him like a friend. She was wry and interested in his life, and out of everyone in the building, they had the most in common. But he didn't feel as comfortable around her as he did with Francis. First of all, she didn't want him calling her by her first name, Penelope—or if she did, she never corrected him. Second, she had a bad attitude. She was gorgeous and rich and had a sexy husband, and her apartment looked like it belonged in *Architectural Digest*, but judging from how mopey she always seemed to be, she took all of those gifts for granted. In Caleb's family, that was an unforgivable offense. So if he had to pick one person to help him out with Sergei, Francis was the one. Sergei was also really close with the old guy, whereas he barely knew Mrs. Hunter.

Caleb had gone back and forth a hundred times over the past few months about whether to bring it up. Now he felt he had no choice. Sergei would never come out on his own.

He forced himself to finish Philip Roth's *Indignation* on the train that morning, thinking its title captured how he felt about the book. Then he texted Francis, asking if they could meet during Caleb's lunch break. Francis's eager response took up seven messages, which missed the point of the 160-character form. At least Francis was more clued in than Caleb's parents, who got flustered when the envelope icon lodged on their screen, refusing to disappear no matter how many times they checked their voice mail.

Caleb waited in the living room while Francis made coffee. Mrs. Levy said hello and ducked into a bedroom: she was a polite but shy woman who looked and sounded like an old-school movie actress. Finally Francis appeared with his antique tea tray holding a cup of coffee for Caleb and a cup of hot water and a used, dried-out tea bag for him, as well as a sleeve of bland-ass cookies that Francis had loved as a kid. Caleb took one to be polite.

"So, what did you think?" Francis asked with an eager smile, as he handed Caleb a bowl of sugar cubes, each with a different wrapper that advertised which European hotel they'd been pilfered from.

"It was interesting," Caleb said, so as not to offend him when he was about to ask such a huge favor.

"What about it did you find interesting?" He dipped the tea bag into his mug a few times and placed it on a saucer.

"I liked the relationship between Marcus and Olivia, at first."

"But then you didn't like it?" Francis asked, seeming worried.

Caleb saw that he couldn't pretend to like a book he had hated, not if they were going to talk about it at length. "To be honest, the whole thing seemed a little paranoid."

Francis looked confused, maybe hurt. "What do you mean?"

"I just got the feeling that if Marcus hadn't been afraid of getting kicked out of school, he would've been fine. Instead, he treated everyone like they were out to get him. I mean, there's a kid who does not understand how to go with the flow."

"Did you see the anti-Semitism in the college? Some of it was subtle." Francis dipped a cookie into his weak tea and bit off the sodden end.

"With them having to go to church? Sure, but Marcus was so nasty to everyone, I didn't feel sorry for him. He was a jerk to his roommates, he was a jerk to that girl, he was a jerk to the dean. . . . It was just hard to feel for him after a point."

"I suppose so, but you have to look at his actions in context. Marcus doesn't want to be labeled as a Jew—he doesn't want to be known as the son of a kosher butcher, but the dean clamps down and won't let go. That's exactly the kind of anti-Semitism I faced in college. They never let us forget that we were Jews. But on the surface, everyone was equal. That's what I love about Roth, how elegantly he communicates those hypocrisies."

Caleb didn't need to argue about this. If Francis liked that unbearable scene, Caleb could take a hint and meet him halfway. He could imagine a dean, then or today, needing to tokenize a black student like that; would it happen to a white gay student, or, more to the point, a gay employee who wanted to be treated like anyone else? Maybe, but Caleb knew it was worth being labeled as different if it meant being able to be yourself.

Of course, if a black student had yelled at a white dean and threatened him like a crazy person, he'd definitely be expelled, maybe arrested. So he didn't have a lot of sympathy for this Jewish kid, who managed to turn everyone against him by treating them all like villains, including his girlfriend.

At the moment, Caleb had run out of patience with paranoid boyfriends. "It's not so different from black history," Caleb said, charitably. "They didn't make it easy for either of us."

Francis smiled wanly. "I was hoping the novel would speak to you."

They talked a little more about the book, about Roth's treatment of mental illness and the different kinds of Jews portrayed. It was an interesting conversation, though Caleb couldn't relate to anti-Semitism the way Francis clearly wanted him to. Jews were doing just fine in this world, and black folks had to fight for what little they had.

Francis gave him another book, *The Trial* by Franz Kafka. "This will teach you everything you need to know about the politics of this building," he said. Caleb's semester was starting pretty soon, and he didn't feel like reading another one of Francis's paranoia manuals before then, but he took the book and thanked Francis.

When it was time to get back to work, Caleb still hadn't figured out how to tell Francis why he had come that day. And he had to tell him, even if he was betraying Sergei. He couldn't live a life in the cage of his boyfriend's paranoia. He tried to stay positive. His father had always said that you never had to apologize for doing what was right. If only he could be sure this was right.

They did their final thank-yous and compliments as he took one step at a time toward the service door in the kitchen, trying to come up with a segue. When Francis gave him a paternal pat on the shoulder and said, "I'm very glad you chose to work in the Chelmsford Arms—you have no idea how helpful you are to me," Caleb decided to spit it out.

"Can I ask you a question?"

"Of course," Francis said.

"Are employees allowed to date? I mean, each other?" Francis knew he was gay, or at least Caleb thought he had picked up on it when they were talking about *The Metamorphosis* in the summer.

Francis smiled. "I don't see why it would be a problem. As long as you put the tenants first while you're on the job. But I don't have to tell you that—you're a model employee. Is there someone you were . . . interested in seeing?"

"Would you be willing . . . willing to talk to . . ." Caleb was losing momentum. He knew it was wrong to out Sergei. He also needed to do it, because Sergei would never leave the closet on his own. And if Sergei broke up with him over this betrayal, it would be for the best, because Caleb couldn't keep living in his closet but didn't have the strength to leave him.

"Talk to whom?" Francis asked, his smile turning to a look of concern.

"To Sergei," he said at last.

"Sergei Avilov? Oh, Caleb, I don't think he's . . . he's not . . ." Caleb watched Francis swallow his surprise as if it were a hard-boiled egg. "You and Sergei are together?"

Caleb nodded.

"For how long?"

"A year. As of today."

"Congratulations," Francis said with a smile that became a grimace. He must have realized that a year in the closet was nothing to celebrate.

"I was hoping you might take him aside, real privately, and tell him that it's okay for us to be together. He thinks people are going to discriminate against him. He really respects you. I think if he heard it from you, he might believe it."

"Of course I'll tell him."

"Thanks. It would mean a lot coming from you. You won't tell anyone else, right? He's pretty sensitive about it."

"Your secret is safe with me," Francis said.

"And could you not tell him I asked you?" Caleb added. "Can you tell him I came out to you, and then you decided to talk to him?"

Francis nodded. "I'll try my best."

It seemed urgent now to leave the apartment. Caleb felt guilty for asking so much of Francis, and it scared him to comprehend the violence of outing Sergei.

"I'm glad you've found each other," Francis said with an encouraging nod.

Caleb thanked him, then bounded down the metal stairs three at a time, as if to escape the scene of a crime he had committed before he could feel the first flush of regret.

◄●►

For their anniversary that evening, Caleb and Sergei ate in a Jersey City Italian restaurant with checkered tablecloths. Then, as snow fell like dandruff on the river, they sauntered along the waterfront without holding hands, because Sergei didn't know what friend of a friend of his parents might live in the high-rises nearby. Caleb had dated a white guy in high school who wouldn't hold his hand, and it occurred to him that Sergei might be ashamed to be part of an interracial couple, despite his fetish-level attraction to black men. But suddenly, when no one on the walkway was looking,

Sergei kissed him on the lips. It was progress, and Caleb felt terrible for having outed him.

Nothing happened for two days, and Caleb worried that he had asked too much of Francis. He also considered taking back his request, though that impulse dissolved when Sergei chewed him out for wearing a pink-and-black cap outside his apartment, as if straight Russians didn't wear crazy-colored gear all the time.

After work on the second day following their anniversary, Caleb was transferring at Union Square to catch the Q toward Sergei's apartment when his phone caught a whiff of signal and delivered two text messages from his boyfriend.

"U fuckin idiot"

"Don't call me"

Caleb stared at his screen, regret rising so fast it felt like nausea. He had known Sergei wouldn't want to hear about how welcoming the building was toward gays. He'd hoped Sergei would be pissed for a while and then forgive him, but he'd also known he might leave him. Why had he been in such a rush to out him? He'd been hiding with Sergei for a year; surely he could have convinced him gradually, without ripping off the Band-Aid. Right? Okay, so he'd made no progress in a year, but maybe Sergei would have come out in two or three.

He climbed up to the street and called Sergei from inside Whole Foods, breathing on his fingers to warm them.

Sergei picked up before Caleb heard it ring. "Why are you trying to ruin me?" Sergei asked.

"I'm not—I'm sorry," Caleb said. He felt a physical ache for violating Sergei's trust.

"Fuck sorry. Now I am needing to find another job. Why did you do this? What do you have against me?"

Caleb had picked a stupid place to stand, right where people were funneling into the grocery store. He walked farther in and stood next to a woman inspecting oranges from a huge pile. "It's 2014, Sergei," he spat. "Nobody cares about your sex life."

"Shh! How dare you say my name where people can hear you?"

Caleb couldn't believe he had fallen in love with a madman. He glanced around; the woman looked away as some oranges avalanched to the ground. Maybe he did need to lower his voice. "Listen, Francis isn't going to tell anyone. No one else has to know."

"Ha, ha, ha," Sergei said, his tone nowhere near laughter. "I will believe that when a crayfish whistles on a mountain. That building is a rat's nest of gossip."

"I think people have better things to gossip about than a gay doorman."

"Your foolishness might be cute if not so destructive."

"I'm the one who's destructive?" Caleb shouted, but he could tell from the dead air in the phone that Sergei had hung up.

◄ ● ►

Sergei called in sick the rest of the week. At first Caleb was grateful not to see him. The guilt he felt for outing him only stoked his anger at his boyfriend for being so obstinate. Each evening, he had time to see the friends he'd practically abandoned, and to run errands for his parents. After a few days of sleeping at home, trying to get used to being alone in the bed, he left a phone message for Sergei, asking if they could get together to talk it out. "If you're really sick," he added, "I could take care of you."

On Monday, Sergei still hadn't come in. Nikolas said he had the flu. Caleb left a second message on his voice mail, again asking if he could help. Maybe Sergei's parents were taking care of him, so of course he wouldn't call. Was it possible that by outing him, Caleb had made him physically ill?

As Caleb retrieved his rubbery ham sandwich and fruit cup from the staff refrigerator in the basement, Ranesh, sitting at the lunch table eating plain yogurt with mango slices, waved him over. "Congratulations to you! I always thought you didn't like Sergei."

"Who told you about us?" He didn't mean to sound defensive. He'd guessed Francis might blab his secret but hadn't thought anyone on the staff would find out.

"I apologize—some of the guys were talking about it. I didn't know it was a secret."

"We were keeping it quiet," Caleb said, hoping Ranesh would get the message.

Clearly, it was too late for "quiet." When he delivered a package to Patricia Cooper the next morning, she said, "Now Caleb, if I may: it behooves me to mention that we don't discriminate based on sexual preference, as I hope you will agree that we have not discriminated based on racial background. However, I would simply remind you that staff must remain professional at all times while on the premises." Francis hated Mrs. Cooper; Caleb was sure he wouldn't tell her. How the hell did she find out? He'd thought no one cared enough about the staff to gossip about them.

"Yes, ma'am. Don't worry, we have been and will be completely professional." As he said it, he wondered, despairing, if a "we" existed anymore, or if he had any right to speak for Sergei, or if he ever had.

◄ ● ►

That afternoon, Caleb rang Sergei's buzzer a few times. No answer. Anger flared in him at Sergei for not giving him a key in a whole year of basically living together, and at himself for not forcing the subject. He'd hated being stuck in Sergei's closet, but what had he done to escape before taking the nuclear option? Just about nothing, that's what.

The apartment buzzers were in a grid to the side of the front door. He pressed the buttons until a stranger buzzed him in, then took the elevator to the eighth floor and banged on Sergei's door. Maybe he really wasn't home. He was probably with his parents, or in a hospital. It helped to believe that, though that meant Sergei's life might be in danger. Or maybe he was naked on his bed, listening to Caleb's knocks with vindictive pleasure, waiting for him to accept that their relationship was over. Caleb leaned against the door and slid downward until he was sitting on the doormat. He rested his forehead on his knee and started to cry. It was bad enough to have screwed things up, but unbearable to have lost Sergei without a goodbye.

◄ ● ►

The next day, whether he was mopping the lobby floor or wiping down the railings, he could almost feel everyone looking at him like he was some kind of zoo animal, the way they had in his first few days working there. He'd wanted the secret to get out, but it sucked to feel like a piece of gossip. He hadn't expected that the news of two gay staff members would spread through the building like a brush fire, as if their love were a scandal. Sergei was right about these people. Not that anyone would be fired, of course, just that no one in the building could be trusted with a secret.

Before going home, he knocked on Francis's door. Over the past week, he'd read about half of *The Trial* to try to get his mind off Sergei, stopping when he couldn't take it anymore. It was more paranoid garbage. The protagonist, Josef K., is put on trial without having done anything wrong. As he bumbles around, trying to figure out where his trial will take place, it seems like everyone else knows more about his fate than he does. Caleb saw the parallels Francis had mentioned, between the Chelmsford Arms and the nightmare of the book, but he refused to take that view—of a world with out humanity. That was Sergei's mentality, being afraid of living because he believed the worst in everyone. Maybe Francis's, too. It didn't have to be his own.

"Caleb," Francis said, both welcoming and surprised. "Did you finish the book already?" He walked over to the stove and nudged some scrambled eggs with a spatula. It was a little late in the day for eggs.

Penelope Hunter was sitting at the small, flimsy kitchen table, eating Peanut M&M's by the handful from a big bag. Bunches of kale and celery stuck out from a canvas tote on the table; she held its handles as though about to pick it up and go. If she had a superhealthy diet, that was news to him: all he'd ever seen her eat was chocolate.

She said hi and waved. He hesitated over confronting Francis, but she probably knew about his relationship, too. Besides, he didn't want his private life being whispered about in the hallways. Much better to make it public. "Mrs. Cooper knows about me and Sergei."

Francis looked stricken. "I'm so sorry, Caleb. I shouldn't have told anyone. Sergei was visibly upset when I talked to him, and I was afraid I had done something very wrong. I asked Birdie for advice. But that was it—I didn't tell anyone else."

Caleb couldn't believe Francis had told Mrs. Hirsch. But he held his anger in: he'd trained himself never to let his anger show, especially in front of people who could have him fired.

"What about you and Sergei?" Mrs. Hunter asked, reaching into the bag for another handful of M&M's. "Want some?"

"We're together," Caleb said, accepting the chocolate, "or at least we were."

"That's great!" she said, with the boost of enthusiasm that people usually added when he came out to them. Then the second half of his sentence sunk in. "I mean, I'm sorry."

Francis's hand found his heart. "I feel terrible."

"It was probably for the best." Even if the words were true, they didn't resonate as he spoke them. It wasn't right that something good would hurt so much.

"I really did tell no one but Birdie. Who else knew?"

"Mrs. Cooper and some of the staff. Probably more—I don't know."

"Well, I can piece together that chain of events," Francis said. "Birdie must have told Ardith, and Ardith told Patricia. As to how the staff knew, I'm not sure. Ardith can't be trusted with a secret, I'm afraid."

She's not the only one, Caleb thought.

"She didn't tell me, and I saw her this morning," Mrs. Hunter said, seeming hurt. "Wait, Sergei broke it off with you because you told Francis that he's gay?"

Caleb nodded. "Yes, ma'am."

"I'm sorry, but that's insane. There are really people who are still embarrassed to be gay in New York City? You can do better."

Caleb didn't want to be told whom he should date. "We love each other. At least I do."

She bit her lip. "Sorry, I didn't mean to be dismissive. It's a bad habit."

"Drat!" Francis said, flipping off the stove burner and picking up the smoking pan. He scraped the dried-out eggs onto a plate. "Can I interest either of you in some eggs? I'm afraid they're a bit burnt."

"Thanks, but I should probably go," said Mrs. Hunter, folding the top of the M&M's bag and putting it in the tote, which she then slung around her shoulder before hugging Francis goodbye. "Bye, Caleb."

"Bye, Mrs. Hunter." Caleb bowed his head so that she wouldn't feel bad about not hugging him too.

"Caleb?" Francis asked, holding out the plate after she had left.

"I just ate," he lied. "And I should get going, too. I just wanted to tell you, I don't think I'm going to be able to finish this." He held out the book. When Francis didn't take it, he put it on the table.

"You can take your time with it," Francis said. "I realize you're busy, and I have another copy."

"Thank you, but . . ." He couldn't think of an excuse. His father would have commanded him to tell the truth: "the only five letters that will set you free." He stared at the linoleum; he felt terrible for disappointing Francis, who had only been kind to him. "The books you recommend, they're all so negative. Right now I need to stay positive."

His face took on an expression Caleb had never seen in him, his eyes pleading and his mouth tense. "Caleb," he said, with rebuke in his voice, "you've got it all backward. Reading an unhappy book doesn't make you an unhappy person. Would you also say you can't talk to unhappy people because they'll rub off on you? I had assumed you were better than that New Age rubbish."

"I just want a break from it, that's all. Just until—"

Francis, in full-on teacher mode, interrupted him. Caleb must have triggered his anger. "Pleasure-reading is all well and good, but that has nothing to do with the power of literature. It shows us our lives on the page, interpreted through the author's insight. We read to feel known, and thereby less lonely."

"The books you're giving me don't make me feel known," Caleb said, surprised at his boldness. "They're not about me; they're about you."

"They're about everyone, Caleb." He looked at the eggs, getting cold on the plate, and Caleb got the feeling he had failed him. "Maybe you could try harder to understand."

He saw, or maybe had seen from the beginning, that through the books they were discussing, Francis was trying to be known, as powerfully as Sergei was afraid of it. Why Caleb had to be the one to know Francis, he couldn't guess. Maybe Francis's neighbors didn't have the patience for it, and Caleb, in trying to get on the old man's good side, had been suckered into being his mirror. Not that their get-togethers had been so bad: Francis was the only resident who cared about Caleb's life, not just about gossip. But Caleb couldn't keep sacrificing himself for the comfort of others. He had to learn to push back.

"I do understand," Caleb said. "I just don't want to dwell on this stuff. I mean, I know life is hard, and people can be mean. But I want to believe the best in people. Because most of the time, people really do try to be good." His voice was faltering. He hadn't been good to Sergei at all, and now they might be broken up forever. "Anyway, I appreciate you having me over so much and encouraging me and all. You've been very good to me."

"You can still stop by and have coffee whenever you want," Francis said. "I didn't mean to quarrel."

"Thank you, but I don't know what people would think if they found out I was coming here. I don't want to be gossip anymore."

Francis stared, panicked, into Caleb's eyes. "I'm sorry I haven't been as good a role model as I should be. But please don't let this be the end of our friendship. I don't have a lot that's keeping me going." A few tears fell from Francis's eyes, though he wasn't crying, exactly. It was a silent weeping that Caleb recognized as despair.

"That's not true," Caleb said, embarrassed to be seeing his employer this way, but honored to know how important he was to Francis. "You have a really nice life. You just have to focus on the positive; it's all a matter of perspective."

"You're very lucky to believe that."

Caleb didn't know what else to say, but he couldn't leave, not with Francis such a wreck. He watched Francis turn toward the small window over the sink that looked out on the cement courtyard.

"I'm dying," Francis said in a strange, quiet voice, as if talking to himself. He put the plate of scrambled eggs on the Formica counter, and the clank of the porcelain startled Caleb.

"Do you need an ambulance?" he asked, realizing as he said it that Francis did not.

Francis drummed his fingers on the counter, still not looking at Caleb. "I've never spoken those words to anyone, not even myself."

Caleb didn't think he was the right person to be hearing this; the old man must have known that he couldn't help him. He thought he should hug Francis but sensed that he shouldn't touch him, as if Francis were made of blown glass. "What are you dying of?" he managed to ask.

"I always feared I would die from an eruption of the intestines, and I put up every protection against that," Francis said in that same distant voice. "Now it has come to my attention that it will be an eruption of the heart. And there is absolutely nothing I can do to prevent it."

An "eruption of the heart" didn't sound medically possible, but he sensed that Francis needed to speak without interruption. A secret like that could eat you from the inside; you had to purge it completely. At the same time, Caleb knew he would not tell anyone about this.

"Kafka understood this fear, that everything I've done will be erased. Everything I've fought for, everything I've lived for, will die with me. When I die, that's it: the world will go on as if I never mattered one bit. And I can't shake the feeling that everyone will be *relieved*."

"No, no," Caleb said, unable to keep silent, hearing this craziness.

"It's true," Francis said, turning back to Caleb. "I don't matter anymore. I don't matter to anyone. My brother hates me, my friends are sick of me, and my wife is counting down the minutes—"

"It's okay," Caleb cut in, afraid to reassure him more specifically or to ask questions, because Francis wasn't talking in his right mind. "Everything's going to be okay." Sometimes Caleb's mother would say that to him, and it always made him feel better.

They stared at each other a bit longer. Then a key turned in the front doorknob and Francis straightened and said, in a deeper voice than necessary, as if he hadn't cried or told Caleb any of his secrets, "You're a good man, Caleb Franklin."

"You're a good man, Francis Levy," Caleb said, also in a deep voice. He smiled; he hoped Francis didn't think he was mocking him.

Mrs. Levy appeared at the doorway to the kitchen, holding a mostly empty plastic grocery bag. "I got the butter," she said, raising the bag. "Hi, Caleb."

"Hi, Mrs. Levy."

"It's too late," Francis said. "I already burned the eggs."

She put the butter in the fridge and poked at the scrambled eggs. "Yum, crispy."

It didn't seem right to leave the minute Francis's tears dried, but Carol's presence had silenced him, and the awkwardness between them was getting worse. He thanked Francis for everything and headed into the stairwell through the back door.

"Wait, Caleb," Francis said, standing in the doorway. "I just had a thought. I've been giving you books that speak to me. Maybe we could read some books that speak to you. Have you read much of James Baldwin?"

He'd read a few short essays in high school and had liked them—but he was ashamed to admit that he hadn't read more. He knew his father wished he would.

"Would you be open to trying that?" Francis asked.

Though he'd just vowed to stop sacrificing himself for the comfort of white people, Caleb decided to make an exception. He could try this new arrangement and see how it felt.

◀●▶

In the morning, Caleb asked Thomas to alert him when he saw Mrs. Cooper going out. He promised he wasn't going to break any rule; he just wanted to talk to Letitia alone. In the past, they'd sometimes make small talk in the lobby or at Mrs. Cooper's service door. He needed a good listener about now, someone who didn't need him to be a certain way for their comfort.

She greeted him in a faded pink housedress and fuzzy socks. "Hello, Caleb."

"Are you busy? Can we talk?"

"Sure. What's going on in your neck of the woods?" He stood in the gray, fluorescent-lit service stairwell, and she made no move to let him inside. He might be fired if Mrs. Cooper found him in her apartment.

"I'm guessing you've heard about me and Sergei?"

She shrugged. "News travels fast in these parts."

"He broke up with me. I just miss him, that's all, and I think I just needed to talk to someone about it." When he said it aloud, he was pulled down anew by the weight of Sergei's absence. "I'm sorry," he said, drying the corners of his eyes with his knuckles.

"You don't have to be. You miss him." She didn't touch him, but her calm presence felt like an embrace.

He nodded, sniffling. "I feel like I messed up the best thing I've ever had, because I couldn't be patient with him. I did the one thing he made me promise not to do. And it's like, of all the people who could understand someone's need to be in the closet, it's me. I was the one person who could love him the way he is, and I betrayed him."

She gazed at him sadly. "It's hard to love people who are limited. You want to fix them more than anything, and all you can do is honor their limitations. I gave up trying to change people a long time ago." She smiled to herself.

"Who did you want to change?"

"Oh, my husband, of course. When he had the slightest bit of liquor, he was something else entirely." She motioned behind her into the apartment. "And that one. I've never met anyone—man or woman—with so much pride."

"Mrs. Cooper?" It seemed insubordinate to talk about her employer that way. "What do you mean?"

"It's been two years now since I retired. But she don't want anybody to know that. And I keep her secret. I don't tell anyone that I pay her maintenance, either."

He grinned: she wasn't doing a very good job of keeping these secrets. "If you don't work for her, why do you . . . can't you live anywhere you want?"

She sighed. "I've worked for Mr. and Mrs. Cooper my whole life, and I've lived here since my husband died. It's my home. I like Carnegie Hill. And I like Patricia—she makes me laugh. I feel sorry for her, too. She's the most fragile woman I've ever met, and there are a *lot* of fragile people in this building."

So she was lying to protect Patricia. It still didn't seem right, but it made him feel understood: she was in the closet, too. "White people," Caleb said with a grin.

Letitia laughed in a velvety, comforting way. "Oh, Lord, don't get me started. Sometimes I could strangle that woman."

"You're not . . . Are you and Mrs. Cooper . . . together?"

Her laugh peaked again. "Oh, no. Not like that. Just friends. Just old friends."

"I didn't mean to suggest . . ."

"No explanation necessary."

"Thanks for hearing me out. I feel a lot better."

"Try to forgive him," she said. "It helps."

He'd assumed Sergei was the one who had to forgive *him*, but he saw that the forgiveness had to go both ways. He hoped it wasn't too late.

◄●►

Caleb still had a long day of cleaning ahead of him, but he grabbed his cell phone from his locker and closed himself inside the janitor's closet off the lobby, where the cell service wasn't terrible and where staff members often made illicit calls. It was dark except for the horizontal bar of light under the door and the glow of his phone screen, and quiet except for the slow drip of the mop sink. He dialed Sergei's number. When he heard his boyfriend's sweet, sticky voice on the greeting, he felt pillaged by desire.

"Hey, it's me," Caleb began, breathing through his mouth to keep from smelling the sweet, nauseating cleaning fluid. "I just wanted to say that I'm really, really sorry for outing you. I promise I won't try to change you anymore. You can stay in the closet as long as you need to, and I'll respect that. But please, *please* call me. Because I miss you, and I really don't know what I'm going to do without you."

He hung up and leaned against the mop sink in the cramped, dark space, letting the pain of missing Sergei gnaw at him, a throbbing ache that stretched from his throat to the bottom of his rib cage. It was unbearable to feel this way, and he didn't want it to stop.

◄●►

Sergei was waiting at the front gate of the Lenox Manor when Caleb got home at four thirty that afternoon, as the calm gray sky was darkening into a freezing night. "Hey, you," Sergei said.

It was strange to see Sergei at Caleb's childhood home, like seeing your barber in the line at the post office or your teacher on a date in a restaurant. His week of anger and grief evaporated when he saw his lover's rosy cheeks and nose boxed in by his wool hat and scarf, leaving him with a mix of relief and regret.

"Hey," Caleb said. "How are you feeling? I heard you had the flu."

"I am fine. I needed some—how do you call it? Mental-sick days."

"Mental-health days," Caleb corrected.

"No need for this hair-splitting while we are freezing our asses off. Can we talk inside?"

"I'm pretty sure my folks are home."

"Maybe I could meet them?" Sergei smiled, which made Caleb want to cry with relief. By some miracle, he had come around.

They climbed the stairs to the fourth floor, and Caleb unlocked the dead bolt, the only one of three locks that worked. His parents' bedroom door was shut; instead of disturbing them, he led Sergei to his bedroom.

"Nice digs," Sergei said, staring at each wall in turn as if memorizing every detail.

Caleb heard that as sarcasm. Assuming no one, not a relative, neighbor, or lover, would ever set foot in his room, he hadn't bothered taking down his teenage decorations—posters of shirtless heartthrobs, a framed inspirational artwork from his aunt about genius being 99 percent perspiration, high school track trophies and medals that his mother didn't want him to throw away, magnetic letters that spelled I AM MY FUTURE on his mini fridge. He hadn't really noticed any of it in years. Now it all came rushing to the forefront, and he was embarrassed that Sergei might think this stuff described him, more so because in a small way, it still did.

"I was going to take all this down; I just didn't have anything to replace it with," Caleb said. It was partly true.

"No, it is cute. You are earnest."

They took off their coats and lay them over the footboard of Caleb's single bed. Caleb plopped down on the mattress, thudding onto the deadened springs.

"Mr. Douglas McAllahan offered me a job," Sergei said. "He is needing a doorman captain for his new condominium tower in Hell's Kitchen."

Mr. McAllahan, the richest member of the co-op board, had developed condo skyscrapers all over Manhattan. He was also known for inviting twink hustlers up to his apartment in the middle of the night. His housekeeper met Sergei for cigarette breaks and told him everything.

"He hired you because you're gay?" Caleb asked.

Sergei smiled. "The people who live there are gay. They want gay doormen, but there are not so many to choose from."

Caleb was a little peeved that Dougie hadn't asked him too. Maybe they didn't need more porters. "You didn't get fired, did you? Not to rub it in or anything."

"I did not. You were right about that."

"And you're taking the job?"

"The pay is better. I am sick of the Chelmsford Arms. Too much gossip."

Caleb laughed. "You wouldn't believe the crazy shit people have been saying to me."

"Bastards," he said with a laugh. "They love their secrets."

"We don't have to be a secret."

Sergei grunted, which Caleb took to mean either that he was tired of hiding or that he didn't want to argue. He sat next to Caleb and put his hand on his leg, and Caleb put his hand on Sergei's hand. They stared out the dirty window, across the air shaft at the brick wall and a window that was curtained off with a flowery bedsheet. It had been that way as long as Caleb could remember. He still didn't know whose apartment it was.

"I have been thinking a lot during my mental-health time," Sergei said. "You have been wanting me to be open since the beginning, and I have not listened to you. I say I love you, and I say I will do anything for you, and I did not do this one most important thing that you have asked again and again. I love you but I have not been good to you, and for that I am very, very sorry. I promise to you now that I will be more open."

Caleb had never been with someone who changed for him. It was gratifying and scary, and it felt like proof that their relationship was going to last. "Thanks. That means everything to me."

"But I need to go slow. You will tell me if it is too slow."

"There's pleasure in being known, you know," Caleb said, remembering Francis's desperation the day before. "If you stop worrying about how much people are judging you, it's kind of important to be honest about who you are. I think it might be the most important thing there is."

Sergei took his hand away. "If you are trying to convince me to tell my parents, the answer is no. Never. It would be cruel. But for now, I will be out at work, and we can go on dates outside of Brooklyn."

"But we still have to ride separate trains to your apartment?" Caleb knew he should be grateful for Sergei's willingness to change—and for still having a boyfriend when he was sure it was over—but it pained him to imagine keeping Sergei's secret to anyone. He didn't think he could do it anymore.

Sergei pursed his small mouth. "Listen, I have done some thinking about this, too. I will be making more money at my new job. You have a dream in life, to be a social worker. I do not have such a dream, and because I love you, my dream is for you to have your dream. So here is my proposition: come live with me and you can quit your job and go to college full-time. I will pay for your living expenses and as much of your tuition as I can. Your loans will be very tiny. And if you move in with me, I will tell my parents that you are my friend from work who is paying the rent while I save money to buy a home. We can be outside together then. We can smile and laugh without fear."

Caleb was dumbfounded. Was this a romantic gesture or just a generous one? He did want to live with Sergei, wanted it badly, and he would need to find a place when the Lenox Manor was torn down, which might happen as early as March. And if he went to college full-time, he could finish in two and a half years instead of ten. He could get his MSW before he turned thirty—and then, with a well-paying job helping New Yorkers with real problems, not just the coffee spills and funky smells that his current employers complained about, he could pay Sergei back. If he did accept, though, he would really be locked in that tower.

"I thought you might be happy to hear this," Sergei added with an uncertain smirk.

"I am, I am," Caleb said, as he realized he was being ungrateful. "It's just . . ." He scooted toward the foot of the bed so that he could look Sergei in the eye. He didn't want to be touching him for what he had to say. "I do want to move in with you, and get to live with you and go to school full-time—that would be a total dream. But I can't live in that apartment. I want to move to a neighborhood where we don't have to be in the closet."

"Caleb—I cannot afford anywhere else. Not if I am supporting you, too."

"I don't want you to support me. I want us to support each other. I'll keep working. It's really okay."

Sergei leaned forward and squeezed Caleb's forearms. "You are right, of course," Sergei said. "Let us move somewhere new. Together."

Sergei cupped Caleb's head in his hand and kissed his forehead, then his nose, then his lips, tenderly. Caleb relished the moment, the first pleasure he'd had all day. "I missed you," Sergei said. "I wanted to punish you for what you did, but I found I could not live without you."

"You don't have to."

They lay back on the narrow bed and kissed some more. Sergei rolled on top and unzipped Caleb's pants.

"My parents are home," Caleb protested, pushing him away.

Sergei grinned. "What do you think they are doing all shut up in their room?"

"Last week you didn't want to meet them, and today you want them to hear our sex?" he whispered.

"The human mind is a miraculous treasure." He kissed Caleb, slow and deep.

PART THREE

13

MADAM PRESIDENT

Stepping into Patricia's dining room for the January board meeting, Pepper caught the last whispers of a conversation between Francis and a willowy woman with rippling gray hair who was wearing an oversize tan sweater, black yoga pants, and white sneakers. In recent years, the most powerful women in New York had taken to wearing workout clothes to business meetings and lunches. Pepper's mother abhorred the shift, probably because she couldn't get away with such a young look. As for herself, Pepper had set out a black sheath dress and pumps but instead put on dark jeans, black medallion flats, and a scoop-necked sequined top. This was going to be a big night, and she wanted to be comfortable.

"Marilyn!" said Ardith, who was setting out appetizer plates by the clipboards around the table. "Welcome to our secret society."

Of course, Pepper realized—the mystery woman was Marilyn Devine, a retired actress who had won a spot on the board after Birdie stepped down. Devine was a name concocted for the silver screen, of course; her original Polish last name crammed about twenty letters into two syllables. After Marilyn won the seat on the board, Pepper watched one of her movies from the early 1970s called *Wounded Love*, in which she was miscast as a nurse who fell for a badly burned patient, only to discover when the bandages came off that the patient was her father. The film had aged poorly and, according to the internet, given rise to a drinking game: every time Marilyn presses the back of her hand to her forehead, you take a shot.

Francis tipped his Yankees cap to Pepper and guided her into Patricia's living room, away from the rest of the board members. He whispered, "Did Ardith give you the all clear?"

Pepper shook her head. "She still hasn't made up her mind."

He had never been able to persuade Ardith to vote for him in the annual officer elections, even after he exposed Patricia's illegal sublet. So he had asked Pepper to talk to her. She had plenty of opportunity. In the weeks leading up to the Beacon of Hope gala in December, Pepper had spent hours every day in Ardith's cavernous apartment, soliciting sponsors, confirming with vendors, and planning seating arrangements using swirls of index cards on Ardith's Tibetan hand-knotted rug. She was excited to be working in a field that she liked, for a worthy cause, though she kept making mistakes: seating archenemies at neighboring tables, inserting a political joke into a speech that might offend the Republicans in the room, or choosing peanut clusters for the dessert table when one of the honorees had a peanut allergy.

Pepper managed to bring up the board elections on Christmas Eve, a few hours before she and Rick were driving up to Vermont to celebrate with her family. All Ardith said was that Patricia's illegal sublet had given her a lot to ponder. Pepper suspected Ardith relished the power of being a swing voter.

"We have no choice," Francis said. "The die is cast." Maybe his whispered conversation to Marilyn had secured her vote.

The problem was, she wasn't sure Francis would make a much better replacement. Sure, he knew everything about the building, and he was honest to a fault, but he had been acting strangely for months. He went on a deranged rant at the last meeting about his not being nominated to the board, which made it patently clear why Dougie and Chess hadn't nominated him. His private scheming about ousting Patricia was also tinged with paranoia. She remembered his wit and cheer when they first met in Patricia's dining room more than a year earlier: the jokes about Empress Pat and the untouchable bar cart. Since then, his roguish humor had become caustic. It seemed he hadn't smiled in months. But she had to vote for him. She couldn't stand another day, much less a year, under Patricia's control.

Ardith hobbled over and kissed Pepper twice on each cheek. Pepper gave her a weightless hug, afraid of applying pressure to her bones. The building's beloved dowager was probably still in her seventies, but it was hard to be sure.

"My dearest Pepper," Ardith said, "meet Marilyn."

"I loved you in *Wounded Love*," Pepper said, shaking her limp hand.

"Thank you," said Marilyn. "It's a pleasure to meet you too."

"Pepper is a veritable whiz at organizing and planning," Ardith said. "She absolutely saved our gala."

Pepper smiled, enjoying the compliment.

"If you're not careful," Ardith said to Pepper, "word will get around of your talent, and you'll become yet another prisoner of the gala circuit."

"Is it really a prison?" Pepper asked.

"Joke, darling, joke! It's a great privilege to improve the lives of those less fortunate without the drudgery of the punch clock. In one of my past lives, a mere nanosecond between husbands two and three, I tried my hand at secretarial work, and I found it not to my liking. I don't think women were meant to work the eight-hour day. It's really quite tedious, don't you think?"

Pepper didn't think anyone in New York worked just eight hours anymore. Rick worked nine or ten most days—and recently had been working twelve and fourteen, and then most of the weekends, too.

"Carol used to love working," Francis said, "far more than I."

"Ah, but Carol has the heart of a man," Ardith said, shaking her fists in the air. "Robust!"

At Ardith's trilled "R," Patricia stepped into the dining room, holding her sleeping Pomeranian like a muff. She wore a long red douppioni-silk coat embroidered with dragons, along with matching emerald earrings and brooch. She always seemed to be dressing for a Chinese emperor's court, but this election-day getup looked borderline insane. Pepper imagined her in yoga pants and couldn't help smiling.

It was 7:30, time for the meeting to start, and Chess, the incumbent secretary of the board, had not arrived. Dougie texted him, mouthing the words as he typed, and the six present board members took their seats.

Pepper had been afraid to ask Rick for the usual two bottles of wine. A week before Christmas, he'd been mugged in Central Park. The whole thing was terrifying: it didn't seem right that they could live in one of the nicest neighborhoods in the city and not be able to prevent a kid with a gun from nearly killing Rick. Now it seemed as though there wasn't going to be any justice, and though she'd put aside all of her needs to take care of him, he just wanted to be alone. So she basically hid from him, hoping his anger would subside. If she'd learned anything in her six months of being married, it was that in a few weeks, everything could be different, maybe better, maybe worse.

Instead of asking for his wine, she'd baked macarons with Birdie. After five hours of exhaustive precision, the tiny sugar sandwiches turned out perfect: airy, crisp, and not too sweet. It had been unnerving to hear George watching TV in the other room while they baked, especially because Birdie wouldn't even refer to him, nor did she mention her plans to move out. If Birdie did end up leaving, Pepper was going to miss her.

Patricia noticeably did not offer to open a bottle of her own—she still provided nothing at the meetings and kept her fancy spring water for herself—but Ardith lived a few flights above Patricia and nabbed three bottles of red from her apartment. "Today, we'll need the extra," she said. Since Letitia wasn't around—Pepper hadn't seen her in months—Dougie poured everyone a glass except Marilyn, who somberly informed all present that she had not touched alcohol in thirty-two years.

"Watch the drips," Patricia said.

"Aye, aye, Madam President," Dougie said as a droplet fell onto the tablecloth and grew into a large purple splotch. "Sorry."

"Douglas!" Patricia hustled into the kitchen for a liter of club soda and a roll of paper towels. For someone who flaunted her wealth and pooh-poohed the middle class, she was awfully anxious about a little stain.

Once the tablecloth was clean, she sat down and composed herself. "Any response from Chess?"

"Not yet," Dougie said. "He was supposed to fly in this morning from Aspen. I hope his plane didn't crash."

"Behind the fear lies the wish," Francis said, widening his eyes.

"You're a laugh a minute, Francis."

"Let's get started without him," Patricia said. "We'll simply delay the officer elections until he shows up."

"That's not in the bylaws, Patricia," said Francis. "We've always done the officer elections at the start of the January meeting. If he's not here, tough." Chess, of course, would be voting for Patricia.

"As board president, the meeting agenda is under my responsibility. And I say that we will vote at the end of the meeting." Her eyes darted to each board member. "How is everyone tonight? Were you all sufficiently fatigued by the holidays?"

"Please call it what it is, and say Christmas," Francis said. "Hanukkah has nothing to do with it."

Pepper had grown accustomed to his gentle corrections, but now he snapped over the slightest annoyance. Maybe he was going senile.

"Francis, darling," Ardith chimed in, "if we just say 'Christmas,' we leave out that delightful little turd known as New Year's Eve."

"Don't forget Kwanzaa," Dougie pointed out with a straight face.

"Please," Pepper said, feeling brazen. "Not only do we have no black shareholders, you don't have a single person of color on your staff."

"We're supposed to say 'person of color' now?" Dougie asked. "As in, 'person of interest'?"

"Enough of that PC rubbish," Patricia said, restraining Helen of Troy, who was trying to poach a macaron off Patricia's plate. "As it happens, we have a—what would you have me say?—colored? No, of course not. We have one such family applying to purchase 14C. So Penelope, you may finally get your wish. Or maybe not." She passed around the binders, which were twice as thick as usual. "On the surface, the financials are respectable, but I do have some serious concerns."

"They've got a parakeet!" Dougie said, flipping pages.

"That apartment shares a wall with my bedroom," Marilyn sighed. "I have enough trouble sleeping as it is."

"Worry not, Marilyn," Ardith said, her plumped lips forming into a semblance of a smile. "It's an absolute breeze to get rid of a bird. One simply opens a window." She opened her binder and took out a magnifying glass from her structured orange-leather handbag.

"I'm not worried about the bird," Patricia said. "If there isn't already a no-birds clause in the bylaws, we can pass one tonight. It's the job, the previous residence, the tax returns, the ex-wife—everything stinks like an old fish." She refilled her wine glass. Pepper wasn't one to police drinking, but Patricia was going to get sloppy at this rate.

"I see what you're talking about," Dougie said, scratching his gleaming, spotted scalp. He turned back to the first page. "They were living in Fifteen Central Park West—Jesus, why are they moving here? Can someone call up what they sold their place for?"

"I already did," Patricia said. "Twelve million. All to buy a four-million-dollar apartment here. I don't like it."

"I'm surprised you would criticize anyone for needing money, Patricia," said Francis.

The room fell silent, and Pepper sensed with cinching despair that everyone knew something she wasn't privy to. Four years of therapy, and her reaction to others' secrets was stronger than ever. Dr. Riffler called it anger against her parents, but she couldn't find any anger in it.

Patricia said, "I would ask you to explain what you're insinuating, but on second thought, forget it."

"I think we all know," Francis said.

"Maybe he's liquidating his assets to buy a country estate," said Marilyn. "Or a house in the Hollywood Hills. I looked up my old bungalow on Zillow, and it was valued at eighteen million dollars. Can you believe it? My little place? I'm glad I'm out of that whole business now. This life is much more sane."

Pepper thought Marilyn seemed more than a little proud of herself.

"Wishful thinking," said Patricia. "I googled him. He owns hotels. He was on a reality television show. His wife of the month is a model. He's exactly the species we don't want in the Chelmsford Arms."

Pepper bristled at the word "species." "Could we at least pretend not to be racist?"

"Oh, bleeding-heart Penelope, you're not going to win this one. You should have seen the list of complaints against him by his employees. Black, white, or purple, he's a crook."

"We don't google any of the white applicants."

"I google all of them," Dougie said, one thick finger raised. "And myself, every week. And all of you too. Penelope's wedding photos are beautiful, by the way. Even a novice googler should be able to find them."

"Thanks," Pepper said, though she'd hated the photos. The portrait that the magazine editors had picked made her teeth and forehead look so huge that it sent her running to the salon to embrace a life of bangs. On the upside, one of her mother's friends who had seen the feature hired Pepper to design her daughter's coming-out party, and a donor to Beacon of Hope asked Pepper to submit a proposal for a museum gala. It seemed she could carve out a meaningful life as an event planner. It would help to have work to fall back on if her marriage didn't last. She tried not to think this way.

"What has this world come to?" Ardith wondered aloud. "I used to go to the opera and the ballet. I used to throw spectacular parties. Now I do nothing but Google and Facebook."

"Don't get me started on Facebook," said Marilyn, who had spent the meeting thus far doodling intricate mazes on her notepaper. "Neither of my kids will friend me. And Twitter! Does anyone in their right mind Twitter?"

"The verb is to 'tweet,'" Francis corrected. "And yes, I tweet sometimes."

"You've tweeted twice," Dougie said. "And the first one was, 'Testing, one, two, three.'"

He sat back, chagrined. "Maybe I'll tweet tonight's election results."

Pepper skimmed the first few pages. Isaiah and Valerie Darden had three young children, plus a fourth who came from Isaiah's previous marriage.

Valerie was his second wife, going on six years, not a "wife of the month," as Patricia had asserted. Also, children were desperately needed in the building; Pepper wanted her eventual child to have friends among their neighbors. The Dardens' adjusted gross income was over two million in 2011 and a little less than a million in 2012, but the disparity could have been a product of accounting wizardry. She looked up Isaiah Darden on her phone. The *Post* seemed to be tracking his every misstep: a failed casino venture, a divorce, a lawsuit from a cocktail waitress who was asked to lose weight. The first two didn't seem scandalous, and he had claimed ignorance of the last one. And these offenses had nothing on Dougie's own checkered history. Ardith said he was battling a passel of lawsuits over one of his luxury apartment buildings that leaked, and he had almost gone to trial that fall for sexually harassing his cook.

"Has everyone come to a conclusion?" Patricia asked after a few minutes. "Are we ready to vote? Since there are only six of us, the bylaws dictate that I do not vote, and therefore three is a majority."

"Can I make a case for giving them an interview?" Pepper asked. "We say over and over again that we want to be welcoming to young, wealthy families, but what are we doing to welcome them?"

Patricia shot her a chilly look: the woman had limited patience for monologues. But Pepper had more to say, and if Francis could tolerate Patricia's disapproval, so could she. One of Dr. Riffler's catchphrases was "It takes two to tango." For Patricia's intimidation to work, Pepper had to want her approval. She told herself it didn't matter if Patricia was disgusted with her, and that her own voice mattered. For the moment, she could believe it.

"Speaking of Google," Pepper continued, "has anyone here looked on the co-op message boards? People say not to even bother applying to the Chelmsford Arms if you're under forty. We're known for our distaste for young children. We're basically considered a NORC. Our rejection rate is twenty-four percent. That's extremely high. And a colleague of mine in real estate told me that we are the whitest co-op in Carnegie Hill. This application is a gift. We'd be stupid not to accept it."

"It's true," Dougie said. "A lot of people complain about us online."

"It should come as no surprise that I disagree," Patricia said in between sips of her third glass of wine. She seemed loose, though not tipsy. "We look for stability in our shareholders. This man has children from multiple marriages, and it's only a matter of time before he leaves this one for a Kardashian or a Real Housewife. Residents of the Chelmsford Arms do not take our marriages for a test drive."

"Speak for yourself," Ardith said. "In my twenties, I was party to a jaunt of a marriage with the most charming sociopath you ever met. I still have a few pennies squirreled away from that lucrative fling."

Pepper tried to imagine Ardith's appearance in previous decades. She might have been a beauty, though her doctored face revealed none of its history. Maybe she'd learned to say outlandish, flirtatious things when she was so beautiful no one could fault her, or maybe she had begun saying them to grasp for attention after her face changed and people stopped taking her seriously. Still, she was likable to the core, and it was hard to understand why she'd tried so desperately to preserve herself.

"That's why you won't see me getting married," Dougie said. "Even with a prenup, it's a fifty-million-dollar mistake waiting to happen."

"Some of them last," said Francis. He'd been with Carol for half a century, though their love wasn't igniting any wildfires.

"A single marriage bespeaks a lack of passion." Ardith tapped the crumbs off a piece of cookie and tossed it into her mouth.

Pepper thought about how fragile her marriage still seemed, even though she was beginning to forgive Rick. She wondered how Patricia's marriage had gone before her husband's death. She must have ruled the nest. It was hard to imagine him having a say in anything.

"We are all entitled to our opinions," Patricia said. "But we pride ourselves on our discretion. People love our building because we don't have celebrities living here. I for one don't want the entire staff of the *New York Post* camping out on our sidewalk."

"Celebrities are fine, in my mind," said Marilyn, who seemed ruffled to hear that she wasn't considered a celebrity, "as long as they want to be out of the public eye. It sounds like the Dardens want just that. I say we give them a chance to start a new life."

"I didn't realize we had so many romantics on the board," Patricia said. "A show of hands: Who is in favor of tendering these people an interview?"

Pepper raised her hand, as did Francis and Dougie. Marilyn and Ardith raised their hands next. Pride welled up in Pepper as she realized that she had convinced them. She had almost quit the board a number of times because Patricia wouldn't listen to her, but she also hadn't offered sturdy arguments. Maybe she could make a difference after all.

"All of you?"

"As long as the bird doesn't come too," Marilyn said.

"I will eat that bird if I have to," Ardith said.

"Very well," Patricia sighed, "we will proffer them an interview."

While they discussed a small assessment to be added to the maintenance fees for sandblasting the grimy exterior, Chess appeared, bleary and disheveled. For the first time, Pepper saw him without a bow tie; a fan of gray chest hairs climbed past his yellow Oxford shirt toward his neck. She would have thought that such a stiff, effete man waxed his upper body, as Rick did. This glimpse of roughness made him seem more human. "I'm sorry I'm late," he said. "There was an accident on the Van Wyck. A truck overturned. Eight-car pileup. My wife and I were stuck for hours."

Pepper had known he was married, but this was the first time he had mentioned his wife. She'd never seen him with a woman in the lobby and had assumed they led separate lives. It was one way of making a marriage work, she supposed, though not one she wanted for herself.

"Worry not, you're just in time," Patricia said. "I've delayed the officer elections for your arrival. We might as well start with the uncontested elections. Douglas is running again for treasurer, and Chess for secretary."

Chess sat in the empty chair next to Patricia, with a glazed look in his eyes as he and Dougie were elected unanimously. Ardith furnished him with a glass of wine and a macaron, then fixed his hair. He barely acknowledged her touch.

"Now, as many of you know," Patricia continued, her words beginning to slur together, "both I and Francis are running for president. It has been some time since we have had a contested election on this board. We will both read our prepared statements, and then we all vote. Think carefully before making that decision. The president of the co-op board is a role of tremendous responsibility, not one to be taken lightly."

"Is this part of your speech?" Francis asked.

She glared at him. "Are you this difficult with Carol?"

He shrugged theatrically. "Give or take."

"Then she earns my profoundest pity." She removed a folded, typed page from an envelope, switched to an electric-blue pair of reading glasses and, as she scratched Helen of Troy behind the ears, began to read. She wasn't too drunk to pronounce the words, though she chose odd moments to breathe. "I have served as president for twenty-three years. In that time, our building has operated smoothly and in the black every single year. The structure is in prime condition, and our community is envied for our peaceful cohabitation and absence of scandal. We do not always agree on every point, but a diversity of opinions makes for right-headed decision-making. I don't think I need to go into just how much work the presidency requires, but I will mention that the average tenure of a board president in New York is two-point-eight years. In other words, if you're not voting for me, you might elect a candidate who will give up before he has learned the complexities of the role. And I don't know about you, but I don't like to take chances with the fortunes of the hundred and four shareholders of the Chelmsford Arms."

Pepper had to admit that the speech was convincing, despite the halting delivery. As unpleasant as the woman could be, Patricia kept the building solvent, and it would remain so, even if it would never change with the times. Maybe that meant Pepper and Rick would have to move to a family-friendly building when they had children. It was a shame, because she finally felt part of the community of residents.

Simpering, Patricia reached into her briefcase and affixed a neatly drawn VOTE PATRICIA! sticker to the lapel of her blazer, which brought forth a consensus of polite laughter, though Pepper cringed at her attempt at self-deprecating irony. "Your turn, Francis."

"I'll keep this short," Francis said, rising from his chair with the help of the table. He clutched his baseball cap against his chest with both hands like an apologetic schoolboy. "Many of the framers of our Constitution wanted to limit presidents to one four-year term, to prevent the possibility of tyranny. Eventually the two-term limit was agreed upon. Franklin Delano Roosevelt, great-uncle to our very own Ardith, was elected to four terms, and although he was one of our greatest leaders, his death in his fourth term guaranteed the presidency to Truman, whose use of the atomic bomb was quite possibly the most shameful act in our country's history."

Dougie groaned, and Patricia stared at the mantel clock. It did seem overblown to make a big deal about term limits when the bylaws were mum on the subject.

"But even Roosevelt's term doesn't hold a candle to Patricia's tenure in office. I don't argue that she is a competent leader. But there is no question that she has become a tyrant. She started the practice of closed-door meetings, and she created an incestuous nominating committee that guarantees her control over the board's makeup. And has anyone else noticed that she tells us how to vote on every issue? Or that she performs backdoor deals constantly? Only last year, she gave the Flints permission to move a bathroom, which is expressly forbidden in our bylaws. I only know this because the resulting move sprung a leak into the Hightowers' ceiling. And I'm sure no one has forgotten Patricia's illegal sublet, which we are supposed to overlook because of her meager financial reserves. To be honest, I wouldn't be surprised to learn that she doesn't pay her maintenance."

Pepper now understood Francis's earlier dig about Patricia needing money. The woman put up such a show of wealth—hosting the meetings around her ornate Duncan Phyfe table instead of in the building's common room, dressing like royalty, looking down her nose at applicants without a seven-figure income—that her insolvency seemed doubly sad. Maybe that was why she hadn't seen Patricia's maid in so long. Poor Letitia must have been let go.

"Is that an accusation?" Patricia asked.

Francis stroked his chin. "It's a contemplation. A meditation. A flight of fancy."

"It's mudslinging, that's what it is. Because I do pay my maintenance and always have."

"Whether or not it's true," Francis said, "I think it's obvious to everyone that, for the good of the building, it's time to take the reins from her. A vote for Patricia Cooper is a vote for corruption and thievery."

"Don't you think that's a bit much?" Dougie asked. He pried a flake of wax from his ear, sniffed it, and flicked it behind him.

Pepper agreed with Dougie. She despised Patricia, but the woman wasn't a thief.

"I hope you enjoyed yourself," Patricia said to Francis as he sat down. "Sometimes I think you simply hate women."

"You are no ordinary woman," Francis said.

"Testy, testy," Ardith said.

The room was silent except for the ticking of Patricia's mantel clock and the drowsy growl of her dog. Chess downed a second glass of red wine. Marilyn returned to her doodling. Everyone around the table, even Francis, looked glum. And Pepper finally accepted what she had known for months: Francis would not make a good president. He was sharp, thoughtful, articulate, and morally upright, but he was not well-liked. And he was becoming angrier by the day. Although he might have secured enough support to win, she realized that she couldn't in good conscience vote for him. She couldn't vote for either of them.

She raised her hand. "I would like to run, too."

Francis looked confused, Patricia appalled. A wicked smile formed on Dougie's face. Pepper couldn't believe what she was doing. She had no idea how to run a building, and if she wanted to pursue a career in event planning, she would hardly have time. And if she didn't win, Patricia would punish her for opposing her. But she couldn't sit back and let this woman continue blocking progress and fairness in the building. Francis might have been losing his mind, but he did what he believed was right, no matter what the cost. She wanted to be that kind of person, too.

"I'm sorry, Penelope, but all candidates must announce their intention to run at least one week in advance of the January meeting," Patricia said, petulantly waving her hand. "Those are the rules."

"I know the rules," Pepper said, thankful that she had finally memorized the bylaws. "I'd like to run as a write-in. The bylaws state that board members may vote for any board member, candidate or not. And I am asking all of you to vote for me." She didn't have a speech prepared—and she wasn't sure if she was authorized to give one—but the words tumbled out of her, things she'd never considered legitimate enough to voice, some of which might have been ludicrous, for all she knew. "I agree with Francis that we should open up our meetings to all shareholders. I'd also like to start a quarterly e-newsletter, to communicate what we do and welcome suggestions for future improvements. I'd update our preferred-vendors list; the contractors this building allows are awful, and the preferred brokers are all white."

"It's not our place—" Patricia began.

"Don't interrupt," Pepper said, and was gratified to watch Patricia shrink back. "I'd like to freshen up the lobby decorations to create a contemporary ambience that will attract young people. I'd like to build a playroom out of the gym that no one uses, with stroller parking: it would be so easy to appeal to families with kids, and we do nothing for them. I'd like to host open houses for our whole community to get to know each other, and I'd look into the feasibility of tenting the roof during the summer for special events. I'd appoint a social media coordinator to improve our standing online. We can be better if we don't make decisions based on discrimination and fear."

Ardith nodded at her, impressed. Chess's eyes came into focus. Even Francis looked on with seeming admiration. Her words had lightened the air.

"Mrs. Hunter," said Patricia, slurring her words, "that was a lovely speech, but this is all very aspirational. You don't know the first thing about running this building. I'm sorry to say that I don't think you'd like the drudgery of it, and you certainly don't have the patience and tact to negotiate with the property manager. I also worry about all the expenses you want to accrue. Running a building is not a shopping spree. It's a serious vocation with serious consequences, and frankly, you seem more than a little naïve."

"This is important to me," Pepper said, uplifted by a swell of resolve that pushed back against Patricia's rebuke. This inner strength, this sturdiness in the face of opposition, was courage, she realized, thrilling, vital, and terrifying. "And if you all are kind enough to vote for me, I hope you'll be kind enough to teach me, Patricia."

"Hear, hear!" Dougie said, raising his glass. Francis and Marilyn raised theirs, too.

"We'll see," Patricia muttered.

"I think you vastly underestimate her, Patricia, darling," said Ardith. "I would trust our spicy Pepper with just about any job. This would be an ideal time to hand over the reins, train the next generation, don't you think? You're not getting any younger."

Patricia chuckled, her head heavy on her neck. "You're a wonderful human being, Ardith, but I'm not sure I trust your judgment of people."

Ardith stiffened. "I'm sorry, but what on earth could you mean by that?"

"Oh, forget I said anything."

"If you are referring to my choice of husbands, you should know that I don't regret marrying any of them, nor do I regret leaving them. You, Patricia, might have been better off leaving that philandering snake of yours. Oh, don't look at me like that."

Pepper was so alarmed to hear about the wreck that had been Patricia's marriage, she couldn't quite process it. The sheer amount of exposure she was witnessing made her feel exposed, too.

"What I have kept secret," Ardith continued, "is that I too numbered among his targets. Of course I told him where he could stuff his little thing. But tell me again, who is the poor judge of character?"

"All right, let's move on," Patricia said, petting Helen of Troy in long, rough strokes until the poor thing decamped from her lap for a peaceful spot on the living room sofa. "Anyone else want to throw their name in? Marilyn, want to give it a go? Douglas? Maybe my Helen wants to do it. Bark twice if you're interested. No takers? Fantastic."

Pepper had never seen her so unhinged. She feared that the old woman might do or say anything. She bowed her head, hoping Patricia wouldn't address her.

"As it is vital that this not become a popularity contest, we will vote by secret ballot." Patricia popped open the rings of a binder and lifted out a sheet of lined paper, which she tore into seven ragged strips.

The bylaws prohibited secret ballots without a majority show of hands first, but it would have been cruel to get in the way of Patricia's efforts to restore her dignity. Pepper had hated the officious crone, but instead of the satisfaction of witnessing her comeuppance—which she had been craving since her first board meeting—she felt sorry for her.

Everyone clamped a piece to their clipboard, scribbled a name, folded the ballots, and placed them in Francis's baseball cap. Patricia mixed the ballots in the hat as if it mattered which one she pulled first, and read a name: "Penelope."

Francis tapped her hand encouragingly. Maybe he really would be happy if she won. His goal, after all, had been to dethrone Patricia, not to run the building himself. He must have known that he would be a terrible leader.

Patricia opened another. "Penelope." She betrayed no upset as she announced Pepper's victory, ballot by ballot. After four votes for Pepper, she stopped, not wanting to embarrass herself further. "There you have it. We can all see who has garnered the most votes. All I can say is, I hope you live up to your acclaim."

Dread seeped into Pepper's belly, and she barely managed to smile. She was proud that her opinions had been taken seriously, proud to have found, within a year and a half of moving in, a sturdy foothold in the building. But as she watched Patricia packing her briefcase and corking the leftover wine, assiduously avoiding eye contact, she saw she had taken this ancient woman's role in life and, if she was indeed penniless, her means of remaining in the building—and a part of her wished she hadn't run. Worse, now she was going to have to be Patricia's pupil for months until she could figure out how to do all the work without help. Maybe Patricia would forgive her. Or maybe someone else on the board would educate her. Not Francis; he had become just as bitter as Patricia. If Pepper was lucky, Ardith would train her.

"Congratulations," Francis said softly, squeezing her hand. "You'll be a great success."

14

ALL THE DAYS OF THY LIFE

It was important not to nap. If George napped, he wouldn't sleep at night, and then he would have to nap again the next day, and so forth. So why not nap when he wanted to and be awake at night? Because then he would never be awake or asleep, just drifting from pole to pole in hermetic twilight. Every day lasted a lifetime; every night lasted a lifetime. All sixty-three years of his life and then the rest, every day and every night. *"All the days of thy life" include the nights also.* It was a line from the Passover Haggadah, the free edition published by Maxwell House, which his parents had picked up at Bohack's and passed around at the start of every seder. As time dragged him further from his family, the stilted Talmudic language of the Passover story burrowed deeper into his consciousness, tendrils of his childhood that would not let him go.

He was going to see Marie that afternoon. Not Marie/Birdie, his soon-to-be-ex-wife who was always leaving—every day was leaving him a little more because he couldn't pull himself out of his sadness and she couldn't withstand any more of it—but Marie, Original Marie, the reason he nick-named the second Marie Birdie. Original Marie wanted to see him. She had never moved out of New York, lived on Riverside Drive, and in the thirty years he and Birdie had lived in New York, their paths had never crossed. He searched women's faces for her, hoping to find her but never did. How was that possible, that he could live less than a mile from her for thirty years without seeing her, and yet run into Bill Wichitt from high school at least once a year, Bill who lived in Forest Hills and worked on Wall Street and had no reason to come to the Upper East Side? Maybe because he wanted to see her and didn't want to see Bill, who was the president of a midsize bank and was probably gleeful that George was no longer anything, and whatever spiteful God lurked in the shadows wanted to punish him for every happiness he had salvaged from his life.

Forty years ago, he had turned down the job in Montreal, director of the Montreal office of the cosmetics company whose name he now detested. He couldn't move away from his family in Flatbush, his parents and his four younger sisters, his family who needed him to flip the mattresses and grease the hinges on their cabinets and chase the raccoons out of the chimney. He turned down the promotion in Montreal but then changed his mind and took it, spent ten years there, met Birdie there.

Had it really been forty years? Ten in Montreal, thirty back in New York as vice president of the cosmetics company, but by the time he returned his parents were dead, the house was sold, and his sisters had moved away.

He wouldn't have said yes to Marie's Facebook message, but Birdie hated him now; he had failed her just as he had failed Marie, and when your wife insisted that she was your ex-wife, there was nothing wrong in seeing your ex-girlfriend from 1973, before you met your current wife/ex-wife. Right?

He squeezed into a dress shirt that Birdie had bought him as an apology after that Yom Kippur when they had fought over him eating when he was supposed to be fasting, their tempers raging over that trifle, which was really just a shadow of the larger disappointment, his disappointing her after forty years. And even fifteen months later he couldn't forget her cherry tart in chunks in the garbage and the roses in their cellophane sleeve shedding petals on the console table and the closed door and the forbidding silence and his secret vows to be better again.

He wore a red fleece jacket because the buttons on his coat strained, and went out to the elevator and pressed the button, and when the doors opened he couldn't step in. He'd been cloistered with one woman for forty years, never had eyes for anyone else. He knew he had to free himself to survive, but like an old dog, his body couldn't break its loyalty.

He stood facing the sealed elevator doors for he didn't know how long, when the neighbors' door opened and out came Penelope Hunter. He barely knew her but felt tender and fatherly toward her, and more than that, he understood her, and she him. Her husband was a fake, anyone could see that, and he had broken her, he saw it in her tired smile and the hunch of her shoulders. Not even thirty-five years old and already living in the stodgiest part of the Upper East Side.

He had always loved kids, loved his little sisters and their kids, badly wanted kids, but Birdie hated noise, didn't see the point of children, wanted to round up all the children of Manhattan and ship them off to Staten Island until they learned manners. And that was that. No discussion. She had her reasons—a vicious set of parents who guilted her mercilessly over her marriage to a Jew—but he was heartbroken nonetheless. He wanted a large family or at least a daughter to spoil but didn't want that enough to leave Birdie, not when he'd been left and could be left again, an endless parade of Maries who couldn't bear his failure.

"You have to push the button if you want the elevator to come," Penelope said, and he laughed as though he'd forgotten and pushed the button, and the elevator came. Outside they walked together but not together, and every time he glanced toward her, she was glancing back. Finally she asked where he was headed, and he told her he was going to lunch with an ex-girlfriend.

"So it's true, then," she said. "You and Birdie are . . . ?"

He nodded.

"I'd wondered about that."

She said she was going to buy some chocolates for her mother's birthday but really just needed to get out of the apartment because she was a little depressed, and Rick was working late every night, and she was tired of staring at the bookshelves and seeing the same books. He wondered if she was going through the same blank misery that he was, and he felt his heart crack and wished he could hold her and cry into her hair. But he hadn't been able to cry in years.

On the frigid walk past the glittering limestone palisades of Carnegie Hill, co-ops one and all, past uniformed doormen lingering inside, fighting their boredom with attentiveness, he told her about Marie, Original Marie, about how she would buy clothes for him, boss around the barber when he got his haircuts, tell him to get into the car and pick left or right turns, and how they would always end up at some park or vista or crowded restaurant with space for two at seven thirty or eight, and they did it five or six times before he asked her if she had an inkling about where they were going, and she laughed, and she called him a dummy, and it was one reason she broke up with him, that he was too simple. *What says the simple son? . . . "What is this?" Then thou shalt tell him: With a mighty hand did the Eternal bring us forth from Egypt, from the house of bondage.* But maybe the children of Israel wanted the bondage. Maybe it was freedom that cursed them with centuries of unhappiness, plagues that circulated in their blood and surfaced generations later with atavistic brutality.

Marie said he was too simple and he wasn't confident enough, and his voice wasn't deep enough, and he wasn't motivated enough, and he was probably going to spend the rest of his life living in his parents' basement in Flatbush working as a low-grade publicist for a makeup company, and wasn't that the most horrifying thing imaginable? And the more she hated him the more painfully he loved her, and on the first night of the Passover seder when he opened the door for the Prophet Elijah she was waiting in her car at the black fire hydrant, and she broke up with him, made him sob in front of his bewildered parents, and she pretended to be sorry, but he could feel the fierceness of her anger in her hot, wet breath.

He admitted all of this to Penelope, these things he hadn't ever told Birdie, but that was the way with strangers and sometimes neighbors—you just told them things to see how they would respond and how you would respond to the telling of things you had never said out loud. Because it was much easier to be honest with a stranger than with your wife. Was that a truth everybody accepted, or was it sad? If he'd been honest with Marie/Birdie about Original Marie, could all of this have been prevented? Or would it have fallen apart before it began?

Penelope had a proposal, a game of pretend, because she needed to step outside of her life and be someone else for the afternoon. It was preposterous but he accepted, because he saw in her eyes that she needed him to say yes, and anyway, he was afraid of meeting Marie alone.

Birdie had gotten so excited about him, adored everything about him, he could do no wrong. And in the glinting sunlight and bracing wind atop Mount Royal, it had been so thrilling, this idea that he could marry her and that he loved her, that the fierceness of her love for him could help him love her enough to marry her, even if he might have loved Marie more. *Dayenu: it would have been enough.*

Marie wasn't at the restaurant, hadn't called or texted, so he and Penelope sat in a burgundy banquette, close but not touching. Penelope filled the air with her news. She had been elected president of the co-op board and had launched an event-planning business, and she said it all made her feel like an adult, but that it was also so scary she wanted to hide. He said, "I'm proud of you," and he could feel how happy it made her. He asked her about life with Rick, and she laughed in an unhinged way and admitted that it was rocky; she loved him but didn't know him, wasn't sure if she'd ever really know him, and he said, "Yep, that's marriage, you have to hold part of yourself back."

"To protect yourself?" she asked.

"To protect the person you love," he said.

"Rick thinks he's protecting me, but he's really just abandoning me." She glanced at him with tears in her eyes and looked away. "When your neighbors split up after forty years, you start to wonder why you're working so hard to make it work."

He didn't have an answer.

She apologized.

He shook his head.

And then Marie was at the door, Marie/Marie, Original Marie, the Marie he had loved too much and disappointed. Marie.

She was fleshy—not like Birdie, who hadn't aged a day in forty years— with a pretty duck face and a drapey silk blouse/pants combo and a jerky gait, hip troubles maybe. And he couldn't see any of the Marie he had loved in her. But when they embraced, and he smelled her powdery perfume mixed with cigarette smoke and deeper body smells, and heard her voice, raspy and sweet, his body remembered everything all at once.

Marie was getting her third divorce, a lawyer this time. She had two daughters and two sons from the first two marriages, a playwright, a baker, a banker, and a pilot. She had become a therapist, with a master's in social work. He told her a version of his story that made sense, not the one that really happened and made no sense at all.

"I took the job in Montreal," he said.

"I know."

"I wouldn't have done it if it hadn't been for you."

"I know." Her smile shimmered with pride, but then he saw that it wasn't pride, it was regret.

They were done with their stories and asked each other pointless little questions about real estate and movies and the horrendous cold, while the food came and went and the wine rose and sank in their glasses. It was one of Birdie's favorite restaurants, and George chose it because he didn't have a sense of what restaurant someone with taste might like, especially Marie who had always thought him tasteless. Penelope talked about her recent trip to Bermuda with Rick and her magnificent success on the co-op board and her volunteer work for a charity helping low-income women succeed, and George could hear how much she wanted these things to add up to something. He understood that she shared his affliction, the chasm between knowledge and feeling through which flowed only unhappinesses of the past.

Marie talked about her patients without using their names: one was a doctor who became a singer, one was a singer who became a priest, one was a man who became a woman, one was a woman who left the world of gender behind. Sometimes she helped them find the courage to flee; other times she helped them find the courage to settle down. "If only they could have traded lives!" she exclaimed, then found her point. "We start in one place and move to another, and sometimes we're not ready to accept a gift when it comes the first time, and we spend our lives preparing ourselves for our second chances. We just have to hope that we're granted a second chance." Marie smiled at him and raised her eyebrows a little. She took a sip of water from the goblet, and condensation dribbled on her blouse, making a dark stain.

Marie had rented a house in San Juan for the winter, was leaving in a week, and her daughter was supposed to join her for the first month but she couldn't go because her son was having a hernia repaired. So here was her proposal: "Would you like to come, George?"

The past rushed up to meet him, and he thought he might vomit.

In 1973 he'd accepted the job offer and left for Montreal the next morning, the morning after she broke his heart. His parents begged him to stay for the second night of the seder, but he couldn't stay another minute; he had to make himself good enough to deserve Marie. His mother cursed and threw the horseradish root from the seder plate at him; the hairy, gnarled lump bounced off his shoulder and floundered on the floor like a flat tire. "The shiksa breaks your heart, so you have to go and break mine?" she cried. Three years later he flew home to bury her in the family plot, where his grandparents and great-aunts and -uncles were buried, and he could see more and more bodies tumbling in around them, cascades of arms and legs and panicking faces, a mountain of flesh scrabbling for a home in the earth. He believed that her cancer began the day he left, the day her body decided to die.

Marie said he would have his own room in San Juan, that they wouldn't rush anything, that they would be friends first.

"I would love that," he said.

"And Penelope, you'll come too, won't you?" Marie asked. "I'm looking forward to getting to know you. It's amazing, the resemblance between you two."

Penelope nodded, grinning, yes she would come, and for that instant they were a family, the family that George was meant to have, the family that would finally help him lift himself out of his funk and return to the world he had thrived in for so many years. Did it matter if it wasn't true?

George and Marie split the check while Penelope busied herself with her cell phone. He walked Marie to the crosstown bus; Penelope followed a few steps behind.

Marie had been in love many times, she said, smoking a Virginia Slims, and no one had loved her as much as he had. At the time she had thought it was a weakness in him, and it made her want to be cruel. But now she wished just one of her husbands, or all of them combined, had loved her so much. "You were a gift that I wasn't ready to accept," she said. "I always cherished you, even if I couldn't let myself have you."

They walked on in silence—past pyramids of shining apples and oranges in the gourmet grocery, past town houses and co-ops armored with brick and stone, past stores that had lived and died and lived again—the antique map store that became a pharmacy, the bistro that became a chain bakery, the fashion boutique that became another fashion boutique that was already out of business—because he didn't want to say something that would ruin everything.

She laughed nervously. "Our child was another gift that I wasn't ready to accept, you know, and I don't regret letting it go, because I didn't want to raise a child alone, but I think about it all the time, what a fine citizen it would have grown into."

He kept walking because he couldn't command his legs to stop.

A child. His child. His child that he had longed for since before Marie, and Marie carried it and Marie killed it. "I didn't know about that," he said.

"You knew," she said. "I told you in my letter. After you went to Montreal. I told you."

There had been a letter.

"Your parents didn't forward my letter," she said, falling into the past. "Then I'm sorry. I had an abortion. I waited a month, in case you wanted to . . . I thought you knew."

"I didn't know," was all he could say.

And I will smite every firstborn: I Myself and not a Seraph. . . . I, the Eternal, I am He, and none other.

Penelope said she had to run, but that she'd see Marie in San Juan.

"Sometimes I think I saved you by letting you go," Marie said to George, when they had arrived at the bus stop. "You needed to be free from your family. They were suffocating you."

And he said, "I never asked to be freed," and his gruffness made her flinch, and for a long time afterward he wished he'd kept his resentment hidden from her so that they could pretend the past had healed itself.

The raccoons had made a nest in the chimney in the house in Flatbush. They hadn't wanted to be freed, but George did what he had to. He opened the flue and lit a fire in the fireplace, and as the smoke drifted upward the raccoons screeched. A thud between the andirons, and the burning logs shook as smoking balls of raccoon, large and small, lurched out into the living room, five or six of them, sparks floating off their tails, and he chased them around the bedroom with a broom, trying to sweep the shrieking creatures out the front door, the singed-hair smell like the taste of fingernails in his nostrils: *blood and fire and pillars of smoke.* The raccoons never came back, and the whole family slept well except for George, who closed the front door and returned to the fireplace just in time to see a baby raccoon release a final shudder as flames consumed its blameless body.

They were silent for a while, he and Marie, and he saw that it was important to say something, to erase the anger he had shown her, but he couldn't think of anything to say. When the bus came she patted his shoulder and said, "I really have missed you." And they kissed lightly on the lips on the steps of the bus, and he remembered those lips, that kiss, tense then soft then tense again, top lip then bottom lip then tongue; forty years apart and the pattern hadn't changed. His lips still tingled after the bus pulled away, and for the first time since he was let go from the cosmetics company, he saw a future for himself. He imagined himself telling Birdie—in the kitchen, maybe, where she often hid from him—imagined her disappointment when she saw that he had someone and she didn't. She'd beg for him back, and he wouldn't come back. He'd find out how his life would have gone if he'd been good enough for Marie.

But she never called. He left three messages for her over two weeks before giving up. She was already in San Juan, anyway; maybe her daughter had changed her mind and went with her. He wished he hadn't gotten angry with her at the bus stop. He wished he'd pretended to know about her abortion. He wished he'd shaved his beard. He wished he'd suggested a restaurant that he liked, one on the Upper West Side so that she could have invited him back to her apartment for drinks. He replayed every word of the conversation inside his memory a thousand times and berated himself for not being more honest or dishonest, and still he could only guess why she had changed her mind. Maybe Marie found out, as he had known for his forty years of happiness with Birdie and somehow forgotten, that you can't open the lid on the past without being obliterated by regret.

Lying half awake at two in the morning, after he'd given up on Marie ever calling him, he heard a scraping in the living room, and he opened his bedroom door and encountered her, Marie/Birdie, dragging the sofa across the floor, a tea towel placed under each leg to keep it from scratching, the doors of the display cabinet flung open, her collection of white marionettes splayed on the floor. She looked up as if caught cleaning a crime scene.

"I'm just rearranging a few things," she explained. "This place is suffocating me."

"Please don't leave," he said.

He saw a flash of hope in her eyes, then remembered that in Birdie, hope always looked the same as desperation. "I need my freedom, George. I have to try to be happy, even if you can't be."

He wanted to tell her that freedom was a curse, but she wouldn't believe him. He lifted the opposite end of the couch and helped her carry it across the room. The small, oddly shaped sofa was much heavier than it looked. They put it down in a new place, and the room didn't look better or worse, didn't even look different. But Birdie was pleased.

"Thank you," she said.

And he went back into his room.

On the first day of Passover he had moved to Montreal and left his family and Marie, and he met the second Marie and nicknamed her Birdie and pretended he was someone who had never been left before, someone who was worthy of love, and he could believe it, too. And they fell in love and married and filled up their lives with happiness, and *it would have been enough*, and she never knew that there was another Marie; he never told her, not once, not ever.

15

WHEN IT BEGINS

There was so much to tell Dr. Riffler, Pepper didn't have time to unpack any of it. She talked about how, since Rick's mugging, his attempts to push down his anger only made her afraid he might snap, and even on vacation in Bermuda, the thrum of his restlessness had put her on edge. She talked about how scared she was to be president of the Chelmsford Arms and how guilty she felt about unseating Patricia. About how overwhelmed she was by her new event-planning business, in filling out exhaustive requests for proposals that were probably deleted without being read, because when it came down to it, her experience amounted to planning her own wedding and helping out with one benefit. About the urgency to have a baby amid her uncertainty about whether she was going to stay with Rick, and how worried she was that she might be infertile. About how much she was regressing: not only had she *pretended to be George's daughter* on that bizarre afternoon in late January, but in the weeks since, she had unplugged the hole between their apartments and was eavesdropping for hours each day. The crazy thing was, she heard almost nothing, just the harried sounds of Birdie's cooking and the occasional tense conversation between her and Francis, who frequently stopped by—and still she kept listening.

She stared at the floor as she talked, because it was hard to meet Dr. Riffler's gaze without feeling reproved.

Sometimes her therapist said something useless: "That sounds frustrating." "How does Rick's anger make you feel?" "What would it mean if you put aside thoughts of a baby for now?" Mostly the old woman listened, sipping the strange brown liquid that she'd drunk from a green-glazed mug since the beginning of their work together. Pepper was curious to know what that stuff was—it was too thin to be coffee and not quite the color of black tea—but if she asked, Dr. Riffler would ask her why she wanted to know, and then they'd travel down a path that had no relevance to anything. She was beginning to wonder if she needed a different therapist, someone who could share "ten tips for a happy life" and send her on her way.

"Rick wants to go back into couple's therapy," she said. "I know we need more of it, but I can't. I just can't." It was strange to talk about their couple's therapy with Dr. Riffler, who had referred her and Rick to Dr. Dixon. Pepper imagined that everything she said to either therapist would be transmitted to the other.

The old woman examined her. Even with her mesh-backed office chair on its lowest setting, the toes of her slippers didn't touch the floor. Pepper often thought that if Dr. Riffler were married, her husband might crush her under his weight. Maybe she was a little person. "Why don't you want to?"

"I'm afraid he's going to tell me something that I can't unhear, and then our marriage will be ruined. Part of me would rather end my marriage now than go back into Dr. Dixon's office." She laughed.

"What are you afraid of learning?"

"I don't know, maybe he has some girlfriend or wife on the side, like Molly but serious. Or that he had a girlfriend before me and he wishes he could leave me for her." That seemed to be true of George. To think that she'd once envied her neighbors' relationship. Now there was almost nothing left of it. She really had no role models for marriage.

Dr. Riffler took a sip of the brown liquid. "I doubt you want to hear this, but The Locked Door locks from both sides."

She usually let her therapist insert that annoying quip without comment, but if the old lady knew she hated to hear it, why did she keep saying it? "I get it," she said through clenched teeth. "I'm keeping secrets and I'm somehow making Rick keep the same secrets. But knowing that doesn't help. Don't you have anything else?"

She set the mug on a square slate coaster. "Only that the opposite of secrecy is intimacy."

Pepper felt hot with rage. She had seen Dr. Riffler every week for the past four years, and all her advice could be reduced to a bunch of coy apothegms. Sure, Pepper had bested Patricia in the election, but she'd made no progress where it mattered: she still couldn't have a conversation with her mother without wanting to scream. She still couldn't move past her childhood blurriness around secrets. She was thirty-four, on the cusp of tossing her marriage into the toilet, and Dr. Riffler just sat there, sipping the goddamned bong water. It was sadistic. "Just tell me: Do you think I have to go back into couple's therapy?"

Dr. Riffler squinted in Pepper's direction. "I don't think we need to think in terms of shoulds."

She couldn't stand these nonanswers when she was in so much pain. "You won't give me any advice? About anything? I need help, Dr. Riffler. Can't you just do your job for once?"

"I can give you all the advice you want, but the insight has to come from you."

If Dr. Riffler was trying to enrage her, she'd gotten an A-plus. Pepper couldn't sit in that room any longer and wait for some magical Freudian epiphany. She was sick of sifting through everything wrong with her life and doing nothing to fix it.

She stood up. "You know what? I'm done. This has been a colossal waste of time."

"You're ending early?" Dr. Riffler asked with what looked like a hint of a smile. "Or are you terminating our work together?"

"The latter. Thanks for everything, nice knowing you, bye." The anger hummed in her fingers. She couldn't remember having gotten mad at Dr. Riffler before. Maybe she'd been afraid to.

"Penelope, it's your decision whether you stay or leave, but for your sake, let's process what led you to this decision."

"Fuck processing. I'm miserable, and my marriage is fucked, and I need help, and you couldn't care less. I'm sick of this shit."

"Stay with it a little longer," Dr. Riffler said softly.

"How much longer? Four more years? Forty? When does it end?"

"Not while you're angry. That's when it begins."

The only thing Dr. Riffler was good at was convincing Pepper to stay for more sessions. "I can't keep sitting on your crappy futon while you feed me the same meaningless bullshit." Pepper didn't feel comfortable standing in front of Dr. Riffler, but she didn't want to sit back down and wasn't ready to leave. She decided to give her therapist one last chance.

"Tell me what's making you so angry." Dr. Riffler took another sip from her mug.

"What the hell is that stuff, anyway?" Pepper asked, bracing herself for a deflection or interpretation.

"This?" she asked, holding out her mug. "It's kukicha. Japanese twig tea."

After wondering about that drink for so long, Pepper couldn't believe the answer had come so easily, but of course it had; she had never asked. Still standing, she looked around the office as if for the first time, searching for more mysteries to solve. She'd stared at the abstract painting of a sunset behind Dr. Riffler but hadn't realized a similar painting hung behind the futon where the patients sat. A miniature Zen garden with three pebbles and a tiny wooden rake was on a side table that Pepper had never looked at. Or had Dr. Riffler put it there recently? On top of the bookshelf sat a small gold Buddha with green gems for eyes. She'd seen that before but hadn't given it any thought. She had sat in this woman's presence for almost two hundred sessions without wondering about these decorations—or anything about her therapist's life. Wasn't that the great thing about therapy, that you could ignore the therapist? Or was that just self-centered?

"Has that always been there?" Pepper asked, pointing to the Zen garden. Her anger had floated away, and she didn't feel like looking for it.

Dr. Riffler nodded.

"Are you Buddhist?"

Dr. Riffler didn't answer, and the rebuff laced up Pepper's belly and tightened like a corset. When she took a breath, it didn't loosen.

"Is this your secrecy reflex?" her therapist asked.

Pepper nodded. Finally it let go, leaving behind a dazed curiosity. She hadn't asked anything about Dr. Riffler in four years because she feared that tightening. What if she ignored it and asked questions anyway? A minute earlier, she'd been ready to leave for good, and now it seemed that growth of all kinds was in reach. "I just realized that I don't need to be scared of it. I've been waiting for it to go away, but maybe it's okay if it doesn't."

Dr. Riffler smiled.

Pepper had the empowering sense that she could change anything about herself if she just looked at it in another light. In the span of a minute, her perspective had shifted on its axis. She sat down and leaned back on the futon, feeling the changes tingling inside her.

"And by the way, the answer is yes," Dr. Riffler said.

"What?"

"I'm Buddhist."

Her therapist might as well have just flashed her. Pepper slowed her breath and tried to calm the buzzing in her head. She felt dizzy; she touched her throat.

Dr. Riffler picked up her mug. "How does it feel to hear me say that?"

Pepper started to tell her that she needed a minute. But no words came out, only ragged, wet sobs that lasted until the end of the session.

16

WRATH

SIX WEEKS EARLIER

Crossing Central Park from west to east, Rick followed the bridle path just south of the reservoir, where cop cars and paddy wagons were parked en masse. It was dark save for lampposts from the road behind him, but he didn't hurry; the gritty New York that he'd read about as a kid growing up in Akron had been swept clean by Giuliani and polished to a shine by Bloomberg. If you wanted to die in this city, you pretty much had to kill yourself.

He'd come from a holiday benefit for the homeless at the Museum of Natural History—had ingratiated himself with a beautiful woman who'd just inherited fifteen million of an oil fortune—and was too sloshed to submit to a jouncing cab. He needed to start setting limits on his consumption. Maybe marriage was making him soft. He was still pissed at Pepper for ending their couple's therapy with Dr. Dixon, for no reason that made sense. She said she couldn't be that open, but what was a marriage if not honesty between two people? On the other hand, they were finally getting along. She had forgiven him for the Molly fiasco, so he could forgive her for dropping out of couple's therapy.

He needed to piss, could have pulled his dick out on the dirt path, it was so quiet. Not wanting to risk arrest, he wandered into the brush to find a big enough tree. Probably should have stopped at three glasses of Johnnie Black, but he couldn't keep handing drinks to the oil heiress without sucking down a few himself. Pepper hated the flirting, but if tossing off a few smiles and winks netted him half a million bucks, she could hardly complain. To be honest, he did want to bang the heiress, and he could tell she was game, but he wasn't going to; he'd learned his lesson. He loved Pepper, and they were married, and he didn't want that to change. End of story.

On the Eighty-sixth Street Transverse, ten feet down an embankment, cars sluiced by, headlights streaking across his vision. The police precinct across the road was dark. That was the thing about New York: you were never alone. He hoped the twigs scraping his hands weren't poison ivy.

Footsteps crunched on frozen dirt, and Rick looked back to see a bone-thin kid in an embossed red-leather jacket with a black balaclava covering his face. In an instant, he foresaw exactly what would happen.

"Hey, man, wait up," the kid said, squeezing between two parked cop cars with one hand awkwardly in his coat pocket.

Rick glanced around. Even if he could jump the ten feet down to the transverse road without breaking an ankle or getting hit by a car, he couldn't outrun anyone in his drunken state. He prayed that the kid was just asking for directions, a few bucks, or a light.

Then the kid took his hand out of his pocket, and the glint of his pistol felt like a smack to the gut. At first Rick thought he'd been shot, that the warmth soaking his inner thighs was blood. But the pain went away, and he smelled piss.

"Don't do anything stupid," the mugger said. The movements of his wide, thin lips didn't sync with the words Rick heard. "Gimme your wallet and phone."

With shaking hands Rick emptied his pockets. He could get another phone, but he was carrying Pepper's gray shagreen wallet. No, his wallet. Pepper had given it to him. Custom-ordered it from a Dutch leatherworker on their honeymoon. Whenever he held it, he felt sappy with affection. He thought he should say something, humanize himself. "There's five hundred dollars in there, and you can have the credit cards," he said, as the mugger grabbed his valuables. "But can I keep the wallet? It was a present from my wife."

"No talking," the mugger said, jabbing the barrel into Rick's ribs, shocking him with pain. "Get down, face on the ground." He flipped through the cash and glanced at the visible edges of the cards. He had trouble holding the gun at the same time, and his finger slid against the trigger. The mugger was shaking—was he afraid or just cold? Rick thought he shouldn't look away. This guy would have to be a psychopath to shoot someone who was looking him in the eye. So instead of lying facedown, he knelt with his hands over his head. That seemed to satisfy the mugger. Rick tried to memorize his features. Nothing was visible except his thin mouth with a sparse mustache and the bright whites of his eyes. His jacket was embossed with cherries, dice, and stacks of bills.

"If you give me back the wallet, I'll take out an extra thousand for you from an ATM."

"Right. I'm not falling for that," the mugger said. Rick didn't know what kind of trick he thought he was playing.

"Why are you doing this?" Rick asked, shivering from the piss in his pants, now ice-cold. "There are better ways to get money."

"Shut up." He kicked Rick hard in the groin. The pain flashed in Rick's eyes, almost making him puke. "Now close your eyes and count to a hundred. Move one inch and I'll kill you."

Rick closed his eyes and heard footsteps receding on the gravel. He counted to a hundred, not because the mugger told him to but because he couldn't think of any other way to remember to breathe.

◄●►

For a moment Rick wasn't sure he was in the right apartment. He saw the sky-blue tailored sofa their interior designer had custom-ordered, the Louis XVI bergères handed down from Pepper's great-grandmother, and the framed black-and-white photographs hanging over the bookshelves, but the living room felt like a stage set. Why hadn't he run for it when he saw the guy? He'd just knelt there like a moron. He couldn't remember exactly what had happened. The events resisted sticking in his mind.

Not wanting Pepper to know he'd pissed himself, he stripped off his tuxedo and stuffed it into a plastic bag for the dry cleaner before showering in the guest bedroom.

Through the distortion of the shower door, Pepper appeared in a vintage kimono she sometimes wore as a nightgown. Seeing her, and thinking of the beautiful wallet, it struck him how much danger he'd been in. "Why so quick to jump in the shower?" she asked, leaning against the doorframe.

He tried to think of a response that wouldn't upset her. He didn't want to put this on her. He shut off the water and opened the door, reached for his towel and swaddled himself. He didn't want her to see him naked. He felt flabby and misshapen.

"What did you do?" she asked angrily.

"Your wallet," he said, struggling to move his lips. "My wallet. I couldn't save it." He tripped on the edge of the shower and fell. He didn't feel pain.

"What's going on?" Pepper asked, helping him up. "What happened?"

The water from his hair soaked into her kimono. He didn't want to get her wet. He pulled out of her embrace, stumbled into the bedroom, and collapsed onto the bed. His vision bleached. The room spun.

She knelt in front of him on the bed, felt his hot forehead, felt his cold fingers. "You're really freaking me out, Rick. I'm going to call an ambulance if you don't say something right now."

"He took the wallet. He had a gun."

"Who had a gun? Were you mugged?"

His neck felt stiff and brittle; when he nodded, he feared it might snap.

"Did you call nine-one-one?" she asked.

"He took my phone."

She gaped at him, then lunged for her phone on the nightstand.

◀◆▶

Rick woke up at noon the next day with a throbbing head and papery mouth. Pepper served him a plate of eggs, Swiss chard, a glass of fresh-squeezed grapefruit juice, and four shots of espresso. He wasn't hungry, but he swallowed as much as he could.

The night before, they'd spent an hour at the police precinct. Describing the mugger to the detectives, Rick realized he wasn't sure of his race. He'd seen him as an inner-city white kid—he hadn't given it much thought. Piecing it together with the cops, though, he wondered if the mugger had been a light-skinned black man or a Latino. He'd seen other black men wear jackets like that. In the dim light, his skin color had been hard to read. When Detective Rojas, the lead detective, radioed him in as a light-skinned black male, Rick assumed he knew what he was talking about. Maybe he already had a suspect in mind.

They had nearby patrol cars keeping an eye out, but considering Rick had waited an hour to call the police, no one was surprised that the mugger wasn't smoking a joint on a park bench. As Detective Rojas dispatched the sheaf of forms for the police report with fatigued virtuosity, seeming almost irritated by the task, Rick wondered if the crime hadn't been so serious after all. He kept telling Pepper to go home, but she refused, even stayed up two more hours to cancel his cards and wipe his phone remotely. Now she looked as if someone had clocked her in both eyes.

While he sipped the thick, bitter espresso, she handed him the black crosshatched Bottega Veneta wallet he'd used before their honeymoon. It looked anorexic without his credit cards and ID. "I got some cash and a new

Starbucks card for you," she said. "Your new license and credit cards should be coming in the next few days."

"I loved that wallet," he groaned.

"I guess we'll just have to go back to Amsterdam and get you another," she said with a wan smile. "I called my dad, too—he's going to make sure they prioritize your case." Her father, a partner at one of the oldest law firms in New York, was buddy-buddy with a deputy commissioner at One Police Plaza.

"You're a goddess," he said. He hadn't felt such pure, disclaimer-free love for her since they moved into the building. He'd been so upset by the mugging, all of his previous quibbles with Pepper—her insanity around the wedding, her telling him she might not love him, her ending couple's therapy—now felt irrelevant. The horror of the previous night seemed a small price to pay for the promise of a happier marriage. At the same time, he was still in shock.

"I knew all those years as a personal assistant would come in handy someday," she said, kissing him on the cheek as she cleared his plate.

◄●►

A week later, Rick managed to smile through Christmas in Vermont with Pepper's family by believing that his phone would ring imminently with news that the mugger had been caught. Come the first week of January, the cops had found zero suspects, and they stopped returning his calls. Detective Rojas had promised they'd find the kid sooner or later—nobody was a one-time felon—but Rick had his doubts. And now he couldn't go five minutes without startling. On crowded avenues he worried that someone might detonate a bomb strapped to his or her chest; on desolate streets he expected someone to pop out of an apartment building with a Glock. In the locker room at the gym, when a muscular black guy in a towel brushed up against him, Rick's insides lurched, and he shouted at the guy to watch where he was going.

To keep his fear at bay, he started leaving for work before Pepper woke up and returning after she'd gone to sleep. He typically didn't spend much of early January in the office—it was so dead, guys could be found napping at their desks—but this year, he appreciated the ordered quiet of the cubicles and the multitude of tasks available to him: there was no limit to how many new investment funds he could spec or how much year-end paperwork he could file. And even though he could poach more business by warming hands and wetting cheeks at one art opening or high-profile birthday party than logging a week's worth of desk time, he stopped going out. When he imagined himself surrounded by people, his throat closed up and he gasped for air.

◄ ● ►

About three weeks after the mugging, his fear had morphed into aimless bouts of rage. As he began to realize the mugger was not going to be caught, Rick was consumed by hatred for him, for pointing a gun at people instead of getting a job like a decent human being. Kids grew up in this city thinking guns were normal, if not necessary. The system was fucked beyond belief. But that didn't let this shit kid off the hook.

He found himself shouting at his assistant until she cried, and he picked a fight with another wealth-management guy down the hall, a lone wolf like himself who hunted for business at cocktail parties. When a high-maintenance Very High Net Worth Individual pulled her investments and gave them to a known slimeball, he chucked his wireless mouse against the wall, sending the battery flying.

He made the mistake of telling Pepper about those incidents. "I think you should see a trauma counselor," she said, lying on the sofa with a cup of mint tea, reading an accounting textbook to prepare for her new role as co-op president. It was great that she'd won the election—she cared about helping their neighbors in a way he never would—but between that and the event planning, he wondered if she needed to cut back. She was showing her typical signs of depression, too—staying inside, leaving dishes everywhere, napping on the floor—and he feared it was a chemical reaction to his anger. He needed to calm down, for both their sakes. He didn't want to let his anger ruin their newfound détente.

"I don't know if I'm ready to be alone in a room with a stranger," he replied. She had been pushing for him to see an individual therapist for God knew how long, but he didn't understand why they couldn't talk about the mugging together with Dr. Dixon. Just four sessions together had gotten them to finally be honest with each other, and then, the second they had a breakthrough, she refused to go back—as if she wanted their marriage to end. It pissed him off when he thought about it, so he clung to the gratitude he'd felt for her in the days after the mugging and tried not to dwell on his irritation. "I'd go back to Dr. Dixon with you, though."

She looked away. "You don't need me there for this."

"But I want you there. You were so helpful after the mugging. I really think you could be the key to my recovery."

"Just see your own therapist," she said, closing the textbook with a pop.

"Hey. What's with the rudeness?"

"I'm sorry, I don't mean to be rude. I just . . . I think trauma counseling is completely different from couples therapy. You need someone who specializes in it."

"I want to work through it together. With Dr. Dixon."

She closed her eyes. "First I think we should work on our stuff separately."

He felt himself getting annoyed again. She could be as chilly and forbidding as a glacier. He imagined himself physically pushing all his anger into his feet, then flicked his toes until it was gone. "All right. I'll see somebody myself."

"Thank you."

He kissed her, and she kissed back, and still the moment seemed to be holding its breath.

◀ ⬢ ▶

Dr. Dixon recommended a hoary Freudian who pronounced the first syllable of "trauma" like in "trousers" and could barely keep his eyes open while Rick narrated the mugging. His patent unfriendliness notwithstanding, Rick would have stuck around more than three sessions if he felt he could be cured by that therapist. They did figure out one important thing: Rick's anger stemmed from his masculinity being compromised, and from feeling powerless when he had devoted his entire life to accumulating power. But knowing these things didn't help him. The upset was in his body; he had to expunge it through action, not words.

Meanwhile, he posted about it on Facebook, asking what any fellow muggees had done to move on. Two friends had been mugged, and though they were afraid to be alone outside for months, eventually they moved on. For the sake of his marriage, Rick couldn't wait that long, and besides, his rage was getting worse. He'd been leaving messages for Detective Rojas every other day, fearing that his case had been forgotten. He lay awake every night for an hour or two, wanting to break something. It felt like a physical illness.

He also googled ways people had gotten over their muggings. A few people had written about returning to the scene of the crime with a friend, to experience their fears from a place of security. One guy had found peace by reenacting the mugging at the scene—he'd asked a friend to play the mugger—and telling the guy how being mugged had made him feel. A reenactment sounded too fake to work, but Rick did walk to the spot where he'd been mugged. During the day, it didn't feel like the same place. He wasn't going back there at night, not even with a friend.

He tried boxing. He went to a shooting range. He screamed into his pillow.

Thinking that relaxation, not violence, might help, he booked a few days in an oceanfront villa in Bermuda; as it was midweek and off-season, the rates were surprisingly cheap. He and Pepper got a couple's massage and rode horses on the famed pink-sand beach, which, he was disappointed to discover, was closer to peach-colored and the texture of driveway salt. They ordered room service and feasted on spicy fish chowder and buttered spiny lobster tails, swam naked in their private pool, made love and slept ten hours a night without interruption. He began to feel better about the mugging and more hopeful about their marriage.

On their last morning in Bermuda, over a breakfast of eggs Benedict and mimosas in bed, Detective Rojas called.

Pepper, chewing on a bite of toast with marmalade, put down her gossip magazine and asked a question with her face. Rick held up a dilatory finger, wriggled out of bed, and walked out to the private pool deck.

"I'll keep it short," the detective said. "Our guys have been on the lookout for your mugger. We've devoted a lot of time to searching for this guy. We got no leads. I'm sorry to say it's a dead case."

"So that's it? You're just going to give up?" He felt his chances of retribution slipping away.

"Mr. Hunter, I've got five homicides on my desk as we speak. Your textbook mugging—we would have let it go a long time ago if your wife's old man hadn't been pulling strings. So if you don't mind, I would appreciate it if you stopped calling and let us do the job we're paid to do."

"Keep up the good work, detective," Rick said. "Another case cracked by New York's finest."

"There's nothing more we can do at this point, sir." The detective hung up.

Consumed by rage, Rick kicked a lounge chair into the pool and chucked his phone as far as he could. "Fuck!" he shouted. A bellhop in a white windbreaker and pink shorts, emerging from an adjacent villa, met his eyes and dashed away.

Pepper opened the sliding glass door and leaned her head outside. "You need to calm down."

"That fucking kid got away."

"Yeah, and another kid is probably getting life in prison for a crime he didn't commit. No one ever said there was justice in this world. But you need to relax. You got mugged. It was terrible. And now it's time to move on."

He didn't want her to dictate the timeline of his recovery. But he saw that she said it out of love. "I'm trying. I just don't know how."

She stepped outside, closed the sliding door behind her, and took him into her arms.

◄ ● ►

It was over in the way of most things, that is, nothing was resolved and he tried not to let it bother him.

During the days, he managed calmness. He could function at work, and he started making dinner for Pepper on nights when he got home at a reasonable hour. When he felt the anger coming on, he took a deep breath and pushed it down. His marriage to Pepper was the best thing in his life. He couldn't let the mugging infect it further.

But he still woke up at night, seething. He remembered how powerless he'd felt when the gun was pointed at him. Lying half awake, suspended for hours in that liminal state when thoughts become dreams, Rick couldn't prevent sickening scenarios from unspooling in his mind: Breaking the mugger's face with his fist. Pointing that gun at him and firing it. Pushing him down the embankment into the transverse road, and watching him get chewed up in the wheels of a truck. He loathed these visions, yet they were his only relief.

◄ ● ►

He found himself thinking about the guy online who had reenacted his mugging. It was a little dumb, but it wasn't crazy, right? It seemed like something a TV psychologist might arrange. Having run out of ideas, the least he could do was try.

A quick internet search unearthed the red embossed jacket, on sale at Target for a hundred dollars. He bought a size medium for overnight delivery, along with a black knitted face mask. He decided against buying a handgun, as he didn't want to break any laws—or get himself killed. A fake gun would be ridiculous, though.

Now he just needed someone to play the mugger, preferably a young, light-skinned black man. There was a junior analyst at work who might do it, but Rick didn't want anyone at work to know he'd been mugged. Otherwise, he didn't know any black men in their late teens or early twenties. After the Molly debacle, he knew better than to find one on the internet.

He'd been pondering this matter for a few days when, on his way to work, he passed Caleb in the lobby, vacuuming a rug. He knew better than to hire a building staffer for this possibly humiliating pursuit, but maybe Caleb knew someone who was hard up for cash.

"Hey, Caleb my man," Rick said, and the porter switched off the vacuum cleaner and locked it upright. "How you been? That was great news about Sergei—my wife told me. Congratulations!"

"Thank you, sir. I mean, we're not engaged or anything."

"No, I just meant, congrats on finding each other. It's hard to find love in this city. How long you been together?"

"About a year. We're planning on moving in together, as soon as we can find a place."

"Great! Great. Hey, listen, do you have any friends who are actors? I'm looking for a guy about your age for a little acting job." He hoped Caleb understood that he wanted the guy to be black. "The pay's really good. It would just take an hour, tops."

"What kind of acting?"

"I need someone to role-play a situation. It might get a little physical, but the actor would be safe."

"Oh," Caleb said, widening his eyes, and Rick wondered if his request had seemed lewd.

"Like a tussle. In Central Park. It wouldn't have to be an actor, just someone who has an hour to kill and wants to earn some cash." It still sounded perverted.

Caleb looked down at the vacuum cleaner while another shareholder walked by. "How much is the pay, if you don't mind my asking?" he mumbled.

"A couple hundred bucks."

"I'd do it. I mean, could I do it?"

He hadn't expected Caleb to volunteer; then again, that was probably a lot of money for a porter. Rick would have preferred a stranger, but the mask and jacket might be an adequate disguise. Anyway, Caleb didn't report to him, and they barely saw each other in the building. Even if things became awkward between them, they'd get over it.

"Sure, you could do it," Rick said, with a pat on Caleb's shoulder.

◄●►

Rather than try to find a time when Pepper wouldn't be home—he sensed she wouldn't approve of this experiment—Rick met Caleb in a tourist-infested café near his office that evening. Rick ordered a small coffee and a Paleo bar, Caleb, a peppermint cappuccino and cranberry biscotto, and Rick's eyes widened when the bill came to nineteen dollars. A boss had once told him that he had become much happier when he stopped getting upset about money in amounts less than twenty dollars. Even though Rick spent thousands without blinking, he had never been able to relax about wasted money of any amount. Maybe that was one reason he'd been upset over the mugging, which only set him back a few hundred bucks but was costing him a few thousand—the therapist, the gun range, the vacation, and now this— in trying to repair it.

At a tiny round table in the back, he and Caleb attempted small talk. It wasn't easy. Rick wasn't great at chatting up men; with women, he could let his eyes do the work.

"Where are you and Sergei moving?" Rick asked. Everybody liked to talk about neighborhoods and real estate.

"We were looking in the Bronx on the four, five, and six lines," Caleb said, glancing around as though worried someone would catch them sitting together. Rick didn't think what they were doing was against building rules. A lot of the guys did odd jobs like painting or washing windows for a little extra cash.

Caleb waxed poetic about a two-bedroom in Parkchester with a big tree out the window and a dishwasher. Unfortunately, Caleb said, they were a few hundred dollars short of the six grand they needed for first month's rent, security deposit, and broker's fee. That surprised Rick, because they each must have cleared a few thousand from their holiday tips. Caleb said his young nephew had had some kind of seizure and needed medical testing; the boy was fine, but his brother and sister-in-law hadn't realized the tests weren't covered by insurance, and the bill came to almost four thousand. Caleb's brother could barely afford living expenses for his family, so Caleb paid it. And much of Sergei's bonus went toward some high-interest credit-card debt that had snuck up on him. Caleb said that they would probably be able to afford the new place in a few months, but he had to evacuate his parents' apartment by March first—less than a month away. Moving in with Sergei apparently wasn't an option.

Rick suspected all this detail was an attempt to convince him to let Caleb have the acting job. Maybe Caleb was trying to convince himself. "Sounds like you and I play the same role in our families," Rick said. "The money man."

Caleb poked his biscotto into his foamy drink and smiled. He was a sweet kid; Rick could see why Pepper liked him so much. "It's hard when there isn't enough."

"And we're the only ones who treat it with respect," said Rick, trying to encourage alliance. "We know you can't just expect money to be there when you want it. You have to work for it, and spend wisely."

Caleb gulped his cappuccino.

"So listen, here's what I'm looking for. Now, I know it's going to sound a little weird, but bear with me. Basically, in a nutshell, I want you to pretend to mug me in Central Park."

Caleb smiled quizzically. "I was under the impression . . . I didn't realize . . . I guess I thought I'd be acting with somebody else."

Rick supposed it would be strange to do this with a staff member. "You don't have a friend who can do it? Maybe it'd be better if it were somebody I didn't know."

"I could ask. How much are you offering again?"

"Five hundred dollars," Rick had decided. He watched as Caleb digested the figure. Everyone had a price.

"I guess I could do it." He looked troubled.

"Great. I have a jacket and face mask for you to wear. You'll need to bring a threatening-looking knife, like a switchblade or something. I'll tell you when and where to wait. When I come by, you'll order me to hand over my wallet and phone, and I won't give it to you. I'll probably tell you off. Maybe I'll push you a little, but I promise I won't hurt you. Just don't stab me, okay?"

A man, pushing a stroller back and forth while waiting for a table, eyed their empty mugs. Rick glared at him, and he looked elsewhere.

"Sorry—I'm still confused," Caleb said. "Is this going to be videotaped?"

"No. No one will be around."

"So then why . . . ? If you don't mind my asking."

"It's like a therapy thing."

"Ah." He nodded a little too long, which made it clear how poorly he understood the concept.

"You still want to do it?" Rick asked. "I understand if you want to find someone else, but if you're in, you gotta be in."

"No, I can do it," Caleb said, very seriously. "Just one thing: Can you write and sign a letter that says you asked me to do this? It's just, if anyone sees me doing it, I don't want to be arrested or anything like that."

"Don't worry, no one will see you. But if someone does, I'll tell them it isn't real."

"Still, if you don't mind."

"Sure, absolutely. Monday at nine P.M.?"

Rick stood up and shook Caleb's hand. "Pleasure doing business with you."

◄●►

Rick hustled along the bridle path just south of the Central Park reservoir. The snowbanks on both sides glowed in the moonlight, brightening his surroundings a bit too much. Thinking that a full bladder and a light buzz would help with the verisimilitude, he'd downed a few glasses of Johnnie Black at a bar on Columbus Avenue, not far from the Museum of Natural History, before heading into the park.

He veered off the path, careful not to slip, and stopped in front of the retaining wall that separated the park from the road. All he heard was the rush of cars. He looked around. No one. Ten minutes passed. Still no one.

Now he was annoyed. Maybe Caleb had balked after seeing how close they were to the police station. At least he hadn't paid him in advance.

Why hadn't he tried another therapist instead of this crazy scheme? Maybe because it was so emasculating, all this therapy. He didn't mind the couple's therapist, but if Pepper had her way, he'd have an analyst and a trauma counselor and probably a guru and a life coach. How had people dealt with their shit before Freud? They sucked it up and went on with life.

He angled himself away from the road and unzipped in front of a sad excuse for a tree, more like a sapling with big ambitions. He soaked the tree, then signed his initials in the snow. He was actually relieved that he didn't have to go through with it, though he couldn't help thinking of the parallels with his coitus interruptus with Molly. He'd been glad to ditch her at the time—and his marriage was better for it—but now he felt like someone who didn't follow through on his plans, at least those that he'd arranged for his mental health.

As he shook himself off, he felt something sharp in the small of his back. Someone was behind him. His body lurched with the memory of the smooth round nose of the pistol.

"Don't move until I tell you," came an unrecognizable growl. It didn't sound like Caleb at all. He must have found a friend to step in. "You're going to lie facedown real slow."

Rick moved his hands to zip his pants, but the mugger hissed, "Hands above your head or I stab you."

He lifted his arms and knelt down. His thoughts swarmed, and he fought to steady his mind. He knew he should spin around and grab the knife, but he wanted a cleaner opportunity. He didn't want to risk being stabbed, even if the mugger was trying not to. He didn't know what Caleb had or had not told this guy. "Can I move a little away so I don't have to lie in my piss?"

"Down!" A foot on his lower back, and Rick was facedown, piss and melted snow soaking into his wool coat and jeans.

The mugger's knee was pushing down on his mid-spine, and his hands were rifling through Rick's pockets. Through his fear, Rick was impressed—this guy was good.

The mugger snatched Rick's wallet from his coat pocket and his phone from his pants. Rick was running out of time: if he didn't do something, he would miss his opportunity.

With all his strength, he jerked up to all fours, knocking the guy off him, then jumped up and spun around. Fighting a momentary dizziness, he grasped that his wallet and phone were in the snow, and the mugger, wearing the red jacket and the face mask, was pointing the knife at him. A serrated knife. Rick nearly laughed. He was being mugged with a bread knife.

But otherwise, this felt right. This felt real. Headlights from the road blinded him as they passed, and the underbrush scratched at his benumbed hands. The mugger looked taller than him, but Rick was very strong. Blazing with adrenaline, feeling the throb of hot blood in his limbs, he leaped forward and grabbed the mugger's arm, then wrenched the knife out of his hand and threw it aside. Rick pushed him onto the ground and, ceding his willpower to his animal brain, pinned him. His knees were on the kid's thighs, his hands gripping his upper arms. He was in control.

He'd thought it might be enough to disarm the mugger and reclaim his valuables, but now he felt compelled to speak. The mugger had threatened his life and taken his dignity; Rick finally had the chance to take it back.

"You stole from me," Rick said, staring into the mugger's fearful eyes, able to speak as if it weren't a reenactment. "You humiliated me. You think it's a game to ruin other people's lives, you selfish piece of shit? You thought you could take from me, but you failed. You're nothing. It's my money and I make the rules. You do what I say now. You don't get a say. You do what I say." The mugger had stopped squirming; he was wide-eyed and unblinking. Rick closed his eyes, letting the sense of triumph cleanse him. This was exactly what he needed.

Finally, Rick hopped up, zipped his pants, and brushed the snow off his arms and legs. He paced in the snow, trying to calm down. He was still flooded with vitality; he wanted to use his body again. He was going to give Pepper the night of her life.

The mugger was still lying supine in the snow. When Rick's heartbeat had slowed and the cold burn in his throat subsided, he extended a hand to help him up. "That was perfect," he gasped, in between breaths. "You were so convincing. I can't thank you enough."

Instead of taking Rick's hand, the mugger scooted back through the snow and grabbed a tree to pull himself up. He peeled off his mask. It was Caleb after all. He stared into space, his lips parted. He looked hollowed out.

"Caleb!" Rick exclaimed. "My hero! Are you okay, man?" What he could remember of his tirade must have been terrible to hear. "I'm sorry if I scared you—I didn't really know what I was going to do. It was just role-playing— it wasn't about you at all. See, I was mugged in this spot in December, and I had this hunch that if I could just, you know, gain some mastery over the incident, I could finally feel like myself again." He grabbed his wallet and phone off the ground, counted out five hundred-dollar bills, and gave them to Caleb, who seemed too stunned to put them in his pocket.

Rick put a hand on Caleb's shoulder. It was unfortunate how much he'd scared Caleb; if he only could understand how helpful he'd been, maybe he could forgive Rick. "Was that worse than you were expecting? I didn't realize I was going to need to say all that. Here, let me give you a little more." He pinched a thick stack of twenties from his wallet and handed them over. Once Caleb got over the shock of their little encounter, the seven or eight hundred dollars in his pocket would surely bring him back to life. He'd get to move in with his lover, all for a few minutes of work. It seemed like a good deal. When Rick was first in New York, sneaking a flask into bars and buying the cheap toilet paper, he would have taken this gig and been glad for it. "Let's get you in a cab."

Caleb nodded. He put all the money in his pants pocket. He wouldn't look at Rick.

"You're okay, bud. Everything's okay." Rick took Caleb's limp arm, then thought better of it. Maybe he didn't want to be touched.

17

THE TRUTH

Pepper had lined up printouts of the building's finances over the past five years on the coffee table, in hopes of understanding what line items had changed and what expenses might come back to surprise her. Ardith knew the basics of communicating with the managing agent and creating an agenda for the board meetings but was a little fuzzy on all the different ways money was spent. As treasurer, Dougie could answer her questions in this realm, but, preferring not to be mentally undressed more than necessary, she decided to figure it out on her own.

Someone knocked on the door. Maybe it was Birdie, who had promised Pepper a stack of *Gourmet* magazine back issues as part of a purge that she would not admit had anything to do with the possibility of moving out. Had Ardith not told everyone about Birdie's plans at the last board meeting, she wouldn't have known; she assumed the Montreal move she'd overheard through the hole had been a dashed fantasy. Pepper looked through the door viewer out to the landing, wondering why her neighbor hadn't simply rung the doorbell, when she realized that the knock had come from the staff entrance off the cramped bedroom that had once been a maid's room.

Indeed, Caleb was standing by the freight elevator, looking nervous and fidgeting with a stuffed letter-size envelope as if it were too hot to hold. It was a little after four; his shift had just ended.

"Hi, there," she said. "What's going on?"

"I'm very sorry to bother you, Mrs. Hunter, but is Mr. Hunter home?" he asked, staring at the envelope.

"I'm sorry, he's at work."

"Do you know when he'll be home? I can come back."

Oddly, Rick hadn't texted or called once that day. He'd come home late the previous night. Usually, he was a meticulous lover, making sure she was fully cared for at each rung in the ladder of her arousal, but that night, the second she gave her consent, he threw her on the bed, unzipped, pulled her underwear to the side, and started thrusting, fully dressed. At first she'd been a little afraid, and then she caught whatever had gotten him fired up, and twenty minutes later, she climaxed so powerfully she feared her organs might burst. She'd never undressed *after* sex before.

"I honestly don't know," she said. "He doesn't get home until seven at the earliest. Tonight it could be later. Can I help?"

Caleb seemed disappointed. He studied the envelope in his hand and, after some consideration, gave it to her. "Would you make sure he gets this?"

She shouldn't have looked inside, but it wasn't sealed, nor was it addressed to him. It was cash, a lot of it. Though she dared not guess the specifics, Rick must have misbehaved. "I'm sorry, but where did this come from? Why are you giving it to him?"

"He gave it to me. I'm giving it back."

"Why did he give it to you?"

He bit his lip and gripped one fist with the other hand. "I promised I wouldn't say. I'm sorry."

She was flooded with reflexive dread. She said, with her best attempt at a friendly smile, "That's fair. You know as well as I do how much people in this building love their gossip. But will you tell me if he did something I should be concerned about?"

The tension in Caleb's face gave him away. What was the opposite of a poker face? A charades face? "No, ma'am," he said. Then he nodded good-bye and pressed the elevator button. As the doors opened, it occurred to Pepper that he might be in real distress.

"Are you all right?" she asked. "Is there any way I can help? I'm a pretty good listener."

He stood in the doors, keeping them open. "No, thank you, Mrs. Hunter. I'm doing very well, thanks."

"And how's Sergei? You guys getting along okay?"

He smiled, briefly seeming to shake off his upset. "Very well, thanks. We're moving in together."

"That's great news! Where's the apartment?"

"In Parkchester." He seemed disappointed as he said, "I'm not sure we can afford it."

"Where is that?"

He pointed upward. "In the Bronx. On the six."

"Well, I hope you get it."

He thanked her again, stepped into the elevator cab, and let the doors close.

She tossed the envelope onto the coffee table and tried to focus on the financial reports, thinking about how uncertain Caleb had been of handing her that money and the torn look on his face when she asked if Rick had done something wrong. Maybe she wouldn't have predicted the worst had Rick not already proven himself to be untrustworthy, with Molly, or if he hadn't been acting so crazy. She understood that he'd been through a trauma, and she was trying to be supportive, but she was beginning to think his skyrocketing anxiety had less to do with the mugging and more to do with the secret, wild part of him that terrified her.

And now this, whatever it was. Maybe he'd asked Caleb to hire him a prostitute, or maybe Caleb had seen Rick misbehaving with a woman, and this was hush money. Then her thoughts diffracted into a thousand worries: he could have done anything. She'd known him for two years, and she barely knew him at all. The Petersons, the couple who had lived in their apartment before they did, had been married ten years before the wife found out that her husband was living a double life with another woman. Pepper had been mystified as to how neither of Roland Peterson's lovers had suspected him, but now she understood: they'd known. They'd known and hadn't wanted to know.

She pulled out her phone and sent Rick a neutral text: "How's your day? When do you think you'll be home?" A few minutes passed, and he didn't respond, so she called. It went straight to voice mail.

She tried Katt and wasn't surprised when her phone also went to voice mail. Katt was now among the top ten brokers in the city and hardly ever took Pepper's calls.

It seemed unfair to tell anyone in the building, including Birdie or Francis, not only because Rick saw them all the time but also because it might affect Caleb's job. She thought better of calling her sister. The last time she'd called, Maisie had her hands full with a screaming Ashwin, and Pepper came away feeling judged for having so little on her plate. She certainly wasn't going to call her mother: she didn't want Claudia to have to suppress her delight in guessing Rick's latest indiscretion. So she speed-dialed her father at work.

"Pepperoni! To what do I owe the pleasure?"

"Daddy—do you have a minute to talk? Something is going on with Rick, and I . . ." She had no idea where that sentence was headed, but it didn't matter, because she knew if she didn't stop, she would cry.

◄●►

Half an hour later, she was in his wintry arms in her foyer, breathing in his pine-scented cologne and coffee breath. He chose a Pinot Noir from the top, least expensive row of Rick's formidable wine cabinet, and she microwaved a bag of popcorn and mixed in a few dark-chocolate peanut butter cups. They nibbled and drank in the kitchen, sitting at the tulip table, which Pepper had recently painted neon orange, thinking it might cheer her up. She hoped her father didn't notice that the paint job was uneven. High-gloss enamel kept no secrets.

"So what's going on?" he asked.

She didn't quite know what to tell him. She didn't want to stir up a cloud of suspicion if Rick hadn't done anything wrong. At the same time, she knew he had. "One of the porters here handed me seven hundred and sixty dollars, which he said was for Rick. And I'm worried that . . ." She composed herself and said into the transparent cavern of her wineglass, "I'm worried that he's done something unforgivable."

"What do you think he did?" Lewis asked.

"I don't know," she said, afraid that speaking her fears would make them real. "But I can't think of a single reason why a porter would give Rick all that money."

"You really can't know until you ask him."

"So why am I so afraid of asking him?"

The dishwasher finished its cycle, and the kitchen fell silent. It was strange in New York not to hear anything at all. It seemed as if the room were floating in space. Then the refrigerator began to whirr, and footsteps thumped above them, and the city resumed its onslaught.

"Do you guys, you know, talk?" he asked.

Maybe it was the momentary quiet or the wine or the absence of her mother or his kindness in an awful situation, but she felt porous and wanted to tell him things, not just the stagnant pleasantries she'd doled out to her parents since college. Her parents kept secrets and called it propriety; it had taken being married to Rick to see how much destruction her secrecy caused.

"We didn't at first," she said. "Then it got better. Then worse. We did couple's therapy. We probably should go back. It's been hard, I guess."

"Marriage is hard."

She tried looking him in the eye but couldn't. "I feel like you have every right to say 'I told you so.' I know you and Mommy saw his faults before I did. I was being stubborn. We really could have waited to get married."

"Do you want to move back home?" he asked.

It was tempting, the idea that she could escape her marriage and cocoon herself in the safety of childhood, but she was finally getting a foothold in the building—she was president of the co-op, for Christ's sake—and leaving would undo everything. She had to at least try to be an adult. "Thank you, but I need to stay here."

"I know Mommy would love to have you."

It used to make her angry that they still called each other Mommy and Daddy and that they presumed to speak for each other a decade after their divorce. Now it felt sad, as though they weren't strong enough to move on. "Why did you two break up? I mean, not the glib answer."

He massaged one palm with his thumb while she waited for the rebuff. "We did it because . . . because I wanted freedom, and your mother didn't want me to have it."

She was struck by his honesty. Not only was it a real answer, but it also sounded accusatory, which pleased her, because they'd led her to believe that their divorce had been bloodless—needless, even. She'd thought no one else in her family knew resentment.

"What do you mean by 'freedom'? You don't mean, like, affairs . . ."

He shrugged. "A bunch of things, but that was part of it."

It would have been easy to play the scandalized daughter, to turn away from her father's honesty and teach him that she didn't want it. But she had been hungry for any scrap of truth about her parents' lives since she was a child. She hoped she was strong enough to hear it.

"So you threw away thirty years of marriage for sex?" she asked. It was appalling, yet she could imagine Rick doing the same thing.

"No, it wasn't . . . I didn't throw away anything," he said, and she feared she had gone too far. "We were married thirty years—we still have that. It didn't go away. And it wasn't really about the sex. It was love. I didn't love her anymore."

"When? When did you fall out of love?" Her parents had seemed sturdy, primordial; she hadn't imagined their love could decay. But Birdie and George's had, too, maybe Francis's, maybe Patricia's. It was a cliché that love was the most powerful force in the world, but in truth, the stuff seemed awfully fragile.

"It didn't happen overnight. But when two people are chained together for decades, it creates an awful lot of resentment, and it takes constant work to keep love going. People get tired, Pepper."

"Tired?"

"Of having the same fights over and over again. Of wanting things from your partner and not getting them. Of reaching compromises that don't make either of you happy. Of working through something and then realizing you were back where you started."

That described her marriage with Rick, less than a year in. She remembered Dr. Dixon talking about the couple he'd seen every week for ten years. At the time she'd been shocked that they still had something to argue about after five hundred sessions, but now it made perfect sense. There were the old arguments and the new ones, and every resolution was temporary. She wanted to believe it was worth it. Maybe it could be, if they could get through this rough patch. But so far, their marriage had been nothing but rough patches.

"I think I stopped loving her pretty early on. I've always liked her—she still makes me laugh—but we kept our distance, emotionally. We almost broke up a number of times while you girls were growing up," Lewis continued. "We stayed together because we wanted to give you a stable home."

Maybe the icy distance she'd always sensed between her parents was not decorum but the absence of love.

"After Maisie went off to college," he continued, "your mother and I were alone in that apartment for the first time in twenty years, listening to the clock tick, and it was like I had woken up from a long sleep. Suddenly I couldn't stand to be tied to her another minute. I told her I'd stay if she'd let me date on the side, and she said no."

"I think I'd say no to that, too."

He shrugged, as if fidelity were a matter of taste.

"I guess I just feel like I shouldn't, you know, leave Rick," she said. "Like the whole world is going to see that I failed."

He swirled his mostly empty glass. "Claudia was terrified of what her friends would think when she announced her divorce. Not only did no one bat an eye, but, lo and behold, a few weeks later, her most till-death-do-us-part girlfriend propositioned me at the fish counter at Citarella." He pointed at her, and she worried for a split second that he was going to ground her. "Don't tell your mother."

She laughed. "You said no, I hope."

He smiled, deepening his dimples. "She wasn't my type."

They changed the subject, and Lewis shared news about their family: her grandmother finally gave up her driver's license after her third fender bender in six months; Claudia won third place in a flower-arranging contest at the botanical garden; Ashwin was going to have minor surgery to fix his frequent ear infections. She told him about the co-op board and her new event-planning business.

Soon they had finished the bottle, and the popcorn bowl was empty except for some greasy unpopped kernels in the bottom and smears of chocolate along the sides. She wanted to extend the moment with another bottle but didn't want to be drunk when Rick came home. She hoped he was okay. She rinsed the dishes and left them in the sink. Her father sensed that it was time to go.

They stood by the door and hugged. "Good night, Pepper."

While he figured out which of their door locks to unlock, another question came to her.

"Wait, Daddy, there's something else I wanted to ask."

"Yeah?"

"I'm sorry, but when I was a kid, I have this memory. . . . You started locking your bedroom door at night, and I slept outside, hoping you would open the door and invite me in."

"We locked our door? I don't remember that."

It didn't seem possible. But she didn't think he'd lie to her to protect his marital secrets, not tonight. "I used to sleep in the bed with you and Mommy, and then one night you weren't there, and the next night, the door was locked. You really don't remember locking me out?" She glanced up at him.

He smiled disarmingly, the way Rick did when he was poking fun at her. "How could I remember it if I wasn't there?"

"Right, but you don't remember locking the door *after* that?" Dr. Riffler said that childhood memories were distorted by emotion, but she couldn't believe she had made up something that had happened multiple times when she was ten or eleven years old, something she remembered physically. She could still feel the doorknob, cold in her hands, and its refusal to budge.

"Sometimes your mother made me sleep on the couch, and I remember that you liked sleeping in the hallway. I'm sure we locked the door when we were, you know, intimate. But most of the time we left it unlocked. I'm positive."

She saw that he was telling the truth. Had The Locked Door, the central conflict of her life, been unlocked all along? After witnessing evidence of a marital rift, she must not have tried to open it. It was easier to believe that they had locked it than to risk walking in on that secret again. "You probably thought I was pretty weird, sleeping in the hallway."

"We were touched by it. We thought you were trying to protect us from intruders."

"I think I was trying to protect myself."

◀●▶

Pepper was finding moderate success in distraction via a TV police procedural when she got a text from Rick: "Just seeing this now! Almost home. Love u!" Soon, a key turned in the lock and Rick bounded into the room, his shoes dangling on two fingers, and kissed her on the lips.

"I had the best day," he said. "I was in the zone for like ten hours straight. I haven't gotten that much work done since college." No wonder he hadn't answered his phone.

She wore a sly, amused expression. "I had an interesting day, too."

"I'm just feeling so *good* right now." Finally her irritation registered in his face. "Hold that thought." She watched him clean the salt and dirt off his shoes with a disposable wipe before heading into the bedroom to put them away. His joyous energy did not reassure her.

He returned to the living room, wearing a Smashing Pumpkins concert T-shirt and pajama bottoms and holding a lowball glass containing an absurd quantity of Scotch. He sat on the light-blue linen-upholstered sofa and enjoyed a plentiful sip.

"Okay, what's up?"

"Do you know who owned our apartment before we did?"

He seemed to tread carefully when he said, "Yeah."

"Deirdre Peterson, right? And do you know why she was in the news?"

"I do . . ."

"Why didn't you tell me?"

"And this is relevant how?"

"I don't know. I'd wondered for a while if you knew, and I never asked, I think because I was afraid you did. It helps me understand something about you." She crossed her legs, the hem of her kimono falling on either side. She noticed him eyeing her bare thighs and wished she'd changed into pants. "So Caleb gave me an envelope with seven hundred and sixty dollars in it."

He seemed confused. "What did he say?"

She narrowed her eyes. "Why do I feel like you're trying to figure out how much of something awful to tell me?"

He stared into his Scotch and took a gulp, then exhaled noisily. "I might have done something unkind."

She closed her eyes and breathed. Her instincts had been right. Had she not talked to her father an hour earlier, she might have snapped at him. "What did you do?"

"Does it make a difference that I thought I was doing something good?"

She looked up at him. "Just tell me what it was."

He proceeded to tell her a story so preposterous, she wasn't sure if she understood. He'd paid Caleb to pretend to mug him? And Rick had turned around and pinned him on the ground and yelled at him?

"I know," Rick said, seeing her bewilderment, "it's weird, right? But here's the thing: I haven't felt this good in months. I think I just needed to be on top for like one minute to reverse what that mugger did. I needed to feel like I was in control, you know?"

"What did you say to him?" She could hear her icy, vindictive tone and did nothing to soften it.

"I don't remember everything—I was just saying things without thinking about them. I remember repeating, 'It's my money,' and 'You do what I say now.'"

She tried to imagine Caleb hearing this. Caleb, who almost definitely did not want to be barked at as if he were a servant or slave. No wonder he had been shaken. No wonder he gave back the money.

"Okay, okay," Pepper said, taking shallow breaths, "I guess I can understand why you did this. Sorry, let me rephrase that: I can imagine a future version of myself understanding why you did it. But what I don't understand is, why did you do it to someone who works for us?"

"I asked him to recommend someone else to do it," he said, defensively. "He's the one who wanted to do it himself. He wanted the money to put a deposit down on an apartment—I didn't force him into it."

She understood the necessity of money, especially in New York. But she wished that it meant less to Rick. "You should have said no. That was an abuse of your power."

Suddenly his manic energy turned into anger. "He's an adult. He can take responsibility for his actions."

"The same could be said of you."

He stood and jabbed a finger toward her. "I see what this is about. You're worried it's going to compromise your position overseeing the nabobs. If he didn't tell you, I highly doubt he'll tell anyone else." He paced the room.

After her breakthrough with Dr. Riffler and her eye-opening talk with her father, the idea of keeping a secret, especially one so nefarious, revolted her. "I hope he tells everyone, if it'll help. I'd resign tomorrow if that could make one iota of difference. You did something disgusting, and the sickest thing is, you don't realize how bad it is."

"Then tell me. Help me understand." He lifted his glass to her, sloshing liquor onto his fingers.

"You scared the living shit out of our staff member. You pinned a black man to the ground and basically told him you owned him. Need I say more?"

"I didn't tell him— Fine, I get it. Jesus."

"I honestly don't think you do."

"What do you want me to say? I'm sorry. I'm a terrible person. Or are apologies not good enough for you?"

"I'm not the one you should apologize to." She stood, feeling almost noble in her indignation. "I'd like you to sleep in the guest room tonight."

"Fine, on one condition. We go back into therapy with Dr. Dixon."

She saw that she could put it off no longer. If she wanted to be married to Rick—and that was a big "if"—she had to agree to this. Maybe she was ready to hear the rest of his secrets. "Fine." She strode into the bedroom, locked the door behind her, and lay on the bed, trying not to let Rick hear her cry.

◄ ● ►

Before their couple's therapy session, Pepper and Rick ate at the hole-in-the-wall noodle shop in Chinatown where he had sometimes taken her during his lunch breaks, back when he worked on Wall Street. She would never have ventured inside this place without Rick. Golden-lacquered Peking ducks hung by the neck in the window, their heads bowed toward a plump chef drawing tins of dumplings from a steaming pot. When Rick first lived in New York after graduating from Princeton, working fifteen-hour days as a securities analyst, he ate at this dingy spot because he could get beef chow fun for five dollars (give or take: there seemed to be no set price). As a couple, they shared each other's memories, and she developed a fondness for this restaurant, a feeling that existed peaceably alongside her disgust at the dirty floor and the stink of rotting trash on the sidewalk. They had resumed civil relations, though she asked that they sleep separately until after meeting with Dr. Dixon, and Rick had been working so much she hardly saw him. Watching him eat in silence, she realized that if she decided to leave him, she probably would never eat here again: it would make her too sad. So she gorged on the wide, chewy noodles, eating well past feeling full, bidding farewell to this joy that she had borrowed from him and was not quite ready to give back.

They arrived at Dr. Dixon's office a few minutes early and waited in the hallway like students outside the principal's office, communicating with raised eyebrows and grins. Pepper found herself giggling in spite of her frustration with him.

Dr. Dixon opened the door a few seconds after one o'clock. It was comforting to return to the long, narrow office where she and Rick had made progress toward each other, its black-painted wood floors, its indigo batik rug making a sort of living room of the armchairs, its curved brass floor lamp standing like a hunchback in the corner. She wondered why she'd so resisted coming back.

The modular armchairs had been rearranged, and she wasn't brazen enough to push her chair closer to the window, in view of her beloved BONDS: GUARANTEED sign, the painted remnant of an earlier era on the building across the alley. It was like a good friend, always within reach, always positive, never judgmental. Now all she could see out the window was another window with its shades drawn.

"Welcome back," Dr. Dixon said. His legs were crossed, a yellow-and-blue argyle sock in view. She'd missed him. "So, tell me what's been going on."

She didn't know where to begin. "It's not great."

"It's kind of hard to explain," Rick said. He was sitting with his legs spread wide, which annoyed Pepper. She didn't want him to look confident right then.

"So I think I told you this when I asked you to recommend a trauma counselor, but I was mugged in December," Rick said, staring at his crossed hands. "At gunpoint."

Dr. Dixon's eyes widened. "You didn't tell me that."

"Well, I really thought I might die that night. For a few weeks, I was afraid all the time. After a while, whenever I felt afraid, I got really angry at the mugger for making me so scared. I wanted to kill that mugger with my bare hands. Our marriage was the one thing keeping me sane, so I tried really hard to keep my anger from hurting our relationship, you know?"

"How would your anger hurt your relationship?" Dr. Dixon asked.

"The mugging brought us together in this weird way. It was like we were reminded of how important we are to each other. But then I couldn't get over it, and that was pushing us apart. It was like all of my frustration was seeping out and making Pepper frustrated with me. And then she started to get depressed, and I felt like it was my fault, because I couldn't protect her from my anger."

He'd hinted at this theory in Bermuda. Even then it felt icky to her, as if she had no autonomy—or reason to be mad at him.

"I don't think you caused my depression," she said. "It's been going on much longer than I've known you."

"I know I didn't *cause* it," said Rick. "But I could feel it happening. I could feel you slipping. How do you explain that?"

"I don't know, maybe you're psychic? Or psychotic? You didn't do it to me."

Rick looked plaintively at Dr. Dixon, as if seeking protection from his bully of a wife. She didn't feel like being nice.

"Rick, what happened to you must have been harrowing. Being mugged is unspeakably awful. I am very sorry."

"Thanks," Rick said, with a tight-lipped smile. "So, long story short, I had this gut feeling that it might help if I reenacted the mugging but came out on top. It worked. It just got a little out of hand, and the guy I paid to be the mugger was kind of traumatized, I think."

Pepper didn't want Rick to get away with the sanitized version, so she added, "He tackled a staff member from our building. And he said some pretty horrific things to him." She didn't mention that Caleb was black, though it seemed relevant. Dr. Dixon probably sensed it.

"We'll have time to get your perspective, Penelope," Dr. Dixon said. "I think it's best if we go slow."

"Got it." She didn't like being silenced but was willing to play along for now.

"What did you say to this person?" asked Dr. Dixon.

"It was all kind of a blur," Rick said. "I was really scared, and when I pinned the guy, all I remember saying is, 'It's my money,' and 'You do what I say now.'"

"So you were taking your power back from the mugger."

Rick nodded. "Bingo. And it worked. Like, instantaneously."

At whose expense? Pepper thought.

"And how much time elapsed between the mugging and this reenactment?" Dr. Dixon pushed his wire-rimmed glasses up on his nose.

"About seven weeks," Rick said.

"That's a long time to be angry," Dr. Dixon said, with more kindness than Rick deserved, Pepper thought. "Penelope, how did it feel to see Rick so angry for so long?"

She could feel Rick looking at her, but she didn't want to make eye contact. "I felt terrible for him, and I tried to be there for him. After a few weeks, that became really difficult." She told Dr. Dixon about Rick's endless hours at work and how he'd yelled at his secretary and, in Bermuda, how he'd kicked the lounge chair into the pool.

"That's why I was trying to protect you from it," Rick said.

"It would have been better if you had just yelled at me," she said, "so we could talk about it."

"No, Pepper. You didn't want to talk about it. You wanted me to get over it by myself. I wanted us to do it together, with Dr. Dixon."

She was getting worked up. "I wanted you to do what everyone does when they get mugged, which is see someone who specializes in trauma."

"I have a hunch about something that I'd like to run by you," Dr. Dixon said, easing his calm voice back into the conversation. "Rick, did you feel any anger *at Penelope?*"

Rick looked surprised. "Me? No, of course not. It was always the mugger. You don't know how much he scared me when he pulled his gun on me."

"Anyone in that situation would have been left with a lot of very powerful and painful feelings. But are you sure you didn't feel any anger toward Penelope? For anything?"

Was he trying to catch Rick in a lie? Then Pepper began to understand his point. In their earlier sessions together, Rick had been angry with her about a litany of offenses: withholding affection, belittling him, resenting him, avoiding him. When he was mugged, all that vanished. In Dr. Riffler's words, *Feelings don't disappear.*

"I'm not sure what you're getting at, Dr. Dixon," Rick said.

Their therapist uncrossed his legs and sat back. "Let me put it this way. Imagine if someone said to you, very nicely, 'I'm trying not to be angry at you because I'm afraid my anger might cause you to suffer.' How would that make you feel?"

Rick's mouth opened into a perfect O, and his eyes darted about as if revisiting each memory of their interactions from this new understanding. Pepper saw it, too. She had assumed she was collateral damage from Rick's fury, not the target. And she'd hated that he thought his anger was dangerous to her; now she grasped why. Because on some level, he'd wanted to hurt her.

"I wouldn't take it literally," Dr. Dixon said. "But remind me what you said in your reenactment? Is that something you wanted to say to Pepper?"

"'It's my money. You do what I say now,'" Rick said again, nodding. "I guess I do feel like I should have a say because I support both of us. I feel like she spends my money and doesn't give me anything in return."

Pepper cringed. She hadn't thought their marriage was a transaction.

"Tell Pepper."

Rick stared at his knuckles as he cracked them. That too seemed angry. "I guess I've been pretty mad at you."

She nodded, bracing herself for a rundown of her mistakes. They had gotten out of the practice of nightly check-ins to talk about how they had pleased and disappointed each other that day.

He shifted in his chair. "I work really hard so that we can live in a nice apartment and do fun things together. I text you a lot during the day because I want to be in touch, and you barely ever get back to me. And when I walk in the door at night, you don't ask me about my day—you don't ask me about anything. It feels like you're sick of me and you don't want to know me."

You don't ask about what I'm going through, either, she wanted to say, but at the same time, he was right. She did want space from him.

"And we still only have sex about once a week. I'd understand it if we had young kids, or if we'd been married twenty years, but I still feel like I'm this great burden because I'm attracted to you."

"I like our sex life," she said, truthfully. She just didn't want it all the time. It certainly felt like more than once a week.

"And I know I should be able to get over this," Rick continued, "but I still can't forget that you told me you didn't love me."

It didn't seem fair for him to bring up things that he'd already complained about, things that she'd naively assumed they'd moved past. She'd tried to change; apparently it hadn't been enough. "I said that I didn't *know* if I loved you," she said, and he flinched. She put it more kindly. "I did love you. I still do. I was just so upset with you that I couldn't feel it."

"Well, for the record, I would never say that to you. It really sucks to hear that from the person you love more than anyone."

"I love you, okay?"

He crossed his arms and looked toward the front door, away from her.

"Pardon my interruption," Dr. Dixon said, "but Rick, you don't seem satisfied."

It annoyed her how high a value Dr. Dixon placed on Rick's satisfaction. At least he had stopped gunning for an open relationship like some perverted wingman. Or maybe that was still on the table. Maybe nothing was ever taken off the table.

"There's one other thing, and it was big for me," Rick said. "We made such great advances so fast in therapy, and just when it seemed like things were really going to work between us, you ended it. You wouldn't discuss it, you wouldn't compromise, nothing. End of story. It felt like—it still feels like you don't want to give me a chance. Like you don't want us to be happy."

He was right: the first breakthroughs had come fast, maybe too fast, and that had scared her. She wasn't ready to withstand any more reveals. With Rick, it could be anything: a fight with their porter, a Ponzi scheme, another wife in another city. His unpredictability had been thrilling when they met, but after more than two years together, she still didn't know him, and she didn't have the stamina to hear any more of his secrets. Dr. Riffler said secrecy was the opposite of intimacy, but intimacy with Rick had begun to feel like hyenas tearing at her flesh.

"I was furious about it," he said, "but I swallowed it and tried not to feel it. And maybe I didn't feel it for a while. And, yeah, now that I'm talking about it like this, I can see that when I pinned Caleb and said those things to him, a lot of what I was trying to release was my anger at you, for shutting down when I needed you to open up."

Of course I shut down: you were running around like a crazy person! How could he demand that she be open when it wasn't safe to confide in him?

"So you were thinking of me when you pinned him?" she asked, daring him to admit it.

"No, of course not. But you've got all these walls up all the time, and it makes it really hard to be in a relationship with you. What's crazy is, I think I fell in love with you because you were uncrackable. I thought I could break through to you, but you're still uncrackable, and I'm realizing that if you can't open up"—he looked down at the blue-and-white rug—"I can't do this anymore."

He might as well have slapped her. She was the one who was justified in leaving him, not the other way around. She hadn't put it together that she and Rick had both been aroused by secrecy.

She looked out the grimy window toward the tan brick wall. In a moment she might apologize for being secretive and promise to be more open with him. She had her list of demands, and she might be willing to compromise. But for now, she basked in the silence, letting both men wait for her response.

18

A GOOD WAY TO GO

"Valentine's Day is coming up, isn't it," Dr. Rothschild said as part of his appointment banter, a discussion of holidays, vacation plans, and the weather. "Are you and Carol doing anything to celebrate?" he asked without intonation, as though it were a thought he'd just had.

Francis displaced a crocheted pillow from a button-tufted chair and sat down. The pillow read BREATHE, YOU ARE ALIVE. Whatever bozo came up with that one must have meant, "If you're reading this, congratulations! You're not dead yet." He covered the message with his black knitted cap.

"Unfortunately, yes," Francis replied. "Carol made reservations at some trendy downtown restaurant that was written up in the *Times*. It's going to cost a fortune, and you can bet it's going to be mobbed. And as I'm sure you recall, my father died from eating in a restaurant."

The upcoming dinner plan was just one way Carol had been acting strangely. If he was critical of anything, from their inconsistent cleaning lady to a suspicious batch of ground chuck, she swooped in to contradict him. He suspected the culprit for this hostile optimism was a self-help book he found hidden under a *New Yorker* on her bedside table: *Present Tense, Future Perfect: Finding Happiness in the Life You Already Lead*. The cover was illustrated with a daisy in a half-full glass of water. Francis couldn't stomach a single page.

"As long as you watch your salt intake, you should be fine," the doctor said. "And be careful in the snow. I hear we're getting a dump."

"One hopes the weather reports are exaggerated."

"How have you been feeling since our last appointment? I know it was a lot to take in."

Francis crossed his legs the other way, which twinged his lower back. "Just trying not to exert myself. We don't want a rupture!"

Dr. Rothschild studied him with pursed lips. "It's not really in your control, but yes, it's good you're not running any marathons."

"I have run not one marathon. Not even a half marathon. Not even a turkey trot."

The doctor laughed. "But seriously, are your affairs in order?"

"I haven't yet crossed all the t's and dotted all the i's, but I have a will, and I just need to make a few last arrangements."

"That doesn't sound like a yes."

The truth was, he still hadn't told Carol. At first he'd kept it to himself because he didn't want to burden her with it. After a point, though, it had become easiest not to think about it. Just the stress of telling her might cause his heart to explode.

The doctor folded his hands together on his desk, empty except for his laptop, nameplate, business-card holder, and a box of tissues. "Mr. Levy, bearing bad news is my least favorite part of the job. But the news is bad, and there's nothing we can do about it. I measured your aneurysm at five centimeters in August. In the MRI you just had, I measured it at nine centimeters."

The room seemed to dim, and Francis's brain began to swim away. He gripped the armrests of his chair to steady himself.

"You could surprise us all and live another ten years, but do your family a favor and put your affairs in order."

"You'd mentioned a possible surgery. . . . Is that still an option?"

He shrugged, not a heartening response. "There is a surgical treatment. We could slide a stent inside the aorta to reinforce it. But I wouldn't recommend it in your case. Your aneurysm is located where your renal arteries branch off to transport blood to the kidneys. If we try to put a stent in, we could block blood flow to the kidneys, and trust me, you don't want that. And we wouldn't give general anesthesia to someone at your age unless the benefits of surgery outweighed the risks. Which, in my opinion, they do not."

What did that mean, *at your age*? Two years earlier, when he turned eighty, the same doctor had told him his heart was as strong as a sixty-year-old's. He'd always thought that if he ate well and didn't take risks, his age didn't matter. Now he was too old to be fixed? "I suppose I need to figure out what to do."

"Mr. Levy," he said, seemingly annoyed, "nobody wants to hear that their life is coming to a close. But there is a silver lining. When it happens, it'll happen fast. You'll have all your mental and physical faculties right up to the end, and the pain, if you feel anything, will be over quickly. Sometimes it only lasts a second. It's really a good way to go, if you ask me."

That was an awfully crude way to put it. "Please address me as Dr. Levy," Francis said as loudly as he could, which was barely above a whisper. "I have a doctorate in comparative literature."

"I'm sorry, Dr. Levy, I didn't know," the doctor said, looking concerned, and Francis regretted snapping. "I'm available at any time if you have questions. You know the number." He shook Francis's hand and kept holding it after the two pumps ended. Neither man seemed prepared to be the first to let go.

◄●►

While putting away the remainder of an orange clove pound cake she'd concocted the previous night and eaten for breakfast, Birdie's gaze caught on a mostly full jar of Little Scarlet preserves. George adored the tiny strawberries suspended in it—though not enough to eat it, apparently. It had expired last June. She'd seen the jar so often over the past two years that it had become invisible to her, like an unpleasant childhood memory, but on Valentine's Day morning, it would not be ignored.

The jar made a satisfying clang at the bottom of the steel trash can. She felt a little lighter.

She dragged the trash can to the fridge and, in a cathartic spree, pitched more evidence of her husband's tastelessness: a saccharine hazelnut spread that George had used just once; Styrofoam clamshell containers of onion rings and hamburger fragments, white with congealed fat; and a tub of gunky, astringent olives he'd bought when she made the mistake of letting him do the shopping. She squealed and cackled with each throw. Her propulsive fury delighted and scared her.

A text message came from George: "Permission to enter the kitchen?"

"You don't have to ask permission!" she shouted, without slowing down.

"Is something wrong?" he asked from the doorway. "You woke me up." His depression thickened his handsome voice, and the antidepressant cocktail made him dopey like a child. In 1974, she had married a man; forty years later, he'd devolved into a toddler.

A french-fry crumb rode in his bushy white beard—God knew for how long; grease spotted the front of his bathrobe, and his light-starved belly peered out from under his T-shirt. He reeked of pork and vinegar.

"You threw away my Little Scarlet!" He gaped into the trash can.

"I'm cleaning out the refrigerator," she said, attacking a dried brown splotch with the scrubber side of a sponge. "It expired ages ago."

"Everyone knows expiration dates are just a marketing ploy." He lifted the jar from the trash, wiped it off on his bathrobe, kissed it, and placed it in the center of the middle shelf of the refrigerator. "There you go, sweet girl. Safe and sound."

It infuriated her, the care he showed that jar of preserves. "It's spoiled!" She threw the jar onto the floor and it shattered, spattering red muck on the lower cabinets, the inside of the refrigerator, and both of their legs. Her hands were shaking.

"You didn't have to do that," he whimpered. He stepped around the asterisk of jam and glass, opened the freezer drawer, and perused a stack of ice cream sundaes she'd purchased that morning for Penelope, trudging across town in the deep snow, still soft and blinding white from a blizzard the previous day. She'd heard a shocking rumor from Dougie McAllahan about Rick, and whatever unsavory doings had or had not transpired between him and Caleb, she thought her next-door neighbor might need cheering up. She'd meant to visit sooner but hadn't wanted to insert herself at such a delicate time. She and Penelope were good neighbors, but not quite friends. She couldn't just drop in the way she did with Francis. But now, on Valentine's Day, Birdie would have taken any excuse to get out of the apartment.

"Those sundaes are for our neighbors."

"No one will notice if I take a little bite."

She put the ice cream cups back in the freezer and shut the drawer. It seemed too great a compromise to give him anything. The compressor whirred, restoring the vacuum seal.

In prior years, Valentine's Day had been more special than their anniversary or their birthdays. All day they'd surprise each other with gifts: a gold-mesh filter for the coffee maker, dress socks embroidered with ants, an orderly lacquered box of Japanese cream puffs, a pair of heart-shaped cuff links. At night, after frolicking through the tasting menu at one of the four-star restaurants in the East Fifties or Sixties, they'd stroll through Central Park, wandering into the Ramble to neck on a bench. She was a small woman married to a large man, and she liked sitting on his lap while they kissed. They'd gotten away with naughtier pleasures, too.

George opened a takeout container from the trash and slurped up a soggy onion ring.

"Did you have something to say to me?" she asked. "Or did you finally tire of the scenery in your cave?"

He glowered at her. "I'm sorry I've disappointed you. I know I'm not good enough to deserve you."

"George . . ." she began. But she couldn't bring herself to toss another "Chin up!" his way. She'd looked forward to his retirement since they married—a chance to travel the world unhindered by work schedules—and he'd gone and spoiled it. His psychiatrist had insisted that the depression wasn't his fault, but after a lifetime of unflappable cheer, it was hard not to see his transformation as revenge. Maybe he was angry at the cosmetics company for laying him off and was taking it out on her. Maybe a lifetime of bottled-up resentments had finally begun to leak. Or maybe she had never understood who he really was, and that after forty years of playing the dauntless leader and gentle lover, he was finally letting his true self show.

He packed more onion rings into his mouth and swallowed without chewing. "I've decided to give you your freedom," he said, then clomped back into his bedroom, shaking the apartment with every thud of his heels.

◄●►

Caleb was fussing with the trash compactor in the refuse room when someone cleared his throat behind him. Ranesh, standing in the doorway, told him that Mr. Hunter had asked to see him.

Caleb felt weak with dread. He'd been able to avoid Mr. Hunter since that unthinkable night the week before, first by calling in sick for three days, the maximum before he needed a doctor's note, and then by working in the back of the house until ten in the mornings to avoid seeing Mr. Hunter on his way to work.

He was trying to move forward and treat that night as a valuable lesson. When he closed his eyes, though, Mr. Hunter's wild glare and bared teeth flashed in his mind, and his shouts played on loop. "You thought you could take from me, but you failed!" and "You do what I say now!" Why had he said those awful things? Who did he think he was yelling at? Inside his fear, Caleb sensed the trauma his ancestors had endured, stolen from their homes by evil men, their humanity torn from them with violence. His parents had always tried to lard the truth with positivity, to medicate themselves with hard work and optimism, but in that gruesome moment, he accessed his inheritance as a black man, a deprivation more powerful than any of them could avert.

Caleb didn't remember how he'd gotten home that night, though he did recall Mr. Hunter offering to get him a cab. At home he'd gone right into the bathroom and filled the tub, sitting in the scalding water as it crept up his hips, then his waist, making islands of his knees. He didn't have the energy to reach for the soap. He was still too stunned to cry.

He'd thought he was going to die. He'd thought Mr. Hunter was going to take the knife Caleb had brought and stab him to death. He had a glimpse of how their fight might have looked to an outsider. Black man attacks white man in Central Park. White man kills black man in self-defense. White man is a hero. He felt stupid for not seeing it before. And Mr. Hunter's letter was in his pocket! If he'd really been thinking, he would have left a copy in his bedroom.

When the water had gone lukewarm and his fingers had shriveled to raisins, he kicked the drain and continued to lie there, too weak to fight the slow return of gravity.

Sergei was at his place in Sheepshead Bay. Of course he'd rush over, probably take a cab at that hour, spend a hundred dollars when they were trying to scrimp for the apartment. Caleb needed to see him, needed to be touching him, but he wanted to calm down first. He didn't want to scare him. So he lay in his bed, hoping some of the fear would soften.

The next thing he knew, it was light out. He had a throbbing headache and muscles so sore he could barely walk to the bathroom. His parents had gone to visit his grandmother that morning, and he was relieved that they wouldn't see him like this, because they would be disappointed and angry that he'd put himself in danger for money, that he'd demeaned himself for a white man. Sergei, his prince, skipped work and rushed over to the Lenox Manor, cuddled the life back into Caleb, and made him a grilled cheese sandwich and tomato soup.

"I will kill him," Sergei kept saying. "I will cut his fucking dick off."

Caleb talked him down. Revenge would make everything worse, and depending on what he did, Sergei would definitely lose his job and maybe go to prison. Caleb didn't even want to hurt Rick; he just wanted to feel human again.

They both knew they couldn't keep the money. They couldn't start a life together on ill-gotten gains. They'd find a way to afford that apartment, somehow. It really was heartbreakingly perfect, and it was hard to imagine their life together without it.

Caleb thanked Ranesh and climbed the ancient marble stairs, worn down in the middle from thousands, maybe millions of footsteps. Rick was pacing near the doorman station, swinging a spotless tan-and-white-leather briefcase as he walked. He came to a halt when he saw Caleb and motioned him away from Thomas, who was peering outside the front doors, waiting to open them should anyone arrive.

"Hey buddy," Rick said, "how's it going?"

Caleb nodded, wishing he could stop smiling so hard.

"So my wife said you returned the money. You didn't have to do that. You earned it."

This was not the place for honesty. Nor was any other place, not as long as Caleb worked for the building, nor at any point afterward. "It was very generous of you," Caleb said quietly. "I just didn't feel right keeping it."

"Well, I'd give you ten times as much if you'd let me," Mr. Hunter said with a nervous laugh. "You really saved me, you know."

The most shocking thing wasn't that Mr. Hunter had paid him to be powerless so that he could feel powerful; it was that he could put a price on humiliation. These people could put a price on anything.

"So I was just feeling so grateful to you," Mr. Hunter continued, "and since you gave back the money, I was hoping I could help you in some other way."

An apology would be nice, Caleb thought. Or maybe this was supposed to be an apology, in the way that men could apologize without ever admitting they'd done something wrong. "You don't have to do anything for me." Caleb was still smiling, though it had hardened into a smile that would fool no one. Mrs. Levy walked past and waved; he returned a slight nod without diverting his attention from Mr. Hunter.

"Well, if you ever think of anything," he said, "I hope you'll let me know."

"Yes, sir."

Caleb saw Mr. Hunter flinch at "sir." They'd been so close to the end of this cringeworthy conversation, and now Mr. Hunter was going to keep it on life support until he could prove to himself that they were friends.

He bit his lip and held his briefcase in front of him in both hands. "My wife said I should find a way to make it up to you. I mean, I definitely would have either way, but she was really upset by what happened. By what I did." He lowered his gaze. "To you."

This still wasn't an apology, but now he began to feel for Mr. Hunter, who clearly didn't know what he was supposed to feel. Caleb felt an urge to apologize, maybe to make up for the lack of apology in the air. Then he felt a detached anger for diminishing himself even in this small way. In a flat tone, he said, "It's very kind of you, but you don't need to give me anything."

Mr. Hunter looked up excitedly. "Maybe I could pay for your movers? Or buy you a couch or something?"

Is that all you have to give? Money? Caleb thought, feeling sad. "Thank you, but it's not necessary." He nodded at Thomas, as if responding to a summons—though Thomas was still minding the front door. "I should probably get back to work."

"We're okay, right?" Mr. Hunter asked, panicked. "Are we okay?"

Even though Mr. Hunter had not done anything to deserve Caleb's forgiveness, there existed only one possible response between an employee and one of the shareholders he served, between a black man and a white man. "Totally," Caleb said with a hearty nod.

◄◆►

Carol had thought it considerate to invite Birdie over for Valentine's Day tea. Although Francis assumed Birdie would just as soon not have the decomposing remains of her marriage rubbed in her face, he also didn't want to be alone with Miss Congeniality, née Carol, any longer than necessary.

"Sorry about the cheese selection," Francis said to Birdie as he plated water crackers and miscellaneous cheese cubes from Zabar's. "The odds and ends aren't what they used to be."

"I think it looks great," Carol said. She set up her tea and snacks by the white sofa, which was odd because she always sat on the brown sofa, and he sat on the white one. He imagined that *Present Tense, Future Perfect* had told her to shake things up. "Sit on the other sofa today," it might have read. "Invite over an unhappy woman, and don't sweat it if the cheese is bland."

"I'm worried about George," Birdie said, surveying the cheese plate with a discerning frown.

"What about him?" Francis asked.

"You know, the thing we sometimes worry he's going to do."

"You mean suicide?" Carol asked, holding her hand to her chest.

Birdie nodded. "I'm sorry, I didn't want to say it so baldly."

Francis managed to splash tea all over the coffee table as he guided the cup in for an emergency landing. His surroundings darkened, and he leaned back on the sofa to keep from tumbling onto the floor. "You're not going to let him, I hope."

"Of course not," Birdie said. "But he's not going to ask my permission."

Francis mopped up the milky tea with a sheaf of napkins. He had stained the sleeve of his sweater. He hoped he wouldn't die before he could get it cleaned. Carol certainly wouldn't think to do it before giving his clothes to her cousins and nephews, and then her family would remember him as a slob, which wasn't true at all.

"Birdie," Carol said carefully, "is there the slightest chance he would do it?"

"I don't think so," Birdie said. "But he gave me a strange apology this morning. And then he said he was going to 'give me my freedom.' Maybe he's finally letting me leave. But it sounded ominous."

Francis wanted to scream. But even screaming might be enough to end his life. Months ago, Birdie had bristled at the idea of sending George to an analyst to confront his unhappiness instead of burying it under pills and shock treatments—and now, if he really was contemplating suicide, he had no one to talk to. Certainly not Birdie, who thought all of life's problems could be solved by a tasty meal with a side of psychoactive drugs.

"You know him better than we do," said Carol, pressing a finger to her mouth to keep the cheese in. She swallowed half a dozen times until her mouth was empty. "But why not sit down with him, tell him you still care about him, and ask what's going on? I find that a little affection goes a long way."

If Francis told Carol about his aneurysm and she responded with something as stock and insipid as "I care about you!" he thought his aorta might rupture on the spot. Death rendered speech useless, and yet people persisted, trying to find words to console the dying and the grieving, to confine that unbearable, insuperable pain into greeting-card platitudes. It wasn't just Carol and Birdie; everyone did it. Everyone did it, and the violence of it was horrific.

"I'll talk to him, but I'm not going to lie," Birdie said. "I can't feel much of anything for a man who treats me like his nanny." She picked up another cheese cube and studied it. "Honestly, I think I'd forgive him for everything if he still wanted me. We haven't made love in almost a year."

Francis had always thought it strange that Birdie, who wouldn't admit her age or how much she tipped the doormen, blabbed about her sex life as if reciting times tables. He and Carol hadn't crossed that threshold in years. Instead of constantly wondering if a peck on the lips would turn into a feature production, or whether they should take pains to arrange simultaneous bedtimes, they silently agreed to dispense with the whole thing. And he wasn't about to start it up again now, not when it could end him. It didn't mean they didn't love each other.

"I don't think you should take chances with a person's life," Francis said. "Bring him to a hospital."

"He said he'd never forgive me if I had him locked up. He said he'd rather die."

"The alternative doesn't sound much better, Birdie."

"Maybe it's time to move out," said Carol.

"Wouldn't I love to!" Birdie exclaimed. "But I can't leave him like this, even if he's allowing it. He can't live on his own."

"Life's too short to be unhappy, Birdie."

"Did you get that one from your self-help book?" Francis asked. "Or was it from today's horoscope?"

Carol glowered at him. "If people say it a lot, it's because it's true."

◄●►

The humid stink of grease, body odor, urine, and wet paper assaulted Francis when he opened George's bedroom door. Blades of light pierced the edges of the drawn shades, but Francis's eyes didn't adjust until after a soggy pile of french fries squished underneath his foot. Slowly he began to make out a craggy landscape of dirty takeout containers and plastic utensils, splayed magazines, heaps of fleece and terry, and, in the corner, a forest of empty beer and wine bottles. George lay on the bed in a dark-blue bathrobe, breathing noisily. When Francis last stepped into George's room a few months earlier, it had been messy. This was postapocalyptic.

"George, hi; it's me, Francis. I'll turn a light on, maybe?"

"No, please," George drawled, staring at the ceiling.

Francis moved a stack of country CDs off an armchair and sat down. He had to be careful not to walk too fast or stand too long. It was hard to say what constituted a marathon. "I'm not going to beat around the bush. You are very sick, and you are not getting better. There is help, but you have to accept it. Now wash up, come out with me for a walk, and let's begin to flush this madness out of your head."

"Francis, I can't. I'm too unhappy to move."

"Who said anything about happiness?" Francis asked, sipping breaths through his mouth. "Do you think I'm happy? Do you think Birdie is happy? It's life, George, and we have a moral obligation to see it through."

George rolled toward him. "When we first moved into the building, you gave us a book, do you remember? It was about the history of Jews on the

Upper East Side. We knew nobody, and you did that thoughtful thing. You've always been such good neighbors."

"I'm glad you liked the book." Francis was admittedly touched that he remembered.

"I wonder if we still have it. Birdie likes throwing things away." He lifted his right arm toward the ceiling and opened and closed his fist. "It's in her nature; she needs to get rid of everything that doesn't serve her."

"You sound pretty angry at her."

"Me? I'm not angry at all. I'm just stating the fact that she doesn't form sentimental attachments to things."

"Listen, Birdie thought you might be thinking about . . ." He knew that the word had to be used, to draw the temptation for self-harm out of his head, like sucking venom out of a snakebite, but now he couldn't say it.

"What's that?" George asked.

"Just tell me one thing, and I'll leave you alone. What would you do if you decided to do it?"

"If I tell you, do you promise they won't lock me up?"

"So you do have a plan."

"I didn't say that."

Francis clutched his chest—was that a pain? George needed him— needed somebody—but Francis wasn't going to spend the last trickle of his life trying to convince him that it was worth living. He stepped backward, crunching a plastic takeout container, and stumbled toward the door.

"Don't leave, Francis. I like your company. Birdie never sits with me anymore. She used to love me. But I've failed her. I've tried to be happy but I can't. God, have I tried. I think I was never happy, and was too busy trying to make other people happy to notice."

Francis paused at the door. "People love you, George." It was the best he could do.

George rolled onto his back and stared at the ceiling.

◄ ● ►

Birdie knocked on Penelope's door, a stack of lidded ice cream sundaes balanced against one arm. Her young neighbor answered the door in a kimono and felted slippers. She'd recently had her blond hair cut short and grown out her bangs. It was an appealing style. She looked tired but sturdy, considering what she must have been through. Birdie had always suspected Rick's morals—a week or two before his marriage to Penelope, she'd shared the elevator with him and a demented floozy, and then she'd seen the girl by herself in the building here and there for months—but she hadn't thought him capable of wrestling their porter to the ground and shouting racial slurs in his face. Apparently there had been a knife, too.

Penelope greeted her with an apologetic smile.

"Are you busy?" Birdie asked. "I brought ice cream sundaes from Emack and Bolio's."

"That's really sweet of you, but it's not a great time." She held the door a quarter way open, neither welcoming nor rejecting Birdie.

"At least let me give you the ice creams. I thought you might need some neighborly cheer after Rick's . . . little mess."

Penelope narrowed her eyes. "Who told you?"

"Dougie did. He said Sergei, our old doorman, told him. Which just goes to show, you can take a fellow out of the Chelmsford Arms . . ." Birdie laughed at her joke.

Penelope surveyed her apartment, looked again at Birdie, and opened the door. "The place is a disaster. Promise not to judge me?"

"Cross my heart."

"Okay, you asked for it." She swung the door open.

Penelope was exaggerating, but not by much. Birdie had to navigate an archipelago of unopened boxes from Williams-Sonoma and Saks Fifth Avenue crowding the foyer. The bottom shelf of the bookcase was empty, the books in small piles nearby. The coffee table was cluttered with magazines—*Town & Country, Vogue,* and some of those that showed up in everyone's mailboxes, glossy vehicles for luxury advertisements. A stack of crinkled pages torn from the magazines had been arranged at the corner of the table, possibly a pile of inspirations for some of her party planning. An empty mug, stained with a residue of coffee silt, served as a paperweight.

"Sorry about the boxes," Penelope said. "We still haven't opened all our wedding gifts. And already I'm thinking of leaving him."

"Don't say that," Birdie said.

Penelope made a cute little grunt and walked into the kitchen. Birdie watched her clear her half-eaten breakfast, Kashi cereal and yogurty milk, off the kitchen table and drop everything into the sink.

"So, ice cream in February," Pepper marveled. "There's an idea."

"No lines at the parlor."

"I like how you think."

"I didn't know what flavor you would enjoy," Birdie said, "so I got creative. We have dark chocolate with salted caramel and peanut butter cup, sweet cream with hot fudge and Heath bar, and mint with strawberries and walnuts. I added a sprig of fresh mint to that one."

"You're a genius."

Birdie blushed. She couldn't remember the last time she'd been given a compliment of any kind. The closest George had gotten was his declarations of love to "Marie" in his half sleep, and she hadn't been Marie since the early seventies. "I do think a lot about food. Especially when I don't much want to think about George."

Penelope looked at her with sad eyes, as if about to say something kind about George. "I guess I'll take chocolate."

Birdie chose mint and tucked the sweet cream in the freezer, over Penelope's protestations—but Birdie didn't want to give it to George. Penelope used a metal tablespoon; Birdie preferred the tiny pink sampling spoon from the ice cream parlor, as it reminded her of sharing sundaes with George in years past. With petite stabs she collected a sample of each ingredient—ice cream, whipped cream, half a macerated strawberry, a walnut piece, and a mint leaf—and, eyelids drooping, let the flavors meld across her tongue. Exceptional. But the sundae didn't transcend its ingredients, not in the way the same concoction would have when she and George first moved to New York in 1983. Maybe a body could only absorb so much pleasure in its lifetime. She hoped she could survive on memory alone.

"Rick hired Caleb to pretend to mug him," Penelope said. "And then he pinned him down and scared the hell out of him."

"I'm sure it was an isolated incident," Birdie said.

"We're in couples counseling. I'm still not sure what's going to happen to our marriage, but I don't know if I can live with someone who's capable of that," she said with a big scoop of ice cream in her mouth. She swallowed and took another big bite. "This is really good."

"I'm sure he wouldn't hurt you," Birdie said. She didn't know why she felt the need to defend him. George had never hit anyone. But she would have preferred him to hit her than to leech her spirit dry. At least then her pain would be visible, comprehensible to others. Then she could leave in good conscience.

I am not going to feel guilty about this, she thought. Francis was probably overcautious with these things. She wasn't sure she could trust him, anyway. He'd made an avocation out of finding fault with other people. She would take George in to see Dr. Clay first thing Monday morning, and once his medications were calibrated, then she could talk to him about her freedom.

"It's not that, exactly—I'm pretty sure he wouldn't hit me. I just have this persistent feeling that I don't know him," Penelope said. "I married a man I didn't really know, and the more I learn about him, the less I like."

"Do you love him?"

"I do—but I don't think that's enough." Penelope scraped the bottom of the paper cup. "I had a bunch of serious relationships before I met Rick. Each of them was flawed in a big way; I think my mother made a game of figuring out the flaw and then telling me. One was too old, one was too stupid, one was too gay—that is, he was gay." They both laughed. "Anyway, the flaw with Rick was that he wasn't honest. That didn't seem so bad to me; the mystery was exciting. In comparison, everyone else felt sort of . . . safe." She shrugged. "Maybe I should have given safe another try."

"Safe! If we wanted safe, we could have stayed single. My George was an adventure from day one, and I wouldn't have had it any other way."

"How is he, by the way?"

"Just fine." Birdie tried to savor another bite but didn't feel like eating anymore. Maybe George couldn't wait until Monday to get his meds fixed. But (and here was something she would never have admitted thinking to anyone) if he really wanted to die, why should she stop him? Of course she loved him—forty years together could not be folded up and locked in a drawer—and of course his death would undo her. But he had been punishing her for almost two years. They had both given up hope for his recovery, and she was ravaged by anger. It was torture to remember loving him. It was torture to consider how much she'd lost.

The plastic spoon snapped lengthwise in her teeth.

When she returned to her apartment, George was gone. Maybe that was a good sign. It was just like him to pretend he'd forgotten her birthday or their anniversary, then spring an elaborate dinner and gift on her. Even a bouquet of roses would make her day. Maybe that's why he'd behaved so strangely that morning. Maybe he really was trying to change. Maybe his meds were finally kicking in. She bundled up in her long down coat, rabbit-fur hat, mittens, and boots to go looking for him. Before she left, she applied the last of her stem-cell serum, enjoying its rubbery smell. Then she found her wedding band in her jewelry drawer and put it on. She put on the engagement ring, too. It was a simple silver ring with a princess-cut quartz gemstone, and although she had worn it proudly for years, happy that she didn't need to prove her love with diamonds, she'd recently begun thinking it looked cheap. Both had sat in the drawer for months, but she wanted to be wearing them if George surprised her. She wanted to believe in the magic of Valentine's Day.

◀ ● ▶

Rick texted Pepper that afternoon, asking to meet at the north end of the Great Lawn, by the pinetum, at four o'clock sharp. So he was planning something for Valentine's Day. She was glad he was trying, at least. They'd been civil, waiting for their next session. It was manageable for the short term.

The snow was deep from the previous day's storm, and she was exhausted by the time she found him, on a bench by the paved path that encircled the expansive oval lawn. The park was teeming with kids tossing snowballs and couples with hands interlocked, believing in the made-up holiday. Rick stood and put his hands in the pockets of his long wool coat. His hair looked good; maybe he'd gotten a haircut that afternoon. She remembered that underneath all her fear and frustration crouched an animal desire. She knew this attraction would fade: her parents had lost it, and so would she. Still, she wanted to kiss him, and so she did, quickly on the lips.

"To what do I owe this sudden burst of affection?" he asked with a grin.

"To spontaneity. It doesn't mean you're out of the doghouse."

"You're also in the doghouse, you know. A different one. Maybe a cat-house."

"Meow," she said drily.

He glanced upward, and she did too. There was nothing to see except cloud rubble scattered across the purpling horizon. The sky above was clear.

"I talked to Caleb this morning," he said.

"And?" She felt a chill and crossed her arms to stay warm.

"I apologized. He wouldn't accept the money, but I think we're good."

"Thanks for doing that. I'm sorry I got so angry about it." She wasn't exactly sorry, just feeling charitable.

"No, no, it makes total sense. You helped me see what I did to him. I'm glad you did. I do wish he'd taken some money, at least enough to get that apartment. But I couldn't force him."

"All you could do was apologize."

He looked up again. "Oh, good, it's happening. Check it out."

She noticed the letter "P," written in contrails in the sky. Five parallel planes flying in a straight line were releasing timed smoke to print the message. As the planes created an "E" and a second "P," she understood that this was not a coincidence. "That's not for me, is it? Oh, Jesus." She watched, bemused, as another "P," then an "E" appeared. The spectacle embarrassed her, but since he had gone to all the trouble, she owed it to him to watch. Around them, fingers and faces pointed upward, and now a crowd of people stared, reverent, as it finished her name. Already the first letters were thickening and becoming diffuse, like a promise forgotten as soon as it's made.

A space, and then the word "I'M." The melting snow had seeped into Pepper's boots, and even in her shearling coat, she was shivering. "Not to sound ungrateful," she whispered, "but how long is this message?"

"Not too much longer."

It was hard to be standing so close for so long without taking his hand, like holding two magnets a few millimeters apart. But as the letters "S" and "O" materialized, it made her sad that he might think this air show would move her more than a simple, heartfelt apology—one she was pretty sure he had never given her—and it sank in, finally, that her marriage was over. Sure, they could stay in couples therapy every week and negotiate their relationship like a peace accord. They could distract themselves with children and find their way to happiness and stability along parallel courses, the way her parents had. They could continue to surprise each other in good and bad ways, and they could forgive each other until the betrayals lost their meaning. All to keep the promise they made in front of their families and friends at the Temple of Dendur.

But the spectacle of this skywritten apology showed her that, despite how powerfully she had resisted the prospect, she and Rick were not a good match. It was as if he could only prove his love by epic gestures. She should have seen it when he arranged the copse of trees in their living room to cheer her up. In retrospect she saw that designing a wedding around those trees was her attempt to appreciate a gift that had, at its core, upset her. Or she should have seen it when he sprang for a Bermuda getaway to try to paint over their feelings. He was showy with his gifts and with his body, brash and impulsive, and so obsessed with money that it formed his moral compass. She didn't want to spend her life with someone capable of seducing a stranger or assaulting an employee. The only thing she really loved about him was that he loved her, more intensely than anyone she had known. She'd thought the purity of that love could sustain their union, but now she saw that it was only the prerequisite.

"SORRY" was all that remained in the sky, and then "ORRY." She had feared destroying their marriage with an accidental insult, and now that she wanted to do it, she couldn't find the words.

"Pretty cool, right?" Rick asked, his expression as unguarded and optimistic as she'd ever seen it.

"I can't stay with you," she said. "I'm sorry."

His eyes cracked with desperation. "All because I lost it with Caleb? Or is it because of Molly?"

"It's not just that," she said. "It's what those things mean about you. It's everything you've done. It's who we are as people." She was trying not to tell him that he was amoral.

"I love you, Pepper," he said. "And you love me, too. Don't say you don't." He reached for her, and she stepped back, nearly falling into the snow.

People around them, having lost interest in the sky, were now gawking at them. A skinny teenage girl in a pink parka and black tights recorded them on her cell phone.

"I do love you," she whispered, motioning for him to follow her, away from the girl with the camera. "It's just, I know now that love isn't enough. When I met you, I didn't know who I was, and it was enough just to be loved. You gave me that gift, to know how it felt to be loved completely. Now I know that I need more than you can give me."

"Of course love is enough," he said at full volume as they clomped through the snow toward Fifth Avenue. "What else could you possibly want?"

"Compatibility," she said, now fleeing the park with him, or possibly from him. "I need to be with someone who shares my values."

"Values? Of course I share your values."

"Rick, you attacked Caleb just so you could feel powerful again. Do you really understand how bad that is? Or were you just agreeing with me because I was angry?"

"Sure I do. He works for us. He's black. I scared him."

"Rick . . ." She glanced at him, and his incredulous anger frightened her into silence.

"Like you're some messiah for black people? You planned one fundraiser to ease white people's consciences. You convinced the co-op board to let in one black family. You're not exactly Sojourner Truth. You've never had to work a day of your life. And you go on, complaining about gentrification and racism and all the black people who can't get into our building, but I don't see you taking responsibility for any of it, when you, a rich white socialite, are literally the problem. So fine, you think I'm an asshole. You think I'm a liar. But please don't talk to me about values and then go have tea with your white friends in our white building with money that I gave you. The hypocrisy makes me sick." He walked away from her in the snow, still heading out of the park.

She'd known all of this, in a small way, all along, but hearing him say it with such disgust in his voice made her furious. "The only thing that matters to you in this whole world is money. You think you can do whatever you want if you throw a wad of cash at someone."

He laughed theatrically. "For someone who wants nothing to do with money, you sure spend a lot of it. I don't know what they taught you in finishing school, but most volunteer party planners don't get to live in four-million-dollar apartments." He was shouting, his breath visible.

She was lucky enough not to have to make what she spent, but that didn't mean she had to get a job at a bank to prove a point. "Well, how about this? Most people who are getting married in a week don't think that's the perfect time to have sex with a stranger."

They reached the mostly shoveled sidewalk of Fifth Avenue, where they could walk more quickly, though the thin layer of gray slush made it slippery. It occurred to Pepper that they were in a race to the apartment, past a minivan making a hopeless attempt at parallel parking in deeper slush.

"So that's it?" Rick said. "You can't forgive anything I've done?"

"I did forgive you for that," she said, "but that doesn't mean it didn't happen. And for the record, you never apologized." The blanket apology in the sky didn't count, not really.

"Well, sorry, okay? Sorry, sorry, sorry for everything I've ever done and ever will do. Sorry. Are you happy now?"

She wasn't going to respond to that. She could find someone with a more genteel personality, someone she could live with. Or she could live on her own. If she really couldn't wait for a baby, she could find a sperm donor. "We can see Dr. Dixon again if you want. But only to help us end it." The light changed, and she crossed the street toward Madison Avenue.

"I worked so hard for you," he said bitterly, as he followed her. "You made me better. You can't just throw it all away."

"I'm better because of you, too," she called behind her. "And now I know that I have to move on."

"But we're married," Rick said. "You married me. You can't just walk away because you figured out that we're different. You promised me a life together."

She hastened toward the apartment building. She knew he was following her and didn't dare look back. She crossed Madison Avenue and stopped fifty feet from the entrance. She didn't want to be together in the apartment again, and if they fought in front of the doormen, the whole building would find out. She turned around. He was a few steps away, a vision of elegance in his long black coat and waterproof leather boots. He never wore a hat because it would ruin his hair.

"I'm going to stay with my dad for a while," she said. "Please go back to work so I can pack."

He took a step forward with a mischievous smile.

"It's over," she repeated. "It's over."

He took her by the waist and pulled her toward him. He was wearing a new cologne, smelling of leather, powder, and grapefruit, and his face and neck warmed her cold nose and cheeks as he kissed her, tongue slashing across her mouth, lips firm. She hated herself for kissing him back, breathing in his breath, absorbing the sensuous blows of his tongue. His hand slid beneath her coat and sweater and gripped her back. The weakest part of her wanted to take back everything she said, to stay in the marriage and let things be wrong between them. Finally, he stopped, rested his forehead against hers, and continued to watch her eyes. Her face tingled with the memory of his stubble.

"How about I come upstairs with you?" he offered.

He could only mean one thing by that, and she craved it, too. But she knew that if she let him make love to her, she might never leave him. And she had to leave him. Or did she? It wasn't too late to change her mind. She needed more time to think. She peeled his hands off of her and stepped back. "I'll see you at Dr. Dixon's."

He put his hands in his pockets and studied her. "Don't go to your father's. I'll stay in a hotel."

"We'll figure this out," she said, taking a tentative step backward, then another, then a third, and when she saw that he wouldn't follow, she turned and hurried toward the building, smiled compulsively at the doorman, and, with one last glance at Rick, went inside.

◄ ● ►

Francis and Carol were seated at a corner table in a windowless back room without a tablecloth, set with dish towels instead of napkins. Someone had stuck dandelions in a bud vase and called it a centerpiece. The ambience was so casual, the *ninety-five dollars* whispered in cursive at the bottom of the prix-fixe menu read like a joke. At least it was quieter than he'd expected.

Nate, their towering waiter in a black T-shirt, rested his hand on Carol's shoulder and asked if he could get them a drink. Francis missed the days when waiters stood up straight and didn't try to be charming. Formality was a lost tradition. Soon he would be gone—maybe any minute now—and who among his survivors would care about the old ways?

Carol ordered a glass of Merlot, and Francis asked for a cup of tea.

"We have Earl Grey, ginger peach, gunpowder green, jasmine green, and lavender mint," Nate recited, bending back the same finger five times.

"You don't have plain black tea?"

Nate pursed his lips. "I'm afraid not."

For what could be his last meal on earth, they didn't even have plain tea. "Then bring me hot water and a slice of lemon. And I want the water to be really hot. Just off the boil."

When the waiter had left, Francis wondered aloud, "What kind of restaurant doesn't have plain tea?"

Carol slathered her roll with butter and bit off two thirds of it. Even fifty-three years of suggestion couldn't give her a little polish. At least she looked nice. She didn't even need the usual convincing. She'd dressed up, brushed her hair, and put on perfume, all without a fight. He couldn't figure out why that annoyed him. "I like that they don't have plain tea. It's nice to change up your routine sometimes."

"How would you feel if all they had was ginger-peach-flavored wine?"

"Sounds heavenly. I'll take two." She sneered.

"Of course you would."

"I have an idea. Just for tonight, just while we're having dinner, can you not say anything negative? Is that possible for you?"

"One more thing, and I'll be as positive as a schoolboy. I think waiters should wear a name tag telling you their sexual preference, so husbands know how to feel when they grope their wives."

"Only Francis Levy would think a tap on the shoulder constituted groping."

"Is that a formal complaint?"

"Forget it," Carol said. "Let's please not bicker tonight."

"Fine. From now on, everything's going to be sunshine and lollipops." He picked up his fork. "This makes me so happy!" He embraced the wine bottle filled with tap water—which Nate had called "our house water." "What a clever idea!" He looked around. "Isn't this place just swell?"

She tightened her jaw. "Actually, I like it very much. You only take pleasure in hating everything. That's not the man I married, and I'm telling you, I'd like my old husband back."

Nate appeared with a tray full of glassware and crockery for the two drinks: a miniature carafe of wine, an empty wineglass, a teacup with spoon and saucer, a teapot on its own saucer, a square appetizer plate with a fan of lemon slices in one corner, and a little vase sprouting tubular sugar and sweetener packets. The preciousness of the setup suggested to Francis that the water would not be hot enough, so he stuck a finger in the teapot. "I asked for it to be just off the boil," Francis said. "This is more like a puddle on a hot day."

"Actually," Carol said, "don't worry about it. It's plenty hot."

"You're sure?" Nate asked, cocking his head with a practiced squint, doubtless learned at surfer academy.

"Positive."

This was not the time to cross her, even if he'd die with a cup of lukewarm water in his hand.

"Okay, well, let me know if you change your mind," Nate said. "It's no trouble to heat it up a bit. Have we made any decisions?"

"I have," Carol said. "Are you ready, Francis?"

"Why don't you give him your order," Francis suggested, still scrutinizing the menu, "and by that time I'll have figured out mine."

Carol smiled at Nate. "I'll start with the rabbit terrine, and then for my entrée, I'd like the appetizer portion of the gnocchi with pancetta."

"My two favorite menu items," Nate said.

"Thanks for giving us your top picks, Nate," Francis said.

Carol kicked him under the table.

While the waiter hid his impatience under a broad smile, Francis tried to choose a dish that he could eat. It seemed the newer the restaurant, the fewer the meal options. And this one had pork all over it, much of it in code: lardons, pancetta, speck. Was this a new way to exclude Jews, subtler but no less disgraceful than the anti-Semitic policies of private clubs in the past? Carol thought kosher laws were quaint, but Francis maintained a modicum of respect for the traditions of his ancestors. He was the last one in his extended family who cared about preserving the past. Within a few generations, the religion as he knew it would probably cease to exist.

The relatively kosher elements of the menu weren't much more viable. The trout was "crispy"—which meant fried—and came with "creamy radicchio slaw" and "pine-smoked morels," all of which spelled disaster for Francis's gut. The "orecchiette with brown sheep's butter and porcini foam" would be far too rich for his vulnerable heart, and the steak came with a spicy au poivre sauce and truffle-dusted french fries: salt, salt, salt. Had his laxity about salt caused the aneurysm in the first place?

He wished he'd fought Carol on such a precious restaurant and its "farm-to-table" baloney. Even if she decided she was sick of being married to a person of sensitivity, even if she didn't care that his father had died from eating in a restaurant, the least she could do was accept his limitations before she had to scrape his remains off the floor. George's forsaken cell was still etched into Francis's vision, his stink in Francis's nostrils. If Francis were ready to hop out the window, would Carol tell him, "Life's too short to be unhappy"? The scream inside him yearned to escape.

"I'll have the salad with no lardons and no dressing, and the pasta without any sauce," he said.

"Really sorry," Nate said, "but Chef doesn't allow substitutions."

"They're not substitutions, they're deletions. For ninety-five dollars a person, I can't get something I can eat?"

"I can ask. . . ." Nate said. "I'll tell him you have a medical issue."

"Forget it," Francis said, rubbing his temple. "Give me the salad and the steak, extra-well-done, with a big stack of napkins so I can wipe off the sauce. And I know ninety-five dollars is not enough to grant me say as to how my food is prepared in this concentration camp, but please tell 'Chef' not to salt the meat. I cannot have any salt at all."

"I'll see what I can do," Nate said. Without writing down a word of their order, he gathered the menus and hurried off.

"Now, who is this old husband you were talking about?" Francis asked. "He sounds sort of interesting."

"Quiet! I'm pretending you're not here," Carol muttered.

He dug out a tea bag from his inside breast pocket, bobbed it in the teapot, gave it a quick squeeze, and set it aside. "What about my old wife? The one who comforts me when I'm down instead of undermining me with positive thinking?"

"It'd be easier to comfort you if you weren't down every minute of every day. Have you had a single pleasant thought in the past six months? Ever since I had that cancer scare, you've been impossible. Maybe I'd understand your upset if I was dying. But it was nothing. I'm healthy." She reached for his hands and squeezed them. He could barely feel her touch. "I'm not going to die on you, Francis. I'm not going to leave you."

It was time to tell her. Whatever her response, it would be better than this hideous estrangement. "The truth is, I've gotten some very bad news," he began.

"Listen, I started on Zoloft a few weeks ago." She spoke over him, pulling her hands away and sipping her wine. "I didn't want to tell you because you hate people who take antidepressants, just like you hate everyone else. But I was tired of being depressed, and, believe it or not, I really like being happy."

He was stunned into silence. He'd known something strange was going on with Carol. He supposed that unhappiness had become so unsightly and unbearable in modern life that everyone was expected to extinguish it with chemicals, but was this really the woman he married? Someone who chose drugs over feelings? Who chose happiness over her husband? "I don't hate people who take antidepressants," he said with effort.

"Really? What about George? And your sister-in-law? And Marilyn Devine? And that girl you like on the co-op board? What's her name? Penny?"

"I don't hate any of them. I just think they want a shortcut through their pain. They think it's inconvenient to be sad. I'm sorry if my unhappiness has inconvenienced you."

"There's nothing heroic or interesting about being depressed."

"On the contrary, I think sadness is very interesting."

"Believe me, it gets old," Carol said. She took a long sip of wine.

◄ ● ►

Something told Birdie to leave the front door unlocked. The apartment seemed too quiet.

She was bone-tired and shivering from two hours of searching for George, scrabbling over snowbanks and navigating slushy gray ponds at every street corner. She'd started at the Turkish café on Eighty-fourth and Third that they'd adored since moving to New York. Next she ran past Emack & Bolio's for the second time that day, in the off chance his seeing the sundaes put him in the mood for one. Then she peered in the two sleepy, mediocre bistros they relied on when she didn't feel like cooking, as well as the Irish pub George liked for prime rib on Saturday nights. She should have given up at that point, but the longer she looked, the more frightened she became. So she had plunged into Central Park, sinking into the deep snow, scanning the Great Lawn for his big red fleece in the oblique afternoon light. Everyone was looking upward: "SORRY" was written in the sky. Could it have been a farewell message from George?

Just in case, she knocked on his bedroom door.

"Come in," George said. "I have a present for you."

Had he been home the whole time? She had looked in his room but hadn't pressed into the pile of covers and pillows. She cautiously opened the door. "George, I don't want any funny business."

"There you are!" came his voice, more confident and rapid than it had been in months.

He was standing in the corner of the room on a blue plastic tarp that hung from the wall behind him. The light from a bedside lamp spattered on the tarp and cut distorted shadows across the wall. His hands were wedged in the pockets of his sweatpants, and a blank, uncontained rictus stretched across his face.

Birdie couldn't breathe.

"Don't be afraid," he said. "I would never hurt you. I've given this a lot of thought. I know this is what you want."

When he took his hands out of his pockets, she saw that he was holding a pistol. Cold burned in her stomach.

"Please put that down," she managed to say. "Let's go out for dinner and we'll talk it over like adults."

"I tried, Birdie. God, I've tried. And I am so sorry, but I can't try anymore. I can't be any better for you."

"Listen, I've decided to stay with you. I'm wearing my rings again, see?" She held up her left hand.

"Shh. Don't say that. I don't want to hold you back anymore. Please let me do this for you. I left a note on the bedside table if you need something to show the cops. All you have to do is let me die."

She put her hand down. It seemed crucial not to lie to him, not now. "I don't want you to die," she said, and it was the truth.

He pushed the barrel against his temple, then reconsidered and pointed it at his chest. "Happy Valentine's Day. We had a good long run."

She couldn't stand it anymore, any of it. "George, I'm freezing and exhausted and I really don't have the patience for this. Now put that gun down and stop all this rubbish."

For a second she thought she had gotten through to him. Then his glare slackened into disgust. "Don't tell me what to do," he muttered. He squinched his eyes and fired.

◄●►

A big, flat package was leaning against the front door when Pepper got back to the apartment. She set it atop some other boxes in the living room, hung up her coat, changed into a kimono and slippers, fixed herself a mug of tea, and lay next to the bookshelf where she could listen to Birdie and George through the hole. She needed to stop doing this, she knew. But she had to calm down from her fight with Rick, and forgive herself for her weakness in letting him kiss her, and listening through the hole worked better than an Ativan. Unfortunately, it was about as addictive.

George and Birdie didn't seem to be home. Usually she could hear George snoring or talking in his sleep, or Birdie opening and closing drawers in the kitchen. She supposed George hadn't gone to San Juan with his ex-girlfriend, and she hoped her presence hadn't ruined his prospects. What started as a lark to cheer both of them up had gotten very heavy very fast. It probably wasn't her fault, she told herself. That whole day had seemed to be made of fantasy, like cotton candy that dissolves into nothing once it hits your tongue.

She lay there a while and soaked in the silence. Maybe love really was enough, with more couple's therapy. Maybe Rick could change, settle down, become a little more predictable.

She needed to take the tea bag out of her mug or else the tea would become bitter, but she was overcome with a numbing, pleasant fatigue. Her mind became active with meaningless dreams. She awoke to a loud snap, like the beat of a snare drum, followed by a wail, and then silence. She looked out the window: taxis flowed up Madison Avenue as if nothing had happened. Had she dreamed it? Then she understood: the wail she had heard was Birdie. She snatched her keys and dashed out of the apartment.

◄●►

The au poivre sauce came in a metal cup, leaning against the steak, as though the chef assumed Francis was one of those dieting ninnies who dipped their meat in the sauce instead of pouring it on. The french fries came in a metal pail lined with newsprint.

"Are you sure this doesn't have any salt?" he asked, prodding the steak with his fork.

"Positive," Nate said.

"Would you wait while I try it? I just want to be sure."

"*Francis*," Carol said.

He cut a piece off the steak and chewed on it. It wasn't just salted, it was salty. He spat it out, fearing that a single bite might be enough to kill him. "Salt!" he yelped, unable to organize a sentence.

"Stop it," Carol said.

He drew his pleading eyes toward Nate, hoping that the waiter would right what he'd done. But Nate revealed no humanity beneath his vapid smile. "There might be a little salt from the pan."

"Taste it!" Francis cried, wondering if he was going crazy but afraid to take another bite. "Someone! Tell me that's not salty, and I'll shut up for all of you."

Carol reached over, cut off a sliver, and chewed on it. "Needs salt."

"Chef does dip it in soy sauce and butter for flavor," Nate said. "I suppose there's a little salt in that."

Francis seethed. It was all he could do not to let out the scream vibrating in his belly and shaking his rib cage. "You couldn't have remembered that *before* serving me this? You could have killed me."

Nate mumbled an insincere apology as he whisked the steak back into the kitchen.

Carol folded her napkin and placed it in front of her. "I thought we could have a nice dinner for once," she said, on the verge of tears.

Francis was too angry to stop. "I think the happy pills clouded your judgment."

"Why are you doing this to me? What have I ever done to you?"

A short-haired woman in a white sateen blouse and black pants hurried toward them. "Hi, I'm Teri. I'm the manager tonight. Nate said you guys were off to a rocky start, and I was hoping I could be of service."

"Maybe you can be a dinner companion for my wife, since she loves eating out so much," Francis said. To Carol he said, "Remember, if I drop dead, a simple pine box, so the worms can get at me."

"I'm sorry," Carol said. "My husband can't help it. He hates life and won't rest until everyone around him wants to kill him. Please give Nate my apologies. We'd like to pay our bill and go." She hammered four gnocchi onto her fork and stuffed them into her mouth.

◄ ● ►

Birdie leaned against the wall in the crowded waiting room. It was the busiest night in the ER in a long time, so said a pair of nurses, and anyone who wasn't dying had to wait.

"Valentine's Day," one of them lamented. "People do crazy things for love."

Penelope brought her a coffee and a packaged Danish from the bank of vending machines. It was still a shock to see the girl's bloodied kimono inside her shearling coat. Birdie should have been the bloody one. She had been paralyzed by fear, yes, but had she resisted intervening for another reason? It was already hard to remember. She couldn't even remember what she'd told the cops when they stopped by the waiting room half an hour ago.

She remembered what she saw, not what she felt. After George had shot himself, he fell, knocking the pistol under the bed. He reached for it, floundering on his blood. He begged Birdie to shoot him. Then Penelope was shouting at her, and she realized her neighbor had been banging on the front door. Penelope pushed a canary-colored throw pillow into George's chest to slow the bleeding and with her free hand dialed 911. Birdie could only gape at the miracle that was her neighbor.

The coffee was watery and flat, the Danish brittle and cloying. Birdie would never have touched these things, wasn't even hungry, but they distracted her from the throbbing disbelief. "I've sometimes thought that, under the right circumstances, George could kill another man," she said. "But I never believed that he could . . ." She saw his deranged smirk and the gurgle of blood from his chest, and promptly forgot what she was saying. She thought about happier times, of watching George enthrall the whole table at press dinners. Or watching him drive through the Quebec countryside. Or watching him glide down a mountain on skis, carving squiggles into the snow.

"I guess you can never really know what men are capable of," Penelope said, staring at nothing. "Or anyone. You can't really know anyone, I guess."

"He was a wonderful man, my George."

Then Francis and Carol were rushing toward them. They were far too dressed up for a hospital. She must have interrupted a romantic evening. She felt terrible.

"How is he?" Francis asked, embracing her. His fingers and cheek were ice cold, and he smelled of shallots.

"They're still operating," Penelope said. "They haven't told us much."

"There was a lot of blood," Birdie said. "The paramedics gave him blood and it poured back out."

"He must be alive, at least," said Carol.

"Can we get you anything?" Francis asked. "Another coffee? Some real food?"

Birdie shook her head. "Penelope has been taking care of me."

"We'll be here as long as you need us." He ordered a middle-aged man

out of his seat and told her to sit down. Coming from anyone else, the so-
licitousness would have been comforting. But something told Birdie that
he was being too nice.

Finally a tired, sallow nurse called her name. When the four of them
approached, though, the nurse said that the limit was two at a time.

Birdie and Francis followed the nurse, past patients looking up from
their beds like meek children, to George's bay in intensive care. "The
doctor will be with you in a moment," the nurse said before enclosing them
within the wheat-colored curtain.

"My God," Francis said.

An oxygen mask covered George's swollen face, globs of congealed blood
were lodged in his beard, his chest was cocooned in bandages, and an IV
sprouted from each forearm, one clear, the other tinged red. It was George,
all right, but he looked like a zombie. In Birdie's memory, he was always in
motion—rushing to a meeting, planning a grand surprise for her, driving
too fast or railing against some or another injustice. Even when he was sleeping, and after he confined himself to his room, the energy hadn't left his
face. Now, at rest, he was barely recognizable.

But when she closed her eyes, tenderness gushed in. Good old George,
friend to all, ever willing to help out in a pinch. The man who always
hungered for her, until he didn't. How long had she tried to help him get
better before giving up? How had she turned cold so quickly?

Francis, still wearing his black wool cap inside, motioned toward the only
chair. "Please sit, Birdie. You must be exhausted."

She did not sit.

"We're going to pull through this," he said. "Everything's going to be
fine."

She tried to be soothed by those words, but he seemed not to believe
them.

The respirator pumped deep, loud breaths into George, one after another as time washed over Birdie, mingling the present and the past. Outside the curtain, doctors and nurses hurried by, giving orders and updates
on patients, some who would live and others who would die. How did the
Yom Kippur dirge go? *Some by water and some by fire, some by sword and some
by beast* . . . Had a celestial being known that George would die this year?
Had he known? Had she?

A doctor pushed the curtain aside and introduced herself to Birdie as
Dr. Naeer. She had almond eyes, a slender nose, and long black hair bound

up in a bun, and she seemed too young, beautiful, and soft-spoken to be working in such a desperate place.

"The bullet missed his heart," Dr. Naeer explained, sitting on the edge of George's bed, "but it nicked his aorta and perforated his lung. When the EMTs reached him, he wasn't breathing and his heart had stopped. His blood volume had dropped drastically, and oxygenated blood was not reaching his brain. We intubated him and defibrillated, and we opened up his chest to repair his aorta and stop some of the bleeding elsewhere in his chest cavity. He is breathing, he is alive, and he is stable.

"I'm afraid, however," Dr. Naeer continued, "that he has a long road ahead of him. He's in a coma. We don't know how long his heart was stopped, so we don't know how much his brain has been compromised. He will probably need to remain on a respirator permanently, whether he wakes up or not. The left lobe of his lung is no longer functional, and his breathing capacity will be limited. His kidneys have failed, and he will need dialysis."

It was hard to believe there could be such a distance between alive and healthy. "You tried," Birdie said, staring into the doctor's eyes to keep from having to look at George. She had sometimes thought it might be a relief to have him gone. She hoped that wasn't what had prevented her from trying to take the gun. Because she felt no relief and knew it would not come. She had thought her love had been destroyed by his depression, but she saw that beneath her anger, she had continued to love him. She loved him still.

"Oh, Birdie," Francis said, taking her hand, "I'm so, so sorry."

"We've secured a bed in the ICU for Mr. Hirsch," Dr. Naeer said. "It should be ready in half an hour. I would urge you to go home and get some rest. Tomorrow we can talk about next steps."

"By next steps," Birdie said, "you mean whether or not to let him die?"

A trace of alarm passed across Dr. Naeer's face. "Withdrawing life support may be an option further down the line," she said, "but we'll need to wait a few days to see how he progresses. We don't know yet how much damage his brain has sustained. That decision, if we have to make it, can wait."

The decision over George's life was easy to make, and not for the reason she would have thought a few hours earlier. She didn't know how she could live without him, even though she'd been doing so for months. But he had wanted desperately to die, enough to buy a gun and put a bullet in his chest. If his final, hideous gift to her was to kill himself, then she could give him a gift, too, and let him go. She felt certain of it. Every moment she kept him alive was a cruelty.

"He didn't want to live, you know," Birdie said. "It's clearly stated in his living will. I'd like to honor his wishes."

Dr. Naeer nodded solemnly. "From my experience, I have found that most patients who do recover their most basic faculties are happy to be alive. Even those who tried to take their own life. And I have faith that ultimately, he will be okay."

"You don't know my George. When he gets an idea into his head, he doesn't change his mind. Ever. And he's always said that if it comes to this, I should pull the plug." If her husband died, she could begin to grieve. But this in-between state, and the agonizing guilt of not having him committed earlier in the day, was too much to bear.

A wail pierced the air, so ripe with pain that Birdie thought someone must be dying in the next bay. But the scream was coming from Francis. His face had turned scarlet, his eyes were squeezed shut, and his lips were slightly parted as he clutched the curtain behind him with both fists.

"I am so sorry," Dr. Naeer said, reaching toward Francis.

Francis ran out of breath and opened his eyes. "'Pull the plug?' This is a human being lying here, a living, breathing person. He needed help, and you complained that his pills weren't working. He told you he was going to kill himself, and you pretended not to hear. Pull the plug? You might as well have shot him yourself." He clutched his heaving chest, betraying an instant of panic.

Dr. Naeer stiffened. "I think you should go."

He fumbled for the opening to the curtain and stormed out, one hand still pressed against his heart.

Birdie wasn't surprised that Francis would accost her when George was half dead in a hospital bed. He always seemed to be withholding judgment, waiting to unleash his bottled-up resentment until she was most vulnerable. He forgave nothing, that one. They were only friends, she realized, because they were neighbors with a lot of time on their hands. She was stuck with him as a neighbor, but she didn't have to be his friend. The odd thing was, even though she'd grown to enjoy his company, she'd known from the minute she'd met him, decades ago, that she didn't like him. She'd sensed his true feelings about her from the start. Why had she struggled for so many years to be nice?

Dr. Naeer's gaze was clear and her lips were tensed. Being looked at with such intensity and care felt as soothing as a touch. "I can't imagine how hard this is for you," she said. "I can't imagine what you must be going through."

"Please don't hate me," Birdie said.

The doctor's face registered nothing. "Of course I don't, Mrs. Hirsch. You've been through a lot, and your trial is not over. We will do our best to help him recover, but if we can't, ultimately you will need to decide your plan of action." Dr. Naeer took Birdie's hand. The doctor's fingers were long and slender, her nails clipped short and painted with a pale-blue polish. "Please stay as long as you like. Talk to him. Touch him. But if you are tired, go home. I promise he will still be alive in the morning."

With that, Dr. Naeer slipped through the opening in the curtain.

Birdie turned toward George and took him in. *George*, she thought, *if you want to live, give me a sign.*

His chest continued to rise and fall, and the heart monitor did not quicken or slow its relentless beeping.

The curtain rippled, and Penelope stepped in. She flinched when she saw George. "Jesus. Sorry—I need to keep some thoughts to myself."

"I thought the same thing when I saw him," Birdie said with another glance at the bloated creature who had replaced her husband.

"He really doesn't look like himself."

"You saved his life, you know." Birdie smiled.

Penelope stared at her fingernails, chewed to the quick. "You would have done the same for me."

It wasn't true—Birdie wouldn't have known the first thing to do if her neighbor had been bleeding on the floor. She hadn't known how to help George, neither that night nor for the past two years. But she nodded anyway. "I knew he would do this," she said, apologizing to no one. "Something in me just couldn't accept it."

"I don't know if this helps or hurts," Penelope began, leaning her hip against the foot of George's bed, "but I spent an afternoon with him a few weeks ago. Did he tell you about our lunch?"

"Really? My George?" As far as she'd known, he hadn't left the apartment in months. Though of course he had left that afternoon, maybe to procure that pistol.

"It was all really strange and spontaneous. We ran into each other on the landing, and we went out to lunch with this old friend of his."

"Who?" The jealousy in her voice surprised her.

"A friend from before he met you. Of course it wasn't romantic or anything, I don't have to tell you that, right? It was just one of those weird days that come out of nowhere and lead nowhere, but we both needed to feel like life had possibility, you know?"

"She was his girlfriend?" Birdie knew he'd had girlfriends before her, but for him to see one without telling her . . . !

"No, no, just a friend. He was so cheerful—I mean, he was obviously depressed, but through all that, there was this hope. I was depressed, too, and I think I needed him, I needed someone who could understand. I guess what I'm saying is George helped me, and he seemed happy. I wouldn't have guessed he was so close to . . . I just wouldn't have guessed." She stared at him, breathing seamlessly in the hospital bed.

Birdie was glad for Penelope's company, glad that she was neutralizing the awful silence with words. But knowing that George had gone out to lunch just weeks earlier with some ex-girlfriend, or friend, or whatever, made everything worse. Had he been miserable without break for months, then she could have declared his case hopeless and seen his death as a gift. But the fact that he could be happy, away from her, and that he hadn't told her about this woman and who knew what else . . . A new jolt of anguish burned in her chest, and hot tears stung her eyes.

"Oh, shit, I shouldn't have told you that," Penelope said. "I'm sorry, I just thought it might help to hear something positive. . . . I don't know what I was thinking."

"No, no," Birdie gasped. "I needed to hear it. I'm crying because . . . because I'm afraid I may have wanted him to die."

Penelope leaned over and collected her into an embrace. "It's okay. It's totally okay."

Birdie couldn't remember the last time she'd been hugged. She hadn't realized how much she'd needed to imbibe the warmth of another person. She also hadn't realized how fond she'd become of Penelope. Friendship was too scarce in this world, especially among neighbors, Birdie thought, and that propelled a fresh burst of sobs. When she finally let go, the shoulder of Penelope's coat was darkened with Birdie's tears.

"Would you like to sleep at my place tonight?" Penelope asked.

Birdie couldn't go home, not with the floor and that awful tarp painted in her husband's blood, and she didn't want to sleep alone. She nodded. "Thank you. I don't deserve all this kindness."

"You deserve every kindness." Penelope hugged her again, then picked up her pocketbook. "I'll be in the waiting room," she said. "Don't rush on my account."

Birdie reached under the sheets and fished for George's hand, but when she came upon it she recoiled: it was swollen and cold. She looked at him and the medical equipment and the curtains enclosing them, and suddenly all of it seemed glaringly distasteful. She didn't want to remember him like this. She would go mad if she let these images soak into her memory.

She relaxed her mind and let the past flow in, filling her vision with images of Paris and Provence, San Francisco and Napa, and dear, dear Montreal. She had enjoyed ten lifetimes' worth of happiness with him, and she could live out her days in fond reminiscence. But suddenly it seemed grotesque to think about who he had been, who they'd been together, when he was lying in front of her on the welcome mat of death, when her memories had blinded her to how angry he had become. For all she knew, he'd been sneaking away to cavort with this ex-girlfriend while she drugged herself with memories in the kitchen.

Soon she would have nothing but memories, but for the moment, she could try to see him. She touched his soft, damp hair and ran an index finger over his earlobe. How many months had she ignored the flesh-and-blood version lumbering about her home? And—it frightened her to consider this—had she spent more time with that sad old man instead of the historical George, godlike in his perfection; could she have prevented this awful night?

She kissed him on the upper cheek, at the edge of his oxygen mask. His flesh was sticky and cool. This was her husband, and she still loved him. It was painful to feel this much love piercing her heart, and she was grateful that she did.

There wasn't much room at the edge of the bed, but she was a petite woman, and she climbed up next to him. With some difficulty, she lay down, taking care not to touch the bandages. His belly rose and fell in time with the hiss of the respirator, and his body seemed asleep, but he was alive, and they were together, and for those precious minutes while she lay with him, nuzzling her face into his shoulder and taking him in breath by breath, undistracted by her memories, that was all that mattered.

◄●►

When Francis opened the door to the apartment, beleaguered by the never-ending day and the brutality of humankind, something wasn't right. String lights were hung along the ceiling, bathing the room in a soft glow. Billie Holiday crooned from the speakers, and the floor was dappled with rose petals.

"Oh, shit," Carol said. "I completely forgot about this. You must think you married a nincompoop."

"No, no," Francis said. "But what is it?"

"I had Caleb set it up. It was supposed to be a Valentine's Day . . . surprise."

He explored the rest of the apartment, Carol following a few steps behind. The bedroom was also festooned with lights. A small plate of chocolates and a card addressed to Francis were positioned near the pillows on the tightly made bed. Maybe the last chapter of *Present Tense, Future Perfect* focused on seducing your man.

He opened the envelope. He recognized the illustration on the card, of a dog and cat nuzzling. Carol must have rooted through his desk drawer and found it. It felt like decades ago, not six months, when he'd bought it for Carol's birthday. Inside, he'd written, *London + Paris + me + you = your happiest dream come true. Yours forever—Francis.* He tried to remember the person he had been who hadn't thought twice about booking eight-hour flights to Europe, who didn't know to be afraid of when his aorta might revolt.

Underneath his little rhyme, Carol had written:

> *What a lovely idea! Count me in.*
> *Happy Valentine's Day!*
> *—You-know-who*

Rereading the card in the dim light, it pained him that Carol had gone to so much trouble just to squeeze a little appreciation out of him. She was trying very hard to be good to him, and he had treated her horribly. Yet he feared that to feel anything for her, to allow his emotions to surge, was to risk explosion. It was too awful to bear, too awful to bear alone.

He was crying. He covered his face.

"I'm sorry, Francis. We don't have to go to Europe. It *is* a lot of money. I shouldn't have gone snooping. I don't know what I was thinking."

He shook his head, unable to speak.

"What is it?"

"I'm dying," he blurted out.

"What?" He couldn't tell if she was angry or distressed.

"I have an aneurysm. A something-something aortic aneurysm." He didn't know how to explain it further, so he reached into his pocket and showed her the diagram Dr. Rothschild had drawn for him six months earlier. He'd carried it every day, somehow afraid that if he put it down, his heart would burst and no one would understand why.

She examined it, turned it upside down and flipped it to see if anything was written on the back. "It looks like a bomb attached to a heart."

"That's the gist of it." He looked at it again. Dr. Rothschild had drawn lines coming out of the aneurysm to represent arteries that, for a reason Francis had never understood, rendered it inoperable. The lines did make it look like a detonating bomb. "He doesn't know when it's going to happen, but he said it would probably be soon."

"How soon?"

"I don't know. Today? Tomorrow?"

"When were you planning on telling me?" she whispered, as if keeping his secret. "If I'd known, we could have skipped . . ." She gestured in every direction. "Oh, God, the hospital must have been torture for you."

"You don't know the half of it."

"I'm sorry about dinner," they said at the same time, and laughed.

"I want to do nice things for you, I do," he said. "But your relentless positivity felt like you hated me. Like you wanted nothing to do with me."

"I wanted us to be happy together."

"I wish that were possible."

"We can try."

They closed their eyes and listened to the trickle of jazz spilling in from the living room. Then Carol went to get a glass of wine. It had always bothered him when she got drunk, as though by letting her guard down, she put him at risk. But right now, he accepted that it wasn't his place to stop her.

"Did he give you any pills or say what to avoid doing?" she asked, sitting next to Francis on the edge of the bed and sipping the wine.

"Nothing. If there were something I could do, I think it wouldn't feel so awful."

"And you'll just die in your sleep?"

"Don't sound so eager! You're just like Birdie."

"Come on, Francis, you know I'll mourn you for the rest of my life. But if you had the choice of dying over several painful years and dying suddenly, wouldn't you choose to go quickly?"

"Dr. Rothschild did say it was a 'good way to go.' But it sounded like you were going to have to clean bits of me off the walls."

She snickered. "That's not possible."

"Don't laugh! Who am I to say what's possible? I didn't even know your aorta could explode."

"No wonder you've been so grumpy."

He didn't like her finding a reason for his grumpiness.

"If you want to take an antidepressant, I highly recommend Zoloft." She grinned, flashing her crooked gray teeth. "It's like a teeny, tiny pillow under your heart."

"There's an idea. We could just sit around and smile all the time."

"Or we could laugh. Or dance." She stood up and reached for him.

"You're insane," he said. But there was no reason not to dance, as long as they did it gingerly. Anyway, dying while dancing with your wife on Valentine's Day was probably a good way to go, if you had to go in the first place.

"Why do you put up with me?" Francis asked, standing up again, bracing himself to be surprised by all the familiar little pains of his body.

"My parents must not have punished me enough. Or maybe they punished me too much, and now I need it all the time."

Dancing wasn't so terrible. His feet knew not to step on hers as he led her in a repeating semicircle around the foot of the bed. When they were apart, it was easy to forget how pleasant it was to be touching her in so many places.

"Tell me something," he said, "something you've never told me in all our fifty-three years."

"Francis, I'm an open book. You know everything there is to know."

"I don't think I do," he said. "I'm afraid I'll die without ever having really known you."

She looked into his eyes and promptly stepped on his foot. "Oh, shit, sorry. Okay, there is something. Don't get mad. I never stopped smoking. I've smoked almost every single day of the past sixty years. I know I'm killing myself, but it's my favorite thing to do."

He'd known that she smoked, but all the same, she'd been smart to keep that from him. If he'd accepted how addicted she was, he would have tried to make her quit, and they would have quarreled even more. "For what it's worth, you have my permission to keep smoking after I die. Not that you need it."

"You're right, I don't need it." The song changed, and their dance slowed. She kissed him. "Now tell *me* something. Besides the fact that you might explode in my arms."

He pondered this. He kept a compartment in his mind filled with things he could never tell anyone, like the time he was thinking about a girl at school and rubbed up against little Jacob in their childhood bed until he messed his underpants, or that same year, when his mother wouldn't stop screaming at him and he struck her across the face. But maybe there was something he could talk about. "I don't like hats. I only wear one because I want to have my head covered when I see a religious man. I've always wished I had the courage to wear a yarmulke."

She craned her head back to examine him. "Why would that take courage?"

"Because I was always trying to seem less observant to you, I guess. I'm always afraid you'll regret marrying me."

"I would never— I don't regret marrying you! Why would you say that?"

Again he began tearing up. He was too tired to stop it. "I thought . . . because of how demanding I can be. I wasn't sure. I thought you might."

"Not for a second. Do you regret marrying me?"

"Certainly not. I'm glad I married you." Francis bumped into the bed and almost fell over. He guided her closer to the window. "Very glad."

"Even though I'm never as good as you want me to be?"

"No, no, no; that problem lies with me. You're perfect. You're more than perfect. Everyone knows that."

"I wish all those people would have clued me in," she said.

"I'm telling you now."

They danced in silence, and he buried his face in her hair. It smelled of the restaurant and baby powder and smoke. For the first time, he didn't mind her smoking. He liked the thought of her smoking after he died; he would have hated to think that, through his fear, he had taken a lifelong pleasure from her.

"I was serious about the pine box," he said. "You can't bury a Jew in a designer casket."

"I know."

They stopped by the window—Francis couldn't tell whether it was Carol's doing or his—and swayed in place. He liked being held like this.

"I've missed you," Carol said, kissing him on the neck.

He closed his eyes, trying to absorb the moment into his senses—her fingers, her lips, her hair—and to slow time before it left him behind. "Don't go missing me yet."

◄●►

After they showered and threw away Pepper's bloodied clothes, Pepper and Birdie sat next to each other on the sofa, lost in thought.

I saved a life today, Pepper reminded herself with mounting pride. She replayed the scene in her head: her fingers remembered pressing George's chest, and the warm, sticky blood seeping through the throw pillow she was using as a compress. She remembered the glare of the lamp in her face—had it fallen over? She remembered trying to explain to the 911 operator what was happening, unable to produce common words like "consciousness" and "wound." And George wheezing "no," and trying to push her away until he passed out. And the cell phone slipping out of her bloody hands, and worrying for a regrettable moment that her screen had cracked. *I saved his life*, she thought. *I knew exactly what to do.*

Birdie stared up at the dentil molding, mouthing words. She didn't respond to her name. Pepper tapped her on the stocking, and she startled. "What is it? What happened?" Birdie asked.

"Nothing—everything's going to be fine."

"Oh, good." Birdie's eyes glazed over again, and her parted lips quivered.

Pepper didn't know whether or not these daydreams were safe or not. She had heard of psychological shock but didn't know how dangerous it was. Best to keep her awake and calm, she decided. She had an idea. In Rick's wine cabinet, she unearthed a rare Château Pétrus from 1982, a landmark year for Bordeaux. Rick had bought it at auction for twelve thousand dollars a few days after they met. He'd given it to her; together they'd planned on opening it on their tenth anniversary. But after the horrors of the night, she was finally able to see her marriage with perfect clarity, and she was finally certain, beyond a shadow of a doubt, that she was right to leave Rick. Because as she knelt over George's body, watching his desperate eyes, she had an instant of déjà vu, recognizing the feeling of helplessness and alarm that she had experienced again and again with Rick. She couldn't let herself be surprised anymore by her unpredictable husband. She didn't have the constitution. She didn't see how anyone was strong enough to be married.

"Did you and George ever taste a Château Pétrus?" Pepper asked, sticking in the corkscrew without waiting for an answer. It was her bottle, and she could do with it what she liked.

"George and I visited Pétrus time and again on our trips to Bordeaux, but we never invested in a bottle," Birdie said, her eyes coming into focus. "We loved good things, but those prices were too dear. You don't have to open it. . . . I couldn't."

She popped the cork and handed Birdie the bottle; it seemed friendlier not to pour it into glasses. "Should we let it breathe?"

With a shrug and a giggle, Birdie placed her lips on the finish and held a sip in her mouth. She swayed side to side as if in pain. *"Mon Dieu,"* she whispered. She took another sip and handed back the bottle.

Pepper took a deep draft. She liked wine but was no connoisseur, and this one could have just as easily cost twelve dollars as twelve thousand. "So this is good?"

"This is unspeakably good," Birdie said, fully roused from her stupor. "It's rich, it's velvety, so perfectly balanced you might think you're drinking water. Then, *kapow!* Your taste buds are struck all at once with a pungent bouquet of plums and cherries and tobacco and rich, peaty soil, and you find yourself soaring over rolling French vineyards."

Pepper took in another mouthful, and she could taste the fruit, but she still didn't understand Birdie's reverie.

"You know," Birdie said, still swaying, "when you get to my age, everything begins to taste like a poor imitation of something else. But a prestige Bordeaux is truly new. I feel as though I'm beginning a new life from this very moment. I'm very grateful to you, for the wine, for the hospital . . . for everything."

"Then you should have the rest," Pepper said, handing her the bottle and the cork, afraid to let the conversation slide into talk of blood and gunfire and wills. "I'll be glad not to see it again."

Birdie corked the bottle and set it on the coffee table amid all the junk Pepper had left there. It occurred to Pepper that she was famished—a refreshing sensation after hours of nausea—but in no shape to cook. She settled for a Greek yogurt and blueberries from the fridge. When she returned, Birdie was inspecting the large, flat package that had arrived that afternoon, atop the other wedding gifts that she needed to return, presents that were already obsolete. On some level, Pepper had known she'd never use them.

"What do you think is inside?" Birdie asked.

"It doesn't matter. How are you feeling now?"

Birdie waved her away. "Please let me watch you open your wedding gifts. George and I didn't get many gifts for our marriage, just a few trinkets from our friends, but my life with George was gift enough. We had the most remarkable . . ." she drifted off.

Birdie didn't respond to her name. When Pepper shook her, she woke up and fell right back into her troubled half sleep. Pepper thought about calling an ambulance, as she didn't feel confident enough to recognize whether Birdie was safe. She'd never heard of anyone dying from psychological shock, though, and Birdie would suffer in the hospital after the hours they'd spent there. She'd try again to rouse her, and if she failed, she'd call 911.

"Would you help me with this? Birdie?" Pepper sliced a serrated knife into the tape of the large, flat package, and Birdie's eyes came back into focus. Together they shimmied the gift out of the box and tore open the craft paper protecting it.

It was a large, glossy impasto painting of her and Rick embracing on their wedding day. Almost half the painting was taken up by the obscene volume of her dress, and between her bouquet and her face, Rick barely squeezed in. He must have commissioned it from a wedding photo, but the way they stared at the viewer made it seem as if they weren't supposed to be together and her real husband had just caught them in an embrace. Had the artist sensed that they were wrong for each other? Had everyone known but her? The artist had also exaggerated their blemishes—Rick's asymmetrical eyes and her embarrassingly large forehead—a technique that made the painting ugly and a little comical. It wasn't realistic, but it was honest, and she liked it despite the fact that it would have to be destroyed.

"It's not to my taste," Birdie said, "but it does have a point of view."

Pepper opened the card. She didn't want to read it, but she also didn't want to throw it away without reading it, and she didn't want to save it, either. So she read it.

> *To the most amazing woman I have ever met, to my one great love, Pepper, Penelope, Sweetheart, Babe,*
>
> *I am writing this on the eve of our wedding night, thinking about how lucky I am to have found you and to be loved by you. You will receive this painting on our first of many Valentine's Days as a married couple. The knowledge that we will spend our lives together makes me happier than I ever thought possible.*
>
> *I will love you forever.*
> *Rick*

She handed the card to Birdie and squeezed her temples until it hurt. It was further evidence of the promise she had failed to uphold. Leaving Rick meant exposing herself as a liar. Her father had already forgiven her, and her mother would be relieved, and nobody would fault her, maybe not even Rick, and she saw how quaint it was to feel ashamed of getting a divorce and to care about marriage in the first place, but she didn't know how to forgive herself. Even though she could blame him for screwing it up, she was the one who'd ended it, sweeping all their memories and plans into the dustbin.

She rubbed the stuccolike canvas with her knuckle, over the ruffles of her wedding dress, up the bodice and around her face. She flicked her forehead, and the canvas made a hollow pop. She willed herself not to cry.

Birdie said, "He loves you."

"Are you comfortable? Can I get you a blanket?" She turned the painting around and leaned it against the bookcase.

Birdie took both of her hands and squeezed. "You love him, Penelope. Don't let him go. Don't make the mistake I made." Her voice was monotone and strange.

"What are you talking about? You didn't make a mistake."

"My mistake was forgetting how much I loved George. A rough patch is just a bump in the road on the wonderful journey of marriage. What matters is that you love him. Don't let him go."

"You're still in shock," Pepper said, touching Birdie's forehead in the way that mothers test for fever in their children, as if a hand could feel the difference of a few degrees, and as if Pepper knew whether to be afraid of Birdie's forehead being too hot or too cool. "Maybe you need to eat something." Seized by another idea, she jumped up and hurried into the kitchen, where she grabbed the remaining sundae from the freezer and gave it to Birdie with a pink plastic spoon.

Birdie ate the sundae as she had earlier that day, closing her eyes with each bite, as if desperate to squeeze out a trace of the pleasure that had once flowed freely. Watching her, Pepper felt that she had been wise to give her neighbor some nourishment.

Next, she made up the guest room with fresh sheets, tossing Rick's dirty clothes and sheets into the hamper and piling the satin throw pillows, so much useless beauty, on the floor. She handed Birdie a frilly nightgown her Grandma Phyllis had given her as a birthday present; it was ugly and she would never wear it, yet she couldn't bring herself to throw it away. Birdie's entire wardrobe was sitting not fifty feet away, through the wall in the living room, but they couldn't enter that apartment, the scene of violence that now felt so distant and unreal that it might have been part of a movie they'd watched. Thinking about it brought her back to those haunted moments: the tarp, the phone, George's hideous moaning, and then, after he'd passed out, the unbearable silence. "Would you mind leaving your door open tonight?" she asked, once she had brushed her teeth and Birdie had changed into the nightgown, which she had to lift at the waist to keep from tripping over the fabric. "It would make me feel less alone."

"Of course, dear," Birdie said, touching her arm. "I want that too."

They retreated to their separate bedrooms. But standing alone now in her room, Pepper worried about Birdie sleeping alone. She knocked on Birdie's half-open door. Her neighbor—her friend—was still taking in her surroundings.

"Actually," Pepper said, "I know this is going to sound ridiculous, and you can say no . . ."

"Whatever it is, I promise I will say yes." Birdie rubbed her slim belly through the flannel of the borrowed nightgown. She looked like a child in all that fabric.

Pepper stared at the gray carpet. Even with the disclaimer, it was hard to say: "I don't want to be alone tonight. Can I sleep in the bed with you?"

Birdie's lips curled into a plaintive smile. "Dearest Penelope, I want that, too."

Pepper pulled back the corner of the bedspread and slipped inside, pulled the duvet up to her neck, and rested her arms on top. Birdie crawled in on the other side, and Pepper looked at her, at that button nose and black pixie hairdo and her tight, tentative smile, and wished this woman had been her mother. But if Birdie could have outshone Claudia in some ways, she surely would have failed in others. The point, Pepper knew, was not to have the perfect mother but to forgive the one you had.

"Good night, Penelope," Birdie said, reaching to switch off her bedside lamp. "Sleep tight, and don't let the bedbugs bite."

Pepper closed her eyes, feeling their shared warmth under the covers. "Good night, Birdie."

◄ ● ►

Birdie rolled to her side, away from her darling bedfellow, and, breathing in the pleasant chemical odor of laundry detergent on the crisp sheets, reminded herself of the love she'd had, and the memories calmed her. Maybe George's life was over, and maybe it was not, but no one could say she hadn't enjoyed those forty years with him, reveling in every sweetness their love had borne. No one could say she'd wasted the love she'd been given. She held her wedding and engagement rings to her lips, and they seemed unbearably precious. She wouldn't fritter away the rest of her life, preoccupied by the past—but a little reminiscence wouldn't hurt.

She could almost feel George spooning her, and she imagined she was gripping his hands at her chest and soaking him in, the way they would sleep most nights. His hands had always been pillowy and warm, hers always cold.

She remembered how much she loved holding his hand when they walked down the street, feeling the pleasure and responsibility of being spoken for. And when he'd slide her hands, one at a time, under his jacket onto his furry belly to warm them, "My extra-strength heating pad," he'd proclaim. "Guaranteed warm or your money back." He could sell anything to anyone, she recalled, wearing the memories like a cloak, drifting into the lucid dream that prepares the mind for sturdier sleep. When she was first working as his secretary at the cosmetics company in Montreal, and they were dating in secret, she'd lose whole afternoons listening to his round, confident phone voice, pitching a beauty editor or shaking up a conference call. At night, she'd ask him to read to her, and she absorbed his low, velvety frequency as he absorbed her into his chest. And it was his voice that first attracted her to him, when she applied for the secretarial position and they giggled like children through the entire interview. They both had seen it instantly, that they were broken halves of the same soul, whole again. A week later, he asked her to dinner—she could hardly understand how he could wait a week, but he must have been anxious about dating his secretary. Of course, all barriers swiftly fell. She was raised a good girl, and her Catholic faith was important to her at that time, but she simply could not wait to make love, and they found relief that first night on his narrow bed in his postage-stamp apartment in Mile End, with no furnishings except a bed and a small, feeble lamp. The rug was a dirty orange, and plaster dust fell from the ceiling like snow every time a truck rumbled past, and she had thought it marvelous that he had his own place.

"I've got a good feeling about you," he said, as they lay crammed in that bed, trying not to burn each other with their cigarettes. "I can tell we're going to have a good run."

"I bet you say that to every floozy you take home," she replied, though his prediction excited her.

"You got me—I've said it before. But I've never been sure until now."

And six months later on a Sunday afternoon, at the top of Mount Royal, with the scintillating city towers upright in anticipation, he knelt and kissed her hand and presented her with a ring. His brown hair flapped in the bracing wind, and he steadied his tortoiseshell glasses.

"It's just quartz," he said. "The diamond is coming as soon as I can afford it."

"Of course I'll marry you," she said, kissing him. He tasted lightly of garlic and smelled of his masculine aftershave. "I've wanted to from the day we met."

"Someday I'll give you all the diamonds you want."

"It's perfect the way it is."

"I just want to be good enough to deserve you," he said with desperate eyes.

As he slipped the ring onto her finger, she sensed that they were embarking on a long season of happiness, a warm, hopeful springtime that might never fall into winter. She promised herself she would remember that moment forever.

◄ ● ►

Caleb got to the diner first and sat in a booth toward the back. Another doorman in Sergei's new building had taken Valentine's Day off, sticking Sergei with a double shift that didn't end until after midnight, so they agreed to meet at this twenty-four-hour diner near the Port Authority Bus Terminal, with hospital-strength lighting and spiral-bound laminated menus so big they had chapters, and where the same sleepy, efficient waitresses had worked for as long as either of them could remember. Caleb had been bummed that they were celebrating their first out-of-the-closet Valentine's Day with no style and after the fourteenth was technically over, but at least it was Friday night, so they didn't have work in the morning. They couldn't afford those inflated holiday prix fixes at the fancy places, anyway, if they were going to get their dream apartment, which was by some miracle still available for a March 1 move-in. Because Caleb had given back Rick's money, they were four hundred dollars short, and neither of them knew how they'd make up the difference.

He was on page 9 of the menu, "Greek Specialties," when Sergei arrived, swigging the dregs of a jumbo coffee. After they ordered—a "health salad" for Caleb and barbecued spareribs for Sergei—Caleb scooted next to his boyfriend on the bouncy aqua banquette and held his hand under the table. Touching Sergei still gave him a giddy thrill.

"I talked to Mr. Hunter," Caleb said.

Sergei was astonished. "Really? What did you say?"

"He did most of the talking. Just about how grateful he was to me and how he hoped I was okay. I guess he thought I'd be happy for him."

Sergei gripped his fork and pressed his thumb against the tines, leaving white dots on his skin. "He is shit."

"I know. But I mainly ended up feeling sorry for him. I mean, he kept trying to give me money. It was like, 'Instead of apologizing or talking about how you feel, here's more cash.' And when I didn't take it, he didn't know what to do." Caleb let go of Sergei's hand and tore his napkin into strips. "You know, I was excited to work in the Chelmsford Arms and see how great these people's lives are. But now when I go in there, all I see is their misery. It's like their money stunted them or something, and they forgot how to be people."

"That is most New Yorkers," Sergei pointed out.

"Not my family."

"Yes my family."

"I'm not saying I don't wish we had more money," Caleb said, pining for the apartment as he balled up the shreds of napkin, "but I'm grateful that we aren't like them."

"Most of them are happy in their way." Sergei seemed insistent on normalizing those people, so Caleb let it go.

The waitress, who wore blue eye shadow on bulging eyelids and had a big mop of curly gray hair, approached their table carrying two enormous white ceramic platters. Somehow the kitchen had cooked a rack of ribs in five minutes flat. Caleb's salad, iceberg lettuce and cucumber wheels with a ball of cottage cheese and canned pineapple on top, was a ridiculous quantity of food.

"You guys are adorable," she said, discreetly placing the handwritten check on their table, as if she wasn't expecting them to order dessert. "You gonna get married? I hear that's the thing these days."

Caleb blushed at her tone-deaf question. It was probably her way of telling them she didn't have anything against gay interracial love, as if they'd been waiting for her approval. He was about to say, "Who knows?" when Sergei asked, "You want to get married?" with a grin.

Caleb gave him two thumbs up. "You know it."

"Then, yes," Sergei said with an official nod. "We are going to get married."

The waitress laughed suspiciously and left them alone. Caleb hadn't been serious, which wasn't to say he didn't want to get married. "Do *you* want to get married?" he whispered.

Sergei kissed him on the cheek; he still reserved deeper kisses for the privacy of their bedrooms. "Of course I do. I want to spend the rest of my life with you."

"So we're engaged?" It was both a question and a statement.

Sergei winked. "Happy Valentine's Day."

The whole thing had happened so casually, and yet that was the best way, wasn't it? An agreement between two people in love, not some improbable seduction complete with a pricey stone. He felt light-headed, and though he hadn't drunk in years, his skin pleasantly buzzed.

In this spirit, Caleb decided to let their perfect apartment go. All his dreams of luxurious domesticity were bits of happiness based on material things. He and Sergei didn't need granite countertops or a balcony or a tree outside the window. They didn't need an ice maker or a dishwasher or a walk-in closet. They had each other, and that wasn't just enough, it was everything.

EPILOGUE

Someone had knocked the stone paperweight off the stack of paper napkins on the buffet table, and now napkins were peeling off and tumbling across the rooftop of the Chelmsford Arms in a giddy bid for freedom. Penelope replaced the stone and gathered what napkins she could without breaking into a run, eyed the levels of the food in the chafing dishes, checked in with the catering manager and bartender, chased away a few nosy pigeons, and took a deep breath.

The engagement party had reached that moment when everyone seemed happy and nothing needed to be attended to, but still she felt nervous. Maybe it was because Birdie and George had not arrived, and she feared that carrying him up to the roof would end in disaster. Standing alone at a highboy table with a glass of sparkling rosé, she surveyed the tented, Astroturfed space, watching the guests eat, drink, and chat in the late-afternoon summer heat. Caleb and Sergei, dashing in suits and ties, were mobbed by shareholders and staff alike, wishing them happiness on their upcoming marriage.

She had funded Caleb and Sergei's engagement party herself, as she knew not to use shareholder funds and hadn't wanted to charge admission. She was glad to spend the money to celebrate a love that she believed would last.

She startled as she felt fingers walking up her spine. It was Ardith. "Excellent work, my spicy Pepper, though of course I'm not surprised in the least. You're my most successful creation."

She couldn't give all the credit for her success to Ardith, though a few of the old woman's whispers into influential ears had secured Penelope more work than she could have hoped for, enough to pay her maintenance, support herself, and put aside a few hundred a month to fund an as-yet-unimagined future. Penelope Bradford Event Design was contracted to organize all of Beacon of Hope's fundraisers and board meetings, plus a benefit to aid low-income schools and a series of luncheons for the Central Park Conservancy. Event planning satisfied her creative appetite while keeping her restless mind busy, and by choosing nonprofits over weddings, she could do more good than harm. She didn't want to be around hopeful couples, anyway—present company excluded. After more than a decade of dead-end jobs and absorbing punishment from unhappy female bosses, it was a relief to be building a career on her own terms.

She'd braced herself for a messy divorce, but the whole thing had gone through in three months. Rick gave her the apartment and everything in it, provided that her father took over the mortgage. Her newly minted ex-husband told her he wanted to do some soul-searching before dating again, but two weeks after the documents were signed, photos of him with his new girlfriend in Los Angeles appeared on his Facebook feed. She was a waifish brunette in her forties whose name, Hermione Crabtree, took Penelope a moment to place. She was one of Rick's millionairess clients.

Once her life was Rick-free, she saw that she had been crazy to stay in the marriage so long. She was now happy almost all the time. She loved living alone. Under Ardith's tutelage, she threw herself into her role as president of the co-op, and in those three months managed to set into motion most of her campaign promises, forwarding listings to several brokers of color in hopes of attracting diverse buyers, growing the stable of preferred vendors, hiring an architect to draw up the plans for a playroom in the basement, and hosting monthly wine-and-cheese receptions in the lobby, all without increasing maintenance fees. The tent on the roof was an expense she split with the co-op, since it could be used for future gatherings. Even bitter old Patricia Cooper was impressed.

So Penelope was moving on, and existing quite successfully as an adult. She hadn't noticed her childish insecurities falling away, but they had, somewhat. She supposed that one needed to come face-to-face with despair to find that inner sturdiness that she called "adulthood" and that Dr. Riffler called "resilience."

But the king-size bed was ludicrously big for one person, and she didn't feel like wandering Central Park without a lover by her side. Her mother encouraged her to date again. A new boyfriend might erase her lingering doubts about leaving Rick, but she didn't want anyone else, not yet.

A handsome dark-skinned Hispanic man who couldn't have been over forty brought Ardith a martini and a pyramid of meat and vegetable skewers on a sturdy plate made from palm leaves—one of the many inexpensive touches Penelope had incorporated to bring elegance to an otherwise simple affair. His powder-blue polo shirt and white chinos accentuated his shoulder-length black hair and dark eyes. He kissed Ardith on the lips. After knowing her for two years, it no longer surprised Penelope that young model types would find her attractive. She was funny, powerful, and rich, and if the gender roles had been reversed, no one would have been surprised. Even the uncanny-valley eeriness of her doctored face normalized once you got to know her. "They didn't have shrimp," he said to Ardith.

"They?" Ardith gasped. "*They* is right in front of you. Meet Pepper—she is the mastermind of this delightful fete. Pepper, this is Andres."

He gave her a thumbs-up. "Great party, ma'am."

She bristled at being called "ma'am." "Thank you. More shrimp should be coming in a few minutes."

"Cool." He went to fetch a plate for himself.

"I would so love to be married again," said Ardith, gazing at Andres, who edged his way through the crowd, toward the buffet under the tent.

Penelope tried not to judge them for the age difference. "Do you think you'll marry him?" she asked.

"I'm afraid I want to very much," Ardith replied, "though I know it's a wretched idea. Somehow I always manage to forget what hell it has been to be chained to the same man. During each divorce, I hide little notes around my apartment, reminding myself not *ever* to do it again. And then—poof!—I fall in love, and each time I am positive I've never felt so happy before, and I honestly believe it will work out. At which point the notes are powerless to stop me. It's as though an entirely different person had written them. I suppose it's the true romantic who marries many times, and it's only the most tediously practical person who stays married for life."

Penelope wondered which category Ardith would put her in. If she'd been romantic in marrying Rick, then foolishly so. She'd been foolishly practical, too. "I'm not sure I'm either of those," Penelope said.

"Silence, darling! Of course you're a romantic. You married out of passion, only to discover your husband's violent tendencies. He was a veritable Heathcliff!" Ardith feigned a swoon.

Penelope didn't love that Rick's temper was the prevailing explanation for her marriage's failure, though she preferred it to the truth, which was that neither of them had been ready to be married. On the other hand, Penelope appreciated that no one seemed to be judging her for her divorce. No one but herself.

Andres returned with a triangular stack of raw carrot and celery logs, and the three of them chatted for a while, when Patricia approached from the bar, enameled cane in one hand and glass of red wine in the other. Her Pomeranian had stayed home. She was wearing Chanel sunglasses with huge round lenses and a floor-length beige linen cloak, cinched at the waist with a wide purple belt. Her hair was redder than usual, and Penelope wondered how she could afford to keep her roots from ever showing. Letitia stood beside her, wearing a yellow blouse and brown polyester slacks, ready to grab Patricia if she toppled. In contrast to Patricia's puff of red, Letitia's hair was now a wiry gray.

"A lovely time was had by all," Patricia said, as if reciting the postevent blurb in the society pages. She put her glass on the highboy and gripped its edge. "Really, Ms. Bradford, tenting the roof was not a terrible idea. I don't agree with all your harebrained schemes, but I'm sorry I pooh-poohed this one."

Penelope smiled. "You're forgiven. For all your harebrained pooh-poohing." After Penelope had become board president, she began to find Patricia droll. Unfortunately, the meetings hadn't improved. The board members still fought over trifles, and Francis resented Patricia no less. Patricia seemed relieved to have relinquished her post, though. She'd always pretended it was a great sacrifice to toil as she did. Penelope had assumed she was just being dramatic, but part of her must have wanted to step down.

It also became clear just how impoverished Patricia was. Birdie had told Penelope that Patricia was eighty-six years old with barely a penny to her name. She also explained that Letitia was now more of a roommate than a maid, which Penelope had found sobering, because she had complained about the building's absence of black tenants while one was dusting the bookshelves in Patricia's living room. In the spring, Penelope had taken Patricia aside and said that if she still wanted to sublet her apartment for the summer to Nikolas Lykandros's mother, she would look for a way for the money not to pass through the resident manager. But Patricia had refused. She said she accepted that the sublet was wrong and would not repeat her mistake. Penelope guessed that she had simply become too frail to leave town for the summer.

"This is very charming," Letitia said, nodding stiffly as she looked around at the neighboring buildings, one topped with a penthouse garden. "You all should hold those board meetings up here!"

"I'm sure one of us would be pushed plumb off the roof," Ardith said, looking scandalized at her joke.

"Do I detect a note of enthusiasm in your voice?" Patricia wondered aloud.

A server eyed their glasses and dishes as if judging whether to clear them. Penelope flagged him down and asked Patricia and Letitia, "Have you had anything to eat?"

"I would take a little something, but I can get it myself," Letitia said.

"Not for me," Patricia replied. "I prefer not to traipse about a party with my mouth full. But speaking of food, Ms. Bradford, a question. What are your plans for the excess provisions from today's gathering?"

At larger events that Penelope had organized, a local charity had picked up unopened trays of food and delivered them to shelters, but that would have been too much effort for such a small amount of leftovers. "I'm sure the staff will take them home," Penelope said.

"If I may . . . Letitia volunteers with a soup kitchen in Washington Heights. I know its patrons would be absolutely thrilled to receive such a bounty. If you would have the staff bring the extra trays to my apartment, Letitia and I will make the appropriate calls to ship them downtown by this evening."

"What soup kitchen is that?" Penelope asked. Neither of them had mentioned it before. "Perhaps I could include a donation—to pay for the shipping."

"No need to go to such lengths," Patricia said.

"It's a very small charity," Letitia said.

Patricia added, with that blend of superiority and disgust that had once enraged Penelope, "You frankly wouldn't recognize the name."

It dawned on Penelope that the soup kitchen in question was located within Patricia's apartment. "Of course. Thank you for handling it. I'm glad the food won't be wasted."

"I'm simply pleased we can help those in less fortunate circumstances than our own." Patricia smiled stiffly, walked off, and sat on a roof vent. Letitia said goodbye and headed toward the buffet.

"Somehow I have the feeling that not a single morsel will go uneaten," Ardith mused, before they were out of earshot.

◄ ◆ ►

Penelope waited until Francis's animated conversation with Caleb and Sergei came to an end before approaching him and Carol. They were standing on the opposite edge of the roof, where the music wasn't as loud, their feet wreathed in hungry pigeons. They had just returned from two months in Europe. While Carol dropped crumbs for the pigeons, Francis spoke animatedly about their trip. He said they'd avoided the museums and tourist sites, instead renting apartments in residential areas of London and Paris, dining in the same few spots they'd known from earlier trips and ingratiating themselves with their neighbors. Penelope found it odd that they would fly across the Atlantic only to recreate their New York routine, but the trip clearly had invigorated them. Or maybe every married couple perked up at an engagement party.

"How have things been with you?" Francis asked Penelope with tentative concern in his eyes.

"You mean being single? I've done it before, but I never enjoyed it quite so much," she replied with a wry smile.

"That reminds me of a classic Yiddish folktale," said Francis, shooing a pigeon that was bobbing its head at his ankle. "A poor man lived with his parents, wife, and six children in a one-room house. They constantly bickered and fought, and the man was very unhappy. He went to his rebbe for advice."

"Oh, lord," Carol said, "not this one again. You'll notice that his wife doesn't get a say in all this."

"Why don't you go mingle with your pigeons?"

"I'll just tune you out." She smiled and bopped her head, as if listening to music. Penelope laughed at their vaudevillian bickering.

"Where was I?" Francis said. "Right. So the rebbe tells him to bring the chickens from the yard inside—"

"Take all the animals out of your house!" Carol blurted out.

Francis glowered at Carol.

"I just gave you back half an hour of your life," she told Penelope. "You're welcome."

Penelope finished responding to Francis's original question. "I'm happy being single, but I still wish I had found the right man."

"You're still very young," Carol said. "You're doing just fine."

"Thanks, but I want to have a child someday, and I'm almost thirty-five. I only have a few years left before it's too late."

"A few years is a very long time," Carol said.

"A few years passes in the blink of an eye," Francis said wistfully, staring off toward Central Park.

"Don't listen to him," said Carol, who picked up a shrimp from her plate, dipped it in her puddle of cocktail sauce, and bit off its body. "You have plenty of time."

◄●►

When just about everyone had arrived but before many had left, Penelope clinked her wineglass with a butter knife and took the microphone from the deejay. She couldn't wait any longer for Birdie and George.

"I hope everyone is having a great time this afternoon," she said, flinching at a squeal of feedback from the speakers. She moved where the deejay directed her, and the microphone behaved with only a brief whine of protest. Beckoning Sergei and Caleb toward her, she said, "I wanted to take a moment to congratulate our guests of honor. In the nine years that he safeguarded our building, Sergei became a friend to all of us. Now that he has moved on to bigger pastures, I know I'm not alone in missing him. But as it turns out, we didn't lose him after all, because although jobs come and go, marriage is forever." Her clichéd witticism drew a laugh. "In the year and a half Caleb has cleaned up our messes and delivered our packages, he also has found his way into our hearts. One day he will march off, diploma in hand, to become a social worker, but for our sake, I hope we get at least a little more time with him."

Caleb grinned at her. Sergei wrapped an arm around him and gave him a noogie.

"The Chelmsford Arms is hallowed ground," Penelope said, "because on Caleb's first day working here, he and Sergei met. They tried to hide their love from us, but our little community has a way of pulling out the truth from even the most secretive of people." Ardith's laugh pierced the rest of the polite chuckling, and now it was Sergei's turn to glare at Penelope in mock annoyance. "Don't look at *me*!" she protested. "I'm the last person who hears anything around here.

"But seriously," she said, focusing on the microphone to remember everything she wanted to say, "it makes me really, really happy to know you found each other. Love is precious in this world. It's the most precious gift we have. Maybe it's the only gift that really matters in life." Without warning, tears flooded her eyes. She placed the microphone onto the deejay table, nodded at the crowd to indicate that she was finished, and dried her eyes on her sleeve. The audience applauded and whistled, and the happy couple kissed. She knew she had been right to leave Rick, and she loved her independence, but still she missed him—or at least the knowledge that she had found someone to share her life with. And she was afraid she would never find that person. It was hard to accept the possibility that she might die alone.

"Your speech was devastating," Ardith said, once the music had begun again and the guests turned back to their conversations. "You are a national treasure."

"Maybe I'm not as evolved as I thought," Penelope said, shying away from Ardith's overstatement.

"Bah to that. Who among us is?"

The happy couple approached, and Ardith wandered toward the ledge with Andres and peered down toward the street.

Sergei and Caleb thanked her without a hug, as their employment relationship, even though Sergei had left the building, remained more salient than whatever friendship they could claim.

"Thank you, Ms. Bradford," Sergei said. "You are very good to us." In the months since Penelope had last seen him, he had transformed, though it was hard to pinpoint how. His hair was a little shorter and he might have lost a few pounds, but otherwise, he was physically unchanged. He hadn't developed new mannerisms, either. No, he exuded a lightness, the relief of unburdening himself from the masculinity he'd worn for so long.

"Yeah, thanks," said Caleb. "This is really nice."

"It's the least I can do," she said. It wasn't just a stock phrase; she really had felt she owed them, particularly Caleb. A few months back, she'd brought up the night Rick assaulted him. She wasn't going to apologize for her ex-husband's behavior, but she did tell him that she was there if he ever wanted to talk about it. He thanked her and never brought it up again, and every time she saw him, she couldn't shake her guilt. Dr. Riffler pointed out that this was another Locked Door, and it somehow served her to believe he was upset with her. Still, it felt wrong to ask him to soothe her conscience, so she tried to let it go. "Have you decided when to tie the knot?" she asked.

"We are not hurrying things," Sergei said. "Maybe next year."

"That sounds wise," she said. "I definitely wouldn't recommend rushing." She resisted making a self-deprecating comment.

"Caleb is wanting me to invite my parents, and I am trying to tell him that it is never going to happen." They performed a brief lovers' tussle that ended with Sergei planting a kiss on his temple. "Maybe I will be able to come out to some more friends."

"Your lips to God's ears," Caleb said.

"Are you still liking your new job?" she asked Sergei.

"Yes, ma'am, very much," he said. "The facilities are brand-new, and the residents are very friendly. But I have a special place in my heart for this wonderful community."

◄●►

Bartenders were slotting the unopened bottles into cases when Penelope noticed George, in his wheelchair, levitating up the stairs and onto the roof. In reality, three staff members were lifting him, one from above and two from below. Birdie waited at the top of the stairs with a smattering of onlookers, holding out a hand as if she could catch George if he slipped off the chair. Penelope hurried toward them.

"I'm so glad you made it! I'm sorry about the stairs," Penelope said.

"No, no, it's quite the adventure," Birdie said, clearly relieved now that George was safely on the roof. "I must apologize for our extreme lateness. We had some difficulties on the way out the door." She patted, then squeezed, his hand. "Didn't we, George?"

He smiled. "Let's not go into the specifics." His speech was slurred but intelligible. Sometimes he'd lose steam before the end of longer sentences, but it was a miracle he could speak at all. In the minutes between his attempted suicide and his blood pressure stabilizing in the ambulance, oxygenated blood could not reach his brain, and multiple knots of neurons had suffocated. But thanks to modern medicine—and a miracle, if you believed in that sort of thing—he recovered most of his faculties, far more than Dr. Naeer had predicted in the ER. It was a full-time job, managing in a wheelchair, especially given that he still couldn't use the toilet on his own. Oddly, Penelope had never seen him so happy. She'd only known him in his deepening depression, and she adored the smiling George, even as it saddened her to know how much he had lost.

"I see we've missed the party," Birdie said, glancing around at the stragglers exchanging protracted goodbyes. She pursed her lips and looked at George, who looked up at her and smiled. His hair was whiter and softer than it had been before his suicide attempt, and he had lost some weight. He was wearing a stylish zip-up sweatshirt and sweatpants with buttons along the outseams—clothes designed for the wheelchair-bound.

"We'll be using this space a lot, I think," said Penelope.

"Perhaps for your next engagement," Birdie said with a meaningful raise of her eyebrows.

"Hear, hear!" George said.

Penelope smiled patiently, withstanding Birdie's prediction. She didn't want to worry about the future and its myriad possibilities; right now, she needed a break from her biological clock. But Birdie needed to be in a relationship so powerfully that she couldn't tolerate uncertainty or ambivalence, in her marriage or in anyone else's singlehood. It was alarming to consider Birdie's reversal. Six months earlier, she had been negotiating a separation from George; now it seemed as if their marriage had never contained one minute of strife. Penelope was glad for them, maybe envious.

"You don't have to say that," Penelope told her. "I'm actually doing really well. I'm staying open to wherever life takes me." She laughed at herself for sounding like a greeting card.

"Life will take you far," Birdie predicted. "But I hope not away from our building."

"Don't worry, I think I'm here to stay."

"That's the spirit," said George.

The remaining staff were still breaking down the party. All the guests had left, and the pigeons were cleaning up the dropped food. "I hate to ask them to cart us back downstairs when we just got here," Birdie said, glancing around and biting her lip.

"Why don't you stay a while?" Penelope offered. "Just call me when you want to come down."

"Thank you, Penelope. You're a gift." Birdie turned George's chair so that he could see down Eighty-eighth Street toward Central Park. Penelope stepped back and watched as Birdie reached into her purse and took out two pairs of sunglasses; after putting hers on, she slid the other pair onto George's face. He murmured gratefully. Birdie perched on the arm of George's wheelchair and scratched his back as they took in the view. He brought her other hand to his mouth and kissed it.

ACKNOWLEDGMENTS

A tremendous thank-you to my agent, James Fitzgerald, and my team of editors at Thomas Dunne Books: Thomas Dunne, Stephen Power, Janine Barlow, and Samantha Zukergood. I'm eternally grateful for their tireless support and spot-on editorial advice. Thanks to my publicity and marketing experts, Dori Weintraub and Marissa Sangiacomo, who helped this book find the widest possible audience.

Every novelist should be so lucky as to have a first reader as positive and supportive as Phil Gates. He adored every iteration of every chapter, even when I sent him ramshackle, unloved short stories that would evolve into the backbone of this novel. Writers get better through criticism, but we get stronger through love.

I'm also indebted to the battalion of writer and editor friends who read my book and offered honest and generous feedback: Carol Bartold, Kathy Berlin, Cindy Carssow, Kathy Crisci, Joel Derfner, Cheryl Fish, Katherine Hurley, Alex Joseph, Laura Mamelok, Spencer Merolla, Judy Padow, Anna Qu, Christine Reilly, Michelle Robinson, Eric Sasson, Amy Vatner, and Rick Whitaker. Without you, this book would not exist.

Thanks to the faculty at Sarah Lawrence College, whose advice I still use almost every time I sit down to write, in particular, David Hollander, Kathleen Hill, Brian Morton, and Joan Silber. Thanks to my former classmates in the MFA program, especially Bethany Ball and Amy Beth Wright, who continue to offer moral support. Thanks to Jonathan Dee and my workshop compatriots at the Tin House Writers Workshop; when Mr. Dee told me this would be published, I believed him.

ACKNOWLEDGMENTS

Part of this novel was written at Wildacres Retreat in North Carolina. Part was written at the home of Jay Michaelson and Paul Dakin and the home of Ken Page and Greg Romer.

I relied heavily on others' expertise in my writing: Eli Berlin told me about the job of asset manager, Dmitry Kurmanov gave me insight into the life of a Russian immigrant, Lucy Lang answered my questions about the police and court systems in New York, Daniel Levinson Wilk and Judy Padow were my experts on co-op staff issues, Joel Derfner's "Intimacy Prescription" helped me write the couple's therapy scenes, Dennis Norris II guided my writing about race, Ralph Vatner taught me about matters of physiology and medicine, and I wouldn't have even written the book if not for Jules Cohn, may he rest in peace.

Lastly and mostly, I'm deeply grateful to my impossibly understanding husband, Morty Rosenbaum, whose incisive editing and effusive support have buoyed me in waters both turbulent and serene.